EX LIBRIS

VINTAGE CLASSICS

KENJI MIYAZAWA

Kenji Miyazawa (1896–1933) was born and raised in Iwate, a rural part of Northern Japan, largely cut off from the modern world. As a boy he was fascinated by glimpses of the modern industrial world – train lines and telegraph poles running into the distance – and he hoarded scientific information. His stories often contain fantastical descriptions of landscape alongside technological details. He was also deeply connected to the folk tales of Japan and interested in both Buddhism and Christianity.

After graduation from agricultural college, he moved to Tokyo to write and work as a proof-reader. When his sister became ill, he returned to Iwate to care for her and remained there for the rest of his life. He devoted himself to the education and protection of the local farming community, even eating the same poor diet in solidarity with his neighbours, contributing to his early death from tuberculosis at the age of 37. Only two of Miyazawa's works were published during his lifetime. His success and fame as a writer came posthumously but his poetry and stories are popular in Japan to this day.

KENJI MIYAZAWA

NIGHT TRAIN TO THE STARS

and Other Stories

TRANSLATED FROM THE JAPANESE BY
John Bester

WITH AN INTRODUCTION BY
Kaori Nagai

WITH A FOREWORD BY
David Mitchell

VINTAGE CLASSICS

3 5 7 9 10 8 6 4

Vintage Classics is part of the Penguin Random House
group of companies whose addresses can be found
at global.penguinrandomhouse.com

Penguin
Random House
UK

First published in hardback in Vintage Classics in 2022
This paperback first published in Vintage Classics in 2024

penguin.co.uk/vintage-classics

A CIP catalogue record for this book is available from the British Library

ISBN 9781784878337

Printed and bound in Great Britain by Clays Ltd, Elcograf S.p.A.

The authorised representative in the EEA is Penguin Random House Ireland,
Morrison Chambers, 32 Nassau Street, Dublin D02 YH68

Penguin Random House is committed to a sustainable future
for our business, our readers and our planet. This book is made
from Forest Stewardship Council® certified paper.

FSC www.fsc.org MIX Paper | Supporting responsible forestry FSC® C018179

Contents

Foreword

The world breathed into being by Kenji Miyazawa's tales is a many-sided place where readers may lose their bearings a little. Some of the tales in these pages evoke Aesop's fables, with their talking animals and clean-cut morals. Others land like otherworldly parables told by a Buddhist preacher with a side-gig in syncretic Christianity, and a contemporary reader might wonder, '*What is it exactly you want me to think?*' Some stories glow in the dark with a simple folkloric charm. Others are tethered to their place in the historical continuum, and (gently) puncture the author's modern times – Japan's late Taishō and early Shōwa periods of the 1920s and early 1930s. Some stories possess an autumnal pathos that recalls Oscar Wilde's 'The Selfish Giant' or 'The Happy Prince'. Some are buoyant with humour. Or whimsy, even. Others ache with loss and bereavement. A few flow with the illogic of a dream-poem. Some belong in the landscape of Japanese narrative, up to and including the films of Studio Ghibli. Others are islands unto themselves, resembling nothing – at all – but a Kenji Miyazawa tale. A handful may feel sketchy and made up on the spot, like a bedtime story. Perhaps they were. Yet a further handful – 'The Earthgod and the Fox', or 'The Restaurant of Many Orders' – are half-buried, cut and polished gems of world literature.

The many-sidedness of Kenji Miyazawa's tales reflect the many-sidedness of their creator. Son of a pawnbroker who profited directly from his neighbours' misfortunes. Misfit dreamer of socialist utopias. Soil scientist and lecturer at an agrarian college. Proselytising convert to Nichiren Buddhism and questing believer in spiritual realms. Amateur farmer trying (and failing) to eke out a living in Japan's wintery Iwate Prefecture. Cello-playing, German- and Esperanto-learning humanist with a passion for Beethoven, Bach and Debussy. Founder of a cultural society closed down by the government in 1928 during a clampdown on foreign influences. Poet, mostly ignored by the Tokyo literary world in his lifetime.

These many selves permeate his many tales. On my first reading I caught myself wondering, 'Which is the real Miyazawa?' The answer, of course, is 'All of them' – and if a unifying field is needed, it is Compassion. While Miyazawa never married during his curtailed life (he died of pneumonia at the age of thirty-seven) he was a devoted brother to his sister Toshi – he moved to Tokyo to nurse her and was plunged into grief by her early death. Compassion for animals led him to lifelong vegetarianism, still a relative rarity in Japan. Social conscience led Miyazawa to reject his family pawnbroking business in favour of lecturing and setting up a model farm to showcase new agricultural methods. While wartime propagandists seized on the opening lines of Miyazawa's poem 'Ame ni mo makezu' – a contender for Most Recognised Line of Poetry in the Japanese Language – as a slogan of *bushido* indomitability, the poem in its entirety is a (not very martial at all) credo to an ego-less life guided by compassion. Appropriately, it was Miyazawa's younger brother Seiroku who nourished the poet's posthumous reputation. Without this fraternal love, Kenji Miyazawa's work may have vanished in the ashes of a firebombed backwater, the wilful amnesia of the Occupation and the material rush of Reconstruction.

Luckily for us, Miyazawa's poetry and tales survived to become an evergreen fixture in Japanese letters and culture, cherished even by non-readers. In her knowledgeable introduction to John Bester's alert translations, Dr Kaori Nagai offers the English-speaking reader the perfect map to go exploring Miyazawa's curious, of-its-time-yet-timeless world. Off you go, then. Enjoy losing your bearings a little.

David Mitchell, 2022

Introduction

Kenji Miyazawa (1896–1933), a Japanese modernist poet and storyteller, a devout Buddhist and an agricultural science teacher, was also a stargazer. He fell in love with the stars while in middle school. He often spent hours on the rooftop gazing at the night sky, with his cardboard planisphere in hand. His younger brother, Seiroku, remembers how Kenji as a young teenager tried to teach him the names of the constellations and the legends of the stars, telling him that we travel through the galaxy daily, riding on a vehicle called Earth. Miyazawa's lifelong fascination with the stars provided the inspiration for his masterpiece 'Night Train to the Stars', in which he sends two boys – Giovanni and Campanella – up into the sky, which he himself always wished to visit.

Reading 'Night Train to the Stars' and other stories by Miyazawa is a unique experience: we are invited to step into a strange world, which feels like (and is described by one of his characters as) a 'fourth dimension of fantasy'. There, many unimaginable things happen (such as travelling across the stars on a night train), which expand our perceptions and sense of reality. It is also a breathtakingly beautiful world as, in Miyazawa's descriptions, earthly things are as starry as those of the night sky – the dewdrops on the grass, the flowers lit by the sun, the waves and bubbles in a river, and so on, glitter and shine, reminding us that we are part of the universe.

Kenji Miyazawa is a much-loved author in Japan and something of a national institution. Most Japanese people know by heart the first few lines of his most famous poem, 'Ame ni mo makezu' ('Not Beaten by Rain'), and have read his best-known stories, such as 'Night Train to the Stars', 'The Restaurant of Many Orders' and 'Gorsch the Cellist'. These texts are so influential that they have become part of the cultural vocabulary: it is very easy to spot the influence of Miyazawa in the Japanese art scene and popular culture (for instance, the Studio Ghibli films show a certain affinity with Miyazawa's works, and the studio's iconic director, Hayao Miyazaki, is one of his many admirers). His fame, however, arrived posthumously. In his lifetime, he contributed several pieces to periodicals and self-published two books – the poetry collection *Spring and Asura* (1924) and the short-story collection *The Restaurant of Many Orders* (1924) – without much success. He died at the age of thirty-seven almost unknown as a writer, leaving behind unpublished manuscripts containing over 100 stories and 800 poems. His subsequent rise to fame as a national poet was largely due to the fact that 'Ame ni mo makezu', discovered after his death as an entry in his pocket notebook, was used as wartime propaganda. The poem expresses his aspiration to lead a humble and altruistic existence, undefeated by all the sufferings and adversities of life. This made it a perfect vehicle to teach the nation the virtues of humility, frugality and personal sacrifice during the war and then in the post-war period of hardship. However, Miyazawa would never have achieved his enduring popularity without the efforts of his family, friends and admirers to make his works available to the world. Seiroku played an especially large part in this effort, guarding the manuscripts which Kenji had entrusted to him throughout the WWII air raids, and overseeing their publication afterwards.

Miyazawa was born and spent most of his life in Hanamaki, Iwate Prefecture, in the Tōhoku (northeast) region of Japan. His stories were shaped by his experiences there in many significant ways. With the Kitakami Mountains running through the middle of it, Iwate is a mountainous region of natural beauty, known for its harsh climate. In the winter, the whole area is covered by heavy snowfalls. The splendour and brutality of this weather are captured in Miyazawa's story 'The Red Blanket', in which the Old Snow Woman, the personification of a blizzard, considers it her right to take human lives. Tōhoku is also a volcanic and earthquake-prone area; it was an earthquake there that triggered the gigantic tsunami and Fukushima nuclear power plant meltdown in 2011. These environmental conditions pose a challenge to the lives of the local inhabitants, especially farmers. In Miyazawa's time, cold weather and other factors frequently caused crop failures, and even famines. He was deeply concerned with the plight of those who lived off the land, despite and because of the fact that he was born into a wealthy family. He loathed the family business of pawnbroking, which profited from the struggling of local farmers, and instead chose to pursue a career as an agricultural scientist, specialising in soil science. He taught in an agricultural school in Hanamaki for five years, and then resigned from the position to be a farmer himself and devote himself to sharing his scientific and technological knowledge to help improve the lives of other agricultural workers. If Miyazawa's stories seem attentive to plants, trees and other creatures of the soil, this is partly because he was an expert in them. Just like Dr Lin Po in 'General Son Ba-yu', he was a plant doctor of sorts, who worked with plants to alleviate people's sufferings.

Many of Miyazawa's stories are set in his homeland of Iwate and richly weave in regional references. For instance, Japan is full of legends about fox spirits that shapeshift into humans to do all sorts of mischief, and Miyazawa's 'Tokkobe Torako' focuses on one of these spirits, which is known in Iwate Prefecture. The story fascinatingly juxtaposes two kinds of foxes that the locals live alongside: the supernatural spirit, which they still believe in and are afraid of, and the real 'Tokkobe Torako', the leader of a fox pack who comes out at night for scraps of food. Other folkloric figures inhabiting Miyazawa's stories include the earthgod ('The Earthgod and the Fox') and the wild man of the hills ('The Man of the Hills' and 'Night of the Festival'). In Miyazawa's world, these beings are irresistibly drawn towards new and modern ways of life: the earthgod is intensely jealous of the westernised fox who becomes his rival in love, and the hillmen wander into towns out of curiosity and get into trouble. In this way, these figures from folklore are made to represent how the old and indigenous ways have been marginalised and left behind by the rapid process of modernisation and westernisation happening in Miyazawa's lifetime. In 'The Man of the Hills', the Seven Hills ('Nanatsu-mori') – a range of seven small hills, all covered with trees – marks the threshold between the two worlds; these hills actually exist in Shizukuishi, a town in Iwate which Miyazawa often visited. Likewise, Ōzora Falls near Hanamaki is said to be the model for the majestic mountain waterfall described at the beginning of 'The Bears of Nametoko', which 'goes thundering down through the thick-growing cypresses and maples' for some three hundred feet.

However, it would be misleading merely to say that Miyazawa's stories are set in Iwate. Rather, he mixed local elements with his imagination to create a literary world that is truly magical. Miyazawa called his fictional world *Ihatov*, which he defines as Iwate as a dreamland that really exists in his mind. In this dreamland, everything is possible: 'one can instantly leap onto an icy cloud and travel north, accompanied by the great wind that circles around the Earth, or one can talk with the ants who pass under the red cups of flowers' (my translation, from the advertisement Miyazawa wrote for *The Restaurant of Many Orders*). He likens *Ihatov* to some other literary dreamlands such as Lewis Carroll's Looking-Glass world and the 'Desert of Tepântar', evoked in a poem by Rabindranath Tagore as a fairy-tale place ('The Land of the Exile'), as well as farmlands cultivated by Hans Christian Andersen's characters ('Little Claus and Big Claus') and the kingdom of Ivan the Fool created by Leo Tolstoy. *Ihatov* is hardly a cut-off, hard-to-reach place, but is conceived of as a cosmopolitan dreamland, connected with every location, in the past and the future, through global literary railway networks. *Ihatov* is also a transliteration of 'Iwate' in Esperanto, the international language that Miyazawa learned in order to become a world citizen.

'Night Train to the Stars' is a typical *Ihatov* story. Although the story is set in an unnamed city and its two main characters – Giovanni and Campanella – have European names, its setting unmistakably evokes Hanamaki City, with its railway lines and the Kitakami River, one of Japan's largest rivers. Miyazawa the stargazer must have based the following description on his own experience: 'Further downstream, the Milky Way was reflected over the whole width of the river, so that it looked not like water but like a continuation of the sky itself.' The whole city's landscape – the train, the river and the sky – inspired him to write the story.

Miyazawa was a Buddhist *and* a natural scientist. 'Night Train to the Stars' is a good example of how he draws on science to explore religious and philosophical questions such as: what is the nature of the phenomena we think we are experiencing; where do we go after our deaths; what is the *true* God; and what is and where do we find true happiness for all? The reference to the 'fourth dimension of fantasy' shows that Miyazawa was aware of Einstein's theory of relativity proposed in 1905. He utilises his knowledge of the stars in creating the Milky Way railway route, which traverses the entire galaxy from the Northern Cross to the Southern Cross, and features many real stars, constellations and nebulae. Moreover, to travel on the Milky Way train is also to travel across deep, geological time. At Swan Halt, the boys make a quick visit to the 'Pliocene Coast', where they find walnuts that are 'some one million two hundred thousand years old'. Miyazawa was a geologist and a lover of stones, and this episode is based on his own discovery of walnut fossils in the riverbed of the Kitakami River – another local and personal reference that he weaves into his dreamland. And this geological and cosmic time, which the Western world had recently 'discovered' through a series of scientific advances in the nineteenth century, has long been part of Buddhist cosmology. This can be seen in Miyazawa's Buddhist story 'A Stem of Lilies', in which the narrator tells of Lord Buddha's visit to a city which took place 'two hundred million years or so ago'.

It might be of interest to Western readers that in East and Southeast Asian cultures, the Milky Way is considered to be the River of the Heavens: our galaxy is a body of silvery water flowing across the night sky, rather than spilled milk from Hera's breast, as we find in Greek mythology. According to a Chinese legend, two celestial lovers, the cowherd (the star Altair in the constellation Aquila) and the weaver girl (the star Vega in the constellation of Lyra) are separated by the river and are only allowed to meet once a year. A flock of magpies make a bridge over the heavenly water to enable their meeting. In many countries, including Japan, a festival is held annually to celebrate their reunion on the seventh day of the seventh month of the year. 'Night Train to the Stars' is indebted to this tradition, as the story takes place on the night of the Milky Way Festival. This legend provides a fitting backdrop to the story of Giovanni and Campanella, two childhood friends who have drifted apart due to Giovanni's family circumstances. They rekindle their friendship on the train, only to be separated again. Indeed, longing for lost loved ones is a recurring theme of the story, as it turns out that the Milky Way railroad carries the dead to the heavens. When Miyazawa's younger sister Toshi, who had been his soulmate, died of tuberculosis at the age of twenty-four, he was inconsolable. He even took a train to South Sakhalin, which was on the northern edge of the historical Japanese Empire (now in Russia), to find her. This train journey is said to have contributed to the making of 'Night Train to the Stars'. But in this story, in which all spaces and times commingle in a dreamland, we meet not only those whom we have personally lost but also all others whom we have not met but nonetheless have been connected with. Among the train's passengers are those who died in the sinking of a ship, which struck an iceberg during its passage. This incident is based on the sinking of *Titanic* in the North Atlantic Ocean in 1912, which happened when Miyazawa was fifteen years old. The fact that the girl and the boy from the sunken ship, who join Giovanni and Campanella, are given Japanese names suggests that he felt a strong connection to the victims of this globally high-profile tragedy.

Miyazawa was deeply aware of the corrupt and exploitative nature of modern society and was especially critical of those in power. For instance, in 'The Spider, the Slug and the Racoon', each of the three titular villains represents the powerful in society who prey on the weak for their own personal gain and worldly success. 'The Fire Stone', a story about a hare child entrusted with a precious stone, shows how quickly power corrupts even the most innocent of us. 'The Police Chief' is a caricature of the criminal nature of the government, featuring a police chief who takes to transgressing the law, which he is supposed to be protecting, and committing the gravest of crimes to his heart's content. Miyazawa's stories were also vehicles in which to present his socialist vision of a better society for all. In this sense, 'Ozbel and the Elephant' and 'The Thirty Frogs' can be read as allegories of socialist revolution. In both stories, the good-natured and hardworking workers are tricked into enslavement and are made to endure life-threatening overwork. Both stories end with the liberation of the enslaved, while the capitalist oppressor meets a dismal end. In 'Wildcat and the Acorns', a human boy is asked by Wildcat to put a stop to a dispute among three hundred acorns, each of which is claiming to be the best. The judgement passed by the child (drawing on a Buddhist sermon) – 'the best is the one who's most stupid, most ridiculous and most good-for-nothing' – is truly refreshing for those of us living in an ever more competitive society. Miyazawa called this 'good-for-nothing' figure a *dekunobou*, and this was the ideal that Miyazawa wished to live up to himself. The desire to be a *dekunobou* is at the heart of his poem 'Ame ni mo makezu', and in this collection this figure is most fully embodied in the protagonist of 'Kenju's Wood.' Kenju is a nature-loving boy, 'a bit soft in the head' and made fun of by everybody, who nurtures seven hundred cedar seedlings into a splendid forest park, which continues to be enjoyed by many long after he dies.

One of the pleasures of reading Miyazawa's stories is that they feature many talking non-humans. It is not just animal characters who talk, for we also get to hear the voices of other kinds of nonhumans such as plants ('The Dahlias and the Crane') and household tools including a bucket, a dustpan and a rat trap ('The Ungrateful Rat'). In 'March by Moonlight', we even witness a military procession of railway telegraph poles, marching to the beat of the song they sing. His stories animate and infuse life into all the objects around us, shedding fresh light on their existence. At first glance, these fables might not look like a truthful representation of nature, as non-human characters are made to represent a variety of human types or ideas. But even these stories are infused with the beauty of the natural world. For instance, in 'The Spider, the Slug and the Racoon', the rise and fall of the three villains is framed by poetically naturalistic descriptions of blue-eyed bees, 'flying about buzzing cheerfully in the sunlight' in the spring, 'busily gathering the last honey of the year' in the autumn, and 'in the six-sided home … sleeping peacefully, dreaming of the spring to come' in the winter, as a real-life model of diligence and simple living. In 'The Wild Pear', we are even invited to see the underwater world from the point of view of two boy crabs, for whom the river surface is a ceiling, leading us to admire the movements of fish, bubbles and the network of light around and above them. According to Miyazawa's own preface to *The Restaurant of Many Orders*, his stories were given to him during his walks 'by rainbows and moonlight in the woods, in the fields and on railway tracks' (my translation): natural elements are his co-writers and collaborators. In this collection, the opening of 'The First Deer Dance' captures the moment in which 'the rustling of the breeze' turns into a human speech in the narrator's ears, telling him the origin story of the Deer Dance, traditionally performed in Iwate. Likewise, in 'Down in the Wood', we find the narrator in deep conversation with an owl, who retells the famous Japanese tale about 'the kite who took up dyeing'.

In Buddhism, it is commonly recognised that all of nature – mountains, rivers, plants, trees and all other beings – possess the potential to be a Buddha, just like humans, and our lives are interconnected through the chains of karma and reincarnation. Miyazawa was a devotee of the Nichiren sect of Japanese Buddhism, which bases its teachings on the *Lotus Sutra*, and this deeply coloured his views about the natural world. He advocated and practised vegetarianism, for the same reason as the nighthawk in his story 'The Nighthawk Star', who finds it unbearable to have to kill so many creatures daily to survive, and who resolves to 'stop eating insects and starve to death.' 'The Bears of Nametoko' likewise draws attention to the cruelty of killing animals when a chased bear stops and asks the hunter 'Why do you have to shoot me?' But the story's exploration of this subject goes much deeper than just the criticism of human cruelty, as there is a deep tie and sympathy between the bears of Nametoko and the hunter who unwillingly shoots them to make his meagre living. The story suggests that to kill or eat an animal is to form a karmic tie with it and not being aware of this makes the action even more sinful.

Talking of vegetarianism, 'The Restaurant of Many Orders' is one of the best stories ever written to critique our custom of eating animals. An entertaining story with a vein of dark humour, it does not just invert our meat-eating habits by turning humans into meat. It also reveals the restaurant to be a kind of slaughterhouse, in which the polite instructions written for the customers turn out to be a recipe for them to turn themselves into a dish.

I started this introduction by mentioning how starry and visual Miyazawa's world is, and I'd like to conclude by pointing out that it is also full of sounds. His stories are remarkably rich in their use of onomatopoeia, a distinctive feature of the Japanese language, and the translator has captured this where possible. Moreover, Miyazawa was a lover of music, especially European classical music and operas. He spent most of his salary on records, and he also composed a few short scores himself. In this collection, references to songs and music are scattered throughout his stories, adding sound effects to their vivid imagery. 'Gorsch the Cellist' best captures Miyazawa's love of music, which fascinatingly intersects with his love of nature. In this story, Gorsch, a 'none too good' cellist, transforms himself into an excellent musician through nightly practice sessions with a series of animals, and as his musical skills improve, he becomes more considerate of and kind towards the animals. But this story is not just about our learning from nature and being in harmony with it. Gorsch learns from the mice who visit him that his music has the power to heal animals and that his animal neighbours who get sick come to listen to it. In our era of climate emergency and environmental destruction, we have learned how destructive we are as a species, but the story encourages us to trust our ability also to heal, nurture and thrive with nature. To cultivate this ability, it feels important to read Miyazawa's stories now, as he was a writer who perpetually improvised with nature and the whole world, spiritually, scientifically and ecologically, to create many beautiful and profound works of art.

Kaori Nagai, 2022

Night Train to the Stars

1. The Afternoon Class

'Now, boys – what about this vague white blur that, as I just told you, people used to say was a river, or a "Milky Way" – do you know what it really is?'

As he put the question to the class, the teacher pointed to the smoky white part, stretching in a galactic band from top to bottom, of the big black map of the constellations hung on the blackboard.

Campanella raised his hand. Then four or five others put up their hands. Giovanni was going to put up his too, but hastily gave up the idea.

He was almost sure he'd read in a magazine somewhere that it was all made up of stars. But every day in class lately he'd been terribly sleepy, and he'd no books to read either, or even the time to read them, so he no longer felt he knew anything at all for sure.

But the teacher had already got his eye on him.

'Giovanni, I'm sure you know.'

Giovanni got smartly to his feet, but once there found he couldn't manage any clear answer after all. Zanelli, sitting just in front of him, turned around and looked at him with a snigger. Giovanni went bright red with confusion.

'When you examine the River of Heaven – or the Milky Way as they call it in some countries – really closely, through a big telescope,' the teacher went on, 'what do you think it turns out to be?'

Giovanni still had the feeling that it was made up of stars, but again he couldn't get the reply out in time.

The teacher looked put out for a moment, then turned his gaze to Campanella and called on him instead:

'Campanella, then.'

But though he'd stuck up his hand so briskly a moment before, Campanella just stood there hesitating, and couldn't get out any answer.

The teacher stared at him, surprised, then with a hurried, 'Very well, then,' pointed to the map of the stars and began to explain.

'If you look at this vague white blur, the "Milky Way," through a big telescope, you see that it's made up of lots of small stars. That's right, isn't it Giovanni?'

Giovanni nodded, his face crimson. And he felt his eyes filling with tears. Yes: he'd known it all along. And Campanella of course knew too. In fact, they'd both read it in a magazine he'd seen once at the home of Campanella's father, the Doctor. Not only that, but when Campanella had seen what was in the magazine, he'd gone straight and fetched a big book from his father's library. He'd opened it up at the page for 'Milky Way,' and they'd pored for ages together over the photograph, so attractive with all the white dots on the jet-black page . . .

Campanella couldn't possibly have forgotten about it, yet he'd held back his answer. Every day lately, in the early morning and again in the late afternoon, Giovanni had had so much work to do that when he was there at school he hadn't had the energy to dash around with the rest, or even talk to Campanella very much. Campanella must have realised this and, sympathising with him, deliberately not answered. Somehow, the idea made Giovanni feel dreadfully sorry not just for himself but for Campanella as well.

The teacher was speaking again:

'So if you see the River of Heaven as a real river, then each small star corresponds to a grain of sand or a piece of gravel on the riverbed. Or if you see it as a great stream of milk, that makes it still more like a river in the sky. I mean, the stars are just like a lot of tiny specks of fat floating in the liquid. In that case, then, what is it that corresponds to the watery part of the milk? It's the vacuum that transmits light at a certain speed and in which the sun and the earth itself are both suspended in the same way.

'In other words, we ourselves are living in the midst of the water of the River of Heaven. And when you look around from inside the river, just as water looks more blue the deeper it is, so the stars look denser the deeper and further away in the river they are, which is why they become a white blur. Take a look at this model here.'

He pointed to a big double convex lens containing a mass of gleaming grains of sand.

'The Milky Way's very much like this in shape. Each of these shiny grains corresponds to a star, a sun that gives out its light in the same way as our own sun. Our sun lies roughly in the centre, with the earth close by it. Now suppose it's night and you stand right in the centre of the lens and look around inside it. The glass is thin in this direction, so you won't see more than a few shiny grains – stars, that is – will you? But here, and here, the glass is thick, so you'll see a lot of grains – or stars – and the furthest of them will show up as a white blur. Which is, to sum it up, the present theory about the Milky Way. As for the estimated size of the lens – time's already up, so I'll talk about that, and about all the different kinds of stars to be found in it, in the next science class. Well, then, today's the Festival of the Milky Way, so I hope you'll all go outside tonight and take a good look at the sky.

'That's all for now, then. You may put away your textbooks and notebooks.'

And for a while after that the classroom was full of the sound of desktops being opened and shut and books put in piles, and before long they all stood to attention, bowed and went out of the classroom.

2. The Printing Works

As Giovanni was going out of the school gate he found that seven or eight of his classmates had not gone straight home but were gathered in a group around Campanella near an ornamental cherry tree at the edge of the school yard. It seemed they were discussing an expedition to gather the snake gourds that, with blue lights in them, would be set adrift on the river that night to celebrate the festival.

Giovanni, though, gave a vigorous wave and marched straight on out of the gate. Outside in the street, he found that the houses and shops were making all kinds of preparations for that night's Milky Way Festival, decorating the whole place with balls of yew needles hung from the eaves and cedar boughs with lights attached to them.

Giovanni didn't go home but went on, rounding the corners of three blocks in turn, until he came to a big printing works. Taking off his shoes and stepping up inside, he opened the big door that lay straight ahead. Inside, the electric light was on, though it was still daytime; a large number of rotary presses were thudding round and round, and people with their hair tied back with cloths and shades over their eyes were reading and counting in singsong voices as they worked.

Giovanni went straight up to the man who was sitting at the third high table from the entrance, and bowed.

The man rummaged about on a shelf for a while, then handed Giovanni a sheet of paper and said:

'D'you think you can pick this much by the time you leave?'

Giovanni took a small, flat box from the foot of the man's table, and went and squatted down in a well-lit corner where cases of type were propped up against the wall. With a small pair of tweezers he set about picking the type, each piece of which was only about as big as a grain of millet.

A man in a blue apron went past behind Giovanni. 'Hi there, Master Magnifying Glass!' he called, and several people nearby, without saying anything or even looking in his direction, gave mean little smiles.

Giovanni picked the type with painstaking care, stopping again and again to rub his eyes as he did so.

A while after it had struck six, he had the flat box full of type he'd picked. He checked once more against the paper in his hand, then took the type to the man at the table whom he'd first spoken to. The man took the box in silence, though with a slight nod.

Bowing, Giovanni went out through the door and walked up to the accountant's desk, where a man in white handed him, again in complete silence, one small silver coin. Giovanni's expression brightened suddenly. With a smart bow, he picked up the bag he'd put at the foot of the desk and dashed outside. Then, whistling gaily, he dropped in at the bread store, bought a bread roll and a bag of cube sugar, and ran off again at top speed.

3. At Home

The house that Giovanni came home to so cheerfully was one of a row of small houses in a back street. By the left-hand one of three entrances lined up in the front, purple kale and asparagus were growing in old wooden boxes, and the shades were still down at the two small windows.

'Hi, Mom! I'm back!' called Giovanni as he stepped out of his shoes. 'Mom, have you been all right?'

'Is it you, Giovanni? I'm sure you must be awfully tired from your work. It's been cool, so I've been fine all day.'

Giovanni stepped up indoors and found his mother in the room immediately inside, lying with a white sheet over her.

He opened the window.

'Mom, I bought some lump sugar today. I thought I'd put some in your milk.'

'Thank you. You have some first, though. I'm not ready for it just yet.'

'Mom, what time did Sister go home?'

'Let's see, around three o'clock. She did all the odd things around the house.'

'Mom, hasn't your milk come yet?'

'Hasn't it come? Really?'

'I'll go and get it.'

'Yes, but there's no hurry for me. You have your meal first. Your sister made something with tomatoes and left it over there.'

'I'll have some, then.'

Giovanni got the dish of tomatoes from by the window and devoured it hungrily with some bread.

'Mom, I feel sure Dad will be coming home soon.'

'I think so, too. What makes you think so, though?'

'Well, I mean, it said in this morning's paper that the fishing up north has been good this year.'

'Yes, but your father may not be out fishing at all, you know.'

'I'm sure he is. I don't believe Dad would have done anything bad enough to go to prison for. You remember that big crab shell and the reindeer horns that he brought back and presented to the school? Well, they've still got them in the specimen room. In sixth grade, the teachers are always bringing them out to show to the class.'

'Your father said that next time he'd bring you back an otter-skin jacket, didn't he?'

'That's what the others always say when they see me. As though they're making fun of me.'

'They say nasty things to you?'

'Mm. But Campanella – he never does. When the others say things like that he just stands there looking sorry for me.'

'Campanella's father and your father were friends right from the time they were small, just like Campanella and you.'

'Yes, that's why Dad always used to take me over to Campanella's house with him. I liked those days. I often used to drop in at

Campanella's on my way home from school. They had a train that ran on an alcohol burner. There were seven bits of rail that made a circle when you fitted them together, and there were telegraph poles and signals to go with it, and the signal was made so that it only turned green when a train went past. One time we ran out of alcohol and used gasoline instead, and the boiler got all sooty.'

'Well, now!'

'I still go there every morning to deliver the paper. But the whole place is always quiet, so . . .'

'Well, it's too early at that time of day, isn't it?'

'They've got a dog called Sauer. His tail's just like a broom. When I go there, he comes snuffling after me. He comes all the way to the corner of the block, sometimes further. Tonight they say they're all going to float gourd lanterns on the river. I bet the dog will go with them, too.'

'Oh yes, of course – tonight's the Festival of the Milky Way, isn't it?'

'Yes. I'll have a look when I go to fetch the milk.'

'Yes, you do that! Mind you don't go in the water, though.'

'I'll just watch from the bank. That's all I ever do. I'll be back in an hour.'

'Mind you enjoy yourself, now! I shan't worry if I know you're with Campanella.'

'Oh, I'll be with him, don't worry. Mom, shall I shut the window now?'

'Yes, please, it's getting quite chilly.'

Giovanni got up and shut the window, put away the plate and the bag of bread, then tugged on his shoes, and with a 'Well then, I'll be back in an hour and a half,' went out through the dark doorway.

4. The Night of the Centaur Festival

His lips puckered wistfully as though he were whistling, Giovanni went down the hill with its avenue of pitch-black cedars, down towards the town.

At the foot of the slope, a single, tail street lamp stood shining with a splendid bluish white light. As Giovanni advanced towards the lamp, his shadow, which had been dragging out long and pale behind him like a ghost, gradually got darker and clearer until in the end, lifting its legs and waving its arms, it came around to walk beside him.

I'm just like a locomotive, thought Giovanni. I go faster here because I'm on a down slope. Now I'm passing the street lamp. There – my shadow's moving like a compass needle. Now it's come all the way around and it's in front!

And he'd just strode by under the street lamp when Zanelli, the boy who'd sniggered at him earlier that day, suddenly came out of the dark alley beyond the lamp, wearing a new shirt with a pointed collar, and slipped across Giovanni's path.

Giovanni was just going to say, 'Zanelli, are you going to float lanterns?' But before he could get it out the other boy shouted at him:

'Giovanni's father's sending him an otter-skin jacket!'

Giovanni's heart froze and a cold wind seemed to wail around him.

'You dare say that again, Zanelli!' he shouted back angrily. But Zanelli had already disappeared into a house with a cedar growing in front of it.

I haven't done anything to deserve it, he thought. Why does Zanelli say such things? I bet he doesn't know he looks just like a rat when he runs! He's stupid. Otherwise he wouldn't say such things when he knows I haven't done anything!

His mind seething, Giovanni walked on through the town, which was decked out with all kinds of lights and branches. The clock shop had bright fluorescent lighting, and an owl made of stone whose red eyes rolled round and round every second, and a thick plate of glass, the colour of the sea, bearing all kinds of jewels that went slowly round and round like the stars, while a copper centaur came slowly turning around from the other side. Right in the middle of everything there was a round black disc showing the constellations, decorated with a sprig of green asparagus. Oblivious of his surroundings, Giovanni gazed intently at the map of the stars.

It was far smaller than the map he'd seen at school earlier that day, but it was made so that when you adjusted it to the right day and time, the oval section of the sky that was visible just then appeared as it actually was. And there today, sure enough, right in the middle, stretching from top to bottom in a blurred, smoky-looking band, was the Milky Way. At the bottom was an area where there seemed to have been a slight explosion and what looked like steam was rising.

In the rear of the shop a small telescope on three legs gleamed yellow, while on the wall at the very back there hung a great chart with all the constellations in the sky shown as strange animals and fish and snakes and ewers and the like. Giovanni lingered there for a while, wondering whether the sky was really crammed with scorpions and warriors and other creatures, and thinking how he'd like to wander among them, on and on, forever . . .

But suddenly he remembered the milk for his mother, and reluctantly turned away

He walked on through the town, bothered by his jacket, which was getting too tight for him, yet deliberately drawing back his shoulders and energetically swinging his arms.

The air flowed crystal-clear like water down the street and between the shops; the street lamps were all swathed in deep green fir and oak branches, and the six plane trees in front of the electric company's office actually had fairy lights, lots of them, among their foliage, so that the whole scene looked like the city of the merfolk beneath the sea.

Children in newly pressed kimonos were whistling the Star-Wanderer's tune or rushing about shouting, 'Centaurus, send down the dew!' or letting off fireworks that gave a blue magnesium light. By now, though, Giovanni had his head down again and was hurrying on to the milk shop as if nothing were further from his mind than the gaiety all about him.

Almost before he realised it, he'd reached a place on the outskirts of town where there were countless poplar trees whose tops seemed to be floating high up in the sky. Going through the dark gate of the milkman's, he stopped in the entrance of the great, murky dairy that smelt of cows and, taking off his cap, called out:

'Good evening!'

The house was hushed, seemingly deserted.

'Good evening!' shouted Giovanni again, still standing there at attention. 'Is anyone at home?' There was a pause, then an old woman came out from the back walking slowly, as though she had something wrong with her, and mumbled something unintelligible.

'Er, we didn't get any milk at our place this morning,' announced Giovanni briskly in his best voice, 'so I've come to get it.'

'Don't ask me – there's no one here. Come again tomorrow,'

said the woman, looking down at Giovanni and rubbing at the lower lids of her red eyes.

'My mother's sick, so we must have it tonight.'

'Well then, come back a bit later, will you?' And she turned away.

'I see. Thank you, then.' And with a bow, Giovanni went out of the dairy.

He was turning the corner of the crossroads in the centre of the town when, in front of the general store on the way to the bridge, in a confusion of black shapes and the vague white of undershirts, he saw six or seven schoolboys coming along whistling and laughing, each of them carrying a lighted gourd lantern. Everything about the way they were laughing and whistling was familiar to him: they were from his own class. Startled, Giovanni had an impulse to turn away, then changed his mind and started walking again still more vigorously in their direction.

'Going to the river?' he was going to ask them; but the words somehow stuck in his throat, and just then Zanelli shouted in exactly the same way as before:

'Giovanni's getting an otter-skin jacket!'

At once, the others sang out in chorus:

'Giovanni's getting an otter, skin jacket!'

Giovanni turned bright red and hurried on past them, hardly aware of what his legs were doing. As he did so, he saw Campanella among them, standing quiet with a faintly pitying smile, looking in Giovanni's direction as though wondering whether he would get angry or not.

Giovanni hurried to escape his gaze, and Campanella's tall form was hardly out of sight when the others all started whistling their own versions of the festival song again.

As he went around the corner, he looked back and saw Zanelli looking back too. And he saw Campanella too, whistling loudly again, walking off in the direction of the bridge that was vaguely visible in the distance. Feeling unspeakably sad, Giovanni broke into a run, whereupon some little children who were hopping around on one leg with their hands over their ears, shouting, thought he was running for fun, and set up a clamour after him.

Before long, Giovanni started running again, making at full speed for the black hills.

5. The Weather Pole

Beyond the dairy farm lay a line of gently sloping hills, their dark, flat tops showing vague and seemingly lower than usual beneath the Great Bear in the northern sky.

Giovanni climbed steadily upwards along a narrow path through woods where the dew was already falling. Beneath the light of the stars, the path was a single thread of white between the looming, pitch-black shapes of grasses and bushes. Among the grass, tiny insects gave out a bluish gleam, so that some leaves showed a transparent green, reminding Giovanni of the gourd lanterns the others had been carrying to the river.

Suddenly, beyond the dense black wood of pines and oaks, the sky yawned vast before him. He could see the Milky Way stretching whitish from south to north, and even make out the pole on the hilltop. All about him flowers – bellflowers and daisies – were blooming; their fragrance came to him as though in a dream, and a single bird called incessantly as it flew across the hills.

Reaching the foot of the pole at the summit, Giovanni threw himself down panting on the cool grass.

The lights of the town below burned in the darkness, for all the world like some fairy palace beneath the sea, and the faint sounds of children singing and whistling, and broken cries, reached him from below. The wind soughed in the distance, the grass on the hill rustled, and Giovanni's shirt, damp with sweat, began to feel chilly.

From the open countryside came the sound of a train. It looked tiny, with a row of small orange windows, and the thought of the travellers inside it, peeling apples and joking and passing the time pleasantly together, made Giovanni feel so terribly sad that he raised his eyes to the sky again.

And yet, however much he looked, he couldn't bring himself to believe that the sky was such a cold, empty place as their teacher had told them. In fact, the longer he looked the more he became convinced that it was a great stretch of countryside, with little woods and pastures and the like. And then, as Giovanni watched, the blue Lyra constellation became three, or even four, and twinkled bluish; it stretched out and drew in its legs any number of times until finally it lay long and mushroomlike, while the town right beneath him began to look like a great blurred gathering of stars, or a single great cloud of smoke.

6. Milky Way Station

And then, Giovanni saw that, without his noticing it, the pole right behind him had turned into a vague shape like the kind of marker set in the ground by surveyors. For a while it glimmered on and off indistinctly, like a glow-worm, then gradually it got clearer and clearer, until finally it became still and clear-cut and took off into the deep blue sky, shooting straight up into the open stretch of the sky that was like a sheet of newly tempered blue steel.

Suddenly out of nowhere came a strange voice, calling 'Milky Way! Milky Way Station!' and the very next moment there was a flood of light – as though the fossils of a million firefly squid had been set out all over the sky, or as though someone at a diamond firm had suddenly upset and scattered all the jewels that the firm had been deliberately hoarding, pretending that there was a shortage so as to keep the price up – a great dazzle of light before his eyes, so that he found himself rubbing them again and again in wonderment.

When he recovered, the little train that he was riding in had been clattering along the tracks for some time. Yes, he was sitting in the carriage, with its rows of small yellow lights, of a little night train, looking out of the window. Inside the carriage, the blue velvet-covered seats were mostly empty, and two large brass buttons gleamed in the grey varnish of the opposite wall.

In the seat directly in front of him sat a tall boy in a black, wet-looking jacket, with his head thrust out of the window watching the outside. Something about the set of the boy's shoulders was so familiar that Giovanni felt an urge to find out who it was. He was just about to stick his own head out of the window to see, when the boy drew his in and looked at Giovanni.

It was Campanella. Giovanni was about to ask him whether he'd been there all along, when Campanella said:

'The others ran like mad, but they got left behind. Zanelli was one of them. He ran as hard as he could, but he couldn't catch up.'

Yes, of course, thought Giovanni, we decided to leave together.

'Shall we wait for them somewhere?' he said.

But Campanella said:

'Zanelli's gone home. His father came to fetch him.'

For some reason Campanella's face went rather pale as he spoke, as though he was in pain; and Giovanni, too, had a funny feeling, as though there was something, somewhere, that he'd forgotten.

But Campanella had already got over it and was looking out of the window, exclaiming:

'Oh dear! I've forgotten my water flask. And my sketchbook. But it doesn't matter. We shall soon be at Swan Halt. I like watching swans, so I don't mind. I'm sure I shall spot them even if they're flying far off over the river.'

For a while he sat twisting round and round a map in the form of a circular board that he had in his hands. Sure enough, it showed a railroad track running steadily down towards the south, following the left bank of the white streak that was the Milky Way.

And a particularly striking thing about this map was that every single halt and marker, every river and lake and wood, was picked out on the midnight black of the board in pretty blue or orange or green lights.

Giovanni had the feeling that he'd seen the map somewhere before.

'Where did you buy that map?' he asked. 'It's made of obsidian, isn't it?'

'They gave it to me at Milky Way Station. Didn't you get one?'

'Mm . . . I'm not sure I went through Milky Way Station,' said Giovanni. 'But this is where we are now, isn't it?' He pointed to a place just north of the sign for the halt marked 'Swan'.

'That's right. Look! Do you think that's moonlight on the dry part of the riverbed over there?'

Giovanni looked and saw that the edge of the bluish white, gleaming Milky Way was completely covered with sky-pampas grass that rustled as it swayed and rippled.

'No, it's not moonlight. It shines like that because it's the Milky Way!' As he spoke, Giovanni suddenly felt like jumping for joy; he drummed on the floor with his feet and put his head out of the window, whistling the Star-Wanderer's tune as loud as he could and straining his eyes to make out the water of the Milky Way.

At first, he couldn't see it distinctly. Gradually, though, he realised that the water was there, clearer than crystal, clearer than hydrogen, silently flowing along; occasionally – or was it just his eyes? – it set up tiny purple ripples or glinted in all the colours of the rainbow; and all over the open countryside round about stood markers gleaming with a beautiful, phosphorescent light. The distant ones were small, the nearer ones big; the former distinct and orange or yellow in colour, the latter a pale bluish white and rather hazy; some triangular, some rectangular, others zigzagged or chain-shaped – all kinds of them, gleaming here and there all over the landscape. Giovanni's heart beat excitedly and he shook his head vigorously, whereupon the beautiful markers that glittered orange and blue and every other colour fluttered and flickered as though each of them was alive and breathing.

'Yes, I'm really here in the Plain of Heaven!' exclaimed Giovanni. 'And this train,' he went on, sticking out his left hand and gazing out of the window towards the front, 'doesn't run on coal, either.'

'It probably uses alcohol or electricity,' said Campanella.

At which, as though in reply, a voice, a sonorous voice like a cello, came out of the haze somewhere far, far away:

This train doesn't run on stream or electricity. It just runs, because that's what it's supposed to do. You may think it makes a clatter, but that's just because you're used to trains that make a noise!

'I've heard that voice somewhere lots of times before!'

'So have I! Lots of times, in the woods and by the river.'

Clatter-clatter, clatter-clatter, went the pretty little train, through the fluttering of the sky-pampas grass in the breeze, through the pale glimmerings of the markers and the waters of the Milky Way, on and on forever . . .

'Look, the gentians are in bloom. It's quite late in autumn, isn't it?' said Campanella, pointing out of the window.

In the short grass that bordered the tracks, fine, purplish-blue gentians were blooming as though carved out of sapphire.

'Do you dare me to jump off, pick some, and jump back on again?' said Giovanni.

'Too late! Look how far behind they are already!'

Hardly had Campanella got these words out when another batch of gentians went past in a blaze of light. And before they knew it, another, and yet another mass of gentian flowers with yellow hearts inside their open cups passed their eyes like fountains, or showers of rain, while the markers, some blurred, some blazing, stood there shining in ever greater numbers.

7. The Northern Cross and the Pliocene Coast

'Do you think my mother will forgive me?'

Campanella said it quite suddenly, as though he'd suddenly made up his mind about something. He stammered a little as he spoke, then had a fit of coughing.

Why, I'd forgotten! thought Giovanni. My own mother's down there now, somewhere near that orange marker so far away it looks like a speck of dust, thinking of me at this very moment. Without replying he stayed sunk in his own thoughts.

'I'd do anything to make Mother really happy,' said Campanella. 'But I'm not sure just what would be best.' Somehow, he looked as though he was trying hard not to burst into tears.

'What do you mean?' exclaimed Giovanni, shocked. 'Nothing terrible's happened to her, surely?'

'I'm not sure. But doing something really good is what makes you most happy. Everybody's the same, aren't they? So I feel Mother will probably forgive me.'

He really looked as though he'd made up his mind about something.

Abruptly, the inside of the carriage was flooded with white light. They looked, and there in the midst of the waters of the Milky Way that flowed silent and formless over a bed resplendent with the glory of diamonds and bright dew on grass, they saw an island surrounded with a vague bluish-white light. On the level top of the island stood a magnificent, dazzling white cross with a clear-cut golden halo around it; silent and eternal, it stood there as though cast from frozen arctic cloud.

'Hallelujah! Hallelujah!' rose voices from before and behind them. They looked around and saw that all the travellers in their carriage were standing, so that the folds of their kimono hung straight down, some clutching black bibles to their chests, some with crystal rosaries about their necks, all of them with their hands folded humbly, praying in the direction of the island.

Before they knew what they were doing, they too had both risen to their feet.

Campanella's cheeks were aglow with the beautiful red flush of a ripe apple.

Gradually the island, and the cross with it, fell to the rear.

The opposite bank too became a shining blur of silver that would cloud over fleetingly from time to time as though someone had breathed on it – it must have been the pampas grass fluttering in the breeze – while blue gentian flowers in great numbers emerged from the grass and disappeared again like so many benevolent will-o'-the-wisps.

But it was only a moment again before the space between the river and the train was barred by a row of pampas grass; Swan Island showed itself twice to the rear, but almost at once went small and distant as though in a picture; then there was a rustling of pampas again, and the island finally disappeared from sight altogether. Behind Giovanni, a tall, Catholic-looking nun in a black habit, whom he had not noticed before, stood with her round, green eyes cast down as though still devoutly intent on some words or voices reaching her from afar. The travellers went quietly back to their seats, and the two boys talked softly to each other, in words that were unconsciously different from before, about the new feeling, a kind of sadness, that filled their hearts.

'We shall soon be at Swan Halt, shan't we?'

'Mm, we get there at exactly eleven o'clock.'

Before long the green light of the signal, and its white-looming pole, flashed past outside, then the lights in front of the points, dim and indistinct like burning sulphur, went past below the windows, the train gradually slowed down, and in no time a platform appeared with an attractive, orderly row of electric lights that gradually got bigger and further apart until the two boys came directly opposite the big clock of Swan Halt and stopped precisely in front of it.

On the face of the clock in the pleasant autumn air, two blue hands of tempered steel pointed exactly to eleven o'clock. The other passengers all got out, leaving the carriage empty and deserted.

'Twenty minutes' stop,' said a sign beneath the clock.

'Shall we get off too?' said Giovanni.

'Let's.'

The two of them jumped up together, dashed out through the door, and went running along to the ticket barrier. But all they found at the barrier was a single purplish electric lamp; there was no one there. They looked around, but there was no sign of either station-master or porters.

They went into the little square outside the station, surrounded by ginkgo trees that looked like cut crystal.

A broad road led straight from the square into the bluish light of the Milky Way.

The people who'd got off the train a while ago must have gone off, for not one of them was now in sight. Shoulder to shoulder, the two walked along the white road, creating countless twin shadows as they went that stretched out in all directions like the shadows of two pillars in a room with windows on all sides, or the spokes of two wheels.

Before long they reached the beautiful riverbed that they'd seen from the train.

Campanella spread out a handful of the gleaming sand on the palm of his hand and made it rasp between his fingers.

'This sand's a mass of small crystals,' he said as though in a dream. 'There's a tiny light gleaming in every one of them.'

'So there is!' said Giovanni absently, wondering just where it was he'd learned about such things.

The pieces of gravel on the riverbed were all transparent, like crystal as Campanella had said, or like topaz, some marked with flaws and faults, and some of corundum that gave out a pale light like mist from the edges. Giovanni ran down to the water's edge and plunged his hands in the water. The mysterious waters of the Milky Way were more transparent even than hydrogen, yet you could tell they were really flowing because the part of his wrists under the water looked bent upward a little and the colour of mercury, while the ripples formed as the water dashed against them created a phosphorescence that sparkled beautifully, as though all afire.

Looking upstream, they could see a bank covered with pampas grass and beneath it a stretch of white rock jutting out along the river as flat as a sports ground. On it, a group of figures seemed to be digging up or burying something, for they kept bending down and straightening up, and occasionally there was the glint of an implement.

'Let's go and look,' the two boys shouted almost as one, and they set off running in that direction. At the entrance to the area of white rock stood a nameplate of smooth white china saying 'Pliocene Beach'. Here and there by the edge of the water beyond, slim iron railings had been set up, and there were pleasant-looking wooden benches.

'Look, here's something funny!' Stopping and looking puzzled,

Campanella picked up from the rock what liked like a dark-coloured, longish walnut pointed at one end.

'It's a walnut. Look, there are lots of them. They weren't brought down by the river, they were in the rock.'

'They're big, aren't they, for walnuts. Twice as big as ordinary ones. Here's one that's not damaged at all.'

'Come on, let's go over there and see. I'm sure they're digging something up.'

Taking the gnarled black nuts with them, they went back to the place where they'd seen the people. At the water's edge to their left, the waves burned like friendly lightning as they approached, and the bank to their right was covered with swaying pampas grass, with fronds that looked as though they were made of silver or mother-of-pearl.

As they drew nearer, they could see a tall man who looked like an eminent scholar and wore boots and spectacles with awfully thick lenses, busily making notes in a notebook as he gave orders to three men who seemed to be his assistants and were hard at work wielding pickaxes and digging with shovels.

'Use your spades so you don't damage that projection there. Your spades! Oh, oh, dig a little further away! No, no, don't! Why do you have to go at it so roughly?'

They saw that a good half of the great, whitish skeleton of some animal had been dug out of the soft white rock and laid out so that it looked as though it had fallen over sideways, then come to pieces. They noticed, too, a dozen or so square pieces of rock bearing cloven hoof marks that had been carefully carved out and numbered.

'You're visitors, I imagine?' The scholarly-looking man flashed his spectacles in their direction as he spoke. 'I suppose you noticed all those walnuts? They're – well, now – some one million two hundred thousand years old, I'd say. That puts them among the most recent. One million two hundred thousand years ago, in the later Tertiary period, this place was on the coast, you know. You find shells too under here. The salt tides used to ebb and flow precisely where the river runs now. This beast here – it's called *bos* (hey! – stop using your pickaxes there – do it carefully, with chisels!). As I was saying, it's called *bos*, and it's the ancestor of our cattle. There used to be lots of them.'

'Are you going to use it as a specimen?'

'No, we need it as evidence. As we see things, this place is a particularly fine, thick geological stratum. It yields all kinds of proof that it was formed one million two hundred years ago, but the question is whether people with different ideas from ourselves will see it in the same light, or whether it'll look no different from the wind or the water, or the empty sky. D'you see? And yet (hey, hey! – you mustn't use spades there, either! Don't you realise that the ribs are most likely buried directly beneath there?).'

He went off at a frantic trot.

'It's time. Let's go,' said Campanella, looking from his map to his wristwatch.

'Right,' said Giovanni. He turned to the eminent scholar and bowed politely. 'I'm afraid we must be going.'

'Must you? Well, goodbye to you then.' And the scholar set off busily again, going around supervising the work.

The boys ran for all they were worth, back over the white rock, so as not to miss the train. They found they really could run like the wind: they didn't get out of breath, nor did their knee-joints get hot and sore.

If only I could always run like this, thought Giovanni, I could run anywhere in the world....

They went along the same riverbed as before, the light over the ticket barrier getting steadily larger as they approached, and before long the two of them were sitting in their seats in the carriage, looking out of the window in the direction they'd just come from.

8. The Bird-Catcher

'I wonder whether I might sit here?' said an adult's voice, rough but amiable, behind them.

It was a man with a stoop and a red beard, wearing a brown, rather shabby overcoat and with a bundle wrapped in white cloth slung in two halves over his shoulder.

'Oh, go ahead,' said Giovanni with a slight shrug of acknowledgement. The man smiled faintly in his beard as he slowly hoisted his bundle onto the luggage rack. Giovanni, feeling sad and forlorn, was watching the clock directly in front of them when, way up front, someone blew what sounded like a glass flute and the train slowly slid into motion. Campanella was peering up around the roof of the carriage; a black stag beetle was perched on one of the lights, and its shadow, much enlarged, was visible on the ceiling.

Redbeard was looking Giovanni and Campanella over with a smile as though they were old friends. By now the train was picking up speed, and pampas grass and river flashed by alternately outside the window.

'Where would you be going, I wonder?' the man with the red beard asked them, rather timidly.

'On and on forever,' replied Giovanni, feeling rather embarrassed.

'Now that's nice. That's just where this train is going, you know.'

'And where are you going?' inquired Campanella abruptly, sounding so aggressive that Giovanni couldn't help smiling. A man in the seat across the aisle wearing a pointed hat and with a big key dangling from his sash, glanced in their direction and smiled too, so that Campanella blushed and finally began to smile in turn. The bearded man didn't seem angry, though, and his cheeks twitched in amusement as he replied:

'I'm getting off a bit further along the line. You see, my business is catching birds.'

'What kind of birds?'

'Cranes and wild geese. Herons and swans, too.'

'Are there lots of cranes?'

'Why, certainly. Their calls have been audible for some time now. Didn't you hear them?'

'No.'

'Why, they're still audible now. There – prick up your ears and listen.'

They raised their heads and listened hard. Amidst the regular clatter of the train and the rushing of the wind in the pampas grass they could hear a gurgling sound like water bubbling up from somewhere.

'How do you catch the cranes?'

'Cranes? Or do you mean herons?'

'Herons, then,' replied Giovanni, feeling it didn't really matter which.

'Oh, it's not difficult. Herons, you see, are all made from the sand of the Milky Way that's taken on the heron's shape and turned cloudy; so they're forever coming back home here. You wait here by the river, and when they start to alight with their legs like this, you grab their feet just before they touch down on the ground. And that's it: the heron goes stiff and dies without worrying about anything more. Then all you have to do – I mean, it's obvious – is press them.'

'You press them, like flowers? You mean, as specimens?'

'Not as specimens. I mean, people eat them, don't they?'

'Seems funny to me.' Campanella shook his head doubtfully.

'There's nothing at all funny or suspicious about it! Here –' he stood up, got his bundle down from the luggage rack, and with swift movements untied it.

'Here, look! I've only just caught them.'

The boys couldn't help shouting, 'They really are herons!'

Ten herons, pure white and shining like the Northern Cross they'd seen earlier, were lying there slightly flattened, with their legs drawn up and looking rather like a row of relief carvings.

'Their eyes are shut, aren't they?' said Campanella, gingerly touching one white, crescent-shaped, closed eye with his finger. The head even had its white crest, sticking up like a spear.

'So you see?' said the bird-catcher, folding up the cloth and tying it round and round with string again.

'Do herons taste nice?' asked Giovanni, wondering who ever would eat herons in these parts.

'Yes. I get orders every day. But the wild geese sell even better. Geese have a far better shape, and, what's more important, they're no trouble. Here –'

The bird-catcher began to undo the other bundle. And there were some geese, speckled yellow and bluish white and with a kind of light about them, lying just like the herons in a row, slightly flattened, with their beaks all pointing in the same direction.

'These are ready for eating. Won't you try a bit?' He tugged lightly at the yellow leg of one of the geese, which came off clean as though it was made of chocolate or something.

'Here, try some!' He broke it in two and gave them one piece each.

Gingerly, Giovanni ate a little. 'What a swindle!' he said to himself. 'It's candy! It's nicer than chocolate, but I can't see this kind of goose ever actually flying. This fellow must keep a sweet shop somewhere in the country around here. Even so, I feel guilty, going on eating the poor man's candy while I find fault with him in my mind.' But he went on munching away at it just the same.

'Have a bit more,' said the bird-catcher, holding out the package again.

Giovanni wanted some more, but politely declined: 'No, thank you all the same.' So the bird-catcher offered it instead to the man with the key in the opposite seat.

'Really, I must say,' said that man, doffing his hat, 'I don't like to take your stock like this.'

'No, no, not a bit of it. Tell me – how are things going with the migratory birds this year?'

'Why, really excellent. You know, during the second shift the day before yesterday, I got telephone complaints from all over the place asking why I was shutting off the lighthouse light at other than the regulation periods. "What do you mean?" I said. 'What's the use of coming to me with such complaints? You'd do better to take them to the boss up there, him in his windblown cloak with his pointy mouth and legs!' That's what I told them!' He laughed.

They had got beyond the pampas grass now, so that the light came flooding in again from the open country beyond.

'Why is it that the herons are more trouble?' Campanella had been meaning to put the question for some time.

'Well, you see,' said the bird-catcher, turning towards him, 'before you can eat the herons, you either have to hang them for ten days in the water-light of the Milky Way, or else bury them for three or four days in the sand. That way, the mercury all evaporates and they can be eaten.'

'This isn't a bird, surely? Isn't it just a piece of candy?' asked Campanella. He seemed to have been thinking the same thing as Giovanni, and to have finally decided to speak out.

The bird-catcher stood up as though in a panic. 'Why, of course, this is where I get off,' he said, and took down his bundle. The next moment, he had disappeared.

'I wonder where he went?' said the boys, looking at each other. The lighthouse keeper grinned and leaned over a little to peer out of the window beside them.

Looking in the same direction, they saw the bird-catcher who'd been with them a moment before standing by the river in a stretch of cottonweed that gleamed with a beautiful yellow and bluish white phosphorescence: he had an earnest expression on his face, and was gazing steadily up at the sky with his arms spread out.

'Look where he's got to! It's awfully queer, isn't it? I bet he's going to catch some more birds. I hope some come down soon, before the train leaves!'

No sooner had Giovanni said this than out of the bluebell-coloured sky a flock of herons like the ones they'd seen a while ago came fluttering down like snowflakes, calling as they came. Gleefully, the bird-catcher planted himself with his legs in a perfect equilateral triangle and, grabbing with both hands the black, drawn-up legs of first one, then another heron as they came down, popped them in a cloth bag. For a while they flashed blue, on and off inside the bag like glow-worms, but finally they turned a vague white, then closed their eyes.

In actual fact, the birds that got caught were far fewer than those that alighted safely on the sand by the river. But then, if you watched the latter carefully you saw that the moment their legs touched the sand, they shrank and went flat like melting snow, spreading out over the sand like molten copper flowing out of a blast furnace. For a while, they left their shapes in the sand, but then, after turning first dark then light a few times, ended up exactly the same colour as their surroundings.

The bird-catcher put some twenty birds in his bag, then suddenly raised his arms in the air like a soldier struck down by a bullet. The next moment, there was no sign of him; instead, a familiar voice was saying next to Giovanni:

'My, that's a load off my mind! I must say, there's nothing so satisfying as a good day's catch!' It was the bird-catcher, who already had the herons he'd caught laid out tidily and was piling them neatly one on the other.

'How did you get from there to here so quickly?' Giovanni asked with a funny feeling, not sure whether he should be surprised or not.

'How? Because I felt like it. And where do you two come from?'

Giovanni was about to reply when he found that he just couldn't think where he did come from. Campanella's face, too, was pink as though with the effort of remembering.

'I see,' said the bird-catcher. 'From a long way off.' And he nodded easily, as though he understood.

9. Giovanni's Ticket

'We're just about at the end of the Swan Zone by now. Look, that's the famous Albireo Observatory.'

Outside the window, right in the centre of the mass of fireworks that was the Milky Way, stood four large black buildings; on the flat roof of one were two large, dazzling, transparent jewels – a sapphire and a topaz – revolving quietly about each other. The yellow one would gradually retreat to the far side, while the smaller, blue one would come around to the front; before long the edges of the two jewels would overlap to form a beautiful green convex-lens shape whose middle would gradually swell until finally the blue jewel was completely in front of the topaz, producing a green centre with a bright yellow ring around it. Then it would gradually slide to one side, re-creating the lens shape on the other side, until the two slipped apart again, the sapphire moving around to the back and the yellow one coming to the front, so that things were just as they had been earlier. Surrounded by the formless, soundless waters of the Milky Way the black observatory buildings lay silent, as though asleep.

'That's an instrument to measure the speed of the water's flow,' said the bird-catcher. 'The water –' But just then a voice said, 'Tickets, please!'

A tall conductor in a red cap had come up and was standing bolt upright beside the seat. Without a word the bird-catcher took a small piece of paper from his pocket. The conductor glanced at it, then immediately looked away and held his hand out in the direction of Giovanni and his friend, waggling his fingers as though to say 'And where are yours?'

'Let me see.' Giovanni hesitated awkwardly, but Campanella produced a small, grey ticket as though it was the most natural thing in the world. In a panic, Giovanni thrust a hand into his jacket pocket on the offchance, and encountered what seemed to be a large piece of folded paper. Taking it out hastily, hardly believing his senses, he found it was a piece of green paper about the size of a postcard, folded in four. The conductor was holding his hand out, so he handed it over in a devil-may-care spirit. But now the conductor shot up very straight again, opened it up respectfully, and stood looking at it. Fiddling busily with the buttons of his jacket, he ran his eyes over it, while the lighthouse keeper too peered at it eagerly from underneath. Giovanni was sure it must be a certificate or something, and felt a thrill of excitement.

'Did you come on this from Three-Dimensional Space, sir?' asked the conductor.

'I'm blessed if I know.' Giovanni looked up at the man and giggled, with a feeling of relief: it was all right.

'That's quite all right, sir. We shall be arriving at the Southern Cross around the next Third Hour.' Handing the paper back to Giovanni, the conductor went off down the train.

Immediately, Campanella peered over at the piece of paper as though dying to find out what it was. Giovanni too was every bit as eager, but in fact it was printed all over with a pattern of squiggly black lines, with a dozen or so funny-looking letters among them. He gazed at it in silence, with a feeling that he might be sucked down into it.

At this point the bird-catcher, glancing over at it, exclaimed excitedly:

'My word, this is really something! Why, this ticket will take you all the way up to Heaven itself. Not just Heaven, either. It's a pass to travel absolutely anywhere you like. With this you should – ah, of course, I see now – be able to go on and on forever in this imperfect fourth dimension of fantasy that is the Milky Way Railway. You have my respect, gentlemen!'

'I'm sure I don't know!' Turning pink as he replied, Giovanni folded the ticket up again and put it back in his pocket. Embarrassed, he gazed out of the window again with Campanella, still vaguely aware of the bird-catcher snatching admiring glances at him from time to time.

'We shall soon be reaching Eagle Halt,' said Campanella, checking on his map a row of three small, bluish white markers on the opposite bank.

Without knowing quite why, Giovanni began to feel terribly sorry for the bird-catcher next to him. The way he'd said so happily that it was 'a load off his mind' because he'd caught some herons: the way he'd wrapped them round and round so carefully in white cloth; the way he stole startled glances at people's tickets, then hastily started praising them. As Giovanni pondered such things, he felt he wouldn't mind giving the bird-catcher, complete stranger though he was, everything he had – his belongings, his food, anything. If it would really make him happy, he wouldn't mind standing there on the shining bed of the Milky Way for a hundred years if necessary, just catching birds for him. And he felt he absolutely had to say something, to ask the bird-catcher just what it was he would like.

But he could hardly say such things out of the blue. Still wondering what to do, he looked around, only to find that the bird-catcher was no longer to be seen. There was no sign of his white bundle on the rack, either. Nor, though Giovanni looked hurriedly out of the window expecting to see him with legs planted firmly apart, gazing up at the sky ready to catch his herons, was there anything but an expanse of beautiful sand and waving white pampas grass. Neither the bird-catcher's broad back nor his pointed hat was anywhere in sight.

'Where do you think we shall see him next? Why didn't I talk to him a bit more, I wonder?'

'Mm. I feel the same.'

'I felt he was a bit in the way. So now I feel awfully guilty.'

This was the first time, actually, that Giovanni had ever had this odd feeling; nor, he realised, had he ever said such a thing before.

'Why, there's a smell of apples,' said Campanella, looking about him wonderingly. 'Do you think it was because I was thinking about apples?'

'Yes, it really does smell of apples,' said Giovanni, looking around him in the same way. 'And there's a smell of wild roses, too.' But it seemed the smell must be coming in through the window or somewhere. It's autumn, thought Giovanni, so there ought not to be a smell of wild roses now.

The next moment, without warning, a boy of about six with glossy black hair and the buttons of his red jacket all undone was standing there barefooted and shivering violently, with a terrified expression on his face. Beside him, grasping his hand firmly, a tall young man neatly dressed in a black suit stood like a zelkova tree in the full blast of the wind.

'Goodness! I wonder where this is? Why, it's beautiful!' Behind the young man was another child, a charming little girl of twelve or so with brown eyes wearing a black overcoat, who clung to the young man's arm as she looked wonderingly out of the window.

'Here? It's Lancashire. No – Connecticut. No – why, we're in the sky! We're going to Heaven. Look at that sign. It's the sign of Heaven. There's nothing to be afraid of now. We've been summoned by God!'

The face of the young man in black was alight with joy as he answered the girl. But then, for some reason or other, his forehead went into deep furrows and he looked exhausted, so that his smile was forced as he sat the little boy down in the seat beside Giovanni.

He pointed gently for the little girl to sit in the seat next to Campanella. The girl took the seat obediently and folded her hands tidily before her.

The boy who'd just sat down looked doubtful. 'We're going to where Father and Kikuyo are, aren't we?' he said to the young man, who had also just sat down in the seat opposite the lighthouse keeper. Unable to answer, the young man just gazed at the boy's curly wet hair and looked sad.

Suddenly, the girl put her hands to her face and started sobbing quietly.

'Your father and your oldest sister still have all kinds of work to do,' began the young man. 'But they'll be joining you before long. Think of your mother, though – how long she's been waiting. She's been so anxious, imagining to herself the songs her dear Tadashi would be singing these days, or picturing him on snowy mornings, hand in hand with the others, playing around the bushes in the garden. So we'll go and see her as soon as possible, eh?'

'All right. But I do wish I hadn't gone on that boat.'

'Mm. But look – there, do you see? That splendid river – remember how you always used to say "twinkle, twinkle, little star" when you went to bed, and how you could always see a white blur from the window? That's it. Look, it's beautiful, isn't it? See how it sparkles!'

At this, the boy's sister stopped crying, wiped her eyes with a handkerchief, and looked outside too.

'There's nothing for us to be sad about any more,' the young man told the brother and sister in a hushed voice. 'We're travelling through a lovely place – look! – and it's so light and full of such sweet smells and such wonderful people. And the people who managed to get into the boat when we couldn't – I'm sure they've all been rescued and are going back to the fathers and mothers who were waiting so anxiously for them, or to their own homes and children. So come, it's only a little way now, let's cheer up and sing a nice song as we go!'

The young man stroked the boy's wet-looking black hair, and his own face began to glow as he worked to comfort them.

'Where have you come from, then?' the lighthouse keeper asked the young man, as though he was beginning to understand at last. 'What happened to you?'

The young man smiled faintly.

'Actually,' he said, 'our ship hit an iceberg and sank. Two months ago the father of these two had some business that took him back home suddenly, so we set off a bit later to join him. I was at college, and they'd taken me on as a tutor. But then, just twelve days after setting sail – yesterday or the day before, it would be – the ship struck an iceberg, tilted over all at once, and started sinking. There was a vague light coming from the moon somewhere, but the mist was terribly thick. Half the lifeboats on the port side couldn't be used, and it was impossible for everyone to get into the rest. The ship was going to sink any moment, so I called out desperately asking them to put the little ones in. The people nearby made way for them at once, and prayed for the children. But there were lots of other small children and their parents and other people between them and the boat, and I didn't have the heart to push them aside.

'Even so, I felt it was my duty to save these children here, I was going to push the other children in front out of the way. But then again, I thought it would be better for these two if all of us went into God's presence as we were rather than save them in such a way.

'The very next moment, I was telling myself that in God's eyes it would only be myself who'd commit the crime against Him; and I felt I must save them. Even so, as I watched, I couldn't bring myself to do it.

'It was a heartrending sight – the children left in the boats by themselves, their mothers, half-crazed, blowing kisses to them, and their fathers standing stiff and upright, trying not to show their grief. Before long the ship started sinking rapidly, so we huddled together ready for the worst; I put my arms around these two here, and we waited for the ship to go down, determined to stay afloat for as long as we could.

'A lifebelt that somebody had thrown came our way. But it slipped out of our grasp and went far away into the distance.

'Using all my strength I tore off part of a deck grating and we clung tightly to it. From somewhere, there came a voice saying, 'Hymn Number 306'. And quite suddenly, everybody began singing all at once, in all kinds of languages.

'Just then, there was a loud noise and we were thrown into the water. It seemed we'd got caught in a whirlpool; I held these two tightly in my arms and everything went black, and the next thing I knew we were here.

'These children's mother died the year before last. I'm sure, though, the boats got away safely. I mean, the sailors rowing them were all experienced, and they'd got the boats clear of the ship in good time.'

People round about could be heard sighing or praying quietly to themselves. Both Giovanni and Campanella found their eyes smarting, vaguely recalling all kinds of things they'd long forgotten.

Ah, thought Giovanni, that great sea must have been what they call the Pacific. Up there now, in the far northern waters, where the icebergs come floating down, there's someone on a small ship, braving the wind and the freezing seawater and the bitter cold, working for all he's worth. I feel really sorry for him, and guilty somehow. I wonder what I could do to make him happy?

He hung his head, sunk in gloom.

'Who can say what happiness is?' the lighthouse keeper was saying consolingly. 'However hard to bear things may be, if they happen when you're on the path of righteousness, then every step, whether on the upgrade or the downgrade, is one step on the way to true happiness.'

'Yes, that's right,' replied the young man. 'One must remember,' he went on in a reverential tone, 'that sufferings borne on the way to the greatest happiness are all God's will.'

The young brother and sister, tired out by now, were slumped in their seats, fast asleep. Their feet, which had been bare only a while ago, had somehow acquired shoes of soft, white leather.

Clatter, clatter, went the train along the bank of the gleaming phosphorescent river. Seen through the opposite window, the countryside was just like a scene projected from a magic lantern. Hundreds, thousands of markers of all sizes stood there, the biggest of them surmounted with survey flags bearing red dots; at the edge of the landscape, they crowded so thickly that they were a vague, pale mist, and from thereabouts or still further off there rose, at intervals, vague forms – first one, then another – that looked like signal fires, fires of all shapes and of a beautiful bluebell colour. The clear, fresh breeze that blew across from them was full of the scent of roses.

'Look, I'm sure this is the first time you've seen apples like these, isn't it?'

The lighthouse keeper on the seat across the aisle had somehow acquired some large apples, coloured a beautiful gold and scarlet, which he held carefully on his lap so as not to drop them.

'My word! Wherever did they come from?' exclaimed the young man as though genuinely surprised. 'They're very fine! Do they grow apples like those in these parts?'

He stared intently, narrowing his eyes and tilting his head on one side, at the pile of apples in the lighthouse man's hands.

'Yes, well, anyway help yourself. Go on, help yourself, now.'

The young man took one, glancing at Giovanni and Campanella as he did so.

'You youngsters there – won't you have some?'

Somewhat annoyed at being called a 'youngster,' Giovanni made no reply. Campanella, however, said 'thank you.'

At this, the young man fetched the apples himself and took them to the two boys, so Giovanni stood up politely and said 'thank you' in his turn.

The lighthouse keeper, his arms free at last, went himself and deposited one apple each on the laps of the sleeping brother and sister.

'Thank you very much,' said the young man again, gazing at them intently. 'Where do they grow such fine apples?'

'There are farmers in these parts, of course, but for the most part things are arranged so that good apples grow by themselves.

'Not that the "farming" is so much trouble, either. Mostly you just have to sow the seed you want and the plants grow steadily of their own accord. The rice, for example, doesn't have husks like the stuff you get around the Pacific, and the grain is ten times as big, with a good flavor too.

'Up where you're going, though, they don't farm at all any more. And neither the apples nor the cakes leave any waste when they're eaten. They just disperse through the pores as a faint fragrance, a different one for each person.'

Quite suddenly, the little boy was wide awake.

'Oh,' he said, 'I just had a dream about our mother! She was in a place with splendid bookcases and books, and she looked at me and held out her hand and stood there smiling and smiling. I asked if she'd like me to go and pick an apple for her . . . and then I woke up. Oh yes, we're in that train, aren't we?'

'Your apple's there – this gentleman gave it to you,' said the young man.

'Thank you, sir. Why, Kaoru's still asleep, isn't she? I'll wake her up. Kaoru, look, somebody's given us some apples! Wake up and see!'

The sister awoke with a smile and put her hands to her eyes as though dazzled by the light, then looked at the apples.

The boy was already eating his, as easily as though he were eating a piece of pastry. The pretty skin that he had peeled so carefully, making it turn round and round as it dropped in a corkscrew, had glowed a pale grey and dissipated even before it reached the floor.

Giovanni and Campanella put their apples away carefully in their pockets.

A large wood with dense green foliage appeared on the opposite bank further downstream, the branches of its trees laden with round fruit that glowed ripe and red, and with a tall, tall marker rising right in the centre. From among the trees, an indescribably lovely sound, melting and persuasive, came floating on the breeze, mingled with the notes of glockenspiel and xylophone.

The young man gave a shudder and shook himself.

As they listened in silence to the music, a bright stretch of countryside – or maybe a carpet – in yellow and pale green, spread all about them, while a dew like pure white wax seemed to brush the surface of the sun.

'Oh, look at those crows!' cried the girl called Kaoru, next to Campanella.

'They're not crows, they're magpies, all of them,' cried Campanella in a vaguely reproving voice. Giovanni smiled despite himself and the girl look embarrassed. Hordes of black birds were, in fact, sitting in rows in the pale light of the plain, quite still in the faint glow from the river.

'Yes, they're magpies,' said the young man in a soothing tone. 'They have the tuft of feathers standing up on the back of their heads.'

The marker in the green wood on the other bank had come up directly opposite the train. As it did so, from far back in the train there rose the familiar strains of Hymn 306. It sounded like a large number of people singing in chorus.

The young man suddenly turned pale; he stood and made as though to go off somewhere, then changed his mind and sat down again.

Kaoru buried her face in her handkerchief.

Even Giovanni felt a tickling in his nostrils. Yet the hymn was steadily taken up, in imperceptible stages and by no one in particular, growing ever clearer and stronger until Giovanni and Campanella found themselves joining in too.

Then the green grove of olives gradually retreated to the rear, shining grief-stricken beyond the invisible waters of the Milky Way as it went, and the mysterious sound of instruments that flowed from it grew fainter and fainter, blotted out by the roar of the train and the rushing of the wind.

'Look, a lyrebird!' cried the boy. 'A lyrebird!'

'That wood is the Lyra constellation, isn't it? I bet the members of some ancient orchestra are having a meeting there in that wood!'

'Yes, there've been lots of them,' replied the girl.

Giovanni looked above the wood – which had got smaller and smaller until by now it was no bigger than a single green button – to where an occasional pale gleam showed the light reflecting from the lyrebird's wings as it folded and unfolded them.

'You're right. A while ago I heard lyrebirds calling, too,' said Campanella to the girl.

'Yes,' she replied, 'there were at least thirty of them, for sure.'

Quite suddenly, Giovanni felt very left out, and had to check an urge to look fierce and say, 'Campanella, let's jump off here and play for a while!'

Just at that moment, though, he saw something strange in the distance further down the river.

As far as he could tell, it was a long, narrow object, black and slippery, that leapt up out of the invisible waters of the Milky Way, moved for a moment in an arc, then disappeared into the water again. Puzzled, he watched closely, and saw what seemed to be similar things everywhere, lots of them, leaping out of the water, flying in a curve, then diving into the water again headfirst. They seemed to be climbing upstream, like fish.

'Why, I wonder what they can be, Tadashi? Look! Why, there are lots of them! Whatever can they be?'

The boy, who'd been rubbing his eyes sleepily, got to his feet as though startled.

'What can it be?' The young man stood up, too.

'Why, it's a funny kind of fish! What do you think it is?'

'Dolphins,' said Campanella, looking in that direction.

'Dolphins? I've never seen them. But this isn't the sea, is it?'

They're not found only in the sea. The same strange, quiet voice as before came again from nowhere in particular.

The dolphins really did look funny: shooting up out of the water, two fins hanging down like hands as though they were at attention, then bowing their heads reverently and, still at attention, disappearing beneath the surface again. As they did so, the invisible waters of the Milky Way set up ripples like blue flames.

'Would dolphins be fish?' inquired the little girl of Campanella. The little boy, apparently worn out, was slumped against the seat, asleep.

'Dolphins aren't fish,' replied Campanella. 'They're animals, like whales.'

'Have you ever seen a whale?'

'Yes, I have. With whales, it's the head and the tail you see first. When they spout, they're just like you see them in books.'

'I suppose whales are awfully big.'

'Yes, they're big. Even the calves are the size of a dolphin.'

'Yes, that's right! I read it in the Arabian Nights.' She played with the narrow silver ring on her finger, absorbed in the talk.

Campanella, I'm getting off! I've never even seen a whale! thought Giovanni, almost beside himself with irritation. But he clamped his lips together and forced himself to look out of the window.

Outside, the dolphins were no longer to be seen, and the river had divided into two. Right in the centre of the dark island, a tall, tall framework tower had been erected and a man wearing a loose robe and a red hat was standing on the top. He had a red flag and a green flag in his hands and was looking up at the sky, signalling.

As Giovanni watched, he suddenly lowered the red flag he was busily waving, and, hiding it behind him, raised the green flag as high as he could and waved it furiously as though conducting an orchestra. At this, there was a rushing sound in the sky like rain, and beyond the river cluster after cluster of black forms flew across the sky as though fired from a shotgun. Giovanni leaned right out of the window to look up at them.

Beneath an utterly beautiful, absolutely empty bluebell sky, tens of thousands of small birds were passing over in countless flocks, each one of them calling busily as it went.

'The birds are flying away,' said Giovanni from outside the window.

'Eh, where?' said Campanella, looking up at the sky too.

Suddenly, the man in the loose robe on the tower put up his red flag and waved it about madly, whereupon, quite abruptly, the flocks of birds stopped coming through, and at the same moment a squelching sound came from further down the river, to be followed by complete silence. But the next moment the signalman in the red cap was waving his green flag again and shouting:

'Off you go now, birds of passage! Now's the time to go!' They could hear his voice quite clearly. And with it, a flock of tens of thousands of birds shot straight off across the sky again.

Putting her head out of the same centre window as Giovanni and Campanella, the little girl gazed up at the sky, her pretty cheeks all aglow.

'Why, what a lot of the birds there are!' she said to Giovanni. 'And just look how pretty the sky is!' But Giovanni just thought how stuck-up and unpleasant she was, and went on looking up at the sky with his lips pressed together.

The girl gave a little sigh and went back to her seat without a word. Campanella drew his head in from the window, looking sorry for her, and occupied himself with his map.

'Do you think he's teaching the birds?' the girl asked Campanella in a low voice.

'He's signaling to the birds of passage,' said Campanella. 'I expect,' he added rather doubtfully, 'it's because they've put up a signal flare somewhere or other.'

And with that the carriage fell silent.

Giovanni wanted to draw his head in too, but, hating the idea of showing his face in the light, forced himself to go on standing there, whistling.

I wonder why I feel so fed up? Giovanni thought. I must make my mind more pure and more open. Look at that small, blue, wispy fire burning, quite silent and cold, far away beyond the bank over there. I must let it teach me how to keep my own mind peaceful.

Pressing his burning, aching head between his hands, Giovanni gazed in the direction of the fire.

Ah, isn't there anybody who'll stay with me all the way? he thought. Look at Campanella, talking to that girl there as though he's actually enjoying it. I'm really fed up!

His eyes filled with tears again, so that the Milky Way was no more than a white blur somewhere in the distance.

Just then, the train began to part company with the river and run along the top of a cliff. On the opposite bank too, a dark-coloured cliff appeared, getting gradually higher the further downstream it went. Then he caught sight of a large Indian corn tree. Its leaves were all curly, and beneath them were great shocks of a beautiful green, sprouting red whiskers and giving glimpses of the pearl-like grain inside.

The number of trees steadily increased until they formed a row between the edge of the cliff and the tracks. On an impulse, he drew his head in from the window and looked at the window on the other side, only to find that almost the whole beautiful expanse of countryside right up to the distant horizon was planted with the same great corn trees, which swayed and rustled in the wind, the tips of their splendid curled leaves loaded with a dew that burned and glittered red and green and many other colours, like diamonds that had been drinking up the sunlight all day.

'It's corn, isn't it?' said Campanella to Giovanni, but Giovanni, who just couldn't get himself into a normal frame of mind, replied abruptly, 'I suppose so,' without taking his eyes off the countryside.

The sound of the train grew gradually quieter, and after passing a number of signals and point lights, it came to a halt.

The pale clockface directly opposite them indicated exactly the Second Hour, and the pendulum, in the great silence of the countryside now that there was no wind and the train was still, marked off the time with a precise tick-tock, tick-tock.

And then, through the spaces between the ticks, a thread of melody came flowing from far, far away across the landscape. The girl in the seat opposite looked across. 'It's the New World Symphony,' she said in a low voice, as though to herself. Soon, all of them – the tall young man in black and everyone else in the train – were wrapped in their own fond thoughts.

It's such a peaceful place, why don't I feel happier? thought Giovanni. Why am I so alone? Even so, I think it's just too bad of Campanella. I mean, he's with me on this train, but all he does is talk to that girl. It makes me thoroughly miserable.

He stared out of the opposite window, his face half buried in his hands.

A crystal-clear whistle sounded, the train started quietly to move, and Campanella sadly whistled the Star-Wanderer's tune.

'Yes, yes,' came what sounded like an old man's voice from behind them, 'it's terribly high up here, you see.' He spoke in a brisk voice, as though he'd just woken up. 'Even corn won't grow unless you make a hole two feet deep with a stick to sow it in.'

'Is that so?' came another voice. 'It must be an awfully long way down to the river then.'

'Why, yes, from two thousand to six thousand feet. It's a huge canyon.'

Of course – it occurred to Giovanni out of the blue – this must be the uplands of Colorado!

The little girl, who had her small brother asleep against her breast, was gazing dreamily into the distance with her dark eyes, seeing nothing in particular, sunk in thought. Campanella was whistling to himself sadly, And the small boy slept soundly, his cheeks the colour of a ripe apple wrapped in fine white silk.

Quite suddenly, the corn trees ceased and a great black plain stretched out in all directions. The New World Symphony swelled up ever more clearly from over the horizon, and a solitary Red Indian, white feathers on his head, ornaments of coloured stone around his arms and on his chest, an arrow fitted to his small bow, came rushing after the train across the dark plain.

'Look, a Red Indian. A Red Indian, Kaoru! Look!'

The young man in black woke up too.

Giovanni and Campanella got to their feet.

'Why, he's riding in this direction! Look, in this direction! He's chasing us, isn't he?'

'No, he's not chasing the train. He's either hunting or performing a dance,' said the young man, standing there with his hands in his pockets as though he'd quite forgotten where he was.

The Red Indian did, in fact, almost look as though he was dancing. The way he put his feet down, for one thing, was too economical and too deliberate for him to be running. Suddenly, he halted in his tracks, the clearly visible white feathers falling forward as he did so, and fired his arrow into the air. A crane came tumbling down out of the depths of the sky, and the Red Indian ran forward again with arms spread out to catch it.

Standing there, the Red Indian smiled happily. Then, even as he stood holding the crane and looking in their direction, his figure dwindled rapidly: the insulators of two telegraph poles floated by in succession, and they were in the corn wood again.

Looking out of the window on his side, Giovanni saw that the train was running along a terribly high cliff, with the river flowing broad and bright as ever at the bottom of the canyon.

'Now then,' said the old man's voice again, 'this is where we start to go down. Which is no easy matter, seeing that this time we go right down to the riverbed in one go. With a slope like this, no trains ever come up from the opposite direction. There, you see – we're going gradually faster, aren't we?'

Down and down, down and down, went the train. Whenever it went close to the edge of the cliff, they got a bright glimpse of the river below.

Little by little, Giovanni's spirits recovered. When the train, for example, passed a small hut, with a child standing dejectedly in front of it looking in his direction, he found himself giving a whoop of delight.

On and on, on and on, ran the train. The people in the carriage sat pressed back, clinging tightly to their seats.

Giovanni found himself exchanging a grin with Campanella. And before long the Milky Way was right there beside them, rushing, it seemed, much more strongly than before, for its waters could be seen sparkling from time to time.

Here and there on the shores of the river, pale pinks were blooming. The train seemed to have calmed down at last, and was chuffing on unhurriedly now.

On this and the opposite bank, banners were flying, each bearing a star, shape and a picture of a pickaxe.

'What do you think that flag is?' asked Giovanni, finally bringing himself to speak.

'Beats me! I mean, it's not on the map. There's an iron boat too, isn't there?'

'Mm.'

'Perhaps they're going to build a bridge?' ventured the little girl.

'Yes, of course! It's the Engineers' flag! They're holding a bridge-building exercise! But there's no sign of any troops, is there?'

Just then, a little way downstream near the opposite bank, the invisible waters of the Milky Way gave a gleam, then shot up high in a column, and there was a loud roar.

'They're blasting! Blasting!' cried Campanella, dancing with glee.

The column of water disappeared, leaving huge salmon and trout up in the air, their bellies gleaming white, describing an arc before falling back again into the water.

Giovanni could have jumped up and down, so much lighter did his spirits feel now.

'It's the Sky Engineers! Wasn't it fun? The trout or whatever they were went just like this as they were thrown up, didn't they! I've never had such fun on a trip before. Wow!'

'Those trout must have been as big as *this* if you saw them close to,' said Campanella. 'There must be lots of fish in these waters.'

'Do you suppose there are small fish as well?' asked the little girl, drawn into the conversation.

'I guess so. There are big ones, so I expect there'll be small ones, too. But it was too far off just now to see the small ones.' Giovanni smiled in delight as he replied to the girl, intent on the subject, his previous bad temper forgotten.

'Look, I bet those are the palaces of Gemini!' cried the little boy suddenly, pointing out of the window.

On a low hill on the right stood two small palaces that seemed to be made of crystal.

'What do you mean, the palaces of Gemini?'

'Mother often used to tell me about them. I'm sure it's them. There are two small crystal palaces side by side, just as she said.'

'Tell us about them. What was it the twin stars did?'

'I know. The twin stars went out into the open country to play, and had a quarrel with a raven, didn't they?'

'No, that's not it. You see, on the bank of the Milky Way, so Mother told me –'

'Then a shooting star came along blowing and wheezing –'

'Stop it, Tadashi, you've got it wrong. That was another story!'

'So are they playing their flutes now?'

'Surely they're at sea?'

'No, they're not! They've come back from the sea by now.'

'That's right – I know. I'll tell you about it.'

Without warning, the opposite bank of the river had turned red.

The willow trees and everything else were thrown into jet black relief, and the invisible waves of the Milky Way gleamed from time to time as red pinpoints of light.

A huge red fire had been kindled in the open country on the

other bank, its black smoke reaching so high that it seemed likely to scorch even the cool pale blue of the heavens. The fire burned as though intoxicated, clearer than ruby, more beautiful than lithium in a flame.

'I wonder what kind of fire that is?' said Giovanni. 'I wonder what you have to burn to make it glow red like that?'

'The Scorpion fire,' replied Campanella, who was poring over his map again.

'Oh, the Scorpion fire. I know about that,' said the little girl.

'What is it?' asked Giovanni.

'The scorpion was burned to death. But the fire is still burning to this day. So Father told me, lots of times.'

'A scorpion's an insect, isn't it?'

'Yes, it's an insect. But a good insect.'

'It's not a good insect. I saw one pickled in alcohol in a museum. It's got a pincer this big on its tail, and Teacher said if you get stung by it you die.'

'That's right. But it's a good insect. Father told me about it. Long ago, in a certain vale, there was a scorpion that lived by eating small insects and so on. One day, a weasel found it and was about to eat it. So the scorpion ran and ran for all it was worth. In the end, the weasel was just about to leap on it, when suddenly, just ahead, the scorpion saw a well, and jumped in.

The scorpion couldn't possibly get out, and began to drown. At that moment, so the story goes, it began to pray. Ah, me,' it said, 'I've taken the lives of I don't know how many other creatures, but look how desperately I run away when my own life is in danger from the weasel! See what's happened to me now! Ah me, you can never be sure of anything! Why didn't I stay quiet and let the weasel eat me? That way, at least, the weasel would have lived a day longer. Please, God, look into my heart, and please, next time, let me not waste my life in this way, but use my body so as to benefit others!' And before he realised it, they say, the scorpion found that its body was burning with a beautiful, bright red flame, lightening the darkness of the night.

'It goes on burning for ever,' Father said. And I'm sure that fire there is it!'

'Yes, it is. Look, the markers in that area are arranged in the shape of a scorpion.'

Giovanni saw that beyond the big fire three markers were arranged just like the front legs of a scorpion while five more on this side were lined up like the tail and sting. And the beautiful, red Scorpion fire burned silent and bright, ever so bright.

As the fire gradually began to fall away to the rear, there came to them an indescribably cheerful medley of all kinds of music, mingled with the smell of flowers, and they could hear whistling and the murmur of many people's voices.

The effect was as though there was a town where a festival or something was being held, right close at hand.

'Send down the dew, Centaurus!' shouted someone suddenly. It was the boy next to Giovanni, who had been asleep but was now looking out of the window opposite.

Giovanni looked, and was surprised to see a deep green cypress or fir tree standing there like a Christmas tree, with an enormous number of fairy lights in its foliage, as though a myriad fireflies had gathered there.

'Why, of course, tonight's the Festival of Centaurus!'

'That's right,' said Campanella immediately. 'This is the village of the Centaurs.'

[Here part of the original manuscript is missing]

'Catchball? I never miss a ball,' boasted the boy.

'We shall soon be arriving at the Southern Cross,' said the young man to the others. 'You must get ready to get off.'

'I'm going to stay on the train a bit longer,' said the boy.

Nervously, the little girl next to Campanella got up and started getting ready. Even so, she looked as though she didn't want to part from Giovanni and Campanella.

'We have to get off here,' said the young man, looking down at the boy with set lips.

'I don't want to! I want to ride on the train a bit more first!'

'Why not stay on with us?' said Giovanni, unable to stay silent. 'We have tickets that will take us anywhere.'

'But we can't stay on any longer,' said the girl sadly. 'This is where you get off to go to Heaven.'

'What do you have to go to Heaven for? My teacher at school said we should build a better place than Heaven right here, where we are now!'

'But Mother's there, and besides, God said so.'

'That kind of God's a fraud!'

'Your God is a fraud!'

'No, he's not!'

'What kind of God is yours?' asked the young man with a smile.

'I'm not sure, actually,' said Giovanni. 'But he's not like that. He's the true God.'

'Of course – there's only one true God.'

'No, I don't mean that. I mean the only *true* God.'

'But that's just it! Let's pray it won't be long before you join us before that one true God.' And the young man joined his hands reverently.

The girl followed his example exactly. All three of them were rather pale, as though they really regretted saying goodbye. Giovanni had a hard job to avoid bursting into tears.

'Well, then, are you ready? We're almost at the Southern Cross.'

And then it happened. Far off downstream on the transparent Milky Way, a cross studded with lights of blue, orange and every other possible colour rose gleaming like a lone tree out of the waters, with a bluish white cloud forming a circle above it just like a halo.

A great stir went through the train. All the passengers were on their feet, praying just as they'd done at the Northern Cross.

On all sides the only sounds were cries of joy, cries like those of children pouncing gleefully on a melon, and sighs of an unspeakably deep piety. Gradually the cross drew level with the windows, so that they could see the cloud, silvery white like the flesh of an apple, revolving slowly, ever so slowly, about it.

'Hallelujah! Hallelujah!' Cheerful and happy rose the voices of the passengers, and from the furthest part of the cold sky they heard the clear, incredibly pure tones of a trumpet. The train, passing between great numbers of signals and electric lights, slowed down, until finally it drew to a halt directly opposite the cross.

'Well, this is where we get off.' The young man tugged at the boy's hand, and the sister set the collar and shoulders of his coat straight as they started moving slowly towards the exit at the other end of the carriage.

'Goodbye, then,' said the girl, looking back at Giovanni and Campanella.

'Goodbye,' said Giovanni, his voice surly with the effort to suppress the urge to cry.

The girl looked back once more with eyes large with the pain of parting, then went out without another word. The train, already more than half empty, looked suddenly deserted and forlorn, and the wind swept unhindered through the carriage.

Outside, they could see people in pious ranks, kneeling on the bank of the Milky Way opposite the cross. And over the invisible waters of the river they saw approaching, hand outstretched, a divine figure in a robe of white. But by then the glass flute was being blown, the train was moving, and almost at once a silver mist came stealing up from downstream, blotting out the scene. All they could make out was a large number of walnut trees rising through the mist, their leaves radiant, with the tiny face of an electric squirrel, with its aura of light, peering out from their midst.

Just then, the mist began to drift aside, revealing what looked like a highway leading to some important place, lined with a row of small electric lamps.

The highway ran for a while alongside the tracks. As the two of them came level with each lamp in turn, the small light popped off, just as though it was acknowledging them, then popped on again once they were past.

Looking back, they saw that the cross had become quite small, so small that you could have hung it around your neck on a chain, and the white shore in front of it was too vague for them to make out whether the girl, the young man and the others were still kneeling there or whether they'd gone to some place unknown in the heavens above.

Giovanni heaved a deep sigh.

'Campanella,' he said, 'we're alone again, aren't we? Let's go on together, on and on forever. You know, I feel like that scorpion: if it would really make people happy, I wouldn't care if my body was burned a hundred times over.'

'Mm, I feel the same.' Bright tears were glistening in his eyes.

'But I wonder what real happiness is?' said Giovanni.

'I don't know,' said Campanella thoughtfully.

'We'll do our very best, won't we?' said Giovanni, breathing in deeply as though a new strength was filling his heart.

But Campanella was pointing to a place in the Milky Way, drawing back a little as he did so. 'See those coal sacks? It's the Skypit!'

Giovanni gave a great start as he looked. At one spot in the Milky Way there yawned a great black hole. However much he rubbed his eyes and peered at it, he only made them feel strained. He could see nothing – neither how deep the hole was, nor what lay at the bottom of it.

'No, I wouldn't be afraid to go down into that great dark hole, even,' he said, 'because I'm going in search of true happiness for everyone! Let's go on together, however far it is!'

'Yes, let's!' said Campanella. 'Oh –' he exclaimed abruptly pointing to a beautiful stretch of countryside far beyond the window, 'look how beautiful the scenery is there! They're all there together! That's the real Heaven! Oh look – that's my mother there!'

Giovanni looked, but to him it was just a vague white blur, and not at all as Campanella had said.

Indefinably sad, he was still gazing absently in the same direction when, on the opposite bank of the river, he saw two telegraph poles standing with their red crossarms lined up as though they were linking arms.

'Campanella,' said Giovanni, turning around as he spoke, 'we'll go on together eh?' But there was no Campanella in the seat where Campanella had been sitting until just now. There was nothing but the dark velvet of the seat, shining all alone.

Giovanni shot to his feet. Leaning out of the window so as not to be heard in the train, he beat his breast and shouted wildly, then burst out crying.

Everything round about seemed suddenly to have turned dark.

And then from behind him there came the gentle voice, like a cello, that he had heard so many times before. *Whatever are you crying about? Come, just look over here.*

With a start, Giovanni brushed away his tears and turned to look in the direction of the voice.

In the seat in which Campanella had been sitting until a while ago was a thin, pale-faced grown-up in a large black hat, smiling in a kindly way and holding a big book.

'Your friend's gone off somewhere, hasn't he? Somewhere very far away. It's no use your looking for Campanella any more.'

'Oh, but why? I said I wanted to go on and on with him.'

'Yes, I know. They all think that. But they can't go along. And everybody's a Campanella.

'Whoever you meet, they're all people you've eaten apples with or ridden on trains with any number of times.

So the best thing to do, just as you thought a while ago, is to seek the greatest happiness for others, then go there as soon as possible to join them. It's only there that you'll really be able to go on with Campanella for ever.'

'Yes, I'll do that! What would be the best way for me to look for it?'

'Well, actually, I'm looking for it, too. You must hold on tight to your ticket. And you must study for all you're worth. You've learned chemistry, haven't you? You know that water's made of oxygen and hydrogen. Nobody doubts it for a moment nowadays. I mean, you only have to do an experiment to prove it.

But in the old days people were always arguing about it, saying it was made of mercury and salt, or mercury and sulphur. And everybody believes that his own particular god is the true god, doesn't he? But people find themselves moved to tears just the same by something done by somebody who believes in a different god from themselves. And they argue, you know, about who's righteous and who's unrighteous. And never reach any decision. But if you really study, and by experimenting distinguish between what's true and what's false – so long as you find the right method for your experiment – then you'll find that religion is just the same as chemistry in the end.

Here, though, take a look at this book and listen. This is a dictionary of geography and history. This page of the book – see? – contains the geography and history of the year 2,200 BC Look carefully now. That doesn't mean of the year 2,200 BC as it was, but the geography and history as people saw it around the year 2,200 BC.

So this single page is the equivalent of a whole volume of geography and history, right? And what's written down here is, for the most part, true – for the year 2,200 BC. Look, and you'll find proof after proof to back it up. But just you start having slight doubts about it, and there, you're on the next page!

Take the year 1,000 b.c., now. Both geography and history will have changed considerably by this time. Here's how it is at this stage. You mustn't make a face about it, though. You see, everything about us – our bodies, our ideas, and the Milky Way, and the train, and history – are all as they are only because we feel that way about them. Come now, try calming yourself down a bit along with me. Ready?'

He raised a finger and lowered it again quietly.

At that, quite suddenly Giovanni saw himself, and his ideas, and the train, and the scholar, and the Milky Way everything lit up all together in a flash of light, then fade silently away, then switch on and disappear again: at each flare-up, a whole world opened and a whole history was there. Then, when it faded away, nothing was left but a simple void, that was all.

Things grew gradually faster until before long, everything was just as it had been in the first place.

'Well, do you see? Your experiment will have to account for all these disconnected ideas from beginning to end. That's what's so difficult about it. Though, of course, you can make do with what you've got at any one time.'

Just then, from beyond the dark line of the horizon, a bluish white signal flare went up, making everything like day, so that the inside of the train was filled with light.

The flare reached high up in the sky, where it went on giving out light.

'Ah, it's a Magellanic Cloud! Right! From now on, I'm going out myself to explore, to search for happiness, real happiness, for myself and for my mother, for Campanella and for everyone else!'

Biting his lip and with his eyes fixed on the distant Magellanic Cloud, Giovanni stood up.

Now then, hold on tight to your ticket, said the cello-like voice. *From now on, you're not in a dream train any longer. You've got to forge ahead through the fires and the fierce waves of the real world. You must never lose that ticket. It's the one real thing in the Milky Way!*

The voice ceased, and soon the Milky Way had receded far, far into the distance, and the wind howled. . . .

Giovanni opened his eyes. Tired out, he'd been sleeping on the grass on the hill all the time. There was a strange excitement in his heart, and cold tears were running down his cheeks.

He sprang to his feet. The town below was a pattern of many lights, exactly as it had been earlier, yet somehow the lights looked more intense than before.

And the Milky Way, where he had been travelling a moment before in his dream, stretched in a white blur across the sky just as it had done a while ago, looking particularly milky above the jet-black southern horizon, and with the red stars of the Scorpion twinkling beautifully to the right, and the whole layout of the sky not so different from what it had been.

Giovanni ran straight off down the hillside, his heart suddenly full with the idea of his mother waiting for him to come before eating her supper. Pressing on through the black pine wood, he skirted the farm fence that loomed pale in the dark, and, passing through the same entrance as before, arrived in front of the dark dairy.

Somebody must have come back a short while ago, for a cart that hadn't been there before was parked, with two barrels of something on board.

'Is anyone at home?' called Giovanni.

'Coming!' Almost immediately, a man in baggy white trousers came out and stood in front of him.

'What can I do for you?'

'Actually, no milk was delivered at our home today.'

'Oh – I'm sorry.' He went and brought back a bottle of milk.

'I'm really sorry,' he said as he handed it to Giovanni. 'This afternoon, I left the gate of the calf's pen open and the little devil went straight to its mother and drank half the milk.' He smiled.

'I see. Well then, I'll take it if I may.'

'Of course. I'm very sorry.'

'Not at all.' Clasping his hands around the bottle of still warm milk, Giovanni went out through the fence of the farm.

Along a tree-lined street for a way, and out into the main street he went; a little further on, he came to the crossroads. On the right, a short way from the street, there loomed vague against the night sky the pillar of the bridge over the river where Campanella and the rest had gone to set their lanterns adrift.

But at each corner of the crossroads, and in front of the shops, groups of women were looking in the direction of the bridge and talking in hushed voices. And the bridge itself was thronged with lights of all kinds.

For some reason, Giovanni felt something cold clutch at his heart. Impulsively, he called to those nearest him: 'Has something happened?'

'A child's fallen in the river,' said one of them, and they all looked at Giovanni.

Desperately, Giovanni ran in the direction of the bridge. The bridge was full of people, the river invisible. There was a policeman in a white coat. Reaching the end of the bridge, Giovanni leapt hastily down onto the broad, dried-up section of the riverbed.

A large number of lights were moving busily up and down along the water's edge. Seven or eight lanterns were moving about on the dark bank on the opposite side of the river. And straight through between them the river, empty by now of gourd lanterns, flowed grey and peaceful, faintly murmuring.

On a kind of sandbank that jutted out at the most distant point downstream, a group of people stood in black silhouette.

Giovanni ran steadily in their direction. As he did so, he suddenly encountered Marceau, who had been with Campanella earlier.

'Giovanni,' said Marceau, running up to him, 'Campanella's gone into the river!'

'How? When?'

'Zanelli was in the boat trying to push a lantern out into the moving stream. Just then, the boat rocked and he fell into the water. So Campanella immediately jumped in after him, and pushed Zanelli towards the boat. Zanelli managed to get hold of Kato's hand – but there was no Campanella any more.'

'They're looking for him, aren't they?'

'Yes. They all got here soon after. Campanella's father's with them. But they haven't found him. They took Zanelli home.'

Giovanni went over to where the others were. In the centre of a group of schoolboys and people from the town, Campanella's father, his jaw pale and angular, stood upright wearing a dark coat, holding a watch in his hand and staring fixedly at the water.

The others too were watching the river. No one spoke a word. Giovanni's legs trembled violently A large number of the acetylene lamps used for fishing were going busily to and fro, so that the black waters of the river were visible, setting up glittering ripples as they flowed.

Further downstream, the Milky Way was reflected over the whole width of the river, so that it looked not like water but like a continuation of the sky itself.

Giovanni had an inescapable feeling that by now the only place Campanella would be found was out there in some distant part of the Milky Way.

The others, though, seemed equally convinced that Campanella would still emerge from the waves with a cheerful 'That was some swim!' or that he had reached some uncharted sandbank and was standing there, waiting for someone to come.

Quite suddenly, though, Campanella's father said briskly:

'It's no good. It's forty-five minutes since he went in.'

Impulsively, Giovanni rushed up and stood there, meaning to say to the Doctor 'I know where Campanella's gone, I was travelling with him.' But the words stuck in his throat and he could say nothing.

The Doctor, though, must have thought that Giovanni had come to offer condolences, for he gazed at him steadily for a while, then said courteously:

'You're Giovanni, aren't you? Thank you for coming to help this evening.'

Giovanni just bowed, unable to speak.

'Has your father come back yet?' the Doctor went on, the watch still clasped tight in his hand.

'No,' said Giovanni with a slight shake of his head.

'I wonder why?' he said. 'I got a most cheerful letter from him only the day before yesterday. He should have been arriving around now. But I expect the ship was delayed. Giovanni – after school tomorrow you must come over with the rest to see me.' And as he said so, he gazed intently at the place downstream where the river was filled with the reflection of the Milky Way.

His heart full of many things, Giovanni took his leave of the Doctor in silence. Then, wanting to take the milk home to his mother and let her know as soon as possible that Father was coming home, he set off running across the dry riverbed, as hard as he could go, in the direction of the town.

The Earthgod and the Fox

On the northern edge of a stretch of open land the ground rose in a slight hillock. The hillock was covered entirely with spike-eared grass, and right in the middle of it stood a single, beautiful female birch tree.

The tree was not actually very big, but her trunk gleamed a glossy black and her branches spread out gracefully. In May her pale flowers were like clouds, while in autumn she shed leaves of gold and crimson and many other colours.

All the birds, from birds of passage such as the cuckoo and the shrike right down to the tiny wren and the white-eye, would come to perch in the tree. But if a young hawk or some other large bird was there, the smaller birds would spy him from afar and refuse to go anywhere near.

The tree had two friends. One was the earthgod, who lived in the middle of a marshy hollow about five hundred paces away, and the other was a brown fox, who always appeared from somewhere in the southern part of the plain.

Of the two of them it was the fox, perhaps, that the birch tree preferred. The earthgod, in spite of his imposing name, was too wild, with hair hanging unkempt like a bundle of ragged cotton thread, bloodshot eyes, and clothes that dangled about him like bits of seaweed. He always went barefoot, and his nails were long and black. The fox, on the other hand, was very refined and almost never made people angry or offended.

The only thing was that, if you compared them really carefully, the earthgod was honest, whereas the fox was, perhaps, just a bit dishonest.

It was an evening at the beginning of summer. The birch tree was covered with soft new leaves, which filled the air around them with a delightful fragrance. The Milky Way stretched whitish across the sky, and the stars were winking and blinking and switching themselves on and off all over the firmament.

On such a night, then, the fox came to pay the birch tree a visit, bringing with him a book of poetry. He was wearing a dark blue suit fresh from the tailor's, and his light brown leather shoes squeaked slightly as he walked.

'What a peaceful night,' he said.

'Oh, yes!' breathed the birch tree.

'Do you see Scorpio crawling across the sky over there? In ancient China, you know, they used to call the biggest star in the constellation the "Fire Star."'

'Would that be the same as Mars?'

'Dear me, no. Not Mars. Mars is a *planet*. This one is a real star.'

'Then what's the difference between a planet and a star?'

'Why, a planet can't shine by itself. In other words, it has to have light from somewhere else before it can be seen. A star is the kind that shines by itself. The sun, now, is a star, of course. It looks big and dazzling to us, but if you saw it from very far away, it would only look like a small star, just the same as all the others.'

'Good heavens! So the sun is only one of the stars, is it? Then I suppose the sky must have an awful lot of suns – no, stars – oh, silly me, *suns*, of course.'

The fox smiled magnanimously. 'You might put it like that,' he said.

'I wonder why some stars are red, and some yellow, and some green?'

The fox smiled magnanimously again and folded his arms grandly across his chest. The book of poetry under his arm dangled perilously, but somehow stopped just short of falling.

'Well, you see,' he said, 'at first all the stars were like big, fluffy clouds. There are still lots of them like that in the sky. There are some in Andromeda, some in Orion, and some in the Hunting Dogs. Some of them are spiral-shaped and some are in rings the shape of fishes' mouths.'

'I'd love to see them sometime. Stars the shape of fishes' mouths – how splendid!'

'Oh, they are, I can tell you. I saw them at the observatory.'

'My word! I'd love to see them myself.'

'I'll show you them. As a matter of fact, I've a telescope on order from Germany. It'll be here sometime before next spring, so I'll let you have a look as soon as it comes.'

The fox had spoken without thinking, but the very next moment he was saying to himself, 'Oh dear, if I haven't gone and told my only friend another fib again. But I only said it to please her, I really didn't mean any harm by it. Later on, I'll tell her the truth.'

The fox was quiet for a while, occupied with such thoughts, but the birch tree was too delighted to notice.

'I'm so happy!' she said. 'You're always so kind to me.'

'Oh, quite,' said the fox rather dejectedly. 'You know I'd do anything for you. Would you care to read this book of poetry, by the way? It's by a man called Heine. It's only a translation, of course, but it's not at all bad.'

'Oh! May I really borrow it?'

'By all means. Take as long as you like over it . . . Well, I must say goodbye now. Dear me, though, I feel there's something I forgot to say.'

'Yes, about the colour of the stars.'

'Ah, of course! But let's leave that until next time, shall we? I mustn't overstay my welcome.'

'Oh, that doesn't matter.'

'Anyway, I'll be coming again soon. Goodbye to you, then. I'll leave the book with you. Goodbye.'

The fox set off briskly homeward. And the birch tree, her leaves rustling in a south wind that sprang up just then, took up the book of verse and turned the pages in the light of the faint glow from the Milky Way and the stars that dotted the sky. The book contained 'Lorelei' and many other beautiful poems by Heine, and the birch tree read on and on through the night. Not until past three, when Taurus was already beginning to climb in the east above the plain, did she begin to get even slightly drowsy.

Dawn broke, and the sun rose in the heavens. The dew glittered on the grass, and the flowers bloomed with all their might. Slowly, slowly, from the north-east, bathed in morning sunlight as though he had poured molten copper all over himself, came the earthgod. He walked slowly, quite slowly, with his arms folded soberly across his chest.

Somehow, the birch tree felt rather put out, but even so she shimmered her bright green leaves in the earthgod's direction as he came, so that her shadow went flutter, flutter where it fell on the grass. The earthgod came up quietly and stopped in front of her.

'Good morning to you, Birch Tree.'

'Good morning.'

'D'you know, Birch Tree, there are lots of things I don't understand when I come to think about them. We don't really know very much, do we?'

'What kind of things?'

'Well, there's grass, for instance. Why should it be green, when it comes out of dark brown soil? And then there are the yellow and white flowers. It's all beyond me.'

'Mightn't it be that the seeds of the grass have green or white inside them already?' said the birch tree.

'Yes. Yes, I suppose that's possible,' he said. 'But even so, it's beyond me. Take the toadstools in autumn, now. They come straight out of the earth without any seeds or anything. And they come up in red and yellow and all kinds of colours. I just don't understand it!'

'How would it be if you asked Mr Fox?' said the birch tree, who was still too excited about last night's talk to know any better.

The earthgod's face changed colour abruptly, and he clenched his fists.

'What's that? Fox? What's the fox been saying?'

'Oh,' said the birch tree in a faltering voice, 'he didn't say anything, really. It was just that I thought he might know.'

'And what makes you think a fox has got anything to teach a god, eh?'

By now the birch tree was so unnerved that she could only quiver and quiver. The earthgod paced about with his arms folded over his chest, grinding his teeth loudly all the while. Even the grass shivered with fear wherever his jet-black shadow fell on it.

'That fox is a blight on the face of the earth!' he said. 'Not a word of truth in him. Servile, cowardly and terribly envious into the bargain!'

'It will soon be time for the yearly festival at your shrine, won't it?' said the birch tree, regaining her composure at last.

The earthgod's expression softened slightly.

'That's right,' he said. 'Today's the third of the month, so there are only six days to go.'

But then he thought for a while and suddenly burst out again.

'Human beings, though, are a useless lot! They don't bring a single offering for my festival nowadays. Why, the next one that sets foot on my territory, I'll drag down to the bottom of the swamp for his pains!'

He stood there gnashing his teeth noisily. The birch tree, alarmed at finding that her attempts to soothe him had had just the opposite effect again, was past doing anything except fluttering her leaves in the breeze. For a while the earthgod strode about grinding his teeth, his arms folded high across his chest and his whole body seeming to blaze as the sunlight poured down on him. But the more he thought about it, the crosser he seemed to get. In the end he could bear it no longer and with a great howl stormed off home to his hollow.

The place where the earthgod lived was a dank and chilly swamp grown all over with moss, clover, stumpy reeds, and here and there a thistle or a dreadfully twisted willow tree. There were soggy places where the water seeped through in rusty patches. You only had to look at it to tell that it was all muddy and somehow frightening.

On a patch like a small island right in the middle of it stood the earthgod's shrine, which was about six feet high and made of logs.

Back on this island, the earthgod stretched himself out full length on the ground beside his shrine and scratched long and hard at his dark, scraggy legs.

Just then he noticed a bird flying through the sky right above his head, so he sat up straight and shouted 'Shoo!' The bird wobbled in alarm and for a moment seemed about to fall, then fled into the distance, gradually losing height as it went, as though its wings were paralysed.

The earthgod gave a little laugh and was getting to his feet when he happened to glance towards the hillock, not far away, where the birch tree grew. And instantly his rage returned: his face turned pale, his body went as stiff as a poker, and he began tearing at his wild head of hair.

A solitary woodcutter on his way to work on Mount Mitsumori came up from the south of the hollow, striding along the narrow path that skirted its edge. He seemed to know all about the earthgod, for every now and then he glanced anxiously in the direction of the shrine. But he could not, of course, see anybody there.

When the earthgod caught sight of the woodcutter, he flushed with pleasure. He stretched his arm out towards him, then grasped his own wrist with his other hand and made as though to pull it back. And, strange to say, the woodcutter, who thought he was still walking along the path, found himself gradually moving deeper and deeper into the hollow. He quickened his pace in alarm, his face turned pale, his mouth opened and he began to gasp.

Slowly the earthgod twisted his wrist. And as he did so, the woodcutter slowly began to turn in circles. At this he grew more and more alarmed, until finally he was going round and round on the same spot, panting desperately all the while. His one idea seemed to be to get out of the hollow as quickly as he could, but for all his efforts he stayed, circling, where he was. In the end he began to sob and, flinging up his arms, broke into a run.

This seemed to delight the earthgod. He just grinned and watched without getting up from the ground, until before long the woodcutter, who by now was giddy and exhausted, collapsed in the water. Then the earthgod got slowly to his feet. With long strides he squelched his way to where the woodcutter lay and, picking him up, flung him over onto the grassy ground. The woodcutter landed in the grass with a thud. He groaned once and stirred, but still did not come to.

The earthgod laughed loudly. His laughter rose up into the sky in great mysterious waves. Reaching the sky, the sound bounced back down again to the place where the birch tree stood. The birch tree turned suddenly so pale that the sunlight shone green through her leaves, and she began to quiver frantically.

The earthgod tore at his hair with both hands. 'It's all because of the fox that I feel so miserable,' he told himself. 'Or rather, the birch tree. No, the fox and the birch tree. That's why I suffer so much. If only I didn't mind about the tree, I'd mind even less about the fox. I may be nobody much but I *am* a god after all, and it's disgraceful that I should have to bother myself about a mere fox. But the awful thing is, I do. Why don't I forget all about the birch tree, then? Because I can't. How splendid it was this morning when she went pale and trembled! I was wrong to bully a wretched human being just to work off my temper, but it can't be helped. No one can tell what somebody'll do when he gets really cross.'

So dreadfully sad did he feel that he beat at the air in despair. Another bird came flying through the sky, but this time the earthgod just watched it go in silence.

From far, far away came the sound of cavalry at their manoeuvres, with a crackling of rifle fire like salt being thrown on flames. From the sky, the blue light poured down in waves. This must have done the woodcutter good, for he came to, sat up timidly, and peered about him. The next moment he was up and running like an arrow shot from a bow. Away he ran in the direction of Mount Mitsumori.

Watching him, the earthgod gave a great laugh again. Again his laughter soared up to the blue sky and hurtled back down to the birch tree below. Again the tree's leaves went pale and trembled delicately, so delicately that you would scarcely have noticed.

The earthgod walked aimlessly round and round his shrine until finally, when he seemed to feel more settled, he suddenly darted inside.

It was a misty night in August. The earthgod was so terribly lonely and so dreadfully cross that he left his shrine on an impulse and started walking. Almost before he realised it, his feet were taking him towards the birch tree. He couldn't say why, but whenever he thought of her, his heart seemed to turn over and he felt intolerably sad. Nowadays he was much easier in his mind than before, and he had done his best not to think about either the fox or the birch tree. But, try as he might, they kept coming into his head. Every day he would tell himself over and over again, 'You're a god, after all. What can a mere birch tree mean to you?' But still he felt awfully sad. The memory of the fox, in particular, hurt until it seemed his whole body was on fire.

Wrapped in his own thoughts, the earthgod drew nearer and nearer to the birch tree. Finally it dawned on him quite clearly that he was on his way to see her, and his heart began to dance for joy. It had been a long time. She might well have missed him. In fact, the more he thought about it the surer he felt it was so. If this really was the case, then he was very sorry he had neglected her. His heart danced as he strode on through the grass. But before long his stride faltered and he stopped dead; a great blue wave of sadness had suddenly washed over him. The fox was there before him. It was quite dark by now, but he could hear the fox's voice coming through the mist, which was glowing in the vague light of the moon.

'Why, of course,' he was saying, 'just because something agrees with the laws of symmetry is not to say that it is beautiful. That's nothing more than a dead beauty.'

'How right you are,' came the birch tree's soft voice.

'True beauty is not something rigid and fossilised. People talk of observing the laws of symmetry, but it's enough so long as the *spirit* of symmetry is present.'

'Oh, yes, I'm sure it is,' came the birch tree's gentle voice again.

But now the earthgod felt as though red flames were licking his whole body. His breath came in short gasps, and he really thought he couldn't bear it any longer. 'What are you so miserable about?' he asked himself crossly. 'What is this, after all, but a bit of talk between a birch tree and a fox out in the open country? You call yourself a god, to let things like this upset you?'

But the fox was talking again:

'So all books on art touch on this aspect.'

'Do you have many books on art, then?' asked the birch tree.

'Oh, not such an enormous number. I suppose most of them are in English, German and Japanese. There's a new one in Italian, but it hasn't come yet.'

'What a fine library it must be!'

'No, no. Just a few scattered volumes, really. And besides, I use the place for my studies too, so it's rather a mess, what with a microscope in one corner and the London *Times* lying over there, and a marble bust of Caesar here ...'

'Oh, but it sounds wonderful! Really wonderful!'

There was a little sniff from the fox that might have been either modesty or pride, then everything was quiet for a while.

By now the earthgod was quite beside himself. From what the fox said, it seemed the fox was actually more impressive than he was himself. He could no longer console himself with the thought that he was a god if nothing else. It was frightful. He felt like rushing over and tearing the fox in two. He told himself that one should never even think such things. But then, what was he to do? Hadn't he let the fox get the better of him? He clutched at his breast in distress.

'Has the telescope you once mentioned come yet?' started the birch tree again.

'The telescope I mentioned? Oh, no, it hasn't arrived yet. I keep expecting it, but the shipping routes are terribly busy. As soon as it comes, I'll bring it along for you to see. I really must show you the rings around Venus, for one thing. They're so beautiful.'

At this, the earthgod clapped his hands over his ears and fled away towards the north. He had suddenly felt frightened at the thought of what he might do if he stayed there any longer.

He ran on and on in a straight line. When he finally collapsed out of breath, he found himself at the foot of Mount Mitsumori.

He rolled about in the grass, tearing at his hair. Then he began to cry in a loud voice. The sound rose up into the sky, where it echoed like thunder out of season and made itself heard all over the plain. He wept and wept until dawn, when, tired out, he finally wandered vacantly back to his shrine.

Time passed, and autumn came at last. The birch tree was still green, but on the grass round about golden ears had already formed and were glinting in the breeze, and here and there the berries of lilies of the valley showed ripe and red.

One transparent, golden autumn day found the earthgod in the very best of tempers. All the unpleasant things he had been feeling since the summer seemed somehow to have dissolved into a kind of mist that hovered in only the vaguest of rings over his head. The odd, cross-grained streak in him had quite disappeared, too. He felt that if the birch tree wanted to talk to the fox, well, she could, and that if the two of them enjoyed chatting together, it was a very good thing for them both. He would let the birch tree know how he felt today. With a light heart and his head full of such thoughts, the earthgod set off to visit her.

The birch tree saw him coming in the distance and, as usual, trembled anxiously as she waited for him to arrive.

The earthgod came up and greeted her cheerfully.

'Good morning, Birch Tree. A lovely day we're having!'

'Good morning, Earthgod. Yes, lovely, isn't it?'

'What a blessing the sun is, to be sure! There he is up there, red in the spring, white in the summer and yellow in the autumn. And when he turns yellow in the autumn, the grapes turn purple. Ah, a blessing indeed!'

'How true.'

'D'you know, today I feel much better. I've had all sorts of trials since the summer, but this morning at last something suddenly lifted from my mind.'

The birch tree wanted to reply, but for some reason a great weight seemed to be bearing down on her, and she remained silent.

'The way I feel now, I'd willingly die for anybody. I'd even take the place of a worm if it had to die and didn't want to.' He gazed far off into the blue sky as he spoke, his eyes dark and splendid.

Again the birch tree wanted to reply, but again something heavy seemed to weigh her down, and she barely managed to sigh.

It was then that the fox appeared.

When the fox saw the earthgod there, he started and turned pale.

But he could hardly go back, so, trembling slightly, he went right up to where the birch tree stood.

'Good morning, Birch Tree,' said the fox. 'I believe that's the earthgod I see there, isn't it?' He was wearing his light brown leather shoes and a brown raincoat and was still in his summer hat.

'Yes, I'm the earthgod. Lovely weather, isn't it?' He spoke without a shadow on his mind.

'I must apologise for coming when you have a visitor,' said the fox to the birch tree, his face pale with jealousy. 'Here's the book I promised you the other day. Oh, and I'll show you the telescope one evening when the sky's clear. Goodbye.'

'Oh, thank you . . . ,' began the birch tree, but the fox had already set off towards home without so much as a nod to the other visitor. The birch tree blanched and began to quiver again.

For a while, the earthgod gazed blankly at the fox's retreating form. Then he caught a sudden glint of sunlight on the fox's brown leather shoes amidst the grass, and he came to himself with a start. The next moment, something seemed to click in his brain. The fox was marching steadily into the distance, swaggering almost defiantly as he went. The earthgod began to seethe with rage. His face turned a dreadful dark colour. He'd show him what was what, that fox with his art books and his telescopes!

He was up and after him in a flash. The birch tree's branches began to shake all at once in panic. Sensing something wrong, the fox himself glanced around casually, only to see the earthgod, black all over, rushing after him like a hurricane. Off went the fox like the wind, his face white and his mouth twisted with fear.

To the earthgod, the grass about him seemed to be burning like white fire. Even the bright blue sky had suddenly become a yawning black pit with crimson flames burning and roaring in its depths.

They ran snorting and panting like two railway trains. The fox ran as in a dream, and all the while part of his brain kept saying, 'This is the end. This is the end. Telescope. Telescope. Telescope.'

A small hummock of bare earth lay ahead. The fox dashed around it so as to get to the round hole at its base. He ducked his head, and was diving into the hole, his back legs flicking up as he went, when the earthgod finally pounced on him from behind. The next moment he lay all twisted, with his head drooping over the earthgod's hand and his lips puckered as though smiling slightly.

The earthgod flung the fox down on the ground and stamped on his soft, yielding body four or five times. Then he plunged into the fox's hole. It was quite bare and dark, though the red clay of the floor had been trodden down hard and neat.

The earthgod went outside again, feeling rather strange, with his mouth all slack and crooked. Then he tried putting a hand inside the pocket of the fox's raincoat as he lay there limp and lifeless. The pocket contained two brown burrs, the kind foxes comb their fur with. From the earthgod's open mouth came the most extraordinary sound, and he burst into tears.

The tears fell like rain on the fox, and the fox lay there dead, with his head lolling limper and limper and the faintest of smiles on his face.

General Son Ba-Yu

The Three Physicians

Long ago, in La-yu, the capital, there lived three brothers who were doctors. The eldest, Lin Pa, was an ordinary doctor for people. His younger brother, Lin Pu, was a doctor for horses and sheep, while Lin Po, the youngest of them all, was a doctor for trees and plants. The three brothers had built three hospitals with blue-tiled roofs. They stood in a row on the tip of a yellow cliff at the southernmost edge of the town, each with its own red or white banner fluttering in the breeze.

If you stood at the foot of the hill, you could see the patients going up it in a steady procession – priests with rashes from touching lacquer leaves, horses that were slightly lame, gardeners pulling carts bearing pots of rather wilted peonies, people with cages containing parakeets – and then, when they reached the top, dividing into three groups, the sick people going to Dr Lin Pa on the left, the horses and sheep and birds to Dr Lin Pu in the centre, and the people with trees and plants to Dr Lin Po on the right.

All three of them were remarkably skilled at medicine and were men of considerable compassion, so that they were all what one might call excellent doctors. Fortune, however, had not yet favoured them; none of them so far had any official rank, nor were their names as yet known far and wide. But one day a strange thing happened that changed everything.

The Guardian of the Northern Frontiers

That day, just as the sun was rising, the inhabitants of the town of La-yu heard, coming intermittently from the direction of the plain that stretched far away to the north, a strange sound like the twittering of a great flock of birds. At first, no one thought anything of it, and people went on sweeping out their shops or whatever they were doing. But shortly after breakfast the sounds grew gradually nearer, and it became clear that they came from flutes and bugles. Suddenly, a stir ran through the town. Mingled with the other instruments, the sound of drums of various kinds could also be heard. Before long, merchants and craftsmen grey alike were quite unable to attend to their work any longer. First the soldiers guarding the gates closed them all tight, then lookouts were posted on the walls encircling the town, and word was sent to the palace.

By around noon on the same day the inhabitants could hear the sound of hooves and see the glint of armour, and voices were heard shouting commands. Whatever it was seemed to have completely surrounded the town.

The men on lookout and the ordinary townsfolk felt their hearts hammer with fear as they peered out through the loopholes meant for firing arrows. Outside the walls to the north there lay a great armed host. A forest of bright, fluttering pennants and spears rose before their eyes. What made the scene particularly striking was that the troops were all grey and shaggy, so that they looked, almost, like a great column of smoke. At their head rode a general with a piercing gaze, a pure white beard and a bent back, mounted on a white horse with a tail that stretched out stiff behind it like a broom. His mighty sword was held aloft in his hand, and in a loud voice he was singing this song:

> Guardian of the Northern Frontiers,
> General Son Ba-yu returns
> From the sands beyond the Great Wall.
> Would that I could proclaim a
> Mighty victory, but in fact
> We're all quite spent. It's cold up there.
> Thirty yellowed years ago,
> Mustering ten thousand troops, I
> Rode out proudly through this gate.
> What to find, though? Sky and sky and
> Still more sky, dry winds that raise the
> Sand where even the wild geese wither
> And come tumbling down.
> All the while I galloped onwards
> Until my faithful steed was weary;
> Many a time he sank exhausted.
> Then his eyes would fill with tears and

Gaze far off across the sands;
And each time I'd take a little
Salt from underneath my armour,
Let him lick it to restore his
Strength. But now he's thirty-five; it
Takes him quite four hours or so
Just to go a dozen miles.
I myself, I'm seventy now.
Never thought I'd make it home, but
We were lucky, for the enemy
Perished – not a sole survivor –
Of the beri-beri. It was
Dreadfully damp this summer, and a
Further reason was, they'd run too
Much across the sand while chasing
Us. In which sense, you might call it
Victory after all, perhaps.
One more thing you may consider
Worthy of your praise, I feel.
Off we went one hundred thousand,
Ninety thousand still return.
Hard luck on the men who died, but
Even if we'd stayed at home, I'm sure
A tenth at least would have died off
In the course of thirty years.
So, our dear old friends in La-yu,
Children too and siblings all,
Here we are back home at last,
General Son Ba-yu and his army
From the north. I think you might, then,
Deign to open up the gates.

Up on the city ramparts there arose a great clamour. Some wept for joy, some rushed about waving their arms in the air, some tried to open the gates by themselves and were sworn at by the guards. A messenger, of course, went in haste to the royal palace, and the gates in the walls of the city opened with a great crash. The soldiers outside were so happy that they clung to their horses and wept.

General Son Ba-yu, Guardian of the Northern Frontiers, all grey about the face and shoulders, scowled deliberately to hide his feelings as he gently took up the reins of his horse and rode in, looking straight before him, at the head of his army, followed by the bugles and the various drums, the spears with their pennants, the copper halberds green with age, and the soldiers with their quivers of white arrows on their backs. The horses stepped in time to the drums, while the knees of the white horse on which General Son rode creaked as though they, too, were keeping time. As they marched, the soldiers sang a martial strain:

On the last day and the first
A black moon rises o'er the desert.
On the nights of south and west winds,
Even in winter the moon is red.
When the wild goose flies up high,
The enemy flees into the distance.
Mount your horse to chase him
And the snow comes pouring down.

The soldiers advanced. The mere sight, even, of ninety thousand troops was overwhelming.

On days when it snows hard,
The sky is dark at noon;
Only lines of wild geese show
Dim and white against the black.
Flying frozen through the air
The sand pulls up the withered weeds.
One by one the weeds uprooted
Fly off towards the capital.

The crowds forming a solid barrier on either side of the road watched in tears.

General Son Ba-yu marched thus for about half a mile and had just reached the city square when a fluttering of yellow banners in the distance told them that someone was coming from the palace. It could only mean one thing: the king had been told, and an emissary was on his way to welcome them.

General Son reined in his horse, raised a hand in a lordly way to his forehead, peered hard to make sure what it was, then suddenly saluted and hastily made to dismount from his horse. But he could not get off. His legs seemed to have become fastened to the horse's saddle, which in turn was stuck firmly to the horse's back.

The stout-hearted general was greatly dismayed despite himself. Turning red in the face and twitching his mouth up at one side, he did his utmost to leap off his mount, but his body refused to budge. Poor general: as a result of thirty long years spent doing heavy duty on the nation's frontiers, in the dry air of the desert and without ever once dismounting from his horse, he had finally become one with it. What was worse, since not even grass could grow in the middle of the desert, the grass must have chosen the general instead, for his face and hands were covered with some strange grey stuff. It was growing on the soldiers, too.

In the meantime, the king's representative drew gradually nearer; already the great spears and pennants at the head of his party were visible.

'General, get off your horse!' said someone in the ranks. 'It's the messenger from the king! General, off your horse!' But though he flapped his arms about again, he still could not get free.

Unfortunately, the minister assigned to welcome him was as shortsighted as a mole and thought the general was deliberately refusing to dismount and was waving his hands as some kind of order to his men.

'Turn back!' cried the minister to his party. 'It's an insurrection!' And promptly wheeling their horses around, they all dashed off in a cloud of yellow dust.

When he saw what was happening, General Son's shoulders drooped and he heaved a sigh. For a while he just sat and stared, then abruptly he turned to summon his chief strategist.

'You –' he said, 'take your armour off at once, take my sword and bow, and get to the palace as quickly as possible. Then tell them this: General Son Ba-yu, Guardian of the Northern Frontiers, spent thirty long years out there in the desert without dismounting from his horse either by day or by night, and in the end his body became stuck to his saddle, and the saddle to his horse, so that it's quite impossible for him to appear before the king. Tell them with all due respect that he is now going to see a doctor, and will present himself before His Majesty as soon as he can.'

The chief strategist nodded, removed his armour and helmet and, taking General Son's sword, rushed off towards the palace.

The general turned to his men.

'Soldiers,' he told them, 'you will now dismount, take off your helmets, and be seated on the ground. Your commander is about to pay a brief visit to the doctor. While he is gone, you are to stay here, without moving or making any noise. Do you understand?'

'We understand, General!' the troops cried in unison.

He held up his hand for silence, then flicked at his horse with his whip. The celebrated white steed that so often had sunk down from fatigue on the sands of the desert summoned his last remaining strength and, with a rattling of bones, went racing off. For some two miles the general urged him on as though in a dream, until finally they arrived at the foot of a large hill.

'Who is the best doctor around here?' he demanded.

'Why, Dr Lin Pa,' said a carpenter.

'Where does this Lin Pa live?'

'Up there at the top of the hill. The left of those three banners is his.'

'Right! Giddy-up!' And giving his white steed a flick of his whip, the general galloped all the way up the hill without stopping.

The carpenter was left grumbling to himself.

'There's an uncivilised fellow!' he complained. 'Asks a man for information and all he can say is "Right. Giddy-up!"'

But General Son Ba-yu couldn't have cared less. Leaping over the other patients who were standing about, he had soon arrived at the gateway to the place. And sure enough, there on the gatepost was a sign that said in gold letters 'Dr Lin Pa, Physician.'

Dr Lin Pa

General Son Ba-yu rode through the great hall and steadily advanced along the corridor. As befitted the clinic of Dr Lin Pa, the ceilings and doors of the rooms were all about twenty feet high.

'Where's the doctor? I want him to examine me!' bawled the general imperiously.

'And who might you be?' said a pupil of the doctor's, who wore a long yellow robe and had his head shaved, as he grabbed the horse's bit. 'Don't you think it's a bit arrogant to come riding in here on your horse?'

'Are you the man I want to see?' demanded the general. 'If so, hurry up and examine me.'

'No. Dr Lin Pa is in the room over there. But if you want an appointment, you'll have to get off your horse.'

'That's just what I can't do. If I could get off when I wanted to, I'd be in the king's presence by now.'

'I see. So you can't get off your horse. You've got a stiffening of the legs. Very well, then. Come this way.'

The student opened a door at the far end. With a clatter of hooves General Son rode in. The room was full of people, in the very centre of whom a small man who seemed to be the doctor sat on a chair examining someone's eyes.

'Here, take a look at me, will you?' said the general in a friendly way. 'Can't get off my horse, you know.'

Dr Lin Pa neither moved nor looked in his direction, but went on examining the person's eyes as intently as before.

'Here, you!' the general shouted. 'Hurry up and have a look at me!'

The patients all started in alarm, but the student said in a quiet voice: 'There's a waiting list here. You're the ninety-sixth, and the doctor's on his sixth patient now, so there are ninety ahead of you.'

'Be quiet, you! Are you saying I have to wait seventy-two turns? Who do you think I am? You're speaking to General Son Ba-yu, Guardian of the Northern Frontiers! I have ninety thousand troops back there waiting in the city square. If I wait even *one* turn, then seventy-two thousand troops will be waiting here with me. If I'm not seen to at once I'll kick the place to pieces!'

He raised his whip, the horse reared up, and the other patients began to weep. But still Dr Lin Pa didn't bat an eyelid or give the general so much as a glance. A young woman dressed in yellow stood up on the doctor's left, took a flower of some kind from a vase, and, dipping its head in the water, held it out gently to the horse. The horse munched it down and heaved a mighty sigh. Then suddenly he folded his four legs beneath him, gave a great snore, dropped his head, and went off to sleep. General Son was most upset.

'Oh, this horse! He's let me down again. Oh dear, oh dear, oh dear!' In great haste he took out a bag of salt from under his armour and tried to make the horse eat some of it.

'Come on, now! Here, wake up! After all the hard times we've had together, what do you mean by letting yourself die just when we've got back to the capital? Come on, wake up! Gee-up, giddy-up! Here, take a mouthful of this salt.' But the horse stayed fast asleep. Finally, General Son burst into tears.

'Look here –' he said, 'it doesn't matter about me, but have a look at the horse, won't you? He worked for me for thirty years up on the northern frontier.'

The young woman smiled without saying a word, but at this point Dr Lin Pa suddenly turned to look at him, and with a keen glance that seemed to take in everything, from the pit of the general's stomach to the horse's head, said in a quiet voice:

'The horse will soon get better. We only made him lie down so that we could examine you. Now, did you get sick at all while you were up north?'

'No, I didn't. Not sick, but sometimes I got badly cheated by foxes.'

'How, exactly?'

'The foxes up there are a particularly bad lot. They can put a whole army of close on ten thousand under their spell. They'll lure you with lights at night, or suddenly produce a great sea in the desert in the daytime. Why, they even make walled cities sometimes. They're a really bad lot.'

'The foxes do all that, do they?'

'The foxes, and sometimes a nasty kind of bird. He flies high up so long as no one's around, but when he sees someone he comes to investigate. Pulls the hair out of horses' tails and things like that. He can go for the eyes too, so whenever they know he's about, the horses shake so much they can hardly walk.'

'Once you've been put under a spell, about how many days does it take to get better?'

'Let's see. I'd say about four days. Though sometimes it seems to take five.'

'Now, how many times have you yourself been bewitched?'

'Not often – about ten times, perhaps.'

'I'd like to ask you something, then. What does one hundred and one hundred make?'

'One hundred and eighty.'

'And two hundred and two hundred?'

'Let's see. Three hundred and sixty, if I'm not mistaken.'

'Just one more, then. What's ten times two?'

'Eighteen, of course.'

'I see. Yes, I see very well. Even now, you're still a bit under the influence of the desert. About ten percent, in fact. Well, then, let's put you to rights.'

Dr Lin Pa waved his hands and instructed his assistants to make preparations. They brought a large copper bowl full of medicine, together with a cloth. General Son stretched out his hands and carefully took the bowl from them. Then the doctor rolled up one sleeve, soaked the cloth in the medicine, squeezed it out all over the general's helmet, and gave the helmet a shake with both hands, whereupon it slipped off without any trouble at all. Another assistant brought another bowl full of a different kind of medicine, and the doctor began to douse the general all over with this second medicine. The liquid was quite black.

'I say, will the horse be all right?' asked the general anxiously, peering around at the doctor.

'Yes, I'll soon be finished,' said the doctor, splashing away. Gradually the liquid turned brown, then a pale yellow. And by the time it had finally lost all its colour, General Son's hair was as snowy as a polar bear's. So Dr Lin Pa threw the cloth aside and washed the general's hands, and an assistant washed his head and face. The general gave a great shudder and sat up straight on his horse.

'How about it? You feel a lot fresher now, don't you? Incidentally, how much does one hundred and one hundred come to?'

'Why, two hundred, of course, doesn't it?'

'Then what does two hundred and two hundred make?'

'Let's see. Four hundred. Quite positive.'

'Then what's ten times two?'

'Twenty, of course,' answered the general quite unconcernedly, as though he had entirely forgotten what he'd said a little earlier.

'You're cured. Something was blocked up in your head, and you were ten percent off in everything.'

'Come now, I'm not interested in sums. Couldn't care less if it's ten or twenty. I'll leave that to the mathematicians. What really interests me at the moment is getting you to separate me and this horse here.'

'Yes, well, it's easy enough for me to separate your legs and your clothes. In fact, they should be separate already. But to get your trousers away from the saddle and the saddle away from the horse is a different matter. My brother next door sees to that kind of thing, so perhaps you'd go and see him? Besides, this horse needs treatment, too.'

'But what about this shaggy stuff growing on my face?'

'My brother on the other side will take care of that later. I'll have an assistant go with you.'

'All right, then, I suppose I should be getting along. Goodbye to you, sir.'

The same girl in yellow blew once into the horse's right ear. The horse sprang up, and the general, suddenly much taller again, grasped the reins and left the house with the student at his side. They cut across the garden and found themselves facing a thick earthen wall with a small door in it.

'I'll get them to open the back gate,' said the student, going in through the door.

'Oh no, there's no need for that. A little wall like this is nothing to my horse.'

The general brought his whip down and, with a gee-up and a giddy-up, the horse leapt over the earthen wall and ended up in Dr Lin Pu's garden next door, trampling his poppy patch out of all recognition.

Dr Lin Pu

General Son was ploughing through the poppy patch when suddenly they heard other horses neighing greetings on all sides. As they entered the large building, at least twenty of them came trotting up all around them, stamping their hooves and nodding their heads in welcome to the general's horse.

On the other side of the room Dr Lin Pu was rubbing some white ointment on a chestnut horse with a crooked neck. When the student who had accompanied the general went forward and whispered something briefly in the doctor's ear, he smiled and turned to face the general. He wore a great iron breastplate almost like a piece of armour; its purpose seemed to be to protect him in case the horses kicked. The general rode right up to him.

'Dr Lin Pu?' he asked. 'I'm General Son Ba-yu. I've a favour to ask of you.'

'Yes, yes, I've heard about it. Let's see, your horse is thirty-nine, isn't he?'

'More or less. Yes, he must be thirty-nine.'

'Very good. I'll perform the operation immediately. I should warn you, though, you may find it a bit smoky up there.'

'Smoky? Why should a little smoke bother me? I'll have you know that when the wind blows in the desert you have to make the horses jump at least forty-five times a minute. If you let them stop for even a few seconds, they're buried up to the head before you know it.'

'Indeed. Well, then, let's start. Here, Fu-shu!' The assistant who answered his call gave a bow and fetched a small jar. Dr Lin Pu removed the lid, took out some brownish medicine, and applied it to the horse's eyes.

Then he called again: 'Pu-shu!' Another assistant bowed, went into the next room and rummaged around for a while before returning with a small red rice cake on a plate. The doctor picked this up and spent a while squeezing it between his fingers and smelling it, until finally he seemed to make up his mind and gave it to the horse, who gulped it down. General Son, who was tired of waiting up there on the horse's back, gave a yawn. But suddenly his white steed began to tremble and tremble, and smoke and sweat began to break out all over his body. The doctor retreated as though in alarm and stood watching from a distance. The horse's teeth and bones rattled and rattled, and smoke went on rising from him. The smoke was acrid; at first, General Son put up with it quite well, but before long he had both hands to his eyes and was coughing in great spasms. After a while, the smoke gradually thinned out, but now sweat began to pour off the horse in cascades.

At this point, the doctor went up to the horse, put his hands on the saddle and shook it twice. All at once, the saddle came clean away and the general, taken by surprise, fell with a thud to the floor. True soldier that he was, however, he was up and standing straight on his feet in a flash. What's more, the saddle and the general were also quite separate again, and the general thumped busily at his bandy legs while the horse gently shook himself as though puzzled at the sudden loss of his burden. Next, the doctor got hold of the horse's broom-like tail and gave it a mighty tug, whereupon a great white lump of something in the shape of a tail fell with a clatter to the floor. The horse flourished his new tail of pure hair as though pleased to find it so light again. Then three assistants, working in a group, gave him a thorough rubdown.

'I think that will do. Now try walking.'

The horse took a few steps. This time, not a sound came from his knees, which had once creaked so horribly. Dr Lin Pu raised his hand to bring the horse back, then bowed briefly to the general.

'Most grateful, I'm sure,' said the general. 'Well, then, I must be off.'

Briskly, he saddled his steed and flung himself on board, while the horses round about neighed loudly in farewell. Then he rode out of the room, cleared the wall, and landed in Dr Lin Po's chrysanthemum patch next door.

Dr Lin Po

The place where Dr Lin Po cured various plants looked almost like a natural wood. It was filled with trees and flowers of every imaginable kind standing in rows, all of them with gold or silver plaques attached. General Son Ba-yu dismounted and made his way slowly through them towards the doctor. The student accompanying him had gone on ahead and seemed to have told the doctor everything, for he stood waiting with an air of the greatest deference, holding a box of medicine and a large red fan. Raising a hand, General Son pointed at his face. 'Here,' he said. The doctor got some yellow powder out of the box and scattered it over the general's face and shoulders, then began busily fanning him. As he did so the whiskery stuff all over the general's face turned red and began to float away like fluff, and the skin became perfectly smooth as they watched. And for the first time in thirty long years, the general smiled.

'Right, then, I'll be off. My body feels lighter too,' said the general in delight, and like a gust of wind he left the room, leapt onto his waiting steed and spurred him away. And running after them came six students carrying bags of medicine and fans to help his soldiers get rid of the same grey fuzz.

The Guardian of the Northern Frontiers Ascends to Heaven

Swift as light, General Son Ba-yu shot out through Lin Po's gateway; like a whirlwind he passed through the Lin Pu clinic next door; then, leaving the Lin Pa hospital behind him, he galloped straight on down the hill again. Since the horse was five times faster than before, he almost immediately came in sight of his resting troops. The soldiers, who were still looking anxiously in the direction he had gone, let out a cry of joy and rose to their feet as one man when they saw him. And at almost the same moment, the chief strategist, who had been sent off with a message for the king, came running from the palace, making straight for where they were.

'The king understands completely,' he announced. 'In his goodness, he even shed a tear when he heard about you, and he now awaits your arrival.'

At that point, the students from the hospital turned up with the medicine. Joyfully the troops shook the powder over themselves and vigorously plied the fans. As a result, the clear-cut outlines of all ninety thousand men were instantly restored.

'On your horses!' came the general's loud command. All straddled their steeds, and soon nothing was to be heard save the snuffling of two horses that were late.

'Forward, march!' The drums and gongs sounded, the army advanced in solemn silence. Before long the ninety thousand troops were drawn up in a square, three hundred men by three hundred men, in the great courtyard of the palace.

Dismounting, General Son quietly climbed the steps of the dais and prostrated himself on the floor.

'You have laboured long and well,' the king told him in a soft voice. 'Will you not remain here henceforth, a general among my generals, a living example to them of loyal service?'

With tears streaming from his eyes, General Son, Guardian of the Northern Frontiers, answered: 'I am overcome by Your Majesty's gracious words. Indeed, I scarcely know for the moment how I should reply to them. By now I am no more than a walking shadow, a thing of no worth whatever. All the while I was in the desert, I went with chest thrust proudly forward and searching gaze, ever wary lest the enemy should try to catch us off our guard. But now in your gracious presence, with your gracious words in my ears, suddenly I seem scarcely able even to see. My back is bowed. I beg Your Majesty, grant me leave to return to my home in the country.'

'Tell me, then, the names of five generals to take your place.'

So General Son Ba-yu named four generals. And instead of the fifth, he asked that the three brothers Lin be appointed state physicians. The king promptly granted his request, so on the spot the general took off his armour and removed his helmet, and in their place he donned a garment of coarse linen. Then he went back to the village at the foot of Mount Su where he had been born, and spent his time doing things like sowing a little millet and, later, thinning out the shoots. Before long the general gradually began to eat less and less, and in the end he only ate a single mouthful of the grain he had taken such trouble to grow, and for the rest drank large quantities of water.

Then, as autumn drew near, he ceased entirely to drink even water, and was often to be seen gazing up at the sky and hiccuping, or something equally unbecoming.

In due course, though no one knew quite when, he disappeared from sight altogether. So everyone said that the good general had gone to the Paradise of Eternal Youth, and they built a small shrine to him on the summit of Mount Su and installed his white horse there as a divine steed. And they offered up candles and millet, and set up hempen banners on poles.

But Dr Lin Pa, who was a celebrated physician by now, would tell everyone he met, 'Come now, you don't think General Son Ba-yu could live by breathing clouds, do you? I examined the general myself, so I know. A man's lungs and his bowels are two quite different things. I'll wager that somewhere, in some forest, you'll find his remains.'

And there were many people who thought, yes, that might very well be so.

Ozbel and the Elephant

The First Sunday

Ozbel? Now, there was a fine fellow! He'd installed six threshing machines – six, mind you! – and got them going with a steady *thumpety-thump, thumpety-thump* . . .

There were sixteen farmhands, all bright red in the face, working the machines with their feet, and a small mountain of cut rice that they were feeding steadily into the machines. The straw was being churned out just as steadily at the back, where it made another, new pile. All around them was a funny yellowish haze from the fine dust rising from the husks and the straw – like a little sand-storm, almost.

Ozbel was strolling up and down with a big amber pipe between his teeth, his hands clasped behind his back, squinting at the pipe to make sure that none of the ash fell on the straw. The barn was quite sturdily built, and big enough for a school. Even so – there being six of those new-fangled threshing machines thumping away all at once – it shook with the vibration. It was enough to make your stomach feel empty when you went inside. And so it was with Ozbel – he'd make himself nice and hungry, then at lunchtime he'd put away a few sizzling hot six-inch steaks or omelettes as big as a man's handkerchief.

Anyway, there they were, all busily thumping away, when what should turn up for some reason but a white elephant.

I mean, a *real* white elephant, not one that somebody had painted white. What was he doing there, you say? Well, being an elephant, I suppose he'd just taken a stroll out of the forest and wandered over. When he slowly put his face in at the entrance to the barn, the farmhands got a shock. I mean, who knows what an elephant mightn't do? But it was safer just to ignore him, so they all went on busily threshing their rice.

Ozbel himself, standing behind the row of machines with his hands in his pockets, just gave a sharp glance at the elephant, then looked down and went on pacing up and down as though nothing had happened.

So this time the white elephant put one foot up onto the raised floor. The farmhands started back. Even so, they had a lot of work to do, and getting involved would have been risky; so, trying not to look at him, they went on threshing.

In the dusky area at the back, Ozbel took his hands out of his pockets and gave the elephant another glance. Then he deliberately gave a big yawn as though he really couldn't have cared less, and clasping his hands behind his head continued walking up and down. But the elephant had got his front legs well forward and was beginning to get up into the barn. The farmhands started in alarm; even Ozbel was a bit shaken, and let out a puff of smoke from his big amber pipe. But he still went on pacing slowly up and down as though he hadn't seen a thing.

So in the end the elephant calmly heaved himself up onto the raised floor. And, cool as you please, he started walking about in the space in front of the machines.

The machines were all working away, though, and chaff was peppering the elephant like hail or a sudden summer shower. This seemed to bother him a bit, because he screwed up his little eyes – though, if you'd looked carefully, you'd have seen he was actually smiling slightly, too.

Finally making up his mind, Ozbel came out in front of the machines to talk to the elephant, but before he could start the elephant spoke up in a beautiful, fluty kind of voice:

'Oh, drat this sand – it keeps hitting my tusks.'

He was right: the chaff was raining against his tusks, and beating against his white head and neck.

Ozbel decided to take his chance. Switching his pipe to his right hand and plucking up his courage, he said:

'Well? Do you like it here?'

'Oh yes, I do,' replied the elephant, leaning to one side and screwing up his eyes.

'How would it be if you stayed on?'

Startled, the farmhands looked at the elephant with bated breath. Ozbel too, now that he had actually got it out, began trembling all over; but the elephant, not a bit put out, said simply:

'I wouldn't mind at all.'

'I see. That's fine, then – let's agree on it.' As he spoke, his face wrinkled up in a smile and turned bright red with pleasure.

So, what do you think? The white elephant was now Ozbel's

property. Was he going to put him to work, or would he sell him off to a circus? Well, I'll tell you one thing, anyway: he wasn't going to lose any money on it – that's for sure!

The Second Sunday

That Ozbel – I can't help admiring him. And the elephant, too – the one he'd so cleverly made his own the other day in the threshing barn – I admire *him*, too, in his own way. He had the strength of twenty horses, for one thing. And his tusks were made of fine ivory. His skin as well was good, strong elephant hide. And he worked hard. Even so, they'd never have made so much if it hadn't been for Ozbel.

'Hey –' he said one day, with his amber pipe in his mouth and his face wrinkling in a smile, standing in front of the elephant house they'd built with logs. 'How would you like a watch?'

'I don't need a watch, thank you,' replied the elephant with a smile.

'You should have one, just the same. You'll find it very useful,' said Ozbel; and he hung a big watch made of tin around his neck.

'It looks all right, doesn't it?' said the elephant.

'I suppose you ought to have a chain, too.'

And – would you believe it? – Ozbel fastened a chain weighing a good two hundred pounds to the elephant's front legs.

'Mm – the chain's not half bad, either,' said the elephant, taking a few steps on two legs.

'Why don't you wear shoes?'

'What would I do with shoes?'

'Go on, try some – I'm sure you'll like them.'

With his face screwed up, Ozbel fitted a pair of big red papier-mâché shoes on the elephant's back feet.

'Not bad at all,' said the elephant.

'You need some sort of ornament on them, though.'

And quickly Ozbel fixed a weight weighing a good eight hundred pounds to each shoe, as a kind of buckle.

'Yes, they're not bad, I must say,' said the elephant, taking a couple of steps and looking rather pleased.

The next day, the big tin watch and the shoddy paper shoes were broken, and the elephant was cheerfully going around with just the chain and buckles on.

'I'm sorry,' said Ozbel to the elephant, screwing up his face and clasping his hands behind his back, 'but I've got a lot of taxes to pay. I'd like you to go and draw a little water from the river.'

'Of course – I'll get you as many buckets as you like.'

A smile crinkling his little eyes, the elephant drew fifty buckets of water from the river that morning, and used them to water the vegetables in the fields.

That evening, looking out at the three-day moon in the west as he ate his ten bundles of straw in his shed, the elephant said to himself, 'Mm, working for your living is fun, isn't it? You feel so good afterwards.'

The following day, Ozbel, wearing a red-brimmed hat and with his hands stuck in his pockets, told the elephant:

'I'm sorry, but taxes are going up again. Today I'd like you to fetch a little firewood from the forest.'

'Yes, of course,' said the elephant with a smile. 'The weather's fine, and I love going to the forest.'

Ozbel was a bit taken aback; in fact he very nearly dropped his pipe, but the elephant had already set off at a leisurely pace, just as though he really did enjoy it. Relieved, Ozbel stuck the pipe back in his mouth and with a little cough went off to see how the farmhands were getting on.

That afternoon, in just half a day, the elephant, his eyes crinkling with satisfaction, brought back nine hundred bundles of firewood.

The same evening in his shed, as he ate his eight bundles of straw, the elephant looked up at the moon in the west, which was in its fourth day, and said:

'Ah, I feel so good!'

Then, the next day, Ozbel told him:

'I'm sorry, but they've increased our taxes by five times. Today I'd like you to go to the smithy and fan the charcoal fire.'

'Of course. Why, if I put my mind to it I could send a rock flying with my breath.'

Again Ozbel was a bit startled, but took a grip on himself and smiled.

The elephant lumbered off to the smithy, plumped down, folding his legs under him, and spent half the day acting as a bellows for the charcoal fire.

That evening as he ate his seven bundles of straw in his shed, the elephant looked up at the five-day moon and said:

'Ah, I'm tired. But happy, too.'

So, what happened then? From the next day on, the elephant had to start work first thing in the morning. And his straw when he got home was just five bundles; you'd wonder how he had all that strength on a miserable five bundles of straw. But elephants are surprisingly economical creatures, you know . . .

The Fifth Sunday

Ozbel? Oh, Ozbel – I was meaning to tell you, but he's not around any more.

Wait – just be patient and listen! That elephant I was telling you about – well, Ozbel treated him a bit *too* badly. As things gradually got worse, the elephant hardly ever smiled any more, and sometimes he would stare down steadily at Ozbel with red eyes like a dragon's.

One evening, he looked up at the ten-day moon as he ate his three bundles of straw and said:

'I'm having a hard time.'

Ozbel heard him, and was even harder on him than ever.

Then, the following night, the elephant tottered and collapsed on the ground in his shed. Leaving his straw untouched, he looked up at the eleven-day moon and said:

'It's goodbye.'

'Eh? What? Good*bye*?' exclaimed the moon.

'Yes, goodbye.'

'But you're much too big a fellow to give in like this!' said the moon, laughing. 'You should write a letter to your friends.'

'I don't have a writing brush and paper,' said the elephant in a faint but beautiful voice. And he began to whimper.

'Here – this is what you want, isn't it?' came a charming child's voice right in front of him. The elephant raised his head and saw a boy in a red robe standing there, holding out an ink block, a writing brush, and paper.

The elephant promptly wrote: 'I'm being treated very badly. Please come down from the woods and rescue me.'

The boy took the message and immediately headed for the forest.

When he arrived in the hills, it was just lunchtime. The elephants who lived up there were resting in the shade of a bodhi tree, playing chess and so on. They put their heads together to read the letter: 'I'm being treated very badly. Please come down from the woods and rescue me.'

Rousing themselves, the herd gathered together and began trumpeting until they were purple in the face.

'We'll let that Ozbel have it!' their leader shouted at the top of his voice.

'Come on – let's go!' the others bellowed.

And in no time they were roaring their way like a hurricane through the woods and towards the open country beyond: furious, every one of them. Small trees and the like were pulled up by the roots, thickets trampled out of recognition. In full cry, they burst onto the plain like rockets. From then on it was run, run, run, until finally in the distance, at the hazy edge of the green countryside, they caught sight of the yellow roof of Ozbel's mansion, and erupted in a frenzy of trumpeting.

It was half past one, and Ozbel was in the middle of a nap on his leather couch, having a dream about ravens. There was such a noise that the farmhands at Ozbel's place went a little way outside the gate and shaded their eyes with their hands to look.

And what did they see but a great wall of elephants, heading straight towards them! They rushed inside and yelled:

'Mr Ozbel! Elephants! They're coming to attack us! Mr Ozbel – elephants!'

But Ozbel wasn't a big boss for nothing. The moment his eyes snapped open, he knew exactly what was happening.

'Hey – is that elephant in his shed? He is? Right – shut the door. Shut the *door*! Get the door there closed as soon as you can. Right. Now, quick – go and get some logs. Shut him in. Shut him *in*! Stop flapping about, you idiots! Lash the logs together, across the door. Don't worry – what do you think he can do? I've deliberately made him weak. Right – get another five or six logs. There – now it's all right. It's all right, I say! Just keep cool. Hey, listen, *listen* – now the gate. Shut the gate! Shoot the bolts! Now put some props against it – props! That's it. Hey – there's nothing to worry about! Nothing at all! Get a grip on yourselves!'

Soon everything was ready, with Ozbel urging them on in ringing tones. But the farmhands, I'm afraid, were scared stiff. They didn't fancy sharing the fate of a boss like him, so they bound their arms around with towels, handkerchiefs and anything else, however dirty, that looked at all white, as a sign that they were surrendering. Ozbel was rushing around the place more and more frantically. Even his dog got excited and dashed about inside the house, barking fit to burst.

Almost immediately, the earth gave a great shudder, everything turned dark, and the herd of elephants surrounded the house, trumpeting fiercely. From out of the dreadful uproar, a gentle voice could be heard saying:

'We'll have you out in a moment, keep calm.'

'Thank you,' came a voice from the elephant shed. 'I'm so glad you're here.'

That set the others outside trumpeting still more loudly. They seemed to be running round and round the outer wall, for occasionally a trunk could be seen from inside, waving angrily above it. The wall was made of cement reinforced with iron, so it wasn't easy, even for elephants, to break it down. In the house, Ozbel was the only one shouting; the farmhands hung about uselessly, their minds numb with fright.

Before long, the elephants set about getting over the wall, using each other to stand on. Soon, their heads loomed over the top; when Ozbel's dog looked up and saw the great grey wrinkled faces, he fainted right away. Then Ozbel began to fire a six-shooter – *bang, roar! bang, roar! bang, roar!* – but the bullets couldn't penetrate their hides, and just bounced off their tusks.

'Drat these things,' said one of the elephants, 'they sting!'

'I've heard the same thing said somewhere else, some other time,' thought Ozbel, reloading his gun with ammunition from his belt. But then the leg of an elephant suddenly stuck out over the wall. Another followed. And five of them came crashing down at once. In a moment, Ozbel was squashed to a pulp, the pistol's chamber still in his hand. In no time the gate was open, and a wave of trumpeting elephants came pouring in.

'Where's the prison?' they cried.

They descended on the shed. Logs were smashed like so many matches, and the white elephant came out into the open air, a shadow of his old self.

'Thank heavens,' they said. 'But how *thin* you've got!' They quietly went up to him and removed his chain and weights.

'Yes. Thank you. You've really saved my life,' said the white elephant, giving a sad little smile.

The First Deer Dance

From a gap in the ragged, gleaming clouds to the west, the red rays of the setting sun slanted down on the mossy plain, and the swaying fronds of pampas grass shone like white fire. I was tired, and lay down to sleep. Gradually, the rustling of the breeze began to sound to my ears like human speech, and before long it was telling me the true meaning of the Deer Dance that the countryfolk still perform in the hills and on the plain of Kitakami.

Long ago, in the days when the area was still covered with tall grass and black forests, Kaju, together with his grandfather and the others, came to live there from somewhere east of the river Kitakami. They settled there, cleared the land and began growing millet.

One day, Kaju fell out of a chestnut tree and hurt his knee a little. At such times, it was the local custom to go to the mountains in the west where there was a hot spring, build a shelter there and bathe in the spring until one was cured.

One fine morning, then, Kaju set out for the spring. With his dumplings, his bean paste and his pot on his back, he walked slowly, limping slightly as he went, across the open country where the plumes of pampas grass were blowing silver.

On he went, over streams and across stony wastes, until the mountain range loomed large and clear and he could pick out each single tree on the mountains like the pins in a pincushion. By now the sun was far gone in the west and glittered palely just above the tops of a stand of a dozen alder trees.

Kaju set the load on his back down on the grass, took out some chestnut-and-millet dumplings, and began to eat. The pampas grass stretched away from him in tuft after tuft – so many of them that they seemed to ripple in shining white waves all over the plain. As he ate his dumplings, Kaju thought to himself what a fine sight the trunks of the alders made, rising perfectly straight up out of the high grass.

But it had been such a hard walk he was almost too tired to eat. He was soon full, and in the end, despite himself, he had to leave a piece of dumpling about the size of a chestnut burr.

'I'll leave 'er for the deer,' he said to himself. 'Deer, do 'ee come and eat!' And he put it down by a small white flower that grew at his feet. Then he shouldered his pack and slowly, quite slowly, set off again.

But he had only gone a short way when he realised that he had left his cotton towel at the place where he'd stopped to rest, so he turned back again in a hurry. He could still see the stand of alder trees quite clearly, so to go back was really not much trouble. Yet before he reached the place, he suddenly stopped quite still, sensing beyond all doubt that the deer were already there.

And there, indeed, they were – at least five or six of them, walking towards something, with their moist noses stretched out far in front of them. Kaju tiptoed over the moss towards them, taking care not to brush against the pampas grass.

No mistake about it, the deer had come for the dumpling he had left. 'Hah, deer bain't wasting no time,' he muttered to himself with a smile and, bending down low, crept slowly in their direction.

He peeped out from behind a clump of pampas grass, then drew back in surprise. Six deer were walking round and round in a ring on the stretch of turf. Hardly daring to breathe, Kaju peered at them from between the pampas stems.

The sun had touched the summit of one of the alder trees, and its topmost branches shone with a strange green light, so that it looked for all the world like some green living creature standing stock-still, gazing down at the deer. Each plume of pampas grass shone separate and silver, and the deers' coats seemed even glossier than usual. Delighted, Kaju gently lowered himself onto one knee and concentrated on watching them.

They were moving in a wide circle, and he soon noticed that every one of them seemed intent on something that lay in the centre of the ring. He was sure of it, because their heads and eyes and ears were all pointing in that direction. What was more, from time to time one or the other of them would break the circle and stagger a few paces inwards as though drawn towards the centre.

In the middle of the ring, of course, was the chestnut dumpling that Kaju had left there a while ago. The thing that was bothering the deer so much, though, was not the dumpling, it seemed, but Kaju's white cotton towel, which lay in a curve where it had fallen on the ground. Bending his bad leg gently with one hand, Kaju sat himself neatly on his heels on the moss in order to watch.

Gradually the deers' circling slowed down. Now they moved at a gentle trot, every so often dropping out of the ring and putting one foreleg forward towards the centre as though about to break into a run, then just as soon drawing back again and trotting on once more. Their hooves thudded pleasantly on the dark soil of the plain. Finally, they stopped circling altogether and came and stood in a group between Kaju and the towel.

Without warning, Kaju's ears began to ring and his body to shake: a feeling as of grass swaying in the breeze – the same thing that the deer were feeling – was coming to him in waves. And the next moment, though he could scarcely credit his own senses, he could actually hear the deer talking.

'Shall I go for to look, then?' one was saying.

'Naw, 'er be dangerous. Better watch 'er a bit longer.'

'Mustn't get caught by no trick like old Fox did. 'Er be only for a dumpling, when all's said and done.'

'Right, right. Only too right.'

So went the deers' talk.

' 'Er may be alive.'

'Aye, 'er be summat like a living crittur, indeed.'

In the end one of them seemed to make up his mind. He straightened his back, left the group and stepped forward. All the other deer stopped to watch.

Inch by inch, he edged towards the towel with his neck stretched out just as far as it would go and his legs all bunched up beneath him. Then, quite suddenly, he shot up in the air and came flying back like an arrow. The other five deer scattered in all four directions, but the first deer stopped dead when he got back to where he'd started, so they calmed down and, sheepishly returning, gathered in front of him.

'How were 'er? What do 'er be? That long white thing?'

' 'Er do have wrinkles all the way down 'er.'

'Then 'er bain't a living crittur. 'Er be a toadstool or something, after all! Poisonous too, I don't doubt.'

'Naw, 'er bain't no toadstool. 'Er be a living thing, all right.'

'Be 'er, now! Alive and lots of wrinkles too –'er be getting on in years, then.'

'Aye, that sentry guarding the dumpling be a very *elderly* sentry. Oh, ho-ho-ho-ho!'

'Eh, he-he-he-he! A blue and white sentry!'

'Oh, ho-ho-ho-ho! Private Blue-'n-White.'

'Shall *I* go for to look now?'

'Do 'ee go now. 'Er be safe enough.'

' 'Er won't bite, will 'er?'

'Naw, 'er be safe, I'd say.'

So another deer crept forward. The five who stayed behind nodded their heads approvingly as they watched.

The deer who had gone forward seemed scared to death. Time and time again he bunched his four legs up and arched his back ready for flight, only to stretch them out gingerly and creep on again.

At last he reached a spot only a step away from the towel. He stretched his neck out just as far as it would go and went *sniff*, *sniff*, at the towel, then suddenly leapt up in the air and came dashing back. They all gave a start and began to run off, but the second deer stopped dead as soon as he got back, so they took courage and gathered their faces close about his head.

'How were 'er? Why did 'ee run away?'

'But I thought 'er were going to bite me!'

'What *can* 'er be, now?'

'No telling. What be sure is that 'er be white and blue, in patches, like.'

'How do 'er smell? Eh?'

' 'Er do smell like willow leaves.'

'Do 'er breathe?'

'I didn't rightly notice that.'

'Shall *I* go now?'

'Aye, do 'ee go now.'

The third deer cautiously advanced. Just then a slight breeze stirred the towel. He stopped in his tracks in fright, and the others gave a violent start. After a while, though, he seemed to calm down, and inched forward again until at last he could stretch the tip of his nose out to the towel.

The five deer left behind were nodding at each other knowingly. But just then the deer out in front went quite stiff, shot up in the air, and came racing back.

'What did 'ee run away for?'

' 'Cause I had a strange feeling, like.'

'Be 'er breathing?'

'Well, I don't rightly think I heard 'er *breathing.* 'Er don't seem to have no mouth, either.'

'Do 'er have a head?'

'I couldn't rightly tell about that, either.'

'Then shall *I* go and see this time?'

The fourth deer set out. He was really just as scared as the rest, but he went all the way up to the towel and, ever so boldly, pressed his nose right against it. Then he drew back in a hurry and scampered straight towards them.

'Ah, 'er be soft.'

'Like mud, would 'er be?'

'Naw.'

'Like the fur on bean pods?'

'Mm – summat harder than that.'

'What could 'er be, then?'

'Any rate, 'er be a living crittur.'

' 'Ee reckon so, after all?'

'Aye, 'er be *sweaty.*'

'I think I'll go and have a look meself.'

The fifth deer in turn crept slowly forward. This one seemed to be something of a joker, for he dangled his nose right over the towel, then gave his head a great jerk as much as to say, 'Now this looks very suspicious.' The other five deer skipped about with amusement.

This encouraged the deer out in front, and he gave the towel a great lick. But then he, too, was suddenly seized with fright and came darting back, with his mouth open and his tongue lolling out. The others were dreadfully alarmed.

'Were 'ee bitten, then? Did 'er hurt?'

But he just shivered and shivered.

'Has yer tongue come loose, then?'

Still he shivered and shivered.

'Now, what be up with 'ee? C'mon, speak up!'

'Phew! Ah! Me tongue be all numb, like!'

'What kind of taste do 'er have?'

'No taste.'

'Would 'er be alive?'

'I don't rightly know. Do 'ee go and have a look now.'

'Aye.'

Slowly, the last deer went forward. The others all watched, nodding their heads with interest as he bent down and sniffed at the thing for a while. Then, quite suddenly, he picked it up in his mouth and came back with it as though there was nothing at all to be afraid of any more. The other deer bounced up and down with delight.

'Well done! Well done! Once we've got 'er, bain't nothing to be afeared of!'

'For sure, 'er be just a big dried-up slug.'

'C'mon now, I'll sing, so do 'ee all dance around 'er.'

The deer who had said this went into the middle of the group and began to sing, and the rest began to circle round and round the towel.

They ran and whirled and danced, and again and again as they did so one or the other of them would dash forward and stab the towel with his antlers or trample it with his hooves. In no time, Kaju's poor towel was all muddy and holed. Then gradually the deers' circling slowed down.

'Ah, *now* for the dumpling!'

'Ah, a boiled dumpling 'n all!'

'Ah, 'er be quite round!'

'Ah, *yum yum*'!

'Ah, luvly!'

The deer split up and gathered about the chestnut dumpling. Then they all ate one mouthful of it in turn, beginning with the deer who had gone up to the towel first. The sixth and last deer got a piece hardly bigger than a bean.

Then they formed a ring again and began walking round and round. Kaju had been watching the deer so intently that he almost felt he himself was one of them. He was on the point of rushing out to join them, when he caught sight of his own large, clumsy hand; so he gave up the idea, and went on trying to keep his breathing quiet.

Now the sun had reached the middle branches of the alder tree and was shining with a yellowish light. The deers' dance grew slower and slower. They started nodding to each other busily, and soon drew themselves up in a line facing the sun, standing perfectly straight as though in homage to it. Kaju watched in a dream, forgetful of everything else. All at once, the deer at the right-hand end of the line began to sing in a high, thin voice.

> See the setting sun decline,
> Blazing out behind the leaves
> That delicately shine
> Green upon the alder tree.

Kaju shut his eyes and shivered all over at the sound of the voice, which was like a crystal flute.

Then the second deer from the right suddenly leapt up and, twisting his body to and fro, ran in and out between the others, bowing his head again and again to the sun until at last he returned to his own place, stopped quite still, and began to sing.

> Now the sun's behind its back,
> See the leafy alder tree
> Like a mirror crack
> And shatter in a million lights.

Kaju caught his breath and himself bowed low to the sun in its glory, and to the alder tree. Now the third deer from the right began to sing, bending and raising his head all the while.

> Homeward though the sun may go,
> Down beyond the alder tree,
> See the grass aglow,
> Dazzling white across the plain.

It was true – the pampas grass was all ablaze, like a sea of white fire.

> Long and black the shadow lies
> On the shimmering pampas grass
> Where against the skies
> Straight and tall the alder grows.

Now the fifth deer hung his head low and started singing in a voice that was hardly more than a murmur.

> See, the sun is sinking low
> In the shimmering pampas grass.
> Ants now homeward go
> Through the moss upon the plain.

Soon all the deer were hanging their heads. But suddenly the sixth deer raised his head proudly and sang:

Shy white flower, content to pass
Your quiet days where none can see
Amidst the autumn grass –
Of all, the loveliest to me.

Then all the deer together gave a short, sharp call like the cry of a flute, leapt up in the air and began to dash round and round in a ring.

A cold wind came whistling from the north. The alder tree sparkled as though it really were a broken mirror. Its leaves actually seemed to tinkle as they brushed against each other, and the plumes of grass seemed to be spinning around with the deer.

By now Kaju had forgotten all about the difference between himself and the deer. 'Ho! Bravo, bravo!' he cried, and rushed out from his hiding place.

For a moment the deer stopped stiff and straight in alarm, then they were fleeing like leaves before a gale. Their bodies bent forward in haste, breasting the waves of silver grass and the shining sunset, they fled far, far into the distance, leaving the pampas grass where they had passed glittering on and on, like the wake of a boat on a quiet lake.

Kaju smiled a rueful smile. Then he picked up his muddy, torn towel and set off towards the west.

And that was all, until I heard the story from the clear autumn breeze in the late sunlight that day on the mossy plain.

The Bears of Nametoko

It's interesting, that business of the bears on Mount Nametoko. Nametoko is a large mountain, and the Fuchizawa River starts somewhere inside it. On most days of the year, the mountain breathes in and breathes out cold mists and clouds. The peaks all around it, too, are like blackish green sea slugs or bald sea goblins. Halfway up it there yawns a great cave, from which the river Fuchizawa abruptly drops some three hundred feet in a waterfall that goes thundering down through the thick-growing cypresses and maples.

Nowadays nobody uses the old highway, so it is all grown over with butterbur and knotweed, and there are places where people have put up fences on the track to stop cattle from straying and climbing up the slopes. But if you push your way for about six miles through the rustling undergrowth, you will hear in the distance a sound like the wind on a mountaintop. If you peer carefully in that direction, you might be puzzled to see something long, white and narrow trailing down the mountain in a flurry of mist: this is the Ozora Falls. And in that area, they say, there used to be any number of bears.

Now, I must confess that I have never actually seen either Mount Nametoko or the liver of a newly killed bear. All this is based on what I've heard from other people or worked out for myself. It may not be entirely true, though I for one believe it.

But I do know that Mount Nametoko is famous for its bear's liver, which is good for stomachaches and helps wounds heal. At the entrance to the Namari hot spring there is a sign that says 'Bear's Liver from Mount Nametoko.' So there are definitely bears on the mountain. I can almost see them, going across the valleys with their pink tongues lolling out, and the bear cubs wrestling with each other until finally they lose their tempers and box each other's ears. It was bears like these that the famous hunter Kojuro Fuchizawa once killed so freely.

Kojuro was a swarthy, well-knit, middle-aged man with a squint. His body was massive, like a barrel, and his hands were as big and thick as the handprint of the god Bishamon that they use to cure people's illnesses at the Kitajima Shrine. In summer, he wore a cape made of bark to keep off the rain, with leggings, and he carried a woodsman's axe and a gun as big and heavy as an old-fashioned blunderbuss. With his great yellow hound for company, he would tramp across the mountains, from Mount Nametoko to Shidoke Valley, from Mitsumata to Mount Sakkai, from Mamiana Wood to Shira Valley.

When he went up the old, dried-up valleys, the trees grew so thickly that it was like going through a shadowy green tunnel, though sometimes it suddenly became bright with green and gold, and at other times sunlight fell all around as though the whole place had burst into bloom. Kojuro moved at a slow and ponderous pace, as completely at home as though he were in his own living room. The hound ran on ahead, scampering along high banks or plunging into the water. He would swim for all he was worth across the sluggish, faintly sinister backwaters, then, when he finally reached the other side, would shake himself vigorously to dry his coat and stand with wrinkled nose waiting for his master to catch up. Kojuro would come across with his mouth slightly twisted, moving his legs stiffly and cautiously like a pair of compasses, while the water splashed up in a white curl above his knees.

The bears in the area of Mount Nametoko were fond of Kojuro. One proof of this is that they would often gaze down in silence from some high place as he squelched his way up the valleys or passed along the narrow ledges, overgrown with thistles, that bordered the valley. Clinging to a branch at the top of a tree or sitting on a bank with their paws around their knees, they would watch with interest as he went by.

The bears even seemed to like Kojuro's hound.

Yet for all that, they didn't like it much when they really came up against him, and the dog flew at them like a ball of fire, or when Kojuro with a strange glint in his eyes levelled his gun at them. At such times, most of them would wave their paws as though in distress, telling him that they didn't want to be treated in that way.

But there are all kinds of bears, just as there are all kinds of people, and the fiercest of them would rear up on their hind legs with a great roar and advance on Kojuro with both paws stretched out, ignoring the dog as though they could crush him underfoot as easily as that. Kojuro would remain perfectly calm and, taking aim at the centre of the bear's forehead from behind a tree, would let fly with his gun.

The whole forest would seem to cry out loud, and the bear would slump to the ground. Dark red blood would gush from his mouth, he would snuffle rapidly, and he would die.

Then Kojuro would stand his gun against a tree, cautiously go up to the bear, and say something like this:

'Don't think I killed you, Bear, because I hated you. I have to make a living, just as you have to be shot. I'd like to do different work, work with no sin attached, but I've got no fields, and they say my trees belong to the authorities, and when I go into the village nobody will have anything to do with me. I'm a hunter because I can't help it. It's fate that made you a bear, and it's fate that makes me do this work. Make sure you're not reborn as a bear next time!'

At times like this the dog, too, would sit by him with narrowed eyes and a dejected air. The dog, you see, was Kojuro's sole companion. In the summer of his fortieth year, his whole family had fallen sick with dysentery, and his son and his son's wife had died. The dog, however, had remained healthy and active.

Next, Kojuro would take out of his pocket a short, razor-sharp knife and in one long stroke slit the bear's skin open from under his chin down to his chest and on to his belly. The scene that followed I don't care to think about. Either way, in the end Kojuro would put the bright red bear's liver in the wooden chest on his back, wash the fur which was all in dripping, bloody tassels in the river, roll it up, put it on his back, and set off down the valley with a heavy heart.

It even seemed to Kojuro that he could understand what the bears were saying to each other. Early one spring, before any of the trees had turned green, Kojuro took the dog with him and went far up the marshy bed of Shira Valley. As dusk drew near, he began to climb up to the pass leading over to Bakkai Valley, where he had built a small hut of bamboo grass to shelter in. But for some reason or other Kojuro, unusually for him, took the wrong trail. Any number of times he started up, then came down and started up again; even the dog was quite exhausted and Kojuro himself was breathing heavily out of one side of his mouth before they finally found the hut he'd built the year before, which was half tumbled down.

Remembering that there had been a spring just below the hut, Kojuro set off down the mountain, but had only gone a little way when to his surprise he came across two bears, a mother and a cub barely a year old, standing in the faint light of the still new moon, staring intently at the far-off valley with their paws up to their foreheads, just as human beings do when gazing into the distance. To Kojuro, the bears looked as if they were surrounded by a kind of halo, and he stopped and stared at them transfixed.

Then the small bear said in a wheedling voice, 'I'm sure it's snow, Mother. Only the near side of the valley is white, isn't it? Yes, I'm sure it's snow!'

The mother bear went on staring for a while before saying, 'It's not snow. It wouldn't fall just in that one place.'

'Then it must have been left there after the rest melted,' said the cub.

'No, I went past there only yesterday on my way to look for thistle buds.'

Kojuro stared hard in the same direction. The moonlight was gliding down the mountainside, which gleamed like silver armour. After a while the cub spoke again.

'If it's not snow then it must be frost. I'm sure it is.'

There really will be a frost tonight, thought Kojuro to himself. A star was shimmering blue, close to the moon; even the colour of the moon itself was just like ice.

'I know what it is,' said the mother bear. 'It's cherry blossom.'

'Is that all? Even *I've* seen that.'

'No, you haven't, dear.'

'But I *have.* I went and brought some home myself the other day.'

'No – that wasn't cherry. It was some kind of beech, I think.'

'Really?' the cub said innocently.

For some reason, Kojuro's heart felt full. He gave a last glance at the snowy flowers over in the valley, and at the mother bear and her cub standing bathed in the moonlight, then stealthily, taking care to make no sound, withdrew. As he crept away, praying all the while that the wind wouldn't blow his scent in their direction, the fragrance of spicebush came sharply to him on the moonlight.

When he went to town to sell the bearskins and the bear liver, that same brave Kojuro cut a much humbler figure.

Somewhere near the centre of the town there was a large hardware store where winnowing baskets and sugar, whetstones and cheap cigarettes, and even glass fly traps were set out for sale.

Kojuro had only to step over the threshold of the shop with the great bundle of bearskins on his back for the people there to start smiling as though to say, 'Here he is again.' The owner of the place would be seated massively beside a large brazier in a room leading off the shop.

'Thank you for your kindness last time, sir,' Kojuro would say; and the hunter who back in the hills was completely his own master would lay down his bundle of skins and, kneeling on the boards, bow low.

'Well, well . . . And what can I do for you today?'

'I've brought along a few bearskins again.'

'Bearskins? The last ones are still lying around here somewhere. We don't need any more.'

'Come on, sir – give us a chance. I'll let you have them cheap.'

'I don't care how cheap they are, I don't want them,' the shopkeeper would tell him calmly, tapping out the small bowl of his pipe against the palm of his hand.

Whenever he heard this, Kojuro, brave lord of the hills, would feel his face twist with anxiety.

Where Kojuro came from, there were chestnuts to be found in the hills, and millet grew in the apology for a field that lay at the back of the house; but no rice would grow, nor was there any soybean paste for making soup. So he had to have some rice, however little, to take back to the family of seven – his old mother and his grandchildren.

If he had lived down in the village, he would have grown hemp for weaving cloth, but at Kojuro's place there were only a few wisteria vines, which were woven into baskets and the like.

After a while, Kojuro would say in a voice hoarse with distress, 'Please – please buy some, whatever the price.' And he'd bow down low again.

The shopkeeper would puff smoke for a while without saying anything, then, suppressing a slight grin of satisfaction, would seat himself in front of Kojuro and hand him four large silver coins. Kojuro would accept them with a smile and raise them respectfully to his forehead. Then the owner of the shop would gradually unbend.

'Here – give Kojuro some saké.'

By now Kojuro would be glowing with delight. The shopkeeper would talk to him at leisure about this and that. Deferentially, Kojuro would tell him of things back in the hills. And soon word would come from the kitchen that the meal was ready. Kojuro would rise to go, but in the end would be dragged off to the kitchen, where he would go through his polite greetings once again.

Almost immediately, they would bring a small black lacquered table bearing slices of salted salmon with chopped cuttlefish and a flask of warm saké.

Kojuro would seat himself very correctly at the table, then start to eat, balancing the pieces of cuttlefish on the back of his hand before gulping them down, and reverently pouring the yellowish saké into the tiny cup …

However low prices might be, anyone would have agreed that two yen was too little for a pair of bearskins.

It really was too little, and Kojuro knew it. Why, then, didn't he sell his skins to someone other than that hardware dealer? To most people, it would be a mystery. But in those days there was an order to things: it was a matter of course that Kojuro should get the better of the bears, that the shopkeeper should get the better of Kojuro, and that the bears – but since the shopkeeper lived in the town, the bears couldn't get the better of him, for the moment at least.

Such being the state of affairs, Kojuro killed the bears without feeling any hatred for them. One year, though, a strange thing happened.

Kojuro was squelching his way up a valley and had climbed onto a rock to look about him when he saw a large bear, his back hunched, clambering like a cat up a tree directly in front of him. Immediately, Kojuro levelled his gun. The dog, delighted, was already at the foot of the tree, rushing madly round and round it.

But the bear, who for a while seemed to be debating whether he should come down and attack Kojuro or let himself be shot where he was, suddenly let go with his paws and came crashing to the ground. Instantly on his guard, Kojuro tucked his gun into his shoulder and closed in. But at this point the bear put up his paws and shouted:

'What are you after? Why do you have to shoot me?'

'For nothing but your fur and your liver,' Kojuro replied. 'Not that I'll get anything much for them when I take them to town. I'm sorry for you, but it just can't be helped. Though when I hear you say that kind of thing, I almost feel I'd rather live on chestnuts and ferns and the like, even if it killed me.'

'Can't you wait just two more years? For myself, I don't care whether I die or not, but there are still things I've got to do. When two years are up, you'll find me dead in front of your house, I promise. You can have my fur and my insides too.'

Filled with a strange emotion, Kojuro stood quite still, thinking.

The bear set his four paws firmly on the ground and began, ever so slowly, to move away. But Kojuro went on standing there, staring vacantly in front of him.

Slowly, slowly, the bear walked away without looking back, as though he knew very well that Kojuro would never shoot him from behind. For a moment, his broad, brownish black back shone bright in the sunlight falling through the branches of the trees, and at the same moment Kojuro gave a painful groan, then headed home across the valley.

It was just two years later. One morning, the wind blew so fiercely that Kojuro, sure that it was blowing down trees and hedge and all, went outside to look. The cypress hedge was standing untouched, but at its foot lay something brownish black that seemed familiar. His heart gave a turn, for it was exactly two years since that day, and he had been feeling worried in case the bear should come along. He went up to it, and found the self-same bear lying there as he had promised, dead, in a great pool of blood that had gushed from his mouth. Almost without thinking, Kojuro pressed his hands together in prayer.

It was one day in January. As Kojuro was leaving home that morning, he said something he had never said before.

'Mother, I must be getting old. This morning, for the first time in my life, I don't feel I want to wade through all those streams.'

Kojuro's mother of ninety, who sat spinning on the veranda in the sun, raised her rheumy eyes and glanced at him with an expression that might have been either tearful or smiling.

Kojuro tied on his straw sandals, heaved himself to his feet and set off. One after the other the children poked their faces out of the barn and smiling said, 'Come home soon, Grandpa.'

Kojuro looked up at the smooth, bright blue sky, then turned to his grandchildren and said, 'I'll be back later.'

He climbed up through the pure white, close-packed snow in the direction of Shira Valley. The dog was already panting heavily, his pink tongue lolling, as he ran ahead and stopped, ran ahead and stopped again. Soon Kojuro's figure sank out of sight beyond a low hill, and the children returned to their games.

Kojuro followed the bank of the river up Shira Valley. Here the water lay in deep blue pools, there it was frozen into sheets of glass, here the icicles hung in countless numbers like bead curtains, and on both banks the berries of the spindletree peeped out like red and yellow flowers. As he climbed upstream, Kojuro saw his own glittering shadow and the dog's, deep indigo and sharply etched on the snow, mingling as they moved with the shadows of the birch trunks.

On the other side of the mountain from Shira Valley there lived, as he had confirmed during the summer, a large bear.

On he went upstream, fording five small tributaries that came flowing into the valley, crossing the water again and again from right to left and from left to right. He came to a small waterfall, from the foot of which he began to climb up towards the ridge. The snow was so dazzling it seemed to be on fire, and as he toiled upwards, Kojuro felt as if he saw everything through purple glasses.

The dog was climbing as though determined that the steepness of the slope would not beat him, clinging grimly to the snow, though he nearly slipped many times. When they finally reached the top, they found themselves on a plateau that sloped gently away, where the snow sparkled like white marble and snow-covered peaks thrust up into the sky all about them.

It happened as Kojuro was taking a rest there at the summit. Suddenly, the dog began to bark frantically. Startled, Kojuro looked behind him and saw the same great bear that he had glimpsed that summer rearing up on his hind legs and lumbering towards him. Without panicking, Kojuro planted his feet firmly in the snow and took aim.

Raising his two massive front paws, the bear charged straight at him. Even Kojuro turned a bit pale at the sight.

Kojuro heard the crack of the gun. Yet the bear showed no sign of falling, but seemed to come swaying on towards him, black and raging like a storm. The dog sank his teeth into his leg. The next moment, a great noise filled Kojuro's head and everything around him went white. Then, far off in the distance, he heard a voice saying, 'Ah, Kojuro, I didn't mean to kill you.'

'This is death,' he thought. All about him he could see lights twinkling incessantly like blue stars. 'Those are the signs that I'm finished,' he thought, 'the fires you see when you die. Forgive me, Bears.' As for what he felt from then on, I have no idea.

It was the evening of the third day after that. A moon hung in the sky like a great ball of ice. The snow was a bright bluish white, and the water gave off a phosphorescent glow. The Pleiades and Orion's belt glimmered now green, now orange, as if they were breathing.

On the plateau on top of the mountain, surrounded by chestnut trees and snowy peaks, many great black shapes were gathered in a ring, each casting its own black shadow, each prostrate in the snow like a Muslim at prayer, never moving. And there at the highest point one might have seen, by the light of the snow and the moon, Kojuro's corpse set in a kneeling position. One might even have imagined that on Kojuro's dead, frozen face one could see a chill smile as though he were still alive. Orion's belt moved to the centre of the heavens, then tilted still further to the west, yet the great black shapes stayed quite still, as though they had turned to stone.

Wildcat and the Acorns

One Saturday evening, a most peculiar postcard arrived at Ichiro's house. This is what it said:

> September 19
>
> Mr Ichiro Kaneta:
>
> Pleased to know as how you're well. Tomorrow I've got a difficult case to judge, so please come. Please don't bring no firearms.
>
> Yours respectfully,
> Wildcat

That was all. The writing was terrible, and the ink so blobby it almost stuck to his fingers. But Ichiro was quite delighted. He put the card in his satchel when no one was looking and took it to school, and all day long he was bouncing up and down with joy.

Even after he'd crept into bed that night, he still kept imagining Wildcat's face with its cat's grin, and the scene at tomorrow's trial, and so many other things that he couldn't get to sleep until quite late.

When he awoke, though, it was already broad daylight. He went outside, and there were the hills lined up beneath a bright blue sky, rising as fresh and clean as though they'd just been made. He hurried through his breakfast and set off alone up the path by the stream in the valley. There was a fresh morning breeze, and at each puff the chestnut trees showered their nuts in all directions. Ichiro looked up at them.

'Hello there, Chestnut Trees,' he called. 'Did Wildcat pass this way?'

And the trees paused a while in their rustling and replied, 'Wildcat? Yes, he rushed past in a carriage early this morning, going to the east.'

'The east? That's the direction I'm heading in. How strange! At any rate, I'll keep going this way and see. Thank you, Chestnut Trees.'

The chestnut trees made no answer but went on scattering their nuts around. So Ichiro went a little further, and came to the Flute

Falls. About halfway up a pure white cliff, there was a small hole through which the water spurted, whistling like a flute before dropping with a roar into the valley below. Facing the waterfall, Ichiro shouted up at it:

'Hello there, Flute Falls. Did Wildcat pass this way?'

'Wildcat?' came a high, whistly voice. 'Yes, he rushed past in a carriage a while ago, going to the west.'

'The west?' said Ichiro. 'That's where my home is. How strange! Anyway, I'll go a bit further and see. Thank you, Waterfall.'

But the waterfall was already whistling to itself as it always did. So Ichiro went on a bit and came to a beech tree. Under the tree, a crowd of white mushrooms were playing together in a funny kind of orchestra: *tiddley-tum-tum, tiddley-tum-tum.* Ichiro bent down towards them.

'Hello, Mushrooms,' he said. 'Did Wildcat pass this way?'

'Wildcat?' replied the mushrooms. 'Yes, he rushed past in a carriage early this morning, going to the south.'

'That's strange,' said Ichiro, in growing puzzlement. 'That's in those mountains over there. Anyway, I'll go a bit further and see. Thank you, Mushrooms.'

But the mushrooms were already busy again, playing their peculiar music, *tiddley-tum-tum, tiddley-tum-tum* . . .

Ichiro was walking on when he noticed a squirrel hopping about in the branches of a walnut tree.

'Hey, Squirrel!' called Ichiro, waving at him to stop. 'Did Wildcat pass this way?'

'Wildcat?' said the squirrel, shading his eyes with a paw as he peered down at Ichiro. 'Yes, he rushed past this morning in a carriage while it was still dark, going to the south.'

'The south?' said Ichiro. 'That's strange – that's twice I've been told that. Ah well, I'll go a bit further and see. Thank you, Squirrel.'

But the squirrel had gone. All he could see was the topmost branches of the walnut tree swaying a little, and the leaves of the neighbouring beech tree flashing for a moment in the sun.

A little further on and the path along the stream grew narrower, then disappeared altogether. There was another narrow path, however, leading up towards the dark wood to the south of the stream, so Ichiro set off up it. The branches of the trees were heavy and so close together that not the tiniest patch of blue sky was to be seen. The path became steeper and steeper. Ichiro's face turned bright red, and sweat fell off it in great drops. But then, quite suddenly, he came out into the light. He had reached a beautiful golden meadow. The grass rustled in the breeze, and all around stood fine, olive-coloured trees.

There, in the middle of the meadow, a most odd-looking little man was watching Ichiro. His back was bent, and in his hand he held a leather whip. Ichiro slowly went nearer, then stopped in astonishment. The little man was one-eyed, and his blind eye, which was white, was moving nervously all the time. His legs were very bandy, like a goat's, and – most peculiar of all – his feet were shaped like spades.

'You wouldn't happen to know Wildcat, would you?' Ichiro asked, trying not to show his nervousness.

The little man looked at Ichiro with his one eye, and his mouth twisted in a leer.

'Mr Wildcat will be back in just a moment,' he said. 'You'll be Ichiro, I suppose?'

Ichiro started back in astonishment.

'Yes, I'm Ichiro,' he replied. 'But how did you know?'

The strange little man gave an even broader leer.

'Then you got the postcard?' he asked.

'Yes, that's why I came,' Ichiro said.

'Badly written, wasn't it?' asked the little man, looking gloomily down at the ground. Ichiro felt sorry for him.

'No,' he said. 'It seemed very good to me.'

The man gave a little gasp of joy and blushed to the tips of his ears. He pulled his coat open at the neck to cool himself, and asked:

'Was the handwriting all right?'

Ichiro couldn't help smiling.

'It was fine,' he said. 'I doubt if even a fifth grader could write that well.'

The little man suddenly looked depressed again.

'When you say fifth grader, you mean at primary school, I suppose?' His voice was so listless and pathetic that Ichiro was alarmed.

'Oh, no,' he said hastily. 'At university.'

The little man cheered up again and grinned so broadly that his face seemed to be all mouth.

'*I* wrote that postcard,' he shouted.

'Just who are you, then?' asked Ichiro, trying not to smile.

'I am Mr Wildcat's coachman!' he replied.

A sudden gust of wind rippled over the grass, and the coachman gave a deep bow. Puzzled, Ichiro turned around, and there was Wildcat, standing behind him. He wore a fine coat of yellow brocade, and his green eyes as he stared at Ichiro were perfectly round. Ichiro barely had time to note that his ears were pointed and stuck up just like an ordinary cat's, before Wildcat gave a stiff little bow.

'Oh, good morning,' said Ichiro politely, bowing in return. 'Thank you for the postcard.'

'Good morning,' said Wildcat, pulling his whiskers out stiff and sticking out his chest. 'I'm pleased to see you. The fact is, a most troublesome dispute arose the day before yesterday, and I don't quite know how to settle it, so I thought I might ask your opinion. But anyway, make yourself at home, won't you? The acorns should be here any moment now. Really, you know, I have a lot of trouble with this trial every year.'

He took a cigarette case from inside his coat and put a cigarette in his mouth.

'Won't you have one?' he asked, offering the case to Ichiro.

'Oh, no thank you,' said Ichiro, startled.

'Ho-ho! Of course, you're still too young,' said Wildcat with a lordly kind of laugh. He struck a match and, screwing up his face self-consciously, puffed out a cloud of blue smoke. His coachman, who was stiffly standing by awaiting orders, seemed to be dying for a cigarette himself, as there were big tears rolling down his face.

Just then, Ichiro heard a tiny crackling sound at his feet, like salt being tossed on a fire. He bent down in surprise to look and saw that the ground was covered with little round gold things, glinting in the grass. He looked closer and found that they were acorns – there must have been over three hundred of them – all wearing red trousers and all chattering away about something at the top of their voices.

'Here they come. Just like a lot of ants,' said Wildcat, throwing away his cigarette. Hurriedly he gave orders to the coachman. 'You there, ring the bell,' he said. 'And cut the grass just here, where it's sunny.'

The coachman took up a big sickle at his side and swished down the grass in front of Wildcat. Immediately, the acorns came rushing out from the surrounding grass, glittering in the sun as they came, and chattering like mad.

The coachman rang his bell. *Clang, clang!* it went. *Clang, clang!* the sound echoed through the woods, and the golden acorns became a little quieter. Unnoticed by Ichiro, Wildcat had put on a long black satin gown and was now sitting there in front of them, looking important. It reminded Ichiro of pictures he had seen of crowds of tiny worshippers before a great bronze idol.

Swish, crack!, *swish, crack!* went the coachman with his whip. The sky was blue and cloudless, and the acorns sparkled beautifully.

'Let me remind you, this is the third day this case has been going on,' Wildcat began. 'Now, why don't you call it off and make it up with each other?'

His voice was a little nervous, but he forced himself to sound important. No sooner had he spoken, though, than the acorns set up a commotion again.

'No, that's impossible! Whatever you say, the one with the most pointed head is best. And it's me who's the most pointed.'

'No, you're wrong, the roundest one's best. I'm the roundest!'

'It's size, I tell you! The biggest. I'm the biggest, so I'm the best!'

'That's nonsense! I'm much bigger. Don't you remember the judge said so yesterday?'

'You're all wrong! It's the one who's the tallest. The tallest one, I tell you!'

'No, it's the one who's best at pushing and shoving. That's what settles it!'

The acorns were making such a racket that in the end you had absolutely no idea what it was all about. It was like stirring up a hornet's nest.

'That's enough!' Wildcat bawled. 'Where do you think you are? Silence! Silence!'

Swish, crack! went the coachman's whip, and at last the acorns were quiet.

'Let me remind you again, this is the third day this trial has been going on,' Wildcat declared, twisting his whiskers until they stood on end. 'How about calling it off now and making things up?'

'No, no, it's no good. Whatever you say, the one with the most pointed head's best!'

'No, you're wrong. The roundest one's best!'

'No, he's not, it's the biggest!'

Chatter, chatter, chatter again, until you had no idea what was going on.

'That's enough! Where do you think you are?' Wildcat shouted. 'Silence! Silence!'

Swish, crack! went the coachman's whip again. Wildcat twisted his whiskers until they stood straight up, then started again.

'I don't need to remind you, this is the third day this case has been going on. Why don't you call it off and be friends again?'

'No, no, it's no good! The one with the most pointed head . . .' Chatter, chatter, chatter . . .

'That's enough!' Wildcat yelled. 'Where do you think you are? Silence! Silence!'

Again the coachman's whip went *swish, crack!* and again the acorns fell silent.

'You see what it's like,' whispered Wildcat to Ichiro. 'What do you think I ought to do?'

Ichiro smiled. 'Well, here's one suggestion,' he said. 'Tell them that the best is the one who's most stupid, most ridiculous and most good-for-nothing. I heard that in a sermon, actually.'

Wildcat nodded wisely and prepared to give his verdict. Pulling open his satin gown at the neck so that the yellow brocade coat showed a little, he put on his grandest air. Then he spoke.

'Right! Be quiet now! Here is my verdict. The best of you is the one who is least important, most foolish, most ridiculous, absolutely good-for-nothing and completely crackbrained!'

A hush fell over the acorns, such a complete hush that you could have heard a pin drop.

Wildcat took off his black gown and, wiping the sweat from his forehead, shook Ichiro's hand, while the coachman cracked his whip five or six times for sheer joy.

'I'm most obliged to you,' said Wildcat to Ichiro. 'I must say, you've taken a most awkward case off my hands in not so much as a minute and a half. I do hope you'll act as an honorary judge in my court again in the future. If ever I send you a postcard from now on, please come, won't you? I'll see you're suitably rewarded every time.'

'Of course I'll come,' said Ichiro. 'But I don't want any reward.'

'Oh, no,' objected Wildcat. 'You must accept one. It's a matter of honour for me, you see. And from now on, I'll address the postcard to "Ichiro Kaneta, Esq.", and call this "The Court" – is that all right?'

'That's fine,' said Ichiro.

Wildcat was silent for a moment, twirling his whiskers as though there was something more he wanted to say. Then he seemed to take courage and went on:

'About the wording of the card – how would it be if I put it like this: "Pertaining to certain business in hand, your presence in court is formally requested"?'

Ichiro smiled. 'It sounds rather funny to me, somehow. Perhaps you'd better leave that bit out.'

Wildcat gazed crestfallen at the ground, still twiddling his whiskers as though regretting that he hadn't put it better. Finally, with a sigh, he said:

'Well, then, we'll leave it as it stands. Oh yes – about your reward for today. Which would you prefer, a pint of gold acorns or a salted salmon head?'

'The acorns, please,' replied Ichiro.

Wildcat turned straight to his coachman, as if relieved that it hadn't been the salmon head.

'Get a pint of gold acorns,' he said, speaking fast. 'If there aren't enough, you can put in some gold-plated ones. And be quick about it!'

The coachman began to scoop the acorns into a square wooden measure. When he had finished, he shouted: 'One pint exactly.'

Wildcat's brocade coat flapped in the breeze. He stretched, closed his eyes and smothered a yawn.

'Right!' he said. 'Now hurry up and get the coach ready.'

A carriage made of a great white mushroom appeared, drawn by a horse of a most peculiar shape and grey in colour – just like a rat, in fact. Wildcat turned to Ichiro.

'And now we'll see you home,' he said.

They got into the carriage, the coachman put the measure full of acorns in beside them, and – *swish, crack!* – off they went. The meadow was left behind, and trees and bushes swayed by in a bluish haze. Ichiro's eyes were fixed on his gold acorns, while Wildcat was gazing quite innocently into the distance.

But as the carriage journeyed on, the acorns lost their glitter, and when – in no time, it seemed – the carriage came to a halt, they were just the plain, ordinary, brown kind. Wildcat's yellow brocade coat, and the coachman, and the mushroom carriage – all had vanished together, and Ichiro was left standing in front of his own home, the measure of acorns in his hand.

From that time on, there were no more postcards signed 'Yours respectfully, Wildcat'. Ichiro sometimes wonders about it. Perhaps he ought to have let Wildcat write 'your presence is formally requested', after all?

Gorsch the Cellist

Gorsch was the man who played the cello at the moving-picture theatre in town. Unfortunately, he had a reputation for being none too good a player. 'None too good,' perhaps, was hardly the word, for if the truth be told, he was worse than any of his fellow musicians and was forever being bullied by the conductor for that reason.

One afternoon they were all sitting in a circle backstage rehearsing the Sixth Symphony, which they were soon to perform at the town's concert hall.

The trumpets were blaring for all they were worth.

The clarinets were tootling away in support.

The violins, too, were playing like fury.

Gorsch was scraping away with the rest of them, oblivious to everything else, his lips pressed tight together and his eyes as big as saucers as he stared at the score in front of him.

All of a sudden the conductor clapped his hands.

They all stopped playing instantly, and silence fell.

'The cello was late!' shouted the conductor. '*Tum-tiddy, tiddy-tee* – take it again from the bit that goes *tum-tiddy, tiddy-tee.* Right?' So they started again from a point just before where they had got to. With his face red and his forehead all sweaty, Gorsch managed somehow to get safely past the tricky bit. And he was playing the next part with a feeling of relief when, once again, the conductor clapped his hands.

'Cello! You're off pitch! Whatever *are* we to do with you? I just haven't got time to teach you the simple scale, you know!'

The others looked sorry for Gorsch and deliberately peered at their scores or set about tuning their instruments. Hastily, Gorsch tightened his strings.

'From the previous bar. Right!'

They all began again. Gorsch's mouth was twisted with the effort to play properly. For once, they managed to get quite far without any trouble, and he was just feeling rather pleased with himself when the conductor scowled and brought things to a halt. 'Oh no – not again,' thought Gorsch, with a lurch of his heart. But this time, luckily, it was someone else. So Gorsch deliberately peered closely at his music, as the others had done for him just now, and did his best to look engrossed in something else.

'Let's go straight on to the next bit. Right!'

But Gorsch, feeling smug, had no sooner started playing than the conductor gave a great stamp of his foot and started shouting.

'It won't do. You're all at sixes and sevens. This part's the heart of the whole work, and look what a hash you're making of it. Gentlemen, we've got just ten days until the performance. We're professional musicians – how can we look people in the eye if we do no better than any old bunch of scrapers and blowers? You, Gorsch. You're one of the main problems. You just don't have any *expression*. No anger, no joy – no feeling at all. And you don't keep in perfect time with the other instruments, either. You always drag along behind with your shoelaces dangling. It won't do – you must pull yourself together. It's not fair to the others to let the name of the Venus Orchestra be dragged in the mud all because of one man. Well, then – that's enough rehearsing for now. Have a rest and be in the pit at six sharp.'

They all bowed, then reached for cigarettes or wandered off outside.

With his cheap, box-like cello held in his arms, Gorsch turned to face the wall. His mouth twisted and great tears rolled down his cheeks, but he soon pulled himself together and, all by himself, began to play again from the beginning, very softly, the part they had just done.

Late that evening, Gorsch arrived home carrying an enormous black object on his back. His home was really no more than a tumbledown old millhouse standing by the river on the outskirts of the town. He lived there all alone. His mornings he spent thinning out the tomatoes in the small field surrounding the mill and picking grubs off the cabbages, but in the afternoon he always went out.

Gorsch went indoors and opened the black bundle. It was, of course, the ugly great cello he'd been playing earlier that evening. He lowered it gently to the floor, then took a glass and gulped down some water out of a bucket.

Then, giving a shake of his head, he sat down on a chair and began to play the piece of music they'd rehearsed that day, attacking his instrument with all the ferocity of a tiger.

Turning over the pages of the score, he played a while and thought, thought a while and played, and when he got to the end he started again from the beginning, rumbling his way through the same thing over and over again.

He went on long past midnight, until in the end he hardly knew whether it was himself playing or someone else. He looked awful, as though he might collapse at any moment, his eyes all bloodshot and his face bright red.

Just then, though, somebody tapped three times on the door behind him.

'Is that you, Horsch?' he called as though half-asleep. However, it wasn't Horsch who pushed open the door and came in, but a large tortoiseshell cat that he had seen around several times before.

The cat was carrying, with enormous effort it seemed, a half-ripe tomato from Gorsch's field, which he set down in front of him.

'Phew. That was tiring,' he said 'Carrying things is a terrible job.'

'What on earth ...?' exclaimed Gorsch.

'It's a present for you,' said the tortoiseshell cat.

All the annoyance Gorsch had been damming up inside him since earlier that day came bursting out at once.

'Who told you to bring any tomato? Why should I want anything from somebody like you? And that tomato, what's more, comes from my field. What do you think you're up to? – picking them before they're ripe! I suppose it's you, then, who's been biting at the stalks and scattering them all over the place? Get out of here, you damn cat!'

All this made the visitor's shoulders droop and his eyes narrow, but he forced a grin and said, 'You shouldn't get so angry, sir, it's bad for your health. Why don't you play something instead? Schumann's "Träumerei", say ... I'll be your audience.'

'I've never heard such damned impertinence. And from a cat!'

Feeling furious, Gorsch spent a while thinking of the things he'd like to do to this creature.

'Come on, don't be shy,' said the cat. 'Please. You know, I can't get to sleep unless I hear you play something.'

'That's enough of your cheek! Enough, I say! Enough!'

Gorsch had gone an even brighter red and was shouting and stamping just as the conductor had done earlier that day. Suddenly, though, he changed his mind and said, 'All right, then, I'll play!' Ominously, he locked the door and shut all the windows, then got his cello out and turned off the light. When he did so, the light of the moon shone halfway into the room from outside.

'What was it you wanted to hear?'

'. . . "Träumerei". By Schumann,' said the cat in a perfectly serious voice, wiping his mouth as he spoke.

'Oh. "Träumerei". Of course. Would this be how it goes?'

Ominously again he tore his handkerchief into strips and stuffed up both his ears. Then he stormed straight into a piece called 'Tiger Hunt in India'.

For a while the cat listened with bowed head, but all of a sudden he blinked his eyes rapidly and made a leap for the door. His body collided with the door, but it refused to open. This threw the cat into a great state of agitation, and sparks crackled from his eyes and forehead. Then sparks came from his whiskers and nose too, which tickled, so that for a while he looked as if he was going to sneeze, and he started trotting around as though he couldn't stay still. Gorsch was delighted at the effect he was producing, and began to play all the harder.

'Mr Gorsch, that's enough, thank you,' said the cat. 'Quite enough. I beg you to stop. I promise I'll never tell you what to do again.'

'Be quiet! We're just getting to the bit where they catch the tiger.'

By now the cat was leaping up and down in distress, then racing around the walls, which gave off a green glow for a while when he rubbed against them. In the end, he was whirling like a merry-go-round.

Gorsch's own head began to spin a little, so he said, 'All right, I'll let you off now.' And at last he stopped.

The cat forced himself to look calm. 'Mr Gorsch, there's something funny about your playing tonight, isn't there?' he said.

Again Gorsch felt deeply aggrieved but, as casually as he could, he got out a cigarette and put it in his mouth, then took a match and said, 'What about it? Are you sure there's nothing wrong with *you*? Let's have a look at your tongue.'

Rather rudely the cat stuck out his long, pointed tongue.

'Ah-ha! Looks a bit rough, I'm afraid,' said the cellist, and without warning he struck the match on it and lit his cigarette. To say the cat was startled would be putting it too mildly: waving his tongue about like a pinwheel, he ran to the door and bashed his head against it, staggered away, went back and banged it again, staggered, went back again, banged it once more and staggered, trying desperately to escape.

For a while Gorsch watched in amusement, then said, 'I'll let you out. So mind you don't come again. Stupid!'

He opened the door, and the cat streaked off through the pampas grass. Gorsch gave a little smile as he watched him go, then went to bed and slept soundly as though a load had been lifted from his mind.

The next evening, too, Gorsch came home with the same black bundle on his back and, after gulping down a great deal of water, began to scrub away at his cello again. Soon twelve o'clock came, then one, then two, and still Gorsch went on. And he was still booming away, scarcely aware of the time or even of the fact that he was playing, when he heard someone tapping on the other side of the ceiling.

'What! . . . Haven't you had enough yet, Cat?' he shouted, whereupon a scuffling sound came from a hole in the ceiling and a grey bird flew down through it and landed on the floor. It was a cuckoo.

'So now I have birds, too,' said Gorsch. 'What do *you* want?'

'I want to learn music,' said the cuckoo quite seriously.

'Music, eh?' said Gorsch with a smile. 'But all you can sing is *cuckoo*, *cuckoo*, surely?'

'Yes,' said the cuckoo earnestly, 'that's right. But it's very difficult to do, you know.'

'Difficult? The only problem for cuckoos is having to sing such a lot. There's nothing difficult about the actual notes, is there?'

'No, actually that's just why it's so hard. For example, if I sing like this – *cuckoo* – and then like this – *cuckoo* – you can tell they're different just by listening, can't you?'

'They sound the same to me.'

'That's because your ear's not sensitive enough. We could sing ten thousand *cuckoos* and to us they'd all be different.'

'I'll take your word for it. If you're so good at it, though, why do you have to come to me?'

'But you see, I want to learn the scale correctly.'

'Why should you care about the scale?'

'Oh, but one needs it if one's going abroad.'

'And why should *you* care about going abroad?'

'Sir – please teach me the scale. I'll sing it with you as you play.'

'Oh, hell! Look, I'll play it just three times, then when I've finished I want you out of here.'

Gorsch took up his cello, scraped at the strings as he tuned them, then played *do, re, mi, fa, sol, la, ti, do.*

But the cuckoo fluttered his wings in dismay.

'No, no. That's not how it should go.'

'There's just no pleasing you. You try it, then.'

'This is how it goes.' The bird bent forward slightly, braced himself, and produced a single *cuckoo.*

'Well! Do you call that a scale? If it is, then an ordinary scale and the Sixth Symphony must sound all the same to you cuckoos.'

'Oh no, they're quite different.'

'How?'

'One of the difficult things is when you get a lot of them in succession.'

'You mean like this, I suppose?' Gorsch took up his cello again and started to play a number of *cuckoos* in succession.

This delighted the bird so much that halfway through he began to bawl *cuckoo, cuckoo*, in time with Gorsch. On and on he went, twisting his body to and fro.

Eventually Gorsch's hand began to hurt, so he stopped.

'Here,' he said, 'that's about enough, isn't it?'

But the cuckoo just narrowed his eyes regretfully and went on singing for a while, until finally he went *cuckoo, cuck – cuck – cuck – cu* – and stopped.

By now Gorsch was getting angry.

'Look – if you've finished, you can clear out.'

'Oh, please. Won't you play it just once more? There's something still not quite right about your side of it.'

'What? I'm not supposed to be learning from you. Come on, go home.'

'Please, just one more time. Please . . . ,' said the bird, humbly bobbing his head.

'Well, then, just this once.' Gorsch got his bow ready.

The cuckoo gave a single *cuck!* then said, 'As long as possible if you don't mind.' He bowed his head again.

'Heaven help us,' said Gorsch, and with a wry smile began to play. Again the cuckoo got quite wrapped up in things and sang for all he was worth, twisting back and forth: *cuckoo, cuckoo, cuckoo.*

At first Gorsch felt very irritated, but as he played on he began to have an odd feeling that it was the cuckoo, somehow, who was really hitting the notes of the scale. In fact, the more he played the more convinced he became that the cuckoo was better than he was.

'Hell! I'll go cuckoo myself if I keep this up,' he said, and quite abruptly stopped.

The bird reeled as though someone had banged him on the head, then, just as he'd done before, sang *cuckoo, cuckoo, cuck – cuck – cuck –* and stopped.

'Why did you stop?' the bird said, looking at Gorsch resentfully. 'Any cuckoo worth his salt would've kept on singing at the top of his voice until his throat was too sore to go on.'

'Why, you cheeky ... Do you think I can go on fooling around like this forever? Come on, now, get out. Look – can't you see it's nearly dawn?' He pointed at the window.

The eastern sky was turning faintly silver where black clouds were scudding across it towards the north.

'Couldn't we just go on until it's light? It's only a little while to wait.'

Again the cuckoo bowed his head.

'That's enough! You seem to think you can get away with anything. If you don't get out I'll pluck your feathers and eat you for breakfast, you stupid bird.' He stamped hard on the floor.

This seemed to frighten the cuckoo, for suddenly he flew up towards the window, only to bang his head violently against the glass and flop down on the floor again.

'Look at you, you fool – banging into the glass!' Hastily Gorsch got up to open the window, but the window never had been the kind to slide open at a touch, and he was still rattling the frame furiously when the cuckoo slammed into it and fell again.

Gorsch could see a little blood coming from the base of his beak.

'I'm going to open it for you, so wait a moment, won't you?' With great difficulty he had just got the thing open a couple of inches when the cuckoo picked himself up and, staring hard at the eastern sky beyond the window as though he was determined to succeed at all costs this time, took off with frantically beating wings. This time, of course, he hit the window even more violently than before and dropped to the floor, where he remained perfectly still for a while. But when Gorsch put a hand out, thinking to take him to the door and let him fly away, the bird suddenly opened his eyes and leapt out of reach. It looked as though he was going to fly into the window again, so, almost without thinking, Gorsch raised his leg and gave the window a great kick.

Two or three panes shattered with a tremendous crash and the whole thing fell outside, frame and all. Through the gaping hole it left the cuckoo flew out like an arrow. On and on he flew into the distance until finally he completely disappeared from sight. For a while Gorsch stayed looking out in disgust, then flopped down in a corner of the room and went to sleep where he was.

The next day, too, Gorsch played his cello until past midnight. He was tired and was drinking a glass of water when again there came a tapping at the door.

Whoever his visitor might be, he told himself, he would take a threatening attitude from the start and drive him away before the same thing happened as with the cuckoo. As he waited with the glass in his hand, the door opened a little and a badger cub came in. Gorsch opened the door a bit wider, then stamped on the floor.

'Listen, you,' he shouted, 'do you know what badger soup is?' But the badger seated himself tidily on the floor with a puzzled look on his face and sat thinking for a while, his head tilted to one side.

'Badger soup?' said the badger in a little voice. 'No.'

The look on the cub's face made Gorsch want to burst out laughing, but he put on a fierce expression and went on: 'Then I'll tell you. Badger soup, you see, is a badger just like you boiled up with cabbage and salt for the likes of me to eat.'

The young badger still looked puzzled and said, 'But my father, you know, he said I was to go and study with Mr Gorsch because he was a very nice man and not at all to be scared of.'

At this, Gorsch finally laughed out loud. 'What did he tell you to study?' he said. 'I'm busy, I'll have you know. And I'm sleepy, too.'

The little badger stepped forward as though he had suddenly taken heart.

'You see, I'm the one who plays the side drum,' he said, 'and I was told to go and learn how to play in time with the cello.'

'But I don't see any side drum.'

'Here – look.' The badger produced two sticks that were slung across his back.

'And what are you going to do with those?'

'Play "The Happy Coachman", please, and you'll see.'

'"The Happy Coachman"? What's that – jazz or something?'

'Here's the music.'

This time the badger brought out from behind his back a single sheet of music. Gorsch took it from him and laughed.

'Well, this is a funny piece of music! All right. Here we go, then. So you're going to play the drum, are you?' And he started playing, watching the cub out of the corner of his eye to see what he would do.

To Gorsch's surprise, the badger started busily beating with his sticks on the body of the cello below the bridge. He was not at all bad at it, and, as he played, Gorsch found himself beginning to enjoy things.

When they got to the end, the badger stayed thinking for a while with his head on one side. At last he seemed to reach a conclusion of some kind, for he said, 'When you play this second string you get behind, don't you? Somehow it seems to throw me off the beat.'

Gorsch was taken aback. It was true: ever since yesterday evening he'd had a feeling that however smartly he played that particular string, there was always a pause before it sounded.

'You know, you may be right. This cello's no good,' he said sadly. The badger looked sympathetic and thought again for a while.

'I wonder where it's no good. Would you mind playing it once more?'

'Of course.' Gorsch started up again. The badger beat away as before, tilting his head to one side occasionally as though listening to the cello. And by the time they had finished there was a glimmering of light again in the east.

'Look – it's getting near dawn. Thank you very much.' Hastily the little badger hoisted the sticks and the music onto his back, fastened them there with a rubber band, gave two or three bows, and hurried out of the house.

For a while Gorsch sat there abstractedly, breathing in the cool air that came through the windowpanes he'd broken the previous night, then decided to go to sleep and get his strength back for going into town, and crawled into bed.

The next day, too, Gorsch was up all night playing his cello. It was almost dawn, and he had begun to doze off with the score still held in his hand, when again he heard someone tapping. It was so faint that it was hard to be sure whether somebody had really knocked or not, but Gorsch, who was used to it by now, heard at once and said, 'Come in'.

The door opened an inch or two, and in came a field mouse leading an extremely small child mouse. Hesitantly, she came towards Gorsch. As for the baby mouse, it was so small – only about as big as an eraser – that Gorsch couldn't help smiling. Peering about her as though wondering what he could be smiling at, the mother set down a green chestnut in front of her and bowed very correctly.

'Mr Gorsch,' she said. 'This child here isn't well, and I'm afraid he may die. I beg you, out of the kindness of your heart, to cure him.'

'How can you expect *me* to do that?' demanded Gorsch rather petulantly.

The mother mouse looked down at the floor and was silent for a while, then seemed to pluck up courage and said, 'I know very well that you cure all kinds of people every day, and that you're very good at it, too.'

'I don't know what you're talking about.'

'But it was thanks to you that the rabbit's grandmother got better, wasn't it, and the badger's father, and even that nasty old owl was cured, wasn't he, so in the circumstances I think it's very unkind of you to say you won't save this child.'

'Wait a minute – there must be some mistake. *I've* never cured any sick owl. Though it's true I had the young badger here last night, behaving like a member of the band.'

He laughed, looking down at the baby mouse in dismay.

But the mother mouse started crying.

'Ah me, if the child *had* to get sick I only wish he'd done it sooner. There you were rumbling away here just a while ago, then as soon as he gets sick the sound stops dead and you refuse to play any more. The poor little thing.'

'What?' shouted Gorsch, startled. 'You mean that when I play, sick rabbits and owls get better? Why, I wonder?'

'You see,' said the field mouse, rubbing at her eyes with a paw, 'whenever the folk around here get sick, they creep under the floor of your house.'

'And you mean they get well?'

'Yes, it improves the circulation wonderfully. They feel so much better. Some of them are cured on the spot, others after they're back home again.'

'Ah, I see. You mean that when my cello rumbles it acts as a kind of massage? . . . Now I understand. All right, I'll play for you.' He squeaked at the strings a bit to tune them, then all of a sudden picked up the baby mouse between his fingers and popped him in through the hole in the cello.

'I'll go with him,' said the mother mouse frantically, jumping onto the cello. 'All the hospitals allow it.'

'So you're going in as well, eh?' said Gorsch, and tried to help her through the hole, but she could only get her face halfway in.

'Are you all right there?' she called to the child inside as she pushed and struggled. 'Did you fall properly as I always tell you you should, with your paws foursquare?'

'I'm all right. I fell nicely,' came the baby mouse's voice from the bottom of the cello, so faint it could hardly be heard.

'Of course he's all right,' said Gorsch. 'So we don't want you crying, now.'

Gorsch set the mother down on the floor, then took up his bow and rumbled and scraped his way through some rhapsody or other. The mother sat listening anxiously to the quality of the sound, but finally, it seemed, she could bear the suspense no longer and said, 'That's enough, thank you. Could you take him out now, please?'

'Well! Is that all?' Gorsch tipped the cello over, put his hand by the hole, and waited. Almost immediately, the baby mouse appeared. Without saying anything, Gorsch set him down on the floor. The baby's eyes were shut tight and he was trembling and trembling as though he would never stop.

'How was it? How do you feel? Better?' asked the mother mouse.

The child mouse made no reply but sat for a while with his eyes shut, trembling and trembling, then quite suddenly jumped up and started running about.

'Look, he's better! Thank you so much, sir, thank you so much.' The mother mouse went and ran about a little with her child, but soon came back to Gorsch and, bowing busily over and over again, said, 'Thank you so much, thank you so much,' about ten times in all.

Somehow Gorsch felt rather sorry for them.

'Here –' he said, 'do you eat bread?'

The field mouse looked shocked. 'Oh, no!' she said, looking about her uneasily as she spoke. 'People do say that bread is very light and good to eat – it seems they make it by kneading flour – but of course we've never been near your cupboard, and we'd never dream of coming to steal it after everything you've done for us.'

'No – that's not what I mean. I'm just asking if you can eat it. But of *course* you can. Wait a moment, then, I'll give some to this boy for his bad stomach.'

He set the cello down on the floor, went to the cupboard, tore off a handful of bread, and put it in front of them.

The field mouse cried and laughed and bowed as though she had gone quite silly, then with infinite care took the bread in her mouth and went out, shooing the child in front of her.

'Dear me,' said Gorsch. 'It's quite tiring talking to mice.' And, flopping down on his bed, he was soon fast asleep and snoring.

It was the evening of the sixth day after this. With flushed faces the members of the Venus Orchestra, each carrying his instrument in his hand, came straggling from the stage of the town hall to the musicians' room at the back. They had just performed the Sixth Symphony with great success. In the hall, the storm of applause was still continuing. The conductor, his hands thrust in his pockets, was slowly pacing about among them as though applause meant absolutely nothing to him, but in fact he was thoroughly delighted. Some of them were putting cigarettes between their lips and striking matches, some putting their instruments away in their cases.

The clapping was still going on in the hall. In fact, it was getting steadily louder and was beginning to sound alarmingly as though it might get out of hand. At this point, the master of ceremonies, who had a large white rosette pinned on his chest, came in.

'They're calling for an encore,' he said. 'Do you think you could play something short for them?'

'Afraid not,' replied the conductor stiffly. 'There's nothing we could do to our own satisfaction after such a major work.'

'Then won't you go out and say a word to them?'

'No. Hey, Gorsch. Go and play something for them, will you?'

'Me?' said Gorsch, thoroughly taken aback.

'You – yes, you,' said the concertmaster abruptly, raising his head.

'Come on, now. On you go,' said the conductor.

The others thrust his cello into his hands, opened the door and gave him a shove. As he appeared on stage holding the cello, beside himself with embarrassment, everybody clapped still more loudly as though to say, 'There – you see?' Some people even seemed to be cheering.

'Just how much fun do they think they can make of a fellow?'

thought Gorsch. 'Right – I'll show 'em. I'll play them "Tiger Hunt in India".'

Quite calmly now, he went out into the middle of the stage. And he played 'Tiger Hunt' with all the energy of an angry elephant, just as he'd done the time the cat had come. A hush fell over the audience, and they listened for all they were worth. Gorsch ploughed steadily on. The part where the cat had given off sparks of distress came and went. The part where he had thrown himself again and again against the door also came and went.

When the work finally came to an end, Gorsch gave not so much as a glance at the audience, but, taking up his cello, made a bolt for it, just as the cat had done, and took refuge in the musicians' room. But there he found the conductor and all his other colleagues sitting quite silent, gazing straight in front of them as though there had just been a fire.

No longer caring what happened, Gorsch walked briskly past them, plumped himself on a sofa at the other side of the room, and crossed his legs.

They all turned to look at him, but far from laughing at him, their expressions were serious.

'There's something funny about this evening,' Gorsch thought to himself. But the conductor stood up and said, 'Gorsch, you were wonderful! The music may not be anything much, but you kept us listening. You've improved a lot during the past week or ten days. Why, comparing it with ten days ago is like comparing a green recruit with an old campaigner. I always knew you could if you tried, Gorsch!'

The others, too, came over to him and said, 'Well done!'

'You see,' the conductor was saying in the background, 'he can do it because he's tough. It would kill any ordinary man.'

Late that night, Gorsch went back home.

First, he had a good drink of water. Then he opened the window and, looking into the distant sky in the direction where he felt the cuckoo had gone, he said, 'You know, cuckoo – I'm sorry about what happened. I shouldn't have got angry like that.'

Tokkobe Torako

I expect you've heard about fox spirits. No doubt there are all kinds of them; but the one I know about is called Tokkobe Torako.

Long ago, Tokkobe Torako lived by the bank of a large river, where he made a thorough nuisance of himself at night, stealing fish from people who'd come to fish with nets, and fried bean curd from people who were coming home late after doing their shopping in the village.

One evening, a greedy old man called Roppei, on his way home drunk from the village, was walking along the riverbank when he met a fine-looking samurai got up in a formal kimono of shining gold brocade. The old man would have gone by with no more than a polite bow, but the samurai stopped in his tracks, glanced up at the sky, then, sternly pulling in his chin, called to Roppei to halt. It was the night of the harvest moon.

'Here, just a moment – what's your name?'

'Yessir, yessir – they call me Roppei, sir.'

'Roppei, eh? You're a moneylender by trade, aren't you?'

'Indeed I am, sir. Absolutely right, sir. But I'm afraid that all the funds are out at the moment.'

'No, no – I'm not interested in borrowing any money. Tell me – I imagine that moneylending is a rewarding occupation?'

'Rewarding? Heh-heh, your little joke, sir. Yes, indeed it is, sir.'

'I happen to have a little capital I don't need at the moment. And I'm on my way to a distant province. Would you take care of it for me? I must tell you, though, that I have enemies all over the place. If anything should happen to me on the way there, it will be yours to do as you like with. How about it?'

'Yessir – I'll be only too glad to take care of it for you, sir . . .'

'Good. Well, I've got the money here. You can open the lid yourself and take a look to make sure.'

With much grunting and puffing, the samurai took out a white cord, bound up the sleeves of his kimono, then drew up the stiff formal skirt and with rapid strides ran over to the embankment. He stooped briefly, then produced a money chest which he carried back to Roppei.

'Ah-ha,' thought Roppei. 'He's almost certainly a thief. Or a forger. But I couldn't care less what he is. If anything should happen to him on this trip of his, then it all comes to little me.'

'Very well, sir,' he said aloud, suppressing a gleeful smile.

He opened the lid and found the box stuffed with gold coins gleaming in the moonlight.

With considerable huffing and puffing, the samurai brought another money chest. Once again, Roppei solemnly inspected it. The second box too was full of gold coins glittering in the light of the moon.

Huff, puff – in the end, there was a pile of ten chests.

'How about it – can you carry all these away by yourself? I'll only leave as much as you can manage, of course.'

Roppei couldn't help finding all this a bit fishy; but then, what did it matter to him even if it *was* suspicious?

'No problem, sir. What are a dozen chests or so to me? I'm quite sure I'll be able to carry them.'

'Good. Well, then – you'd better get started.'

'Whatever you say, sir. Here we go – heave-ho! Heeeeave-ho!'

'Splendid, splendid! You're not such a big man, but you've got big ideas. I'm impressed – truly I am. Right, then, I'll leave them in your good care.'

The samurai flicked open his silver fan and bowed formally. But the boxes were far too heavy for Roppei to think of replying.

Shielding his eyes with his fan as he gazed ahead, and murmuring some lines from what sounded like a Noh play, the samurai went on his way.

Tottering under the weight of the ten chests, in such a state that he was hardly aware of the moon shining or the bends in the road, Roppei finally got back to his own house and, dumping his load in the garden, bellowed in a funny-sounding voice:

'Open up! Open up, there! He's back – the millionaire is back!'

Roppei's daughter snapped back the wooden shutters.

'Why, Father – whatever are you carrying all that gravel for?'

Startled, Roppei himself looked at the load he had just set down – and to his amazement found that it was ten perfectly ordinary bags of gravel from the embankment.

Roppei foamed at the mouth and fainted right away. Soon

afterwards he came down with a dreadful fever, and could do nothing for two months but shout:

'I was cheated by Tokkobe Torako! Cheated!'

Well, what do you think – is the story true? Of course, it all happened too long ago for anyone to tell by now, but I myself suspect it was all made up, don't you?

If you ask why, it's because I was told one more story that quite certainly somebody invented. The events it describes happened so recently, too, that there's no doubt about it at all. In fact, they happened only last night.

On the bank of that same big river, about a mile away from the place where the fox lived, there's the house of a man called Heiemon.

Heiemon was made a member of the village council this spring, so last night they were having a party to celebrate, with all the relatives invited. They were all enjoying themselves immensely, laughing and joking, with people calling 'Here – drink up!' and 'Here – have another.' It was a fine do. But there was one man among them who sat there without smiling even once. This was a pale, short, ill-natured farmer called Kokichi.

Kokichi had been feeling disgruntled for some time.

'There's a chip in the rim of my rice bowl . . . ,' he thought in disgust. 'The place is filthy . . . The fish on that plate is goggling at me with its white eyes . . . No one's handed me his saké cup to drink from . . . Oh, what the hell!'

He decided he'd had enough, and went out in a huff.

'Hey, don't go yet, Kokichi,' called Heiemon. 'Have another drink. Come on, sit down!'

But Kokichi put on his wooden sandals and left the house in high dudgeon.

The sky was clear and the thirteen-day-old moon was at its zenith. Kokichi was going out through the gate when he happened to look down and saw, standing by a path along the paddy fields to one side of the gate, a 'General Minamoto' put there to ward off sickness.

It was a bamboo stick with a big sheet of paper stuck on it, on which someone had painted a fierce face.

In the pale light of the moon, General Minamoto, with his lopsided face, seemed to be glaring angrily at Kokichi.

This put him in an even worse temper, so he promptly uprooted the general and was going to throw him into the rice field when a sudden thought made him grin and, instead, he set it up again in the very middle of the road.

Then, muttering discontentedly to himself, he went on his way, crossing two low hills before reaching his own home, where he roundly scolded his children, who had been expecting a present, then crept into bed without another word.

Just around that time, the drinking party had ended at Heiemon's house, and the guests, having wrapped up the remains of the feast to take home to their families, had come out to the gate in groups of three or four, colliding and tangling with each other, the packets dangling at their sides.

Heiemon, who had come out onto the veranda to see them off, was saying goodbye.

'Well, take care, then. Mind those presents of yours don't get stolen by Tokkobe Torako! Ho-ho-ho!'

One of the guests looked around and replied, with a peal of laughter:

'Tokkobe Torako – why, if he turns up I'll take the old devil on myself and eat *him* up!'

He had hardly finished saying this when lo, the elusive Tokkobe Torako was standing there in the middle of the road outside the gate, his pure white fur on end, glaring in their direction.

'Help, he's come! Get back, get back!'

There was a fearful uproar. Weak at the knees, they fled back into the front room without bothering to remove their muddy sandals. Swiftly, Heiemon took down a halberd that was hanging on the wall, unsheathed it, and swung the bare blade around with such vigour that one guest all but had his red nose chopped off.

Leaping down from the veranda, Heiemon advanced barefooted towards the white face beyond the gate. This emboldened the rest to follow, crowding in his wake and uttering hoarse cries of encouragement.

Faced with the white fox in the flesh, as it were, Heiemon shook with fear, but with the others watching he hadn't much choice but to give a loud yell and rush in, slashing with his blade. Unmistakeably, the blade contacted something – and the next moment a white object lay quivering beneath his weapon.

'I got him! Come and look!' cried Heiemon.

'Only a poor, weak animal, after all,' they declared in glee, forming a circle around the body of the fox.

What they actually saw, though, gave them quite a shock. And no wonder: the cunning old fox had made his escape, leaving in his stead a paper face on a stick.

'That cunning old fox!' they told each other. 'Oh, his eyeballs were like fire!'

'And his fur, too – like silver needles!'

'His mouth was split right back to the ears. I only hope he doesn't take it out on us!'

'Don't worry – tomorrow we'll take some fried bean curd to the riverbank and leave it there for him.'

They were all far too done in to go home, so they spent the night at Heiemon's place.

Slashed halfway through, General Minamoto looked as though he was gnashing his teeth in the moonlight.

Sometime after midnight, Tokkobe Torako turned up again with a whole bunch of followers and dragged away the straw packets of food that had been left lying in the garden. The guests were sure they'd heard the rustling sound – or so they told me, just a while ago.

A Stem of Lilies

'At seven tomorrow morning, they say, the Lord Buddha will cross the Himukya River and enter the town.' Thus came the word on the clear breeze, spreading to all the houses in the walled town of Hamukya.

The people who lived there were as eager as children, for who knows how long and how fervently they had been waiting for the Buddha. Besides, many people from their town had gone to join him and become his disciples.

'At seven tomorrow morning, they say, the Lord Buddha will cross the Himukya River and enter the town.'

What would the Buddha's countenance be like, they wondered, and what colour were his eyes? Would he have dark blue eyes like lotus petals, as it was rumoured? Would the nails on his fingers truly gleam like copper? What would they have to say, the men who had gone to join him from the town, and how would they be dressed? . . . As eagerly as children, the people set their houses in order, and when that was done they went out and thoroughly cleaned the streets. Here, there, everywhere, they were to be seen outside their homes with brooms. All the cow dung and stones were carefully removed, and the surface sprinkled with water, then strewn with white quartz sand.

'At seven tomorrow morning, they say, the Lord Buddha will cross the Himukya River and enter the town.'

The news, of course, reached the royal palace in no time.

'Your Majesty, at seven tomorrow morning, they say, the Lord Buddha will cross the Himukya River and arrive in this town.'

'Indeed! Are you certain?' demanded the king, forgetting himself so far as to rise from his agate-inlaid throne.

'It seems it is indeed so, sire. Two merchants from Hamura claim to have heard him preach this very morning on the far bank of the river.'

'Indeed? Then it must be so. Ah, how long we have awaited him! Give the command at once for the town to be cleaned.'

'Sire, the town has already been swept clean: so delighted were the people that they took up their brooms without awaiting your bidding.'

The king made a sound, as if unconvinced. 'Go, even so, and make sure that nothing has been overlooked. Then give word that food be prepared for a thousand persons.'

'Very well, Your Majesty. The Master of the Royal Kitchens has been pacing up and down the kitchens for some time, in expectation of Your Majesty's command.'

'I see . . .' The king thought for a while. 'Then the next thing is suitable lodgings. Go now and tell the carpenters to construct a lodging place for a thousand people in the oak grove outside the walls.'

'Very well, Your Majesty. Your Majesty is most thoughtful. As it happens, the carpenters have already set about surveying the forest, foreseeing just such a royal command.'

'Indeed!' murmured the king in surprise. 'Verily, the virtues of the Buddha impart themselves to others as swiftly as the wind. Tomorrow morning, I will go in person to the bank of the river to greet him. Let the news be spread abroad. You are to come at five, at the break of day.'

'Very well, Your Majesty.' The white-bearded minister left the royal presence joyfully, his cheeks as rosy as a child's.

Dawn broke the next day.

Behind his curtains the king heard the soft footfall as his prime minister entered, and in a flash was sitting up.

'Your Majesty – it is just five o'clock.'

The king grunted. 'I did not sleep all night,' he said, 'yet my person this morning is as fresh as crystal. What of the weather?' He emerged from his curtains and stretched himself up straight.

'Fine weather indeed, Your Majesty. The lapis lazuli on the south side of Mount Sumeru can be seen as clearly as through crystal. How handsome the Lord Buddha will surely look on such a day as this!'

'It is well. Is the town as spotless as it was yesterday?'

'Your Majesty, as spotless as the shore of the Pure Lake itself.'

'Are the provisions ready?'

'All preparations are complete.'

'And the lodgings in the oak grove?'

'They will be ready without fail before the morning is over. It only remains to install the windows and sweep them out.'

The king set out for the banks of the Himukya River, taking everyone with him.

The wind rustled, and the leaves glittered on the trees.

'By this wind one may tell that it is September,' said the king.

'Indeed, Your Majesty. The dust in the air is the dust of autumn, sharp and clear as specks of crystal.'

'Are the lilies in bloom yet?'

'The buds have all formed. Even now the dust is wearing away the golden fastenings at their tips; it seems likely that the flowers will all open together this morning.'

'No doubt. I have a mind to give the Buddha a lily as an offering.' He turned to the chancellor of the exchequer, whose face was buried beneath a black beard. 'Chancellor, go to the forest and find me a lily in bloom.'

'Very well, Your Majesty.'

The chancellor went off alone to the woods. The woods were all hushed and blue, but, peer about as he might, he could find no lilies.

The chancellor roamed the woods until, hidden among the trees, he found a large house. The sun shone bright and white, and the house looked half-bright as though in a dream. Beneath a chestnut tree that stood in front of the house, a child with bare feet stood watching him, holding in his hand a lily stem bearing ten white flowers, pure white as though carved out of shell.

The chancellor went forward.

'Sell me those flowers, will you?'

'All right,' said the child, pursing his lips as he spoke.

'How much are they?' asked the chancellor with a smile.

'Ten pennies,' said the child briskly, in a loud voice.

'Ten pennies is too much,' said the chancellor, who really felt that it was too expensive.

'Five pennies,' replied the child briskly again.

'Five pennies is too much,' said the chancellor with a smile, truly believing that it was still too expensive.

'One penny,' shouted the child, his face bright red.

'I see. One penny. Then I imagine this will do, won't it?' The chancellor took off his necklace of crimson rubies.

'Fine,' shouted the child happily, looking at the red stones. The chancellor handed over the necklace and took the lilies from him.

'What do you want them for, the flowers?' the child asked, as though it had only just occurred to him to wonder.

'To give to the Lord Buddha.'

'Oh, then I can't let you have them.' The child flung the necklace on the ground.

'Why not?'

'I thought of giving them to him myself.'

'Did you? Then I'll give them back to you.'

'No, you can have them.'

'May I?' The chancellor took the flowers again. 'You're a good boy. When the Lord Buddha arrives, come with him to the palace. I'm the chancellor of the exchequer.'

'All right, I'll come,' the child shouted gleefully.

The chancellor went back through the woods to the bank of the river.

'Thank you. They are perfect,' the king said, taking the flowers from him and raising them reverently before his forehead.

Suddenly, they saw a faint flush of gold rising like a rainbow into the sky on this side of the green woods beyond the river. They all prostrated themselves. And the king knelt with them there on the sand . . .

All of which happened, I am sure, somewhere, two hundred million years or so ago.

The Restaurant of Many Orders

Two young gentlemen dressed just like British military men, with gleaming guns on their shoulders and two dogs like great white bears at their heels, were walking in the mountains where the leaves rustled dry underfoot. They were talking as they went.

'I must say, the country around here is really awful,' said one. 'Not a bird or beast in sight. I'm just dying to let fly at something: *bang, bang!* Anything, so long as it moves.'

'Yes, what fun it would be to let a deer or something have a couple of shots smack in his tawny flank!' said the other. 'I can just see him spinning around, then flopping down with a thud.'

They really were *very* deep in the mountains. So deep, in fact, that the professional hunter who had come as their guide went astray and wandered off somewhere. Worse still, the forest was so frightening that the two bearlike dogs both got dizzy, howled for a while, then foamed at the mouth and died.

'Do you realise that dog cost me two thousand four hundred silver pieces?' said one young gentleman, casually turning its eyelids back.

'*Mine* cost me two thousand eight hundred,' said the other, his head tilted ruefully to one side.

The first young gentleman went pale.

'I think I'll be getting back,' he said, gazing into the other's face.

'As a matter of fact,' said his friend, 'I was just beginning to get a bit cold and hungry myself, so I think I'll join you.'

'Then let's call it a day. What does it matter? On our way back we can drop in at yesterday's inn and buy a few game birds to take home with us.'

'They had hares too, didn't they? So it'll come to the same thing in the end. Well, why don't we go home, then?'

But the annoying thing was that by now they no longer had the faintest idea of the way back.

A sudden gust of wind sprang up; the grass stirred, the leaves rustled, and the trees creaked and groaned.

'I really am hungry!' said one. 'I've had an awful hollow feeling under my ribs for quite a while.'

'So have I,' said the other. 'I don't feel like walking any further.'

'O for something to eat!' said the first.

The pampas grass was rustling all about them as they talked.

Just then, one of them happened to look around, and what should he see standing there but a fine brick building. Over the entrance was a notice that said, in large letters:

RESTAURANT WILDCAT HOUSE

'Look! This is perfect,' said one. 'The place is civilised after all. Why don't we go in?'

'Funny,' said the other, 'finding it in a place like this. But I expect we'll be able to get a meal, at any rate.'

'Of course we will, silly. What do you think the sign means?'

'Let's give it a try. I'm just about collapsing with hunger.'

They stepped into the entrance hall, which was very splendid, being done all over in white tiles. There was a glass door, with something written on it in gold letters.

PLEASE COME IN. NO ONE NEED HAVE A MOMENT'S HESITATION.

They were tickled pink.

'Just look at that!' said one of them. 'Things always turn out right in the end. Everything's been going wrong all day, but look how lucky we are now. They're telling us not to worry about the bill!'

'I must say, it does seem like it,' said the other. 'That's what "no one need have a moment's hesitation" suggests.'

They pushed open the door and went through. On the other side was a corridor. Another notice in gold letters on the back of the glass door said:

PLUMP PARTIES AND YOUNG PARTIES ESPECIALLY WELCOME.

They were both overjoyed at this.

'Look, we're especially welcome, it says,' said one.

'Because we satisfy both conditions!' said the other.

They walked briskly along the corridor and came to another door, this time painted bright blue.

'What a strange place! I wonder why there are so many doors?'

'This is the Russian way of doing things, of course. It's always like this in cold places or in the mountains.'

They were just going to open the door when they saw a notice in yellow letters above it:

WE HOPE YOU WILL APPRECIATE THAT THIS IS A RESTAURANT OF MANY ORDERS.

'Awfully popular, isn't it? Out here in the mountains like this!'

'But of course. Why, even back in the capital very few of the best restaurants are on the main streets, are they?'

As they were talking, they opened the door. A notice on the other side said:

THERE REALLY ARE RATHER A LOT OF ORDERS, BUT WE HOPE YOU WILL BE PATIENT.

'Now just what does *that* mean?' said one young gentleman, screwing up his face.

'Mm – I suppose it means they're busy, and they're sorry but it will be a while before the food appears. Something like that.'

'I expect so. I want to get settled down in a room as soon as possible, don't you?'

'Yes, and ready to tuck in.'

But it was most frustrating – there was yet another door, and by the side of it hung a mirror, with a long-handled brush lying beneath it. On the door it said in red letters:

PATRONS ARE REQUESTED TO COMB THEIR HAIR AND GET THE MUD OFF THEIR BOOTS HERE.

'Very right and proper, too. And back in the hall just now I was thinking this was just a place for the locals.'

'They're very strict on etiquette. Some of their customers must be rather grand.'

So they neatly combed their hair and got the mud off their boots.

But no sooner had they put the brush back on its shelf than it blurred and disappeared, and a sudden gust of wind moaned through the room. They huddled together in alarm and, flinging the door open, went into the next room. Both of them felt that unless they fortified themselves with something warm to eat very soon, almost anything might happen.

On the other side of the door there was another unexpected sign:

PLEASE LEAVE YOUR GUNS AND CARTRIDGES HERE.

Sure enough, there was a black gun rack right by the door.

'Of course,' said one young gentleman. 'No one ever ate with his gun.'

'I'm beginning to think their customers must *all* be rather grand,' said the other.

They unshouldered their guns and unbuckled their belts and put them on the rack. Now there was another door, a black one, which said:

KINDLY REMOVE YOUR HATS, OVERCOATS AND BOOTS.

'What about it – do we take them off?'

'I suppose we'd better. They really must be *very* grand, the people dining there in the back rooms.'

They hung their hats and overcoats on the hook, then took their boots off and padded on through the door. On the other side was the notice:

PLEASE REMOVE YOUR TIEPINS, CUFF LINKS, SPECTACLES, PURSES, AND ANYTHING ELSE WITH METAL IN IT, ESPECIALLY ANYTHING POINTED.

Right by the door a fine black safe stood open and waiting. It even had a lock on it.

'Of course! I imagine they use electricity at some point in the cooking. So metal things are dangerous, especially pointed things. I expect that's what it means.'

'I suppose so. I wonder if it also means you pay the bill here on the way out?'

'It seems like it, doesn't it?'

'Yes, that must be it.'

They took off their spectacles and their cuff links and so on, put everything in the safe, and clicked the lock shut.

A little further on, they came to another door, with a glass jar standing in front of it. On the door it said:

PLEASE SPREAD CREAM FROM THE JAR ALL OVER YOUR FACE, HANDS AND FEET.

'Why should they want one to put cream on?'

'Well, if it's very cold outside and too warm inside, one's skin gets chapped, so this is to prevent it. I must say, it does seem they only get the very best sort of people coming here. At this rate, we may soon be on speaking terms with the aristocracy!'

They rubbed some cream from the jar on their faces and hands, then took their socks off and rubbed it on their feet as well. Even so, there was still a bit left, so they both ate some surreptitiously, pretending to be rubbing it on their faces all the while.

Then they opened the door in a great hurry – only to find a notice on the other side which said:

DID YOU PUT ON PLENTY OF CREAM? ON YOUR EARS TOO?

There was another, smaller jar of cream here.

'Of course – I didn't do my ears. I might well have got them chapped. The proprietor of this place is really very thoughtful.'

'Yes, he's got an eye for every little detail. Incidentally, I wouldn't mind something to eat, but it doesn't look very likely with all these eternal corridors, does it?'

But the next door was already upon them, bearing another message:

THE MEAL WILL SOON BE READY. WE WON'T KEEP YOU AS MUCH AS FIFTEEN MINUTES. IN THE MEANTIME, JUST SHAKE SOME OF THIS PERFUME OVER YOUR HEAD.

And there in front of the door stood a shiny gold bottle of scent.

Unfortunately, when they splashed some on themselves, it smelled suspiciously like vinegar.

'This stuff's awfully vinegary,' said one young gentleman. 'What's wrong with it, do you suppose?'

'They've made a mistake,' the other said. 'The maid must have had a cold or something and put the wrong stuff in.'

They opened the door and went through. On the other side of it was a notice in big letters that said:

> YOU MUST BE TIRED OF ALL THESE ORDERS, YOU POOR THINGS. THIS IS THE LAST ONE, SO BE GOOD ENOUGH TO TAKE SOME SALT FROM THE POT AND RUB IT IN WELL ALL OVER YOU.

A fine blue china salt cellar was indeed standing there, but this time both the young gentlemen were thoroughly alarmed. They turned their cream-smeared faces to look at one another.

'I don't like the look of this,' said one.

'Nor do I,' said the other.

'"Lots of orders" means *they're* giving *us* orders.'

'Yes – and I've an idea that "restaurant" doesn't mean a place for serving food, but a place for cooking people and serving *them*. And that m-m-means that w-w-we . . .'

He began to shake and tremble, and tremble and shake, so that he couldn't go on.

'Then w-w-we . . . Oh *dear!*' And the other one, too, began to quake and shiver, and shiver and quake, so that he couldn't go on either.

'Let's get out!' Still shaking all over, one of the young gentlemen pushed at the door behind him. But, strange to say, it refused to budge.

At the other end was another door with two big holes and a silver knife and fork carved on it. It said:

> SO NICE OF YOU TO COME. THAT WILL DO VERY NICELY INDEED. NOW JUST POP INSIDE, PLEASE.

What was worse, two blue eyeballs were ogling them through the keyhole.

'Oh dear!' cried one, quivering and trembling.

'Oh *dear*!' cried the other, trembling and quivering.

And they both burst into tears.

Just then, they heard voices talking furtively on the other side of the door.

'It's no good – they've realised. It doesn't look as if they're going to rub in the salt.'

'What d'you expect? The way the boss put it was all wrong – "you poor things" and the like – stupid, I call it.'

'Who cares? Either way, *we* won't get as much as the bones even.'

'How right you are. But if they won't come in here, it's us who'll get the blame.'

'Shall we call them? Yes, let's. Hey, gentlemen! This way, quickly – this way! The dishes are washed, and the vegetables nicely salted. All that's left is to arrange you nicely with the greens and put you on some snowy white dishes. This way now, quickly!'

The two young gentlemen were so distressed that their faces went all crumpled like pieces of wastepaper. They peered at each other and shook and shivered and silently wept.

There were chuckles on the other side of the door, then a voice shouted again, 'This way, this way! If you cry like that, you know, you'll wash off all the cream you put on specially. (Yes, sir, coming, sir. We'll be bringing it in just a moment, sir.) Come on, we haven't got all day!'

'Yes, hurry up! The boss has his napkin tucked in and his knife in his hand and he's licking his lips, just waiting for you.'

But the two young gentlemen just wept and wept and wept and wept.

Then, all of a sudden, they heard a *woof, woof,* and a *grr!* behind them, and the two dogs like white bears came bursting into the room. The eyes behind the keyhole disappeared in a twinkling. Round and round the room the dogs rushed, snarling, then with another great *woof!* they threw themselves at the other door. The door banged open, and they vanished inside as though swallowed up. From the pitch darkness beyond came a great miaowing and spitting and growling, then a rustling sound.

The room vanished in a puff of smoke, and the two young gentlemen found themselves standing in the grass, shivering and shaking in the cold. Their coats and boots, purses and tiepins were all there with them, hanging from the branches or lying among the roots of the trees. A gust of wind set the grass stirring, the leaves rustling, and the trees creaking and groaning.

The dogs came back, panting, and behind them someone called, 'Gentlemen! Gentlemen!'

'Hey! Hey!' they shouted, suddenly recovering their spirits. 'We're over here. This way, quickly!'

The professional hunter in his straw cape came rustling towards them through the grass, and they really felt safe at last.

They ate the dumplings the guide had brought with him, then returned to the capital, buying some game birds on their way.

But even back in the capital, and however long they soaked themselves in hot baths, their faces that had gone all crumpled like wastepaper would never go back to normal again.

The Man of the Hills

The Man of the Hills, with his golden eyes as big as saucers and his body all hunched up, was walking through the cypress wood on Mount Nishine, after rabbits.

It wasn't a rabbit he caught, though, but a pheasant.

The pheasant was just flying up in alarm when the Man of the Hills drew in his hands and pounced on it, so that the poor creature was half squashed.

With a bright red face and his great mouth twisted in a grin of delight, the Man of the Hills came walking out of the forest twirling the limp-necked pheasant in his hand.

Then, flinging his prey down on a sunny southern slope of dry grass and scratching at his untidy mop of red hair, he curled up on the ground.

A small bird twittered somewhere, and shy purple flowers swayed here and and there among the grass.

Turning over to lie on his back, the Man of the Hills gazed up at the blue, blue sky. The sun was like a red-and-gold speckled wild pear, and a pleasant smell of dried grass drifted about; on the mountain range just behind him, the snow formed a shining white halo.

'Now candy floss, I think, is delicious. But though old Sun spins plenty of it, he never gives any of it to *me*.'

He was idly thinking such thoughts when a fleecy, vague white cloud drifted purposelessly across the absolutely clear azure sky towards the east. The Man of the Hills made a rumbling sound deep in his throat and thought to himself again: 'Clouds are funny things, if you ask me. Depending on the wind, they come and they go, they disappear – *poof* – and they suddenly appear again. That's why they call the kind of man who just drifts around doing nothing a "cloudhead'."

Even as he was thinking this, he felt his legs and his head going terribly light, and had a strange feeling as though he were floating upside down in the air. The next thing he knew, it was *he* who had become a 'cloudhead'. Whether carried by the wind or moving on his own, he was drifting gently through the air, going nowhere in particular.

'Why, those are the Seven Hills,' he said to himself. 'There are seven of them, all covered with trees – one of them all pines, another one bald at the top and yellow . . . But at this rate, I'll soon be in the town. And if I'm going there, I'll have to change into something else, or they'll beat me to death.'

Whereupon, he turned himself into quite a passable woodcutter. And in no time he found himself at the edge of the town. His head still felt very light, so that his whole body seemed to be out of balance, but he plodded on just the same.

Among the first houses he passed was a fish shop, with stands bearing messy-looking straw bags of salted salmon, bundles of sardines and the like, as well as five blackish red boiled octopuses hanging from the eaves. The octopuses made him stand and stare. 'Just look at the curve on those knobbly red legs – now there's something!' he thought. 'Much more impressive, even, than that man at the county office looks in his riding breeches. Just imagine one of these crawling about with its eyes wide open in the dark at the bottom of the deep blue sea!'

The Man of the Hills stood there staring, his thumb, unconsciously, stuck in his mouth.

But just then a Chinaman in a grubby, pale blue robe and carrying a big pack on his back came by, gazing nervously all about him. Tapping the Man of the Hills without warning on the shoulder, he said:

'You – you like Chinese cloth? "Six Gods" pills, too – vellee cheap.'

The Man of the Hills looked around, startled.

'No thank you!' he bellowed. Then he noticed that the loudness of his voice had brought out the owner of the fish shop, who had carefully parted hair and wooden clogs on his feet, and held a curved hook in his hand. Some other townspeople had turned out, too, and were watching him, so he flapped his hand and said quickly in a quieter voice:

'I'm sorry – I didn't mean that. I'll take some, yes I'll take some.'

'Don't buy, no matter don't buy. Just one little look,' said the Chinaman, setting his pack down in the middle of the road. The Man of the Hills couldn't help feeling scared by his watery-looking pink eyes, which reminded him somehow of a lizard.

But while he was feeling this, the Chinaman had swiftly untied the braid around his bundle, undone the wrapping cloth, and taken the lid off the wicker basket inside to reveal rows and rows of cardboard boxes sitting on top of the fabric. From amongst them he grabbed what looked like a small red medicine bottle.

'Oh dear,' the Man of the Hills thought to himself. 'How long and thin his fingers are! And his nails are so pointed, which scares me all the more.'

By now the Chinaman had got out two little glasses no bigger than the tip of your little finger, and handed one to him.

'You – you take medicine. No poison. Absolute no poison. Swear no poison! You take! Me take too – no worry. Me drink beer, drink tea – no drink poison. This medicine for long life. You take!'

And he gulped down a dose himself.

The Man of the Hills was wondering whether it was really all right to drink it when, looking around him, he found that he was no longer in the town but in the middle of an open stretch of country that was the same turquoise colour as the sky, standing opposite the Chinaman with the red-rimmed eyes. The two of them were alone, with the bundle placed between them and their two shadows lying black on the grass.

'Here – you drink! Good for long life. You drink!'

Eagerly the Chinaman thrust out a pointed finger, urging him on. Not knowing what to do, the Man of the Hills finally decided it would be better to get it over with and leave. So he downed the medicine in one go. But then, strange to say, all the bumps and hollows of his body seemed to start disappearing, and he shrank and got smoother, until finally, examining himself carefully, he found he'd become what appeared to be a small box, lying there on the grass.

'Hell, I got caught after all! I *thought* there was something fishy about him, with those pointed nails. He pulled a fast one on me!'

Furious, he tried to struggle, but since by now he was just a little box of Six Gods pills, it was obviously no use.

The Chinaman, though, was gleeful. He jumped up and down, nimbly lifting each of his legs in turn and dealing great slaps to the soles of his feet with his hands. The sound rang out over the countryside like someone beating a hand drum.

Then suddenly the Chinaman's enormous hand appeared before his eyes, and the next moment he was swept up and up until he came to rest among the other boxes in the Chinaman's pack.

'Oh dear,' he thought as the lid of the wicker basket descended with a thud over his head. 'I've finally landed up in jail.' And though he tried to cheer himself up at the sight of the sunlight still shining through the basket's mesh, even that was soon blotted out.

'Oh, oh – he's put the wrapping cloth around. Things are looking worse and worse. This is going to be a dark journey,' said the Man of the Hills, as calmly as he could manage.

But then, to his astonishment, someone spoke up right by his side:

'And where did he get hold of *you*?'

At first he was startled, but the next minute he thought, 'I *see* – the Six Gods pills are all human beings who've been turned into medicine in the same way as me. That explains it!' He braced himself and replied:

'In front of a fish shop.'

Hearing him, the Chinaman bellowed menacingly from outside:

'Voice too loud – you be quiet!'

But the Man of the Hills was feeling so angry with the Chinaman by now that he burst out:

'What? Be *quiet*? You damned thief! As soon as we get to a village, I'm going to shout out: "This Chink's up to no good!" How d'you like that!'

The Chinaman fell silent. The silence went on for quite a while. The Man of the Hills began to imagine him crying, with his arms folded across his chest in that Chinese way of theirs. And that made him think: perhaps all the Chinamen he'd seen in the past, on paths over the hills or in the woods, with their packs on the ground, looking as though they were deep in thought, had all been spoken to in the same way by someone or other. It made him feel so sorry for them that he was just about to say 'I didn't mean it' when the man outside said in a sad, hoarse voice:

'You see, nobody care 'bout me. Me no earn money. No eat rice. Maybe going die. So, nobody care.'

The Man of the Hills, now full of pity for him, felt he'd do anything to help the Chinaman make a little money, so that he could go into some inn for a meal of sardine heads and vegetable soup.

'It's all right,' he told him, 'you don't have to cry like that. When we get to a village I'll be careful not to make too much noise. Don't worry.'

That seemed to calm the Chinaman down at last, and he heard a deep sigh of relief, together with the sound of feet being slapped. Then the Chinaman must have put his pack on his back again, for the cardboard boxes of pills rattled against each other noisily.

'Hey –' said the Man of the Hills, 'which of you was it who spoke to me just now?'

'It was me,' came the reply from right next to him. 'And to go on with what I was saying – if, as you say, he found you in front of a fish shop, you can probably tell me how much a sea bass costs and how much shark's fin you get for ten taels, can't you?'

'I don't think there was anything like that in *that* fish shop. Though they *did* have an octopus. Lovely fat legs it had, too,' he added wistfully.

'Really? It was that good, was it? I'm partial to octopus myself, too.'

'Who isn't? Anybody who says he doesn't like it ought to have his head examined.'

'I couldn't agree more. There's nothing in the world to beat a nice piece of octopus.'

'Absolutely. Anyway, where do *you* come from?'

'Me? Shanghai.'

'That makes *you* a Chinaman too, then. I feel sorry for you people – going around turning each other into pills and selling each other.'

'You're wrong. The ones you see around here are the lowest of the low – like Chen here. But there are any number of fine upstanding people among *real* Chinese. You see, we're all descended from the great saint Confucius.'

'Well, I wouldn't know about that . . . But you say the man outside is called Chen?'

'That's right . . . Ah, but it's hot! If only he'd take the lid off.'

'Yes – hey, Mr Chen! It's awfully stuffy in here. Couldn't you let a bit of air in?'

'You wait,' said Chen.

'If you don't let some air in soon, we'll all suffocate. And you'll be the loser!'

At this, Chen showed his face uneasily outside.

'That vellee inconvenient,' he said. 'Don't die, please.'

'Don't die? You don't think we *want* to suffocate, do you? Get the lid off, quickly!'

'You wait twenty minutes more.'

'Oh well, walk quicker, then, damn you!' He turned to the box next to him. 'Are you the only other one here?' he asked.

'No, there are lots more. Crying all the time.'

'Poor things. Chen's a bad fellow. Isn't there some way we could get back our original shapes?'

'Well, there *is*, in fact. You, now – *you* haven't become a Six Gods pill through and through yet, so you only have to take a different pill to get back to normal. Look, there, right by your side – the bottle of black pills.'

'Well, *that's* a relief. I'll take one, then. What about you and the others, though – won't the pills work for you?'

'No. But once you've had one and recovered, I want you to soak us all in water and soften us up. Then if we take the pills, I'm sure we'll all get back to normal, too.'

'Really? Right, I'll do it, then. Don't worry – I'll soon have you all in good shape again, I promise. These are the pills, aren't they? And this bottle of liquid is the stuff that turns people into Six Gods pills, right? But Chen took this liquid medicine at the same time as me – I wonder why he didn't turn into a Six Gods pill too?'

'That's because he took one of the black pills along with it.'

'Oh, I see. What would happen, then, if Chen took this black pill by itself? Somebody who was still a human being to start with could hardly turn *back* into one, could he?'

Just then they heard Chen's voice outside saying:

'You like Chinese cloth? You – you buy Chinese cloth!'

'Oh, oh – he's at it again!' said the Man of the Hills in a low voice, and was waiting to see what would happen when the lid was suddenly raised and he was dazzled by a flood of light. Forcing himself to look, he saw a child with a fringe standing there in front of Chen with a blank look on his face.

Chen already had a pill between his fingers, holding it close to his own month as he proffered the liquid medicine.

'Now, you drink,' came his voice. 'This long life medicine. Now, you drink!'

'There he goes again,' said someone inside the wicker basket, '– the same old story.'

'Me drink beer, drink tea, no drink poison. Now, you better drink. I drink too.'

At that moment, the Man of the Hills quietly helped himself to one of the pills. And he began to swell and bulge ... and in no time he was his old self again, complete with red hair and sturdy body. Chen, who was just about to swallow the pill along with the liquid medicine, was so startled that he spilled the liquid and only took the pill.

That did it: Chen's head began to grow visibly, swelling to twice its normal size, and his body shot up taller and taller. With a wild cry, he made a grab for the Man of the Hills. The Man of the Hills ducked and ran for all he was worth, but try as he might to escape, his legs seemed to be running on the spot without getting anywhere, until finally a hand seized him from behind.

'Help!' he cried. 'Aaah! . . .'

The clouds raced shining across the sky, the dry grass was warm and fragrant.

For a while he lay with his mind a blank, gazing at the bright feathers of the pheasant lying where he'd flung it, and thinking he should be soaking the cardboard box of Six Gods pills in water, getting them softened up. But then he gave a great yawn and said:

'Eh? What the devil . . . ? It was all a dream! Then Chen can go to hell for all I care. And take his Six Gods pills with him!' And he gave another yawn.

The Police Chief

Four icy mountain streams springing from the glacier on Mount Karakon descended in a flurry of white foam into the country of Puhara. At the town of Puhara, the four streams came together to form one large, placid river. The river's waters were usually clear, and clouds and trees were reflected in the still pools that formed along its course. But when the floods came, the broad river flats – a good twenty-five acres, with willow trees growing on them – were filled with fiercely roaring water. Then, once the water receded, the pleasant white flats appeared again.

Here and there on them were what looked like long, narrow ponds, bordered with reeds and bulrushes. These were signs of where the river had flowed in the past; their shape changed somewhat each time there was a flood, but they never disappeared completely. They contained large quantities of fish, particularly loach and catfish, and since the people of Puhara considered these unfit to eat, they went on increasing steadily. Next after catfish in numbers came, as you might expect, carp and roach, but there were dace as well.

One year – rumour had it – a great sturgeon had turned up, having fled there from the sea. But the adults and the brighter of the children dismissed the story with a smile. After all, it had started with a barber called Richiki, who had only two razors, was bad at his trade, and was generally unreliable. Even so, the smaller children went there every day for a while in the hope of seeing the newcomer. However solemnly they stared, though, there was no sign of the great fish, either near the surface or swimming down below, so that Richiki ended up the object of great scorn.

Now, Article One of the country's Law states that 'It is forbidden to use gunpowder to kill birds, and it is forbidden to use poison bags in order to catch fish', the poison bags in question being described by that same Richiki the barber in the following fashion:

'You peel some *sansho* bark on a dark night on a Day of the Horse in spring, dry it twice in the hot sun, and grind it with a pestle and mortar. With two pounds of this, you mix a pound and a half of wood ash made by burning maple wood on a fine day, put the mixture in a bag, and squeeze it out into the water with your hand.'

The fish swallow the poison and float to the surface with their bellies up and their mouths gasping, a way of dying that is known in the local language as *hepp-kapp* – a most apt expression.

In any case, one of the most important tasks of the Puhara police was to stop people using these poison bags.

One summer, a new chief of police came to the town.

With a red moustache that stuck out stiffly, he somewhat resembled an otter; and his teeth were all capped with silver. As chief of police, he wore a long red cloak with magnificent gold braid, and every day he went around keeping a careful eye on things.

If he saw a mule with its head hanging down, he would ask the mule driver if the load wasn't too heavy, and if he heard a baby crying too loudly inside a house, he would tell the mother to perform rites against smallpox before it was too late.

Around that time, though, there were people who began to ignore Article One of the Law. Some of the bigger pools on the river flats ceased to yield any fish at all. Sometimes there were dead fish floating, rotting, on the surface. And very often, after a Day of the Horse in the spring, the *sansho* trees of which the town had many were found stripped clean of their bark during the night. But both the chief and his policemen seemed doubtful whether such things had really happened at all.

One morning, however, two of a group of children standing on the grassy stretch in front of the calligraphy teacher's house were talking to each other:

'I got a good telling-off from the police chief.'

'You were told off by the *chief*?' said the other, slightly bigger child.

'I was! I threw a stone. I didn't know anybody was there, but he and three or four other men were hiding on the bank of the pond, trying to catch the people who use poison to catch fish.'

'What did he actually say to you?'

'"Who's that, throwing stones?" he said. "Don't you know we're here all day, on the lookout for the criminal who's breaking Article One? So go away, and keep your mouth shut, too."'

'Well, it won't be long now before the person's caught, then, will it?' said the other.

In fact, though, half a year passed without anything happening, and the children began talking again:

'Listen. I've got definite proof!' one of them said. 'Last night just as the moon was coming up I saw the chief, dressed in a black cloak with a hood over his head, talking to a funny-looking man – I mean, that funny little man who goes hunting with a gun – and he was saying to him, "Look here – I want it powdered a bit more thoroughly before you bring it along." Then the hunter said something, and the chief went on: "What, you charge two taels a bundle even though you mix oak ash with it? Come off it!" I bet they were talking about powdered *sansho* bark!'

At this another of the children shouted, 'Hey, I've just remembered! The chief – he bought two bags of ash at our place. I mean, you mix it with the powdered bark, don't you?'

'Yes! That's it!' they shouted, clapping their hands and waving clenched fists. 'That's it for sure!'

Richiki the barber, who didn't have many customers and had plenty of time to spare, heard about this later and immediately started calculating:

Balance Sheet for Poison-Bag Fishing

1. Expenses:

One bag of bark	2 taels
One bag of ash	30 mace
Total	2 taels, 30 mace

2. Income:

Thirteen eels	13 taels
Others (estimated)	10 taels
Total	23 taels

3. Police chief's profit 20 taels, 70 mace

The talk got so bad that eventually even the small children, when they saw a policeman, would make a great show of running away, then stop and, leaning forward, yell from a distance: 'Poison-bag policeman – you might at least let us have the catfish!'

Things got so serious, in fact, that the mayor of Puhara reluctantly took six members of his staff and went to see the chief.

As the two of them sat down side by side on the sofa in the

visitors' room, the police chief's golden eyes had a kind of faraway look.

'Chief,' said the mayor, 'I wonder if you're aware of the talk going around – that someone keeps breaking Article One of the Law? What do you feel about it?'

'Why – is it really true, then?'

'I'm afraid it seems so. The *sansho* tree at my place was stripped of its bark, and they say, you know, that dead fish are often found floating on the water.'

At this the chief gave a funny sort of smile. Or perhaps it was just the mayor's imagination?

'Oh, is *that* what people are saying?'

'They certainly are. I'm afraid that . . . er . . . the children are saying that *you're* responsible. It's rather awkward, isn't it?'

The police chief sprang up from his chair.

'It's awful! It reflects on my honour, for one thing. I will arrest the offender immediately.'

'Do you have any clues?'

'Let me think. Yes, of course – in fact, I have definite *proof*.'

'You know, then . . . ?'

'Without a shadow of a doubt. You see, the poison bag man is myself!'

And the police chief turned his face towards the mayor as though to say, take a good look. The mayor was startled.

'You? So it was you, after all?'

'That's right.'

'You're quite sure, then?'

'Absolutely.'

And calmly clanging the bell that stood on the table, the chief summoned a senior detective with a bushy red beard.

Thus it was that the police chief came to be tied up, put on trial and sentenced to death.

Just as the great curved sword was about to lop off his head, the chief smiled and said:

'Well, it was fun! As far as I'm concerned, I'd be happy doing nothing but catch fish with poison bags all day. And now I think, perhaps, I'll try it in hell.'

They were all immensely impressed.

The Spider, The Slug and the Raccoon

A red spider with long arms, and a silver-coloured slug, and a raccoon who had never washed his face all started at the Badger School together. There were three things that Mr Badger taught.

First, he taught about the race between the tortoise and the hare. Next, he taught that, as this showed, it was up to everyone to overtake his fellows and become bigger and more important than they. The third thing was that the biggest person was held in most respect.

From then on the three of them worked with all their might, vying with each other to be top of the class.

In their first year, the slug and raccoon were punished for always being late, so the spider came out on top. The slug and the raccoon shed tears of vexation.

In their second year, Mr Badger made a mistake in calculating their marks, so the slug came first. The spider and the raccoon ground their teeth in vexation.

In their third-year exam, the light was so bright that it made Mr Badger's eyes water and he kept shutting them. So the raccoon looked into the textbook as he wrote his answers and came first.

Thus the red spider with long arms and the silver slug and the raccoon who had never washed his face all graduated from Mr Badger's school at the same time.

The three of them, who on the surface were very good friends, did all kinds of things to mark the occasion. They held a party for Mr Badger to thank him for all he'd done, followed by a special farewell party for themselves, but deep in their hearts they were all busy thinking about one another and saying to themselves, 'Huh! And what have *they* got to be proud of? Just wait and see who becomes the biggest and most important!'

Once the get-togethers were over, they all went back to their own homes to put the things they had learned into practice. Mr Badger was already busy again, chasing a sewer rat every day in order to enrol him in school.

It was the time when the dogtooth violets were in bloom. Countless blue-eyed bees were flying about buzzing cheerfully in the sunlight, giving greetings to each small pink flower before they took its honey and scent, then carrying the golden balls of pollen to other flowers in return, or collecting the wax that the new buds on the trees had no more need of, for use in building their six-sided homes. It was a busy, cheerful day at the beginning of spring.

What Befell the Spider

The evening after the parties, the spider returned to the oak tree where he lived at the edge of the wood.

Unfortunately, he had used up all his money at the Badger School and hadn't a single thing to call his own. So he put up with his hunger and began to spin a web in the dim light of the moon.

He was so hungry that he had hardly any thread left in his body. But he muttered to himself 'They'll see! They'll see!' and went on spinning for all he was worth, until at last he had made a web about as big as a small copper coin. Then he hid himself behind a branch and all night long peered out at the web with gleaming eyes.

Around dawn, a baby horsefly came flying along humming to himself and ran into the web. But the spider had been so hungry when he spun it that the thread wasn't as sticky as it should have been, and the horsefly had soon almost broken free.

Quite beside himself, the spider rushed out from behind the branch and sank his teeth into him.

'Don't, for pity's sake!' wept the little horsefly, but without a word the spider ate him up – head, wings, feet and all. He heaved a satisfied sigh and for a while lay looking up at the sky and rubbing his belly, then set about spinning a little more thread. So the web grew one size bigger.

The spider went back behind the branch, and his six eyes gleamed bright as he sat motionless, watching the web.

'Where would this be, now?' enquired a blind mayfly who came along, walking with the aid of a stick.

'This is an inn, sir,' said the spider, blinking all his six eyes separately.

The mayfly seated himself in the web with a weary air. The spider ran out.

'Here's some tea for you,' he said, and without warning sank his teeth into the mayfly's body.

The mayfly raised the hand with which he had been going to take the tea and threshed about helplessly, at the same time beginning to recite in a pathetic voice:

> Ah, pity on my daughter when
> The dreadful tidings drear . . .

'Here, that's enough of that! And stop your struggling!' said the spider, whereupon the mayfly pressed his palms together and begged him:

'Have pity, kind sir. Let me at least recite my last poem!'

'All right, but be quick!' said the spider, feeling a bit sorry for him. And he waited, keeping a firm grip on the mayfly's legs.

So the mayfly began to recite in a truly pitiful, tiny voice, going back to the beginning of the poem again:

> Ah, pity on my daughter when
> The dreadful tidings drear
> Of parent's doom so far from home
> Shall reach her sorrowing ear!
> Most pitifully, a pilgrim's staff
> She'll take in her small hand,
> And on a weary pilgrimage
> She'll set off through the land.
> A-wandering from door to door
> Through wind and rain she goes.
> 'Oh, give me alms,' she begs, 'that I
> May pray his soul's repose.'
> Dear daughter, be forewarned and shun
> The cruel spider's lair.
> Of this my last advice take heed –
> Of webby inns beware!

'How dare you – that's enough!' exclaimed the spider, and swallowed the mayfly in one gulp. For a while he lay looking up at the sky and rubbing his belly, then he gave a wink, sang playfully to himself 'Too late to learn respect,' and started spinning thread again.

The web grew three sizes bigger, so that it was like a large umbrella. Quite easy in his mind by now, the spider hid himself again in the leaves. Just then, he heard someone singing in a pleasant voice down below:

Oh, the red long-legged spider
Crawls about up in the sky
As he lets out, soft and bright,
His silver thread of light
In a shining web spun high.

He looked and saw it was a pretty female spider.

'Come up here,' said the red spider, letting a long, long strand hang down for her.

The female spider got hold of it at once and came climbing up. So the two of them became man and wife. There were all kinds of things to eat in the web every day, and the spider's wife ate a great deal and turned it all into babies. So lots of baby spiders were born. But they were all so small you could hardly see them.

What with the children sliding on the web, and wrestling, and swinging, things were quite lively. And, best of all, the dragonfly turned up one day to inform them that the insects had passed a resolution making the spider vice president of the Society of Insects and Worms.

Soon after this, the spider and his wife were hidden in the leaves drinking tea when they heard someone singing down below in a smug-sounding voice:

Oh, the red long-legged spider,
Of sons he had ten score,
But the biggest of them all
Was incredibly small –
Like a grain of sand, no more.

They looked and found it was the silver slug, who had grown enormously fat since they last saw him.

The spider's good lady was so put out that she cried and cried and wouldn't be consoled.

But the long-legged spider sniffed and said:

'He's jealous of me, that's all. Ho! Slug – I'm being made vice president of the Society of Insects and Worms! How d'you like that, eh? I can't see the likes of you doing that, however fat you get. Ha-ha, ha-ha!'

The slug was so furious that he came down with a fever for several days and could say nothing but 'Oh, that hateful spider! What an insult! That hateful spider!'

From time to time the web would break in the wind or be damaged by some lout of a stag beetle, but the spider soon spun out a smooth length of new thread and mended it again.

Of their two hundred children, a full one hundred and ninety-eight were carried off by ants, or disappeared without trace, or died of dysentery. But the children were all so much alike that their parents soon forgot about them.

And the web by now was a magnificent affair. A steady stream of insects got caught in it.

One day, the spider and his wife were again hidden in the leaves drinking tea when a travelling mosquito came flying along, took one look at the web, and swerved away. The spider put three of his legs out into the net and watched in disgust as it went.

Just then, a great peal of laughter came from down below, and a rich voice began to sing:

> O red long-legged spider,
> Long-legged spider red –
> Your web is such a poor affair
> The travelling mosquito there
> Just hummed and turned his head.

It was the raccoon who had never washed his face.

'You wait, you fool raccoon!' said the spider, gnashing his teeth in rage. 'Before long I'll be president of the Society of Insects and Worms and then I'll have you bowing to me – you wait and see!'

From then on, the spider set to work furiously. He spun a full ten webs in different places and kept watch over them even at night.

But, sad to say, the rot set in. So much food piled up that in time things began to go bad. And the rot spread to the spider and his wife and their children. All four of them began to go soft and squashy, beginning at the tips of their legs, until finally they were washed away by the rain.

This was around the time when the clover was in bloom, and the many blue-eyed bees had scattered over the countryside, where they took the honey from each small flower as though taking a light from a little hand lamp.

What Befell the Silver Slug

At about the time the spider first spun his copper-coin web in the oak tree at the edge of the wood, a snail turned up at the silver slug's fine residence.

By then, the slug had quite a reputation in the wood. He was educated, everyone said, and he was good-natured and considerate to others.

'Slug,' said the snail, 'I'm having a hard time of it just now. There's nothing for me to eat, and no water, so I wonder if you'd let me have a little of the butterbur juice you've got stored?'

'Why, of course,' said the slug. 'Come inside, won't you?'

'That's very kind of you. You're a friend in need,' said the snail as he gulped down the butterbur juice.

'Have some more,' said the slug. 'I mean, we're almost brothers, aren't we? – ho-ho-ho. Come on, have a bit more.'

'Well, then, perhaps just a little. Thank you, thank you.' And the snail drank a little more.

'Snail,' said the slug, 'when you feel up to it, shall we have a little wrestle? We haven't wrestled for ages – ho-ho-ho – not for ages.'

'I'm too starved to have the strength,' said the snail.

'Then I'll give you something to eat. Here, help yourself,' said the slug, getting out some thistle buds and the like.

'Well, if you insist . . .' And the snail ate them up.

'Now let's wrestle, ho-ho-ho,' said the slug, getting up as he spoke.

'I'm afraid I'm rather weak,' said the snail, reluctantly getting to his feet, 'so please don't throw me too heavily.'

'There! Over you go!' The snail hit the ground with a crash. 'Let's do it again, eh? Ho-ho-ho!'

'No, I'm tired already.'

'Oh, come on. There you go, ho-ho-ho!' Again the snail crashed to the floor. 'And once more, ho-ho-ho.'

'No, I've had enough.'

'Come on, just once. *Over* you go. Ho-ho-ho . . .' Crash went the snail again.

'No, I'm . . .'

'Oh, come *on*! *There* you go! Ho-ho-ho-ho.' Crash went the snail. 'And one last time.'

'I'm dying. Goodbye.'

'On your feet, now! Here, let me help you up . . . up, and *over*, ho-ho-ho-ho . . .'

And the snail died. So the silver slug munched him down, the hard outside parts and all.

About a month after that, a lizard came limping along to the slug's splendid residence.

'Slug,' he said, 'I wonder if I could have a little medicine?'

'What's wrong?' asked the slug with a smile.

'I've been bitten by a snake,' said the lizard.

'Oh, that's easy,' said the slug, smiling. 'I'll just give it a little lick for you. If I lick it the snake poison will soon disappear. It ought to, seeing that I can dissolve the snake itself, ho-ho-ho!'

'Well, if you wouldn't mind,' said the lizard, putting out his leg.

'Why, of course, of course. We're brothers in a way, aren't we? And so are you and the snake, eh? Ho-ho-ho!' And the slug put his mouth to the lizard's wound.

'Thank you,' said the lizard after a while.

'Hang on, we haven't finished yet,' mumbled the slug as he went on licking. 'I don't want you asking for help again later, ho-ho-ho.'

'Slug –' said the lizard in alarm, 'I do believe my leg's starting to dissolve!'

'Ho-ho-ho,' replied the slug, as indistinctly as before, 'that's nothing to worry about.'

'Slug –' said the lizard anxiously, 'I'm feeling sort of hot around the middle.'

'Ho ho ho,' mumbled the slug, 'you shouldn't let it bother you.'

'Slug –' cried the lizard tearfully, 'I do believe my body's half melted away. Now stop it, please!'

'Ho-ho-ho,' said the slug, 'it's all right – honestly it is.'

As he heard this, the lizard at last stopped worrying. He stopped worrying because just at that moment his heart melted.

So the slug slurped up the lizard whole. And he became quite ridiculously big. And he'd felt so pleased with himself that he couldn't resist teasing the spider.

But the spider had taunted him in return, so that he had taken to his bed with a fever, and day after day he would say, 'You just wait. I'll get as big as I can, then I'll almost certainly be made an honorary member of the Society of Insects and Worms. And if the spider says anything, I won't answer but just give him a contemptuous sniff.'

The trouble was, though, that for some reason or other his reputation began to decline around then.

The raccoon in particular would always pooh-pooh any mention of the slug, saying with a smile, 'I can't say I think much of the slug's way of doing things. Why, anybody could get big the way he does it!'

When the slug heard this he got still angrier and frantically tried to get himself elected an honorary member of the society as soon as possible.

Before long the spider rotted and dissolved and was washed away in the rain, which made the slug feel a bit easier. And he waited eagerly for another visitor to turn up.

Then one day a frog came along.

'Good day, Slug,' he said. 'Could you let me have a little water?'

'Nice to see you, Frog,' said the slug in a determinedly pleasant voice, since he was longing to slurp him up. 'Water? Take as much as you like. There's been quite a drought lately – but you and I are almost brothers, aren't we, ho-ho-ho!' He took the frog to the water jar.

The frog drank his fill, then looked at the slug for a while with an innocent expression and said, 'How about a bit of wrestling, Slug?'

The slug was delighted. The frog had made the very suggestion that he had been about to make himself. A feeble creature like that would probably be ready for slurping up after five throws or so.

'Yes, let's,' he said. 'There! Over you go, ho-ho-ho!' The frog was flung to the ground. 'Let's try it again. And *over* you go, ho-ho-ho!' And again the frog was thrown.

At this point the frog quickly got a bag of salt out of his pocket.

'Sumo wrestlers always purify the ring with salt,' he said, tossing a handful of the stuff around.

'Come on,' said the slug, 'I'm sure you'll beat me next time. You're pretty tough. There! *Up* and over, ho-ho-ho!' And, yet again, the frog hit the ground.

He lay there spread-eagled, with his pale belly turned up to the sky as though he were dead. But when the silver slug made to go and slurp him up, for some reason he couldn't move his legs. He looked, and found they were half dissolved.

'Oh god! The salt!' cried the slug.

At this the frog leapt up and, seating himself cross-legged on the ground, opened wide his great holdall of a mouth and laughed.

'Goodbye, Slug,' he said with a bow. 'This must be most distressing for you.'

The slug was nearly in tears.

'Frog,' he said, 'goo . . .' But just then his tongue dissolved.

The frog laughed and laughed.

'I expect you were going to say "goodbye",' he said. 'Well, goodbye to you, then. When I get home, I'll have a good cry for you.' And off he sped without looking back once.

The white flowers of the buckwheat sown in autumn were just beginning to bloom, and countless blue-eyed bees were moving about among the pinkish stalks that filled one square field, swaying on the tiny branches that bore the flowers, busily gathering the last honey of the year.

What Befell the Raccoon

The raccoon did not wash his face on purpose.

By the time the spider had spun his first web the size of a copper coin in the oak at the edge of the wood, the raccoon was back at the temple where he lived in the country. But he, too, was very hungry, and he was leaning against a pine tree with his eyes closed when a rabbit came along.

'Raccoon,' the rabbit said, 'it's dreadful to be hungry like this, isn't it? One might as well die and have done with it.'

'Yes indeed,' said the raccoon. 'There doesn't seem much hope. But it's all the will of Wildcat, the Blessed Feline. Ave feles, ave feles!'

The rabbit joined him in reciting the Ave Feles.

'Ave feles, ave feles, ave feles!' The raccoon took the rabbit's paw and drew him a little closer.

'Ave feles, ave feles,' murmured the raccoon. 'Everything is the will of the Blessed Feline. Ave feles, ave feles . . .' And he took a bite of the rabbit's ear.

'Ouch!' cried the rabbit in alarm. 'What are you doing, Raccoon?'

'Ave feles, ave feles,' mumbled the raccoon, his mouth full of the rabbit's ear. 'Everything on earth is ordained by the will of Wildcat. Ah, the ineffable wisdom that decrees that I should chew your ears down to a reasonable size! Ave feles . . .' And he ended up eating both the rabbit's ears.

As he listened, however, the rabbit was gradually filled with joy and began to shed great tears.

'Ave feles, ave feles,' he chimed in. 'Blessed be Wildcat! How great a love that troubles itself even with the ears of such a wretch as I! What are two ears, or more, if only one's soul is saved? Ave feles.'

The raccoon, too, shed great false tears.

'Ave feles, ave feles. Thou bidst me chew the rabbit's legs this time? Because he hops too much, perhaps? Yes, yes – I chew, I chew! Ave feles, ave feles! Thy will be done!' And he took a good mouthful of the rabbit's back legs.

'Ah, praise be!' cried the rabbit ever more joyfully. 'Now, thanks to holy Wildcat, my back legs are gone and I need walk no more! Ah, praise be! Ave feles, ave feles!'

The raccoon seemed to be almost soaked in his own tears.

'Ave feles, ave feles. Everything is according to thy will. So now thou sayest that a humble creature such as I must live on to carry out thy will? Very well, if this be thy command . . . Ave feles, ave feles, ave feles. Thy will be done. *Mumble, munch . . .*'

The rabbit disappeared completely.

'You cheated me!' he called from the raccoon's stomach. 'Your belly is pitch dark! Ah, what a fool I was!'

'Be quiet, you!' said the raccoon angrily. 'Hurry up and get digested.'

'Listen everybody!' the rabbit called again. 'Don't be tricked by the raccoon!'

Peering anxiously around, the raccoon shut his mouth and kept it like that for a while, covering his nose with his paw as well so as to smother any sounds.

Just two months after this, the raccoon was performing his usual devotions when a wolf came carrying half a bushel of unhulled rice and begged him for a sermon.

'The lives that you have taken,' began the raccoon, 'will not be easily atoned for. What living creature is there that dies willingly? But you have eaten many, have you not? Hasten to repent, else dire torment awaits you! Oh, the horror of it! Ave feles, ave feles!'

Scared out of his wits, the wolf looked anxiously about him.

'Then what do you think I should do?' he said.

'You must do exactly as I say, since the Blessed Feline speaks through me. Ave feles, ave feles!'

'And *what* must I do?' asked the wolf in alarm.

'Well, now,' said the raccoon. 'Just stay still, and I'll take your fangs out. Ah, how many innocent lives have these fangs taken! The horror of it! Now I'll gouge your eyes out. How many creatures have these eyes stared to death! A dreadful thought. And now (Ave feles, ave feles, ave feles!) I'll just chew your ears a little. This is by way of punishment. Ave feles! Ave feles! Bear up, now. Now I'll chew your head. *Mumble, mumble.* Ave feles. The important thing in this world is endurance. Ave ... *mumble, munch* ... Now I'll eat your legs. Very tasty. Ave feles, *munch, mumble*. Now your back ... mm, this is good too. *Mumble, mumble, munch, munch* ...'

In the end, the wolf was eaten up entirely. And he called out from inside the raccoon's stomach:

'It's pitch dark in here. But there are some rabbit bones. Who could have killed him? Listen, anyone out there, I'm warning you – don't let this raccoon give you a sermon or he'll chew you up.'

'You make too much noise,' said the raccoon. 'I'm going to put a lid on you.' And in one great mouthful he swallowed the bundle containing half a bushel of rice that the wolf had brought with him.

The next day, though, the raccoon just didn't feel at all well. For some reason, his stomach hurt dreadfully, and he had a pricking feeling in his throat.

At first he eased the pain by drinking water, but it grew worse with each ensuing day, until in the end it was almost more than he could bear.

Finally, on the twenty-fifth day after he had eaten the wolf, the raccoon, whose body was swollen up like a rubber balloon by now, burst open with a great boom.

When all the animals in the wood gathered in alarm, they found that the raccoon's body was stuffed with rice plants. The rice that he had swallowed had sprouted and grown.

Mr Badger came too, a little late. He took one look and said with a great yawn, 'Dear me, what a pity. All three of them were such clever children.'

It was early winter by then, and each of the blue-eyed bees in the swarm was in the six-sided home that he had made of wax, sleeping peacefully, dreaming of the spring to come.

The Red Blanket

The Old Snow Woman was away, far away. With her pointed ears like a cat's and her swirling ashen hair, she was far, far away beyond the ragged, gleaming clouds over the western mountains.

Wrapped in a red blanket, his mind full of thoughts of homemade candy, a solitary child was hurrying impatiently homeward past the foot of a snow-covered hillock shaped like a great elephant's head.

'I'll make a cone of newspaper,' he told himself, 'and I'll puff and puff until the charcoal burns up bright and blue. Then I'll put a handful of brown sugar in the candy pan, and a handful of rock sugar. I'll add some water, then all I have to do is boil it, *bubble, bubble, bubble . . .*'

He really had no thought for anything but homemade candy as he hurried on his way.

All the while, up there in the cold, crystal-clear regions of the sky, the sun was busy stoking its dazzling white fires. The light shone out straight in all directions; some of it, falling down to earth, transformed the snow on the hushed uplands into a sheet of gleaming white icing.

Two snow wolves, with their bright red tongues lolling, were walking near the top of the hillock shaped like an elephant's head. Snow wolves are invisible to human beings, but once the wind has set them raging, they will leap up off the snow at the edge of the uplands and rush hither and thither about the sky, treading the swirling snow clouds.

'To heel! Didn't I tell you not to go too far away?' came a voice behind the snow wolves.

It was the Snow Boy, who came walking slowly with his pointed cap of polar-bear fur set on the back of his head and his face bright and ruddy like an apple.

The snow wolves shook their heads and wheeled around, then were off again, panting, their red tongues lolling. The Snow Boy gazed up at the bright blue sky and shouted a greeting to the hidden stars beyond it. The blue light pulsed down in steady waves, and already the snow wolves were far in the distance, their red tongues darting like flames.

'To heel, I said! To heel!' cried the Snow Boy, dancing with rage until his shadow, which had lain clear and black on the snow, changed to a pale glitter. And the wolves came darting back in a straight line with ears pricked.

Swift as the wind, the Snow Boy climbed the hill shaped like an elephant's head. The snow on the hill had been raised in lumps like seashells by the wind, and at its summit stood a great chestnut tree bearing a clump of mistletoe with beautiful, golden, spherical fruit.

'Fetch me some!' ordered the Snow Boy as he climbed the hill. At the first flash of his master's small white teeth, one of the wolves had bounced like a ball into the tree and was chewing at a small branch bearing the golden berries. His shadow, with his head bent busily on one side, fell far and wide over the snow. In no time, the green bark and yellow pith of the branch were ripped through, so that it fell at the Snow Boy's feet just as he reached the top of the hill.

'Thank you,' said the Snow Boy. As he picked it up, his gaze swept over the landscape to the handsome town standing far away on the white and indigo plain. The river glittered, and white smoke rose from the railway station. The Snow Boy dropped his gaze to the foot of the hill. Along the narrow path through the snow that skirted it, the child in the red blanket was hurrying intently towards his home in the hills.

'That's the boy who was pushing a load of charcoal on a sledge yesterday,' thought the Snow Boy. 'He's bought himself some sugar and is coming back alone.'

He laughed and flicked the sprig of mistletoe he held in his hand towards the child. It flew straight as an arrow and landed before the child's very eyes.

The child was startled. He picked up the branch and looked about him wide-eyed. The Snow Boy laughed and cracked his whip. Then from all over the cloudless, polished, deep blue sky, white snow began to fall like feathers from a snowy heron; it made that quiet, lovely Sunday of snow on the plain below, of amber light and brown cypress trees, more beautiful than ever. The child began to walk as fast as he could, still clutching the mistletoe in his hand.

But then, just as this harmless snow stopped falling, the sun seemed to move further away in the sky, to the place where it replenishes its white-hot fire. A slight breeze sprang up from the north-west. The air had turned bitterly cold. From far off to the east, in the direction of the sea, there came a tiny sound as though something had slipped in the sky's mechanism, and small shapes seemed to pass rapidly across the face of the sun, which was a great white mirror now.

The Snow Boy tucked his leather whip under his arm, folded his arms tightly, pressed his lips together, and gazed steadily in the direction from which the wind was blowing. The wolves stretched their necks out straight and stared intently in the same direction.

The wind grew steadily stronger, and the snow at their feet rustled as it streamed away behind them. Soon, what looked like a column of white smoke was to be seen standing on the peaks of the distant mountain range, and all at once the west was dark and grey all over.

The Snow Boy's eyes blazed fiercely. The sky turned white, the wind seemed to be tearing everything apart; the snowflakes came, dry and powdery. Then the air was full of ashen snow, though whether it was really snow or cloud was hard to tell.

All of a sudden, the ridges of the hills began to give out a sound, a kind of creaking and swishing. Horizon and town disappeared beyond the dark vapour, leaving only the white shape of the Snow Boy dimly visible as he stood erect in the storm.

Then, from amidst the rending and the howling of the wind, there came another, stranger voice.

'*Wheeew!* Why do you tarry? Come, snow! *Wheeew! Wheeew!* Come, snow! Come, blow! Why do you tarry? Is there not work to do? *Wheeew! Wheeew!* See, I bring three with me from yonder! Come, snow! *Wheeew!*'

The Snow Boy leapt as though electrified: the Old Snow Woman had arrived.

Crack! went the Snow Boy's whip, and the snow wolves bounded forward. His face grew pale, his lips tightened together, his hat flew away in the wind.

'*Wheeew! Wheeew!* To work, to work! No idling, now! *Wheeew!* To work! To work! *Wheeew!*'

The Old Snow Woman's icy locks swirled about in the snow and wind; her pointed ears and glittering gold eyes were visible among the scurrying dark clouds. Already the three snow boys she had brought with her from the western plain were rushing to and fro, their faces deathly pale and their lips clamped tight, too busy even to exchange greetings with one another. Soon hills and driving snow and sky were quite indistinguishable; the only sounds were the shrieks of the Old Snow Woman as she moved back and forth, the cracking of the snow boys' whips, and the panting of the nine snow wolves as they dashed about in the freshly fallen snow.

And then, in the midst of it all, the Snow Boy heard the sound of a child crying. A strange light gleamed in his eyes. He stopped for a moment and thought. Then, cracking his whip fiercely, he rushed off to look for him.

But he must have mistaken the direction, for he collided with a black, pine-clad hill far off to the south. So he tucked his whip under his arm and pricked up his ears.

'*Wheeew! Wheeew!*' came the Old Snow Woman's voice. 'I'll have no idling! Come, snow! Snow! *Wheeew! Wheeew-wheeew! Wheeew!*'

Once more, from amidst the raging of wind and snow, he caught the thin, transparent sound of a child crying. Straight as a die, the Snow Boy ran in its direction, the Old Snow Woman's wild hair wrapping itself unpleasantly around his face as he went. And there, on the pass over the hills, he found the child in the red blanket, alone in the storm where he had toppled over with his feet stuck firmly in the snow. He was crying and thrusting one hand into the snow in an effort to lift himself up.

'Lie face down and pull the blanket over you!' shouted the Snow Boy as he ran. 'Lie down and cover yourself up. *Wheeew!*'

But the child heard only the voice of the wind and saw nothing.

'Fall over on your front,' cried the Snow Boy, running past him. '*Wheeew!* You mustn't move. It will soon be over, so lie down with the blanket over you!'

But the child still struggled to get up.

'Lie down!' cried the Snow Boy, rushing past again. '*Wheeew!* Be quiet and lie there on your face. It's not so cold today, you won't freeze.'

Again the child tried to get up, weeping all the while, his mouth twisted and trembling with fear.

'Lie down! ... Oh, it's no use!' And the Snow Boy deliberately gave the child a great buffeting, so that he fell over.

'*Wheeew!*' The Old Snow Woman had come up. 'Work, work harder, now! On, on! *Wheeew!*' He could see the purple slit of her mouth and her pointed teeth looming through the storm. 'Ah-ha!

Look, a funny little child! Good! – we'll have him. Why, at this time of year we've a right to one or two at the very least.'

'Of course we have!' said the Snow Boy. 'Here, that'll finish him!' And he made a show of buffeting the child again. But softly he whispered to him, 'Lie still. You mustn't move, do you hear?'

The snow wolves were still rushing madly about, their black paws darting in and out of sight amidst the whirling snow.

'Well done! That's right!' cried the Old Snow Woman as she flew off again. 'Come, snow! Keep at it! *Wheeew!*'

The child made one more effort to stand up. Laughing, the Snow Boy gave him another great buffeting. By now everything was dim and murky; though it was not yet three in the afternoon, it was as though the sun had already set. The child's strength had given out, so with a smile the Snow Boy stretched out a hand and pulled the red blanket right over him.

'Now go to sleep. I'll cover you with lots of quilts, so you'll not freeze. Dream now of homemade candy until the morning.'

Over and over again he repeated the words as he piled layer after layer of snow on the child. Soon the red blanket had disappeared, and the snow above it was smooth all over.

'He's still got the mistletoe I gave him,' muttered the Snow Boy to himself, looking tearful for a moment.

'To work, to work!' came the Old Snow Woman's voice through the wind from afar. 'No rest for us until early morning. No rest for us today! Come, snow! *Wheeew! Wheeew-wheeew! Wheeew!*'

At last, amidst wind and snow and ragged grey clouds, the sun really did set. All through the night, the snow went on falling. Then, when dawn was near, the Old Snow Woman rushed one last time straight through from south to north.

'Come, it'll soon be time to rest,' she cried. 'I must away to the sea again. You need not follow me. Rest all you want, to be fresh for our next meeting . . . It went well! A good day indeed!'

Her eyes had a strange blue gleam in the darkness as she flew off to the east with her rough, dry hair swirling and her mouth chattering.

Plain and hills seemed to relax, and the snow shone with a pale light. The sky had cleared, and starry constellations were twinkling all over the deep blue vault of heaven.

The snow boys collected their wolves and greeted each other for the first time.

'Terrific today, wasn't it?'

'Mm.'

'Wonder when we'll meet again?'

'I wonder. But not more than twice again this year, I expect.'

'I'm longing for us all to go home up north together.'

'Mm.'

'A child died just a while ago, didn't he?'

'It's all right. He's only asleep. I'll leave a mark there to show where he is in the morning.'

'We'd better go. Have to be back beyond the hills by dawn.'

'Goodbye, then.'

'Goodbye.'

The three snow boys with their nine wolves set off homeward to the west. Before long, the eastern sky began to glow like a yellow rose, then gleamed amber, and finally flared all gold. Everywhere, hills and plain alike, was full of new snow.

The Snow Boy's wolves had collapsed, limp and exhausted. The Snow Boy himself sat down and smiled. His cheeks were like apples, and his breath had the fragrance of lilies.

The sun rose in all its glory, with a bluish tinge today that made it more splendid than ever. The whole world flooded pink with sunlight. The snow wolves got up and opened wide their mouths from which blue flames flickered.

'Come on, all of you, follow me,' said the Snow Boy. 'It's dawn. We must wake up the child.'

He ran to where the child was buried beneath the snow.

'Now scratch away the snow just here,' he ordered.

With their back legs, the wolves kicked up the snow, which the breeze scattered at once like smoke.

A figure wearing furs, with snowshoes on its feet, was hurrying from the direction of the village.

'That'll do,' shouted the Snow Boy, seeing the edge of the child's red blanket peeping out.

'Your father is coming,' he cried, racing up the hillock in a column of powdery snow. 'Wake up!'

The child seemed to stir a little. And the figure in furs came running for all it was worth.

The Dahlias and the Crane

At the top of a small hill amidst the orchards there grew two yellow dahlias as tall as sunflowers and one dahlia that was taller still, with a great red flower.

The red dahlia was hoping to become the queen of the flowers.

When the wind came raging from the south, dashing great raindrops against the trees and flowers and shrieking with laughter as it tore green burrs and even twigs from the small chestnut tree on the hill, the three splendid dahlias would merely sway gently and seem to glow all the more intensely.

And when the mischievous north wind, for the first time that year, went wailing like a flute through the blue sky, the wild pear tree at the foot of the hill shook its branches busily and shed its fruit, yet the three tall dahlias merely gave the very slightest of dazzling smiles.

One of the two yellow flowers said as though to herself, her attention fixed on the southern sky near the horizon:

'Today the sun seems to be scattering rather more of its sparkling blue powder than usual.'

Peering earnestly into her friend's face, the other yellow dahlia said:

'You look a little pale today. I'm sure I'm the same.'

'Yes, you are,' said the first. 'But you,' she said to the red dahlia, 'why, you look wonderful today! I feel you might almost burst into flames.'

The red dahlia gazed up at the blue sky and, shining in the sunlight, smiled faintly as she replied:

'It's not enough, though. I shan't be happy until the whole sky seems to blaze red with my light. It makes me so frustrated!'

Before long the sun went down, the twilight sky of yellow crystal sank in turn, the stars came out, and the heavens were an immense abyss of bluish black.

'*Pee-tri-tri*,' called a crane as he flew by, dark beneath the starlight.

'Crane,' said the red dahlia, 'I'm very beautiful, aren't I?'

'*Very* beautiful. So red!'

The bird disappeared into the dark depths of the marsh beyond, calling softly as he went to a single white dahlia that bloomed there unnoticed, 'Good evening.'

The white dahlia smiled shyly.

The waxy clouds over the hills turned a muddy white, and day broke.

'Oh!' cried one yellow dahlia in surprise. 'You look even lovelier, as though surrounded by a reddish halo.'

'Yes, honestly,' said the other. 'It's as if you'd gathered all the reds of the rainbow around you.'

'Oh, really? But I'm still not satisfied, even so. I want to turn the whole sky red with my colour. The sun's sprinkling rather more gold dust around than before.'

Both the yellow flowers fell silent and made no reply.

Golden evening gave way to a cool, fresh night of indigo. The feathery crane went flying urgently across the star-studded sky.

'Crane, I shine quite a bit, don't I?'

'Oh yes, *quite* a bit.'

And as he descended into the dim white mist in the distance, the crane murmured softly again to the white dahlia, 'Good evening. How are you this evening?'

The stars revolved, and to Venus's last song the sky turned silver all over and a new day dawned. This morning, the sunlight was all gleaming waves of amber.

'Oh, how beautiful you look today! Your halo is five times bigger than yesterday!'

'Really dazzling! Look, your light reaches as far as that pear tree over there.'

'Yes, I know. But I'm still miserable. Nobody's said that I'm queen yet.'

So the yellow dahlias gave each other a sad look, then turned their wide eyes towards the hills that rose deep blue in the west.

The fragrant, bright autumn day drew to a close. The dew fell and the stars moved around, and the same crane flew silently across the sky.

'Crane, how do I look tonight?'

'Let's see. Why, magnificent, I think. But it's getting quite dark, you know.'

And as he passed over the edge of the marsh beyond, the crane said to the white dahlia, 'Good evening. A lovely evening.'

Day began to break, and in the violet half-light the yellow dahlias glanced over at the red dahlia, then suddenly turned frightened faces towards each other and said not a word.

'Oh, I'm so frustrated,' said the red dahlia. 'How do I look this morning?'

'Bright red – of course – but not quite so red as before, perhaps,' said one yellow dahlia.

'How do I look, then? Tell me! How?'

'Well, we're the only ones who think so,' said the other yellow dahlia, fidgeting uncomfortably, '. . . so please don't take it to heart . . . but it seems to us as though you've got dark specks on you.'

'Oh, no! Don't go on! You're tempting fate!'

The sun shone all day, and the apples on the hill turned a glossy red on one side.

Twilight descended, dusk drew nearer, and night came.

The crane flew across the sky crying, '*Pee-tri-tri, pee-tri-tri.*'

'Crane, Crane, can you see me tonight?'

'Well, not very clearly, I'm afraid.'

The crane flew on hastily towards the marsh, calling to the white dahlia as he went, 'It's a bit warm this evening, isn't it?'

Another day dawned.

In the pale light that smelled of apples, the red dahlia said:

'Quick, tell me how I look today. Quick!'

However hard the yellow dahlias peered in her direction, they could only make out something darkish and hazy.

'It's still night, we can't tell.'

'No, tell me the truth,' said the red dahlia, on the verge of tears. 'Tell me the truth. You're trying to hide something from me, aren't you? Am I dark? Am I dark?'

'Y-yes, it looks like it. But we can't really see properly.'

'Oh dear! And I do so hate red with black spots!'

Just then, a short man with a yellow, pointed face and a strange, pointed hat came along with his hands in his pockets. When he saw the red dahlia, he shouted:

'Ah, this one has it! The Mark of the Reaper.'

And he snapped the stem clean through. The red dahlia was borne off helpless in his hand.

'Where are you going? Oh, where are you going?' cried the yellow dahlias, racked with sobs. 'Here – hold on to us! Oh, where are you going? . . .'

Faintly from afar they could hear the red dahlia's voice.

The voice grew more distant and more distant still, until finally it was lost in the murmur of the branches of the poplars at the foot of the hill. And the glittering sun rose through the tears of the yellow dahlias.

The Thirty Frogs

Long ago, there were thirty small tree frogs who all worked happily together.

They earned their living chiefly by taking orders from insects to collect fallen pepper and poppy seeds and make flower beds, or to gather well-shaped stones and moss and fashion them into beautiful gardens.

The results, quaint and carefully composed, are still to be found in all kinds of unexpected places – under the bean plants in a field, at the foot of an oak tree in the woods, or hidden beneath a dripstone.

Now, the thirty frogs thoroughly enjoyed their daily tasks. They would start work early in the morning, taking deep breaths of cool, clean air as the golden rays of the sun cast the first, far-reaching shadows of the corn along the ground, and would work away – singing, laughing and shouting to each other all the while – until evening, when the foliage of trees and plants was thrown into relief in the amber light.

On days after a storm, they were *really* busy: 'Come as soon as possible, please, and remove a board that's hiding our garden'; or 'Would five or six of you come urgently to set up some hair-moss trees that have blown over?' The busier they were, the happier they felt, because it made them feel useful.

'*Right – let's give a good tug there. Here goes – heave! Hey – Puchko, the rope's going slack! Right, haul away. You, there, Pikiko, let go of that. Tie the rope! Heave-ho, nearly there, heave! . . .*' and so on: that was how it went.

One day, though, the thirty tree frogs had just put the finishing touches to a park for some ants and were heading home in high spirits when, passing beneath a peach tree, they saw that a new shop had opened up. It had a sign saying 'Imported whisky – two and a half rin a cup.'

Their curiosity aroused, the frogs crowded into the place. There they found an olive-green bullfrog sitting in a stolid sort of way, looking bored and amusing himself by seeing how far he could stick his tongue out. As they came in, he said in his very best voice:

'Good evening, gentlemen! Why not sit down and relax for a bit?'

So one of them said: 'Well, then – I see you've got something called imported whiskroak. What exactly is it? Could I have a cup, please, to see what it's like?'

'Imported whisky, sir? Of course, sir. Two and a half rin a cup – will that be all right, sir?'

'Yes, fine.'

The bullfrog scooped some of the liquor into a cup made of a hollow grain of millet.

'Phew!' exclaimed the tree frog. 'This is powerful stuff! Your throat burns as it goes down. And – wow! – it sets your belly on fire, too. Aaah, now that feels good! Could I have another cup, please?'

'Very well, sir. I'll be with you as soon as I've served this customer over here.'

'And one for me as well.'

'Coming, sir, coming. First come, first served, you know. There, that's for you, sir.'

'Thanks. Wow – this stuff is terrific!'

'Hey, what about mine?'

'Right – this is yours, sir.'

'Ouch!'

'Here – another one for me!'

'Over here – come on!'

'The same again – and make it quick!'

'All in good time, gentlemen. You don't want me to spill it when I've measured it out so carefully, do you? Let's see, now – this is yours, sir.'

'Thanks. Phew, *croak, croak* – it gets better and better.'

In this way, the tree frogs had one cup after the other, drinking a great deal and wanting more the more they drank.

Admittedly, there was a whole oil drum full of the bullfrog's whisky, so that you could have ordered ten thousand of those hollowed-out millet cups without making any great difference.

'Hey, one more for me!'

'Here – I asked for another one, didn't I? Get a move on, will you!'

'Come on, I can't wait forever!'

'Yes, sir, right, sir. That'll be your three hundred and second cup – that's all right, is it?'

'Of course it's all right – when I say another, I mean another.'

'Very well, sir, you shall have it if that's what you want. Here we are . . .'

'Aaah, that's better!'

'Hey, don't forget mine!'

Before long, the tree frogs were drunk, and with a series of long, whistling snores, first one then another of them went off to sleep.

At this, the bullfrog gave a smirk and, putting the lid back tight on the oil drum, quickly shut his shop. Then he got a set of chain mail out of the closet and drew it on carefully over his head, letting it reach all the way down to his feet. Next, he got a chair and table and seated himself carefully at the table. The tree frogs were still filling the room with thin, piping snores, so the bullfrog brought a small stool and placed it on the other side of the table from himself. Then he went and took an iron rod down from the shelf, plumped himself down in the chair again, and dealt the first frog a smart blow on his green head.

'Hey, wake up, you! Time to pay the bill. Come on!'

'*Snore, snore* . . . Ouch, that hurt! What the hell are you up to – hitting a fellow on the head like that!'

'Come on, pay your bill!'

'Eh? – oh yes, of course – how much does it come to?'

'You had three hundred and forty-two cups, so that'll be eighty-five sen, five rin. Well – can you pay?'

The tree frog got out his purse and had a look inside, but he only had three sen, two rin.

'You mean you've only got three sen, two rin? You *are* in trouble, then. Well, what about it? Shall I report you to the police?'

'No, don't, please don't!'

'It's no good, come on – pay up!'

'I really don't have it. Let me off it, please. If you let me off, I'll stay and work for you.'

'I see. All right, then – from now on you can be my servant.'

'Yes, sir, whatever you say, sir.'

'Right. In you go . . .'

Opening the door to the next room, the bullfrog pushed the flabbergasted tree frog inside and slammed the door. Then he smirked and plumped himself down in his chair. Next, he took hold of the iron rod again and gave a second frog a smart tap on his bluish-green head.

'Hey, you – time to get up! It's bill time! Bill time!'

'*Snore, snore, croak, urgh* . . . The same again, please.'

'You fool, you're still half asleep. Wake up! It's time to pay.'

'*Urgh, yawn, urgh*. What's up? What are you hitting me on the head for?'

'Still groggy, are we? Come on, pay your bill. Your bill, I say!'

'Oh, of course – you're quite right – how much is it?'

'You had six hundred cups, so that'll be one yen, fifty sen. How about it – have you got that much?'

The tree frog turned so pale he was almost transparent. He turned his purse upside down, but all that came out was a mere one sen, two rin.

'I'll give you everything I have – will that do, do you think?'

'Mm . . . one yen, twenty sen, eh? Wait, though – this is only one sen, twenty rin! What kind of a fool do you think I am? That's a hundredth of what you owe me, you cheeky devil! Come on, pay up! Quickly!'

'But I don't *have* it.'

'Then you'll just have to stay and work here, won't you?'

'Yes . . . I suppose I will.'

'Right. This way, then . . .' And the bullfrog pushed the second tree frog into the next room too. He was just about to slam the door shut when something seemed to occur to him, and he marched up to where the other tree frogs were snoring their piping snores, dragged out their purses one after the other, and looked inside.

Not one of them contained more than three sen. There was just one that seemed full and bulky, but when he opened it he found not a single coin – nothing but a camellia leaf, folded up small. Grinning with delight, the bullfrog took out his iron rod and tapped all the tree frogs in turn on their green heads. That did it.

'Ouch! Ow!' they complained as they awoke. 'Who the . . . ?'

For a while they simply goggled. But then, realising that the owner of the drink shop was responsible, they set upon him from all sides:

'Here – what d'you think you're up to, hitting people like that! . . .'

But one bullfrog was more than a match for thirty tree frogs, and, besides, he was wearing chain mail, while they were still reeling from the effects of the imported whisky. So he floored them one after the other, flinging the last eleven of them down in one untidy heap.

Utterly subdued by now, the tree frogs lay flat out on the floor, trembling and so pale they were almost invisible.

'You drank my whisky,' the bullfrog said self-righteously. 'None of your bills is less than eighty sen, but not one of you has got more than three sen to his name. Well? Does anyone have more? I don't imagine so . . .'

The tree frogs, breathing hard, could only look at one another helplessly.

'You don't, do you?' said the bullfrog, very pleased with himself. 'Now: two of your friends have already promised to work for me instead of paying up. How about the rest of you?' And at that very moment the two frogs who, as you know, were inside the other room, peered out through a gap in the door and wailed softly.

They all looked at each other.

'There's no other way. Shall we, then?'

'Yes – we'd better accept his offer.'

'If you please, sir,' they said to the bullfrog.

And in that way the tree frogs, being gentle and obliging creatures, became the bullfrog's minions with almost no resistance at all. So the bullfrog opened the door at the back and dragged out the other two, and with them all assembled he declared in a solemn voice:

'Listen. From now on, we'll call ourselves the "Bullfrog Group". And I will be its boss. From tomorrow you take your orders from me. All right?'

'Yes, sir,' they replied.

The next day, the golden light of the sun cast the shadow of the peach tree behind the house far into the distance, and the sky shone a bright blue, but nobody came with jobs for the Bullfrog Group. So the boss called them together and said:

'We're not getting any clients. If we're not going to get any work, what's the point in keeping you lot fed? It puts me in a fix, it really does. However, when there's no work, the best thing to do is to prepare for busier times. So this is a chance to collect material for future jobs . . .

'The first thing, then, is wood. Today I want you to go out and get me ten decent trees. No, wait – that's not enough. Let's see – a hundred – but no, even that's too few – a *thousand* trees. If you don't bring in a thousand of them, I'll complain to the police immediately. And you'll all be sentenced to death. You'll have your fat necks sliced clean through. No, not sliced – they're too fat for that – *hacked*!'

The frogs' green arms and legs twitched and trembled with fright. Furtively, they crept out and started busily searching for the required number of trees – just over 33.33 each, as they calculated. But they'd already used up most of what timber was available, and however frantically they hopped about the neighbourhood, by evening they'd got no more than nine trees.

They hung about helplessly with tearful faces, which only made matters worse. Just then, however, an ant happened to pass by, and seeing them sitting there crying, a translucent green in the amber-coloured evening sunlight, he said in surprise:

'Hello, Frogs – and thanks for the job you did the other day. But whatever's up?'

'Today we were supposed to bring in a thousand trees for the bullfrog. So far, we've only found nine.'

'Heh-heh-heh-heh!' went the ant when he heard this, but then he said: 'If he wants a thousand, then bring him a thousand. See those mould trees over there, the ones so fine they look like wisps of mist? One handful of them will give you five hundred trees at a go.'

'Why didn't *we* think of that?' they wondered happily. And they each gathered just over 33.33 of the wispy mould trees, then, thanking the ant, went back to their new headquarters.

The boss was very pleased.

'Good, good,' he chuckled. 'Well, then – you can all have one cup of imported whisky each before you go to bed.'

So they each had one tot of whisky in the millet-grain cups, then, with heads swimming and many a piping snore, went off to sleep.

The next morning when the sun rose the bullfrog called them all together again.

'There are no orders for work today either,' he said. 'So listen – you're to go to the flower beds in the neighbourhood and pick up seeds. I want you each to collect a hundred – no, a hundred is too few – even a thousand isn't enough for a long day like this – *ten* thousand seeds each. Got it? If you don't, I'll hand you straight over to the police. And they'll have your heads off in no time.'

With the sunlight shining clean through them, the tree frogs set off for the flower beds.

Luckily that day the seeds were falling like rain, with the bees buzzing busily about them, so the frogs squatted down and started picking them up as fast as they could. As they worked, they talked to each other:

'Hey, Bichko – do you think you can collect ten thousand seeds?'

'Doesn't look like it unless I hurry – I've only got three hundred so far.'

'The boss said one hundred at first, didn't he? I wish he'd left it at that.'

'And then he said a thousand. We could still have managed that, couldn't we?'

'Yes, we could.'

'I wonder what made me drink as much as that, though? . . .'

'I've been wondering the same thing, too. It was almost as if they were all tied together in a row – the first cup led to the second, the second to the third, and so on. If you ask *me*, there were three hundred and fifty cups all tied together.'

'I know . . . But we'd better get a move on or there'll be trouble.'

'You're right.'

So they went on picking up seeds, until by dusk they had just about met their target. Then they took them back to the boss's place.

The boss was pleased.

'Mm, good,' he said. 'Right – you can all have one cup of imported whisky each, then go to bed.'

That made the frogs pleased, too. They each drank a cupful of whisky, then went to bed and snored.

When they woke up the next morning, another bullfrog was there talking to the boss:

'Either way, you've got to do it in style if you do it at all. Otherwise people will laugh at you.'

'I know. What do you say – how would ninety yen per frog be?'

'Mm. That'd be about right, I'd say.'

'I think so too. (Hello there – you're up, are you?) Now, what work shall I have them do today? Things are looking bad, you know – all this time without any orders.'

'Yes, I know just how it is.'

'I think I'll get them to carry stones today. Listen, you

people – today I want each of you to bring back three ounces of stones. No – three ounces is too little.'

'A ton would be more like it,' said the other bullfrog.

'You're right – much more like it. Hey – today I want each of you to collect a ton of stones. If you don't, I'll turn you in to the police on the spot. The circuit judge always stops in here, you know; it'd be no trouble at all to have your heads hacked off.'

The tree frogs went a transparent pea green. No wonder, either: a ton of stones would have been too much even for a human being, let alone a tree frog, who weighs next to nothing himself – about a third of an ounce at the most. The idea of each of them carrying that much in one day was enough to make them turn giddy and collapse with a despairing croak.

Swiftly, the bullfrog got out his iron rod and went around beating them on the head, so that in the end they went off to work feeling as though the whole world had turned blue and was whirling round and round. Even the sun seemed to be triangular and to be frantically spinning in a far-off corner of the sky.

Reaching the place where there were lots of stones, they fastened a rope to one that weighed no more than four ounces, and with much heave-ing and ho-ing began to tug at it. They worked until the sweat burst out all over their bodies, until their heads felt as light as thistledown and everything loomed black about them. Even so, by the time the thirty of them had managed to drag the four-ounce stone to the boss's place, it was already noon. They were reeling with exhaustion; they could hardly stand or even keep their eyes open – and yet, if they didn't bring in another one thousand nine hundred and ninety-nine pounds, twelve ounces of stone by the end of the day, they would all have their heads chopped off!

The boss was asleep and snoring inside his house at the time, but he managed to rouse himself and stroll outside to look. Some of the tree frogs were sitting, sighing, on the stone they'd just dragged in, others were sprawled on the ground asleep. Their shadows were green. Furious, the boss hurried into the house to fetch his iron rod, but while he was gone one of the frogs who wasn't sleeping shook the others awake, so that when the boss came out again they were all on their feet.

'What a bunch of – !' declared the boss. 'You mean to say you've taken until now just to carry this little thing? I've never seen such weaklings! Why, I'll carry a ton of stones in thirty minutes myself, just to show you!'

'But for *us* it's quite impossible. We're nearly dead as it is.'

'You gutless wonders! Go out and get it, right now. If it's not done by this evening, I'll turn you all in. And you'll all lose your heads, you idiots!'

At this point, the tree frogs suddenly shouted together in desperation:

'All *right*, then – hand us over to the police, and the sooner the better! Let them chop away – it might be interesting.'

'What!' cried the boss in a fury. 'Why, you idiots, you lily-livered, you *gaaaaaaaaaa* ...'

Suddenly, with a funny look on his face, he clamped his lips shut, but the *gaaaaaaaaaa* went on just the same. It hadn't come from his throat at all. It was the sound of the snail-shell megaphone, the sound that always heralded the latest command from the king, echoing across the blue sky.

'Listen – it's a new royal command!' exclaimed the tree frogs and their boss together, hastily standing to attention. The voice of the snail-shell megaphone rang out with great serenity:

'The latest command from His Majesty the King, the latest command from His Majesty the King! Concerning how to give orders to others: 1. When giving orders, divide your own weight by the weight of the person taking the order, and note the answer. 2. Multiply the amount of work involved in the order by that answer. 3. Try doing that amount of work yourself, for two days. Whoever does not obey this rule will be sent to the Island of the Birds.'

The tree frogs' joy knew no bounds. One of them, who was called Chekko and was good at arithmetic, immediately began calculating:

'Let's see ... the weight of the people who've been taking the orders is a third of an ounce; the weight of the person who's been giving the orders is four ounces. Divide one by the other and you get 1.3 ounces. The work involves a ton. A ton multiplied by 1.3 is two thousand six hundred pounds.

'Right! Between now and tonight, boss, you've got to drag one thousand three hundred pounds of stone here.

'Come on, now, it's His Majesty's order. Get to work!'

This time it was the bullfrog's turn gradually to fade in colour; soon he was a transparent shade of amber and trembling all over.

Surrounding him, the tree frogs led him off to the place where the stones were. Then they tied a rope to one stone that weighed about two pounds and said: 'There – you have to carry six hundred and fifty of these by tonight,' and tossed the rope over his shoulder.

The boss must have resigned himself to his fate, for he threw aside the iron rod he was holding and set his face firmly in the direction in which he was to drag the stone. But still he didn't seem serious about actually hauling it, so the tree frogs joined in a chorus of encouragement:

'Yo, heave, ho! Yo, heave, *ho*!'

Egged on by their cries, the boss planted and replanted his feet five times, then heaved at the rope; but the stone refused to budge.

He broke out into a sweat and began breathing in great gasps, his mouth open as far as it would go. The world before his eyes began to go dark and whirl around him.

'Yo, heave, ho. Yo, heave, *ho*!'

Four times more the bullfrog planted and replanted his feet, but the final time his legs suddenly gave a *clunk* and buckled up.

The tree frogs couldn't help bursting into laughter.

But then, strangely enough, they fell silent – a genuine, unbroken silence. A wretched feeling had come over them, though I don't quite know how to describe it. Perhaps *you* know what I mean – the wretched feeling that sometimes comes when a group of you have burst out laughing at somebody, and you suddenly stop . . .

But just at that moment, high up in the heavens, the snail-shell megaphone rang out again:

'The latest command from His Majesty the King, the latest command from His Majesty the King! Each and every living being is well-intentioned, and deserves compassion. It is wrong for anyone to hate him.' Then the voice receded into the distance again, and could be heard echoing across the sky: 'The latest command from His Majesty . . .'

So the tree frogs ran up to the bullfrog and gave him some water, and set his bent legs straight, and pummelled his back for him.

The bullfrog shed great tears of remorse.

'Tree Frogs,' he said, 'I was wrong. I'm not your boss or anything, not any more. I'm just a frog, after all. From tomorrow I'll become a tailor.'

The tree frogs all clapped their hands in delight. And the next day they happily set to work again as they had always done.

Perhaps you've heard it yourself: after a shower of rain, or the day after a storm – or even on a fine day, for that matter – the babble of little voices in the fields or hidden in the flower beds:

'Hey, Bekko – level the ground there a bit more, will you? Of course it's all right! . . . Hey – it's not sparrow-wort you're supposed to plant there, it's sparrow's-bane! Yes, that's right. It's easy to get them wrong, both being sparrows, eh, ha-ha! . . . Bichko – hey, Bichko! Fill that hole in there . . . All right? I'll throw it, here it comes! Oh, damn! Come on, all together now, heave! . . .'

The Ungrateful Rat

In the pitch-dark space in the ceiling of an old house there lived a rat.

One day, the rat was walking along a passage under the floor, peering about him as he went, when a weasel came dashing along from the other direction carrying a lot of something that looked good. When he saw the rat, he paused a moment and said quickly:

'Hey, Rat! A lot of sugar balls have come through the hole in the closet at your place. If you hurry you'll get some, too.'

His whiskers twitching with delight, the rat ran straight off without so much as a thank-you to the weasel. When he got to the place beneath the closet, however, he suddenly felt something pricking at his leg, and a tiny, shrill voice called:

'Halt! Who goes there?'

The rat looked down in astonishment and found it was an ant. Soldier ants had already set up a series of barricades around the sugar balls, and were brandishing their black battle-axes. Twenty or thirty of them were busy breaking up or dissolving the sugar balls before taking them back to their quarters. The rat quaked with fright.

'Turn back!' boomed a sergeant-major ant. 'This is a no-entry area. Go home!'

The rat spun around and dashed straight back to the space in the ceiling, where he got into his nest and lay still for a while. He was very disgruntled. Nothing could be done about the ants – they were soldiers, after all, and tough. But that smooth fraud of a weasel – it was infuriating, the rat thought, that he should have run all the way to the closet and got turned back by the sergeant-major ant just because of what the weasel had told him. So the rat sneaked out of his nest again and went to the weasel's place behind the timber shed.

When he saw the rat, the weasel, who was grinding some corn into powder with his teeth, said:

'Well? Did you find any sugar balls?'

'Weasel – I think it's shocking, the way you led me on like that.'

'What d'you mean, led you on? There were some left, quite definitely.'

'Oh, there were, but the ants had already got at them.'

'Had they, now? They're awfully quick, those ants.'

'They took the lot. You should pay me compensation, for leading me astray. Yes, compensation!'

'It's not my fault. You were a bit late, that's all.'

'That's nothing to do with it. You shouldn't let people trust you, people weaker than yourself. I want compensation!'

'You're a fine one, aren't you? – throwing somebody's kindness in his face. All right. If you like, I'll give you my own sugar balls.'

'Compensation! Compensation!'

'Here, take them, then! Take as many as you can carry and get out of here. I'm sick of you and your whining. Take all you can carry and get out.'

In a fine rage, the weasel flung the sugar balls at him. The rat gathered up just as many as he could, then bowed.

'Get out!' shouted the weasel still more angrily. 'I don't want what you've left, either. I'll give them to the maggots.'

The rat dashed straight back to his nest in the ceiling, where he crunched his way through every single sugar ball.

In this way, the rat gradually got himself disliked, and in the end there was nobody who would have anything to do with him. So for want of anyone better, he began to associate with pillars, broken dustpans, buckets, brooms, and the like. He was especially friendly with a pillar.

One day, the pillar said to the rat, 'Rat, it'll soon be winter. We pillars will be creaking with the cold before long. You ought to get some good bedding together before it's too late. Luckily enough, just above my head there's a lot of feathers and other stuff that the sparrows left in the spring. Why don't you fetch some down and take it home while the going's good? I may feel a bit cold up there around my head, but I'll manage somehow.'

The rat thought it was a sensible idea, so that day, without delay, he set about carrying the bedding home. Unfortunately, though, there was a steep slope on the way, and on the third journey he fell plump off it.

The pillar was startled. 'Are you hurt, Rat? Are you hurt?' it called frantically, bending in an effort to see.

After a while the rat got up, then, with his face all twisted, said,

'Pillar, I'm shocked at you, letting this kind of thing happen to someone like me who's not strong.'

'I'm sorry, Rat,' it kept repeating, feeling horribly responsible. 'Do forgive me!'

'It's not a matter of forgiving,' said the rat, taking advantage of the situation. 'If only you hadn't been so keen to give me your advice, this wouldn't have happened. I want compensation. Come on, pay up!'

'But you know very well I can't.'

'I don't like being picked on by people like you, so I'm not backing down. Come on, now, pay up!'

Unable to do anything, the pillar wept bitterly, while the rat had to go home empty-handed. From that time on, the pillar was too scared to speak to him again.

It was one day some time after this that the dustpan gave the rat half a cake that someone had left. And it happened that the very next day the rat had an upset stomach. So, as usual, the rat demanded at least a hundred times that the dustpan pay him compensation. The dustpan was so disgusted that it would have nothing more to do with him.

Later still, the bucket gave the rat a piece of washing soda and told him to wash his face with it each morning. The rat was very pleased, and from the next morning on he used it every day. But before long ten of his whiskers fell out. So, sure enough, the rat went to the bucket and demanded at least a hundred times that he be paid compensation. Unfortunately, however, the bucket had no whiskers of its own, nor any other way of repaying him, so at a complete loss it just wept and apologised. And from then on it never said another word to him.

One by one, all the inhabitants of the kitchen in turn had the same trouble and learned to avoid the rat; in the end, they would turn away hastily at the mere sight of him.

There was, in fact, just one of them that hadn't yet had any contact with the rat. This was a rat-trap made of wire mesh.

Rat-traps ought, in theory, to be on the side of human beings, but this one had been feeling fed up recently because of the advertisements in the papers with pictures showing a trap along with a cat, both labelled 'disposable.' Not that human beings had ever treated the rat-trap properly, even before that. No, not once. And they all avoided touching it, as though it were something unclean.

So the trap had less sympathy with human beings than with rats. Most rats, even so, were too frightened to go anywhere near it.

Every day it would call to them in a gentle voice, 'Come on, Ratty, there's a mackerel head for dinner tonight. I'll hold the catch down firmly while you eat it. Don't be frightened. Come on, I'm not the kind to slam the door behind you. I don't like human beings any more than you do.'

But the rats all said, 'Hah, I'm not going to fall for that one,' or 'Really? I see . . . I'll have to ask the others in my family about it sometime,' as though it hardly mattered anyway.

Then, the next morning, a servant with a bright red face would come to look at the trap and say, 'Nothing in it again. The rats know, that's the trouble. They learn about it at rat school. Still, let's try it just one more day.' And he would change the bait in the trap.

One night as usual the trap was calling, 'Come on, come on, tonight there's some nice soft fish cake. You can just have the bait, it's quite safe. Hurry up, now!'

The rat who lived in the ceiling happened to be going past just then.

'Will you really just let me have the bait?' he asked.

'Well, hello,' said the trap. 'You're a new rat around here, aren't you? Yes, of course – just the bait. Here, come in and help yourself.'

The rat popped inside, gobbled up the fish cake, popped out again, and said, 'That was very nice. Thanks.'

'Was it? I'm glad. Come again tomorrow night.'

The next morning the servant came to look and said angrily, 'Damn it! He's got away with the bait. This rat's a crafty one. Still, he went inside, that's something. There – there's a sardine for today.' And he left half a sardine as bait.

The trap hooked onto the fish and waited eagerly for the rat to come along.

As soon as it was dark the rat appeared.

'Good evening. I've come, as you asked me to,' he said in a patronising way.

The trap was a little annoyed, but swallowed his pride and said simply, 'Here, help yourself.'

The rat popped inside, chewed up the sardine, and popped out again. Then he said loftily, 'I'll come and eat it again for you tomorrow.'

'Umph,' replied the trap.

When the servant came to look the next morning he got angrier still.

'The sly brute! But I don't see *how* he can just get away with the bait every night. If you ask me, this trap here has taken a bribe from him.'

'I did nothing of the kind! What an insult!' shouted the trap, but of course the servant couldn't hear it. Once again he put some bait inside, this time a piece of mouldy fish cake.

All day the trap fumed at the idea of being so unjustly suspected.

Night fell. The rat turned up and said, as though it was all a tremendous nuisance, 'Ah me, it's not easy to come all the way here every day. And all for a fish head at the most. I've just about had enough. Still, I'm here now, so I might as well do it the favour of eating it . . . Good evening, Trap.'

The trap was quivering so with rage that all it could get out was, 'Help yourself.'

The rat promptly popped inside, then saw that the fish cake had gone bad and shouted, 'This is going too far! This stuff is rotten. How could you do this to a poor creature like me? I want compensation. Compensation!'

The trap was so angry that it couldn't stop its wire from rattling and shaking.

It was the shaking that did it.

With a *snap* and a *swish*, the catch to which the bait was attached came free and the door to the trap fell shut. That really did it.

The rat went nearly mad.

'Liar! Cheat!' he cried, biting at the wire and dashing round and round in circles and stamping on the floor and shrieking and crying. It was a dreadful commotion. But this time even he wasn't up to asking for compensation. The trap, too, what with pain and indignation, could do nothing but rattle and shake and quiver. This went on until the morning.

When the servant with the bright red face came to have a look, he danced in triumph.

'Got him! Got him!' he cried. 'Caught him at last! And a nasty-looking brute he is, too. Right, out you come now! Out you come, my beauty!'

Night of the Festival

It was the night of the festival of the mountain god.

Wearing his new light-blue sash and armed with fifteen pennies that his mother had given him as pocket money, Ryoji set off for the place where the portable shrine had been installed. One of the side-shows set up nearby was called 'The Air Beast' and was doing a roaring trade, he'd heard.

A man wearing baggy trousers, with long hair and a pockmarked face, was standing in front of the curtain of the booth. 'Come one, come all!' he boomed. 'Come and see the show!' Ryoji happened to be glancing idly at the placard, so the man called out to him: 'Hey, kid, come on in! You can pay on the way out.'

Almost without thinking, Ryoji found himself drawn in through the entrance. Inside, he found Kosuke and quite a number of other people he knew, all staring with half-amused, half-serious expressions at something displayed on a platform in the centre.

Clinging to the top of the stand was the air beast. It was big and flattish and wobbly and white, with no particular head or mouth. When the showman poked it with a stick, it gave way on this side and swelled out on the other side, and when he poked it on the other side it came out on this side, and when he poked it in the middle it swelled out all round. Ryoji didn't like it at all, and was getting out as quickly as he could when his wooden clog caught in a hole in the bare earth. He nearly fell over, and collided heavily with the tall, solid-looking person next to him. Looking up in surprise, he saw a man with a red, heavy-boned face, wearing an old white-striped summer kimono and a peculiar garment resembling a shaggy straw cape over his shoulders. The man looked down at him, just as startled as he was. His eyes were perfectly round and a kind of smoky gold in colour.

Ryoji was still staring at him when all of a sudden the man blinked his eyes rapidly, turned away, and made in a hurry for the exit. Ryoji went after him. On the way out, the man opened his large right hand, which had been tightly clenched, and produced a ten-penny silver coin. Ryoji took out a similar coin, gave it to the person waiting to be paid, and went outside, only to bump into his cousin Tatsuji. The man's broad shoulders disappeared into the crowd.

'Did you go into that show?' asked Tatsuji in a low voice, pointing at the placard. 'They call it an air beast, but people say it's really just a cow's stomach full of air. I think you're stupid to pay to see something like that.'

Ryoji was still staring vacantly at the placard with its oddly shaped creature when Tatsuji said, 'I haven't had a look at the portable shrine yet. See you tomorrow.' And he went off into the crowd, hopping on one leg.

Ryoji, too, quickly moved away. The green apples and grapes piled on the rows of stalls that lined both sides gleamed in the light of the acetylene lamps.

He walked on between them, thinking to himself vaguely that the blue flames of the lamps were pretty but gave off an unpleasant smell, like a dragon's breath.

Over in the enclosure they used for the festival dance, five paper lanterns cast a dim light. It seemed that the dance was about to begin, as a small cymbal was sounding quietly. Ryoji hung about there for a while, remembering that his friend Shoichi was due to appear in it.

Just then he heard loud voices from the direction of the refreshment stalls that stood in the dark shadow of some cypress trees, and everybody started running in that direction. Ryoji hurried over with the rest and peered around the sides of the grown-ups.

The big man he'd seen a while ago was standing there, his hair all dishevelled, being bullied by some young men from the village. The sweat was running down his forehead as he bowed to them again and again. He was trying to say something, but stuttered so badly that he couldn't get the words out.

One young fellow with a neat parting in his sleek hair was gradually shouting louder and louder because he knew people were watching.

'Oh no you don't – no outsider pulls a trick like that. Come on, where's your money? You don't have any, eh? Then why did you eat them? Eh?'

The man was in a terrible state and barely managed to stammer, 'I'll b-b-b-bring you a hundred bundles of firewood instead.'

The fellow running the tea stall seemed to be slightly deaf, for his voice got even louder still:

'What's that – only a couple of dumplings, you say? What do you expect? I'd let you have 'em free, but I don't like the way you talk. Yes, you!'

Wiping away the sweat, the man just managed again to get out, 'I'll b-bring you a hundred bundles of firewood . . . so let me go.'

That made the other burst out: 'You rotten liar! Who'd hand over all that firewood for two dumplings? Where're you from, anyway?'

'Th-th-th-th-that's something I just can't tell you. Let me go now.' The man was blinking his golden eyes and wiping furiously at the sweat. He seemed to be wiping away some tears as well.

'Beat him up! Come on, beat him up!' someone shouted.

Suddenly, Ryoji understood everything. 'I know –' he thought, 'he got terribly hungry, and he'd paid to see the air beast, then he went and ate the dumplings forgetting he hadn't got any money left. He's crying. He's not a bad man. Just the opposite – he's too honest. Right. I'm going to help him out.'

Stealthily he took from his purse the one remaining coin, clutched it tightly in his hand, and, pushing his way through the crowd as unobtrusively as possible, went up to the man. The man was hanging his head, with his hands resting humbly on his knees, furiously mumbling something.

Ryoji crouched down and, without saying anything, placed the nickel coin on top of the man's big foot in its straw sandal.

The man gave a start and stared down into Ryoji's face, then swiftly bent down, took up the coin, and slammed it on the counter of the stall, shouting:

'There, there's your money! Now let me go. I'll bring the firewood later. And four bushels of chestnuts.' No sooner had he said this than he thrust the people surrounding him aside and fled like the wind.

'It's a wild man. A wild man of the hills!' they all cried and ran after him, chattering to each other excitedly; but he'd already disappeared without a trace.

The wind suddenly howled, the great black cedars swayed, the bamboo curtains at the tea stall flew up, and lights blew out here and there.

Just then the flute began to play for the festival dance, but instead of going to watch it Ryoji hurried home along the dim white paths between the paddy fields. He was in a hurry to tell his grandfather about the wild man of the hills. Already the Pleiades was shining dimly quite high up in the sky.

Back at home he went in past the stable and found his grandfather all alone, cooking some soybeans over a fire in the open hearth. Ryoji quickly sat down opposite him and told him everything that had happened. At first his grandfather listened quietly, watching the boy's face as he talked, but when he got to the end he burst out laughing.

'Oh yes,' he laughed, 'that's a wild man of the hills, all right. The wild men are very honest. I've often met them up in the hills myself on misty days. But I'm sure no one's ever heard of one coming to see a festival before.' He laughed again. 'Or maybe they've come before and nobody's noticed, eh?'

'Grandpa, what do they do up there?'

'Well, they say they make fox traps, for one thing, using the branches of trees. They bend down a branch as thick as this and hold it down with another branch, then they dangle a fish or something from the end so that when a fox or bear comes to eat it, the branch springs up again and kills it.'

Just then there was a great thud and rattling outside, and the whole house shook as in an earthquake. Ryoji found himself clinging tightly to his grandfather. The old man, who had gone rather pale himself, hurried outside with a lamp.

Ryoji followed after him. The lamp blew out almost immediately, but it didn't matter, for the moon in its eighteenth day was rising silently over the dark hills to the east.

And there, in the open space in front of the house, a great pile of thick faggots lay flung down on the ground. They were massive pieces, roughly broken, with thick roots and branches still attached to them. His grandfather gazed at them for a while in astonishment, then suddenly clapped his hands together and laughed.

'The wild man of the hills has brought *you* some firewood. And there I was thinking he was going to give it to the fellow at the festival. The wild man knows what he's up to!'

Ryoji was stepping forward to get a better look at the firewood when suddenly he slipped on something and fell over. Looking closer, he found the ground was strewn with shiny chestnuts.

'Grandpa!' he shouted, getting up again. 'The man brought chestnuts too!'

'Well! So he even remembered them,' said his grandfather in

astonishment. 'We can't possibly accept all this. Next time I go into the hills, I'll take along something and leave it for him. I expect he'd like something to wear best of all.'

Suddenly Ryoji had a funny feeling, as though he wanted to cry.

'Grandpa, I feel sorry for him. He's too honest, isn't he? I'd like to give him something nice.'

'Yes. Next time, perhaps, I'll take him a quilted coat. A wild man might prefer a thick, quilted coat to a thin, padded one for the winter. And I'll take him some dumplings.'

'But that's not enough – just clothes and dumplings!' shouted Ryoji. 'I want to give him something that'll make him cry and dance about the place for joy, something so nice he'll think he's in heaven.'

His grandfather picked up the unlit lamp.

'Mm. That's if we can *find* such a thing,' he said. 'Come on, then, let's go indoors and have the beans. Your father'll be back from next door before long.' And he led the way inside.

Ryoji said nothing but looked up at the pale blue, lopsided moon.

The wind was roaring in the hills.

The Fire Stone

The hares were already in their short brown clothes.

The tall grass on the stretch of open country glinted in the sun, and here and there on the birches pale flowers were in bloom. The whole area was full of fragrance.

'Mm, how nice it smells,' said Homoi the young hare as he hopped happily about. 'Mm, delicious. The lilies of the valley are so crisp.'

A breeze came, and the lilies of the valley tinkled as their leaves and bell-shaped flowers brushed together.

Homoi was so happy that he went bouncing over the grass without pausing for breath. Then he stopped for a moment and, folding his front paws, said gleefully, 'It's like doing spring-jumps on the water of a river.'

He had, in fact, come to the bank of a small stream. The cold water was gurgling to itself as it ran, and the sand on the bed glittered down below.

Homoi tilted his head to one side and said to himself, 'Now, shall I hop across this stream? I could of course, perfectly easily. But somehow the grass on the other side doesn't look so good.'

Just then he heard a shrill squeaking and spluttering further up the stream, and something bushy and darkish and shaped rather like a bird came flapping and struggling down the current.

Homoi rushed to the bank and watched intently until it drew level with him. It *was* a bird – a skinny young lark, in fact – that the stream was carrying along. Without hesitating, he jumped into the water and grabbed hold of it with his front paws. But that only frightened the lark even more, and it opened wide its yellow beak and shrieked until Homoi thought he would go deaf. Desperately, he kicked at the water with his back legs.

'It's all right, all right!' he said, looking into the lark's face. But that gave him such a shock that he very nearly let go of it, for the face was all crinkled, with a beak too large for it and, what was worse, a look rather like a lizard.

But the young hare was tough, and refused to let go with his paws. His mouth was twisted with fright, but he fought the fear down hard and held the lark high up out of the water.

Both of them were being carried steadily on. Twice Homoi's head went under the surface and he swallowed a lot of water, but he didn't release his grip.

Then, just at a bend in the stream, he saw a small willow branch smacking against the surface of the water.

Homoi sank his teeth into the branch, so deep that he opened up the green pith underneath. Then, with all his might, he threw the baby bird onto the soft grass of the bank and in a single bound leapt out himself.

The lark collapsed on the grass and lay shaking with the whites of its eyes showing.

Homoi was so tired he was staggering, but he forced himself on; pulling off a branch of pale willow blossoms, he covered the little bird with it. But when the lark raised its grey face as though to thank him, Homoi let out a yell of fright, and took to his heels.

Just then something came hurtling like an arrow from the sky. Homoi stopped and looked back. It was the mother lark. The mother bird said nothing, but held her child as close as possible, shaking all the while. Reassured, he ran on, making straight for home.

Homoi's mother, who was indoors putting together a bundle of white grass roots, was startled when she saw him. 'Heavens, is something wrong?' she said, getting the medicine chest down from a shelf. 'Your face is terribly pale.'

'Mother, I saved a bushy little bird from drowning,' said Homoi.

'A bushy little bird?' she asked as she took out a dose of all-purpose powder and gave it to him. 'You mean a lark?'

'I suppose so,' said Homoi as he took the medicine from her. 'Oh dear, my head's going around. Mother – my eyes are going funny . . .' And he flopped down on the floor. He had a terrible fever.

By the time that Homoi, thanks to his parents and Dr Hare, was quite well again, the lilies of the valley had small green berries on them.

One quiet, cloudless evening Homoi tried going out for the first time.

Looking up, he saw something like a red star racing diagonally across the southern sky. He was watching it in wonder when, quite unexpectedly, there was a fluttering of wings and two birds came flying down. The bigger of the two carefully placed something round and red and shining on the grass, then pressed her wings together respectfully and said:

'Mr Homoi, my child and I owe you a debt we can never repay.'

Homoi took a good look at their faces by the light of the red object and asked, 'Are you the larks I met the other day?'

'Yes,' said the mother lark. 'I don't know how to thank you for saving my son's life. We hear you were actually *ill* because of what you did. But I hope you're better now.'

She bowed a great deal, then went on. 'We flew around this area every day, waiting for you to come out again. This is a present from our king.' And placing the red, shining thing in front of Homoi, she undid its wrapping, a handkerchief so thin it looked like smoke. Inside was a perfectly round gem about the size of a horse chestnut, with red flames flickering inside it.

'This is a jewel known as the Fire Stone. The king said I was to tell you that it will become still more beautiful if you look after it well. I hope you will accept it.'

Homoi smiled. 'I don't deserve this, Mrs Lark,' he said. 'Please take it back with you. It's so beautiful, it's enough just to look at it. I'll come and call on you next time I want to see it.'

'No, I beg you to accept it,' said the lark. 'You see, it's a present from our king; if you don't accept it, we'll be in trouble.' She turned to the baby lark. 'Come on, boy, say goodbye. Bow properly, now. Well, we must be going.'

And with two or three more bows, the mother lark and her son hurried off.

Homoi picked up the jewel and looked at it. Though it seemed to be alive with red and yellow flames, in fact it was cold and beautifully transparent. When he put it to his eye and looked up through it, there were no flames, and he could see the Milky Way as though inside a piece of crystal. When he removed it from his eye, the lovely flames flickered up again.

Holding the jewel gently in his paws, Homoi went indoors and took it straight to his father. Mr Hare removed his spectacles to examine it carefully.

'This is the famous jewel known as the Fire Stone,' he said eventually. 'It's no ordinary jewel, mind you. They say that two birds and a fish were the only ones who ever managed to keep it all their lives. You'll have to take great care of it so that it doesn't lose its light.'

'Don't worry, Father,' said Homoi. 'I'll never let that happen. The larks said the same kind of thing, too. I'll breathe on it a hundred times every day and polish it a hundred times with a linnet feather.'

Mrs Hare also took the jewel in her paws and gazed at it for a long time. 'They say this stone is very easily damaged,' she said. 'Even so, when the late Minister Eagle had charge of it, there was a big volcanic eruption and he took it with him as he went around helping the birds get away safely. It was hit by bits of rock and even got caught in a stream of red-hot lava, but it didn't get scratched or go cloudy – no, it actually became more beautiful than ever.'

'That's right,' said Mr Hare. 'It's a well-known story. I'm sure you'll be a great man like the minister, too, Homoi. But you'll have to be very careful not to be unkind to people.'

Suddenly, Homoi felt tired and sleepy.

'Don't worry,' he said calmly as he lay down on his bed. 'I promise you I'll be a big man, Father. Give me the stone, now – I want to hold it while I sleep.'

Mrs Hare gave it to him. He clasped it to his chest and went to sleep at once.

The dreams he had that night were so beautiful – with yellow and green fires blazing in the sky, and the whole countryside turning into a sea of golden grass, and hordes of tiny windmills flying through the sky humming faintly like bees, and Minister Eagle wise and kind, with his glittering silver cape rippling as he looked over the landscape – that time and time again Homoi cried out 'Hooray! Hooray!' for sheer joy.

The next morning, Homoi awoke around seven o'clock and before doing anything else took a look at the jewel. It was even lovelier than the previous night.

He peered into it. 'Look, look!' he exclaimed to himself. 'There's a crater! There – it's erupting! Erupting! What fun, it's just like fireworks. Oh dear – the fire's pouring out of it. But now it's split in two. Oh, it's lovely! Fireworks, fireworks! Now it's just like lightning. There, it's started to flow. Now it's gone all gold. Hooray! There, it's erupted again!'

Mr Hare had already gone out. Mrs Hare came in smiling, carrying some nice white grass roots and green rose hips.

'Come along, now,' she said. 'Get your face washed and then you can try a little exercise today. Here, let me have a look. Well now, that really *is* pretty. Do you mind if I go on looking while you're washing?'

'Of course not,' said Homoi. 'This is our family treasure, so it's yours too, Mother.' Getting up, he went and collected six large drops of dew from the leaf tips of the lilies of the valley outside the entrance to their house and gave his face a thorough wash.

After he'd had breakfast, he breathed on the jewel a hundred times and polished it a hundred times with linnet down. Then he carefully wrapped it in linnet breast feathers, put it in the agate box that he'd been keeping his telescope in, and gave it to his mother for safekeeping. Then he went out.

A breeze was blowing, and the dew on the grass was spilling in great drops. The bellflowers were ringing their morning chimes, *ding-dong, ding-ding-dong, ding-ding-a-dong* . . .

Homoi hopped on until finally he stopped beneath a birch tree.

Just then, an elderly wild horse came along from the opposite direction. Homoi was rather frightened of him and was going to turn back, but the horse bowed politely and said:

'Would you be Mr Homoi, by any chance? I hear that the Fire Stone has come into your good hands, and I wanted to congratulate you. They say that twelve hundred years have passed since the jewel was last given to us animals. Why, even this old fogey wept this morning when he heard the news.' And great tears rolled from the horse's eyes.

Homoi felt embarrassed, but the horse cried so much that in the end he found himself getting a bit snuffly too.

'We're all most grateful to you,' said the horse, getting out a pale blue handkerchief the size of a small tablecloth and wiping away his tears. 'Please take the greatest care of your health.' He bowed politely again and went off in the other direction.

Homoi walked on, lost in thought, half pleased and half dismayed at what had happened, until he came to an elder tree. Under the tree, two young squirrels were nibbling together at a sticky white rice cake, but when they saw Homoi coming they stiffened in alarm, hastily setting their collars straight and blinking their eyes as they tried to gulp down the sticky cake.

'Hello, Squirrels,' said Homoi, greeting them as usual. But the two of them just stood there quite rigid, unable to get a word out.

'Squirrels,' said Homoi in alarm, 'let's go somewhere and play again today, shall we?' But they just gazed at each other with big round eyes as though the idea was quite outrageous, then suddenly whipped around and ran off as fast as they could go.

Homoi was horrified. He went home in a great state and said to Mrs Hare, 'Mother, there's something funny about the way everybody's behaving. The squirrels – they won't have anything to do with me.'

'I'm not surprised,' said Mrs Hare with a smile. 'They'll be shy because you've become so important. So you've got to be careful not to do anything undignified.'

'Don't worry, Mother, I won't,' said Homoi. 'Does that mean I'm like a big general, then?'

'Well . . . yes, it does,' said Mrs Hare looking pleased.

Homoi jumped for joy.

'Hooray, hooray! Then they're all my soldiers now. I'll never be scared of old Fox again. Mother – I think I'll make the squirrels major generals. And the horse – let's see, the horse can be a colonel.'

'Yes, why not?' said his mother with a smile. 'But you mustn't get too high-and-mighty, you know.'

'Don't worry,' said Homoi. 'Mother, I'm going out for a while.'

And without further ado he hopped outside into the fields. And there he met the nasty old fox, who came dashing past right in front of him.

Homoi trembled a little but took his courage in both hands and called, 'Fox! Stop! I'm a general now, didn't you know?'

The fox looked around, startled, and turning pale said, 'Why, dear me, yes! Would there be anything I can do for you?'

'You've always bullied me, haven't you?' said Homoi as impressively as possible. 'Well, from now on you're under *my* command.'

The fox put a paw to his head as though he might well faint, and softly replied, 'I really do apologise most deeply. Won't you please forgive me?'

Homoi beamed with pleasure. 'Then as a special favour I'll let you off,' he said. 'You can be my lieutenant. I hope you'll make yourself useful.'

The fox spun round and round four times, he was so pleased.

'Thank you, thank you very much. I'll do anything you wish. Shall I go and steal a little sweet corn for you?'

'No, that would be bad. You mustn't do things like that.'

'Very well, sir,' said the fox, scratching his head in embarrassment. 'I'll never do it again. I'll await your orders in everything.'

'Good. I'll call you if I want something, so don't go too far away.'

The fox spun around again, bowed, and trotted off.

Homoi was beside himself with delight. He ran to and fro across the open countryside, talking to himself and laughing, thinking all kinds of pleasant things, until finally the sun, like a broken mirror, went down behind the distant birches and he hurried back to his house.

Mr Hare was already home, and that evening there were all kinds of good things to eat. That night again, Homoi had wonderful dreams.

The next day, at his mother's bidding, Homoi took a winnowing basket and went out into the country to pick lily-of-the-valley fruit.

'Really!' he muttered to himself as he worked. 'It's not right for a *general* to be doing this sort of thing. If anyone saw me I'm sure they'd laugh at me. I wish the fox would come.'

But just then he felt the ground stirring under his feet. It was a mole, slowly burrowing away from him down there.

'Mole, Mole, Master Mole,' he shouted. 'Did you know that I'm a great man now?'

'Is that Mr Homoi?' said the mole in the ground. 'Yes, I'm well aware of it.'

'I see. That's all right, then,' said Homoi, adding very grandly: 'You can be my sergeant major. But you'll have to do a bit of work for me.'

'Why, of course. And what kind of work might it be?' asked the mole nervously.

'I want you to gather some lily-of-the-valley fruit.'

'I'm terribly sorry,' said the mole down in the ground, in a cold sweat of embarrassment, 'but I'm just no good at doing work in the light.'

'Very well, then,' shouted Homoi crossly, 'I won't ask you. But you just wait!'

'I'm really very sorry,' said the mole, bowing busily. 'Too much sunlight would be the death of me, you see.'

'All right. All *right*,' said Homoi, flapping his paws irritably. 'Now shut up and go away.'

But just at that point, five squirrels came sneaking out from under an elder tree. They bobbed their heads obsequiously and said:

'Please, Mr Homoi, won't you let us collect the lily-of-the-valley fruit for you?'

'Of course,' said Homoi. 'Go ahead. From now on you can all be my brigadiers!'

The squirrels set to work, chattering cheerfully as they did so.

Then six ponies came running up and stopped in front of him.

'Mr Homoi,' said the biggest of them. 'Please give us something to do as well.'

Homoi was delighted. 'Certainly,' he said. 'I'll make you my colonels. Be sure to come on the double whenever I call you.'

The ponies jumped for joy.

'Mr Homoi,' called the mole tearfully from beneath the ground. 'Won't you please ask *me* to do something that I can manage? I promise to make a good job of it.'

But Homoi was still annoyed. 'You keep out of it,' he said, stamping on the ground. 'The fox'll be here soon, so I'll have him take care of you and your friends. You just see!'

Not another murmur came from down below.

By dusk the squirrels had collected masses of lily-of-the-valley berries, which they carried to Homoi's house with a good deal of fuss and fanfare.

Startled by the noise, Mrs Hare came out of the house. 'Gracious, whatever's happened, Squirrels?' she said when she saw them.

'Mother, you see what I can do?' put in Homoi. 'There's nothing I *can't* do nowadays.'

Mrs Hare stood thinking to herself for a while, without replying.

Just then, though, Mr Hare came home. He stood and stared for a minute, then said, 'Homoi – I wonder if you haven't got a bit of a fever still. I hear you've been scaring the life out of Mr Mole; they're all crying their eyes out at his place. And whoever do you think is going to eat all this fruit?'

Homoi began to cry. The squirrels watched sympathetically for a while, but in the end they all crept away.

'You've done it this time,' Mr Hare went on. 'Have a look at the Fire Stone. I'm sure it's gone all cloudy.'

Even Mrs Hare was weeping, and she furtively wiped her eyes with her apron as she took the agate box containing the precious stone out of the cupboard. Mr Hare took the box from her and lifted the lid, then stared in astonishment.

The jewel was blazing still redder and still more fiercely than the night before. They gazed at it in rapture. Silently Mr Hare handed the jewel to Homoi and started to eat. Soon Homoi's tears had dried, and, laughing happily together, they ate their dinner, then went to bed.

Early the next morning Homoi went out into the country again.

The weather was still fine, but the lilies of the valley, whose fruit had been picked, were no longer tinkling as before.

The fox came running eagerly from the far, far side of the green grassland and stopped in front of Homoi.

'Mr Homoi, I hear you got the squirrels to gather lily-of-the-valley berries for you yesterday. Today, how would it be if *I* went and got something nice for you? Something yellow and crisp – something even you have never seen before, if you'll excuse my saying so. And I hear you said you'd punish the mole, didn't you? He's a tricky fellow, that mole – shall I drive him into the river?'

'No, leave him alone,' said Homoi. 'I'm letting him off this morning. But bring me a little of that nice food, would you?'

'Right you are,' said the fox. 'It'll only take me ten minutes. Just ten minutes!' And off he ran as swift as the wind.

So Homoi called in a loud voice, 'Mole, Mole, Master Mole! I've forgiven you now, so you don't have to cry.'

But not a sound came from under the earth.

The fox soon came running back again across the open grassland.

'Here, try this,' he said. 'It's really rather special.' And he held out a crisp slice of bread that he'd just stolen.

Homoi took a bite and found it very good indeed.

'What tree does this grow on?' he asked the fox, who turned his face away and covered a laugh with a little cough before replying:

'Why, the kitchen tree. Yes, the *kitchen* tree. If you like it, I'll fetch some for you every day.'

'Then be sure you bring three pieces, will you?' said Homoi.

'Very well, sir,' said the fox, blinking his eyes to show he'd understood. 'But if I do that for you, you won't stop *me* from catching chickens, will you?'

'Of course not,' said Homoi.

'Well, then, I'll go and get you the other two pieces for today,' said the fox, and in a flash he was gone.

Homoi's head was full of how he would take them home and give them to his parents. 'I'm sure even Father has never had anything as nice as this,' he thought. 'I really am a very good son to them, aren't I?'

The fox returned with two slices of bread in his mouth, placed them in front of Homoi, said a hasty goodbye, and vanished.

'I wonder what the fox does with himself every day?' murmured Homoi to himself as he set off home.

That day, Mr and Mrs Hare were drying the lily-of-the-valley fruit in an oven in front of their house.

'Father, I've brought you something nice!' said Homoi, holding out the bread. 'Try some of this.'

Mr Hare took it from him and removed his spectacles to have a closer look: 'You got this from the fox, didn't you?' he said. 'It's been stolen. I won't eat it.' And he snatched the piece that Homoi was about to give his mother, threw it on the ground together with his own piece, and trampled on them.

Homoi burst into tears. Mrs Hare cried with him.

'Homoi,' said his father, pacing to and fro, 'you've gone too far this time. Go and look at the jewel – I'm sure it's all in pieces by now.'

Weeping, Mrs Hare got out the box. But when the light of the sun fell on the stone inside, it blazed so beautifully it seemed about to rise and soar towards the sky. Mr Hare handed the jewel to Homoi without saying another word. Homoi gazed at it and soon forgot his tears.

The next day, Homoi again went out into the country.

The fox came trotting up and promptly handed over three pieces of bread. Homoi ran home to put them on the shelf in the kitchen, then went outside again, where he found the fox still waiting.

'How about having a little fun?' said the fox.

'What kind of fun?' asked Homoi.

'How about punishing the mole? He's a real pest in this part of the country. And he's lazy, too. You've told him you'd leave him in peace, so let *me* lean on him a bit, and you can just watch. Why not?'

'All right. If he's a pest, I don't see why we shouldn't be a bit nasty to him.'

For a while the fox went to and fro sniffing at the ground and stamping on it, then finally he turned up a large stone. There, underneath, the mother mole and her children, all eight of them, were shivering together in a silent huddle.

'Go on, run!' said the fox. 'Run, or I'll tear you to pieces!' He stamped his foot.

'Don't, please don't!' cried the moles, trying to escape, but they were blind and their legs refused to work, so that all they did was claw at the grass.

The smallest mole was lying on his back as though he'd fainted. The fox gnashed his teeth. Homoi too, almost without thinking, went 'Shoo, shoo!' and stamped his foot.

All of a sudden, a loud voice said, 'Here, what are you two up to?' and the fox spun round and round four times and shot straight off.

Homoi's father was standing there watching. Hastily, he put the moles all back in the hole and covered them with the stone again, then grabbed Homoi by the scruff of the neck and dragged him all the way home.

His mother came out and clung to his father, weeping.

'Homoi,' said Mr Hare. 'You've really done it this time. I'm sure the Fire Stone's broken. Get it out and see.'

Her eyes pouring tears, Mrs Hare went and got out the box. Mr Hare opened it and looked inside.

But Homei's father was quite astonished. The Fire Stone had never looked so beautiful. Reds and greens and blues were surging against each other, exploding in great bursts and showers of light; one moment lightning flashed and red light flowed like blood, then pale blue flames would flare and fill the jewel, and suddenly it seemed to throng with scarlet poppies and yellow tulips, with roses and masses of firefly flowers trembling in a breeze.

Mr Hare handed the stone to Homoi in silence. Before long Homoi forgot his tears and was gazing happily at it.

Mrs Hare, too, stopped worrying at last and started preparing the midday meal. They all sat down and ate their bread.

'Homoi,' said his father, 'you should be careful of that fox.'

'Don't worry,' said Homoi. 'What's a fox to me? *I've* got the Fire Stone. It's not the kind of jewel to break or go cloudy!'

'No, of course not,' said Mrs Hare. 'It's such a *nice* jewel!'

'Do you know, Mother,' said Homoi, puffing himself up proudly, 'I'm sure I was born to keep the Fire Stone with me always.

Whatever I do, you won't find it flying off anywhere! And besides, I'm breathing on it and polishing it a hundred times every day.'

'I only hope you're right,' said his father.

That night, Homoi had a dream. He was standing on one leg on the tip of a tall, tall mountain pointed like an awl.

He woke up crying with fright.

The next morning, Homoi went out again into the open country. Today, a damp, melancholy mist was falling. Trees and grasses all stood still and silent. Even the beeches gave not so much as a flick of their leaves.

Only the morning chimes of the bellflowers rang high, high up into the sky, *ding-dong, ding-a-dong, dong*, and the last *dong* came echoing back out of the distance.

Along came the fox, wearing a pair of shorts and carrying the usual three crisp slices of bread.

'Good morning, Fox,' said Homoi.

The fox smiled an unpleasant smile.

'I got a nasty surprise yesterday,' he said. 'Your father's rather a stickler, isn't he? But I expect he soon got over it. Today I've got a much better idea. Do you happen to have any objections to zoos?'

'No, not particularly,' said Homoi.

The fox took a net, folded small, out of his pocket.

'Look,' he said. 'If you set this, you can catch dragonflies and bees and sparrows and even jays and other bigger things. Why don't we collect them and start a zoo of our own?'

Homoi pictured the zoo to himself, and suddenly wanted one very badly.

'Yes, let's,' he said. 'But are you sure you can catch them with that net?'

'Oh, quite sure,' said the fox as though vastly amused at the question. 'You hop along and leave the bread at home. And by the time you get back, I bet you I'll have caught at least a hundred of them.'

Homoi took the rusks, hurried home with them, put them on the kitchen shelf, then hurried back again.

The fox, he found, had got the net over a birch tree that stood there in the mist, and was grinning with his mouth wide open.

'Look! I've got four already,' he said, still smiling, pointing at a large glass box he must have brought from somewhere.

Sure enough, Homoi could see a jay, a nightingale, a linnet and a siskin flapping about inside. As soon as they recognised him, however, they calmed down, as though their fears had vanished.

'Homoi,' called the nightingale through the glass. 'Please rescue us – I know you can. The fox has caught us and he'll eat us tomorrow, for sure. Please, Homoi!'

Homoi immediately went to open the case.

But the fox frowned until dark creases formed in his forehead, and his eyes narrowed in anger.

'Homoi!' he shouted. 'Watch out! Touch that case and I'll tear you to pieces!' His mouth was twisted with rage.

Homoi felt so scared that he ran straight home. Mrs Hare was out in the fields that day, and there was no one in the house.

Homoi's heart was beating so hard that he got out the box containing the Fire Stone and opened the lid to have a look at it.

It was still blazing brightly. But could it be his imagination, or did he see on it a tiny, cloudy speck, as though it had been pricked with a needle?

The speck bothered Homoi a great deal, so he huffed on the jewel as he always did, and rubbed it lightly with a linnet's breast feather. But the speck refused to come off.

Just then, Mr Hare came home. He soon noticed from his son's face that there was something wrong and said, 'What's up, Homoi? You're looking very pale. Has the Fire Stone gone cloudy? Here – show me.' He held the gem up to the light, then laughed. 'What's all this fuss about? We'll soon get this off. Why, the yellow flames are burning almost brighter than ever. Give me some linnet feathers.' And he began busily polishing the stone; but instead of coming off, the cloudy patch seemed to get steadily bigger.

Mrs Hare came home. Without saying anything, she took the stone from her husband and held it up to the light, then gave a sigh and, breathing on the jewel, began rubbing it herself.

They took turns at polishing it as hard as they could, saying not a word but sighing all the while.

Dusk began to fall. All of a sudden, Mr Hare stood up as though he'd suddenly remembered something.

'Come on, let's have dinner, shall we? We'll try leaving it to soak in oil tonight. They say that's the best thing.'

'Gracious!' said Mrs Hare, startled. 'I'd forgotten all about dinner. I haven't made anything at all. Shall we just have the lily-of-the-valley berries from the day before yesterday and this morning's bread?'

Mr Hare grunted. 'That'll do,' he said. Heaving a sigh, Homoi put the stone in its box and stood staring at it for a long time.

They ate their meal in silence.

'Here, I'll get the oil out for you,' said Mr Hare, taking down a bottle of nut oil from the shelf. Homoi poured some into the agate box. Then they put out the light and went to bed early.

Homoi woke up in the night.

Fearfully, he sat up and took a stealthy look at the Fire Stone by his bed. The stone was gleaming silver, like a fish's eye, in the oil. There were no red flames any longer.

Homoi burst into tears.

Mr and Mrs Hare got up in alarm and lit the lamp.

The stone now looked like a ball of lead. Crying, Homoi told his father about the fox and his net.

'Homoi,' said his father as he hurriedly got dressed, 'you're a fool. I've been stupid, too. You were given the Fire Stone because you saved the baby lark's life, weren't you? But the day before yesterday you were talking about it being yours by *birth*. Come on, let's go out into the country, the fox may still have his net up. You've got to fight him, even if it kills you. I'll help you, too, of course.'

Still crying, Homoi stood up and went with him. Mrs Hare, weeping too, followed after them.

The mist was falling in great clammy drops, and dawn was beginning to break. The fox was beneath the birch tree with his net still over it. And when he saw the three of them, he cheered and laughed out loud.

'Fox!' shouted Homoi's father. 'Clever, aren't you, tricking Homoi like that! Come here and fight!'

'Hah! I could easily bite all three of you to bits,' the fox said with a really villainous expression, 'but I don't feel like going to the trouble. Anyway, I've got other, better things to eat.'

He heaved the glass case onto his shoulder and made to flee.

'No you don't!' said Homoi's father, putting a paw firmly on the case.

The fox lost his balance and, abandoning his load, turned tail and ran.

The case was full of about a hundred birds, all of them in tears: not just sparrows and jays and nightingales, but a great owl too, and even the mother lark and her son.

Homoi's father lifted the lid.

The birds all flew out and, bowing to the ground, said in chorus, 'Thank you very much. We're very grateful for your help again.'

'Not at all,' replied Homoi's father. 'The fact is that we weren't sure how to face you. You see, we've made the jewel that your king gave us go cloudy.'

'Why, whatever can have happened?' the birds said all together. 'Won't you let us take a look at it?'

'Come along, then,' said Homoi's father, leading the way towards the house. The birds crowded after him. Homoi followed in the rear, snuffling and looking contrite. The owl walked with great, slow strides, glancing back at Homoi every now and then with a stern expression.

They all went indoors.

The birds took up every inch of space in the house – the floor, the shelves and even the table. The owl turned his eyes in the most outrageous directions, harrumphing to himself from time to time.

Mr Hare picked up the jewel, which looked like nothing more than a white pebble by now.

'You see! So go on – be as rude as you like – it only serves us right,' he said. And at that instant, the Fire Stone split in two with a sharp crack. The next moment, there was a fierce crackling noise, and before their very eyes the stone crumbled up into a cloud of powder.

Homoi in the doorway gave a loud cry and fell down. The powder had got into his eyes. Startled, they were moving towards him when this time there was a sputtering sound and the cloud of dust began gradually to condense until it formed a number of solid pieces again. Then the pieces resolved themselves into just two, which finally snapped together and once more became the Fire Stone, just as it had always been. The jewel flared like the fires of a volcano, it shone like the sunset, and with a swishing sound it flew up, out through the window, and away.

The birds lost interest and began to leave, first one, then another, until in the end only the owl was left. The owl peered about the room. 'Only six days! Boo-hoo,' he said mockingly. 'Only six days, boo-hoo!' And with a shrug of his shoulders he strode out.

What was worse, Homoi's eyes had gone white and cloudy just as the stone had done, and he could see nothing at all.

Mrs Hare had been crying steadily from start to finish. Mr Hare stood for a while with his arms folded, thinking, then patted Homoi gently on the back.

'Don't cry,' he said. 'This kind of thing could happen to anybody. You're luckier than the rest. Because you *know* now. Your eyes will get better, I'm sure. I'll see that they do. So come on, don't cry.'

Beyond the window the mist had cleared, the leaves of the lilies of the valley were glittering in the sunlight, and the bellflowers went *ding, ding, dong, ding-a, ding-a-dong*, as they tolled clear and loud their morning carillon.

March by Moonlight

One night Kyoichi, in his straw sandals, was walking briskly along the level ground beside the railway tracks.

He'd have been fined, of course, if he got caught. Worse still, if a train had come along with a long pole or something sticking out of a window, he'd almost certainly have been knocked down and killed.

That evening, though, no linesman appeared, nor did Kyoichi encounter a train with a pole sticking out of a window. What *did* happen, though, was something else – something quite extraordinary.

A nine-day moon was hanging in a sky full of mackerel clouds. The clouds seemed almost to be reeling with all the moonlight they'd soaked up into their bellies. Occasionally, a cold-looking star would wink through a gap in them.

Proceeding at a smart pace, Kyoichi had got to a point where the lights of a small station shone plainly in the distance. There were bright red points of light, and vague purple lights like burning sulphur, so that if you looked at them through half-closed lids it was if a great castle was standing there.

Without warning, a signal pole on the right shook itself with a clatter and let the horizontal white bar at the top drop to a diagonal position.

There was nothing the slightest bit strange about this: all that had happened was that the signal had changed – something that occurred at least fourteen times in the course of an evening.

What happened *next*, though, was a shock.

The line of telegraph poles that had been moaning in the wind on the left-hand side of the tracks began, all at once and with great dignity, to march off to the north. Each of them had six china epaulettes and was crowned with a zinc hat with a spike sticking out of it. Each bounced along on its single leg and, as it passed Kyoichi, gave him a hard sideways glance as though it didn't think much of him. The moaning grew louder and louder, until finally it turned into a real old-fashioned marching song:

Rum-tiddy tum, rum-tiddy tum,
We're stiff and well-ordered,
A disciplined breed –
Rum-tiddy tum, rum-tiddy tum –
Yet no other army
Can beat us for speed.

One particular pole went past with its shoulders squared so tight that its very crosspieces seemed to creak.

Then Kyoichi noticed that opposite them another column of poles, with six crosspieces and twenty-two china epaulettes, was also on the move, singing the same kind of song:

Rum-tiddy tum, rum-tiddy tum,
A full fifteen thousand
With one single thought –
Rum-tiddy tum, rum-tiddy tum –
In single file marching
To keep the wires taut.

For some reason, two poles came limping along together with their arms linked. Their heads lolling as though they were completely worn out, they were puffing out of the corner of their mouths and staggering as though they might fall down at any moment.

Just then, a brisk-looking pole behind them bellowed:

'Move along there, you two! Look – the wires are going slack!'

'We can't, we're too tired,' they moaned. 'Our feet have started to rot. The tar on our boots and everything is all a sticky mess.'

'I said, get a move on!' shouted the other pole impatiently. 'If either one of you gives in, you get fifteen thousand men in trouble! Come on, get going!'

The two were obliged to totter on again, and the rest of the column came marching on behind them:

Rum-tiddy tum, rum-tiddy tum,
Oh, see on his shoulders
The pride of each pole –
Rum-tiddy tum, rum-tiddy tum –
The white epaulettes that
Are proof of his role.

The figures of the two poles slowly disappeared in the direction of the distant blue-green woods; the moon emerged from behind the mackerel clouds, and suddenly all around was light.

By now, the troops were in high spirits. Some of them deliberately swaggered and smiled sideways at Kyoichi as they went past. Just then, to his surprise, he saw that other soldiers with three arms and bright red epaulettes were marching beyond the poles with six arms. He got the impression that their marching song had a different tune and different words to it, but the song on this side was so loud that he couldn't catch what they were singing.

The soldiers on this side came tramping steadily on:

Rum-tiddy tum, rum-tiddy tum,
The coldest of winters
Won't make a pole flag –
Rum-tiddy tum, rum-tiddy tum –
Nor fierce summer heat cause
His shoulders to sag.

On and on they came like the flow of a river, until Kyoichi began to get tired just watching them, and let his mind go blank. They all looked at him as they went by, but his head hurt and he stared down at the ground in silence.

Suddenly he heard a hoarse voice in the distance mingling with the sound of soldiers singing:

'Hup, hup! *Left*, right!'

Startled, he raised his head and saw a short, yellow-faced old man in a scruffy grey greatcoat striding along beside the column, looking it over as he came and shouting orders:

'*Left*, right! *Left*, right!'

When the old man's eyes fell on them, the troops went as stiff as ramrods and marched on looking neither to left nor right. Drawing level with Kyoichi, the man peered at him for a while out of the corner of his eye, then turned and gave the command:

'Break – *step*!'

At this, the poles began to move in a more relaxed way and picked up their song again:

Rum-tiddy tum, rum-tiddy tum,
Lances to left of them
And lances to right . . .

The old man stopped in front of Kyoichi and bending forward a little said:

'Good evening! Been watching the march, have you?'

'Yes, I have.'

'I see. Well, then, I suppose it can't be helped. Let's make friends. Here – shake hands.'

Pushing back the tattered sleeve of his greatcoat, he extended a large yellow hand. Reluctantly, Kyoichi put out his hand, too.

'There –' the old man said and grasped it in his own.

As he did so, his eyes gave off crackling blue sparks, and Kyoichi's body tingled all over, so that he almost fell over backwards.

The man chuckled.

'You *felt* that, didn't you? But that's only a mild one. If I shook hands just a bit more strongly – well, you'd be charcoal!'

The troops were still marching relentlessly by:

> *Rum-tiddy tum, rum-tiddy tum,*
> Come hill or come dale,
> We take all in our stride –

Kyoichi was quite scared by now, and his teeth began to chatter. The old man, who had been looking up to see what was happening to the moon and the clouds, noticed how pale and shaky he was and must have felt sorry for him, as he said in a rather quieter voice:

'I'm General Electricity, you know.'

That calmed Kyoichi down a bit.

'General Electricity? What kind of electricity is that?'

This made the old man look a bit sulky.

'What a stupid child!' he said. 'I'm a *general* – in charge of everything to do with electricity. The chief, the boss.'

'It must be fun to be the boss,' said Kyoichi wistfully.

'Oh yes, it is!' the general said, his face crinkling with delight. 'I mean, they're all *my* troops – the engineers, and the dragoons, and the fusiliers over there.'

He suddenly looked solemn and, puffing out one of his cheeks, gazed up at the sky. Then he bellowed at a soldier who happened to be going by:

'You there – what are you gawking around you for?'

The pole all but leapt in the air with alarm; his leg sagged and he hastily faced the front again as he marched on. The other poles came on in a steady stream.

'You know the famous story, I suppose? There was a man who lived in England and his father who lived in Kirkshire, in Scotland. The son sent his old man a telegram. Wait – I have it here, I took it down in my notebook.'

The general took out his notebook, then a large pair of spectacles which he put on with an air of importance before continuing:

'Do you understand English? "*Sendo mai buutsu atto wansu*" – "Send my boots at once" – right? So this stupid old fellow in Kirkshire gets in a panic – and hangs the boots up on my telegraph wires!'

He chuckled. 'It put me on the spot, I can tell you. It isn't just in England that you find that kind of thing, either. I was over at a barracks last December, and there were five or six recruits – you'll find them in any army – who, if they were told by the sergeant to go and put out the lights, would huff and puff trying to blow them out! You wouldn't find anyone like that among *my* soldiers, mind you. It was the same in your village, too, when they first got electricity – people there were always saying, "Oh, they must burn at least a hundred drums of oil every month to produce so much light"!'

He roared with laughter. 'Funny, eh? But it's not so funny if, like me, you understand the principle of the conservation of energy, or the second law of thermodynamics . . . What d'you think, though – they're a fine-looking lot, aren't they? They say so themselves, actually, in that marching song of theirs.'

With stern faces looking straight ahead, those of them passing at the time raised their voices even louder:

> *Rum-tiddy tum, rum-tiddy tum –*
> No wonder we poles are
> So famous world-wide!

Just then, far off down the line, two small burning red lights appeared. This threw the old man into a panic.

'Damn it, there's a train coming! It would be awful if somebody saw us. We'll have to stop the march.'

Holding up one hand, he turned to the column of telegraph poles and shouted:

'Army, *halt*!'

The poles all stopped dead in their tracks and quickly assumed their usual appearance; and the marching song turned back into an ordinary moaning in the wind: *whoo, whooo . . .*

The train came roaring along. The coal burned bright red in the driver's cab, with the stocky black figure of the stoker standing in front of it.

The windows of the passenger cars, though, were all in total darkness.

'Oh hell, the lights are out!' exclaimed the old man. 'We can't allow that. It's a disgrace!'

And doubling up like a rabbit he darted underneath the moving train.

'Look out!' cried Kyoichi, trying to stop him, when suddenly the windows of the passenger cars filled with light and a small child at one of them raised his arms in passing and shouted:

'The lights have come on! Hooray!'

The telegraph poles hummed softly; a signal clattered as it went up; the moon went behind the mackerel clouds again.

And the train seemed already to have arrived at the station.

Kenju's Wood

With his kimono fastened by a piece of rope and a smile on his face, Kenju would often stroll through the woods or along the paths between the fields. When he saw the green thickets in the rain, his eyes would twinkle with pleasure, and when he caught sight of a hawk soaring up and up into the blue sky he would jump for pure joy and clap his hands to tell everyone about it.

But the children made such fun of him that in time he began to try to hide his feelings. When a gust of wind came and the leaves on the beech trees shimmered in the light so that his face couldn't help smiling with pleasure, he would force his mouth open and take big, heavy breaths as he stood gazing and gazing up into the boughs.

Sometimes as he laughed his silent laugh with his mouth wide open, he would rub his cheek with his finger, as though it itched. Seen from a distance, Kenju looked as though he was scratching himself or maybe yawning, but from close up, of course, you could hear he was laughing and you could tell that his lips were twitching, so the children made fun of him just the same.

If his mother had told him to, he could have drawn as many as five hundred bucketfuls of water at one time. He could have weeded the fields, too, in a single day. But his parents never told him to do such things.

Behind Kenju's house lay a stretch of open ground, as big as the average sports field, which had been left uncultivated. One year, while the mountains were still white with snow and the new grass had yet to put out buds on the plain, Kenju suddenly came running up to the other members of his family, who were tilling the rice fields.

'Mother, could you buy me seven hundred cedar seedlings, d'you think?' he said.

Kenju's mother stopped wielding her shiny new hoe and stared at him.

'And where are you going to plant seven hundred cedars?' she asked.

'On the open land at the back of the house.'

'Kenju,' said his elder brother, 'you'd never get cedars to grow there. Why don't you help us a bit with the rice field instead?'

Kenju fidgeted uncomfortably and looked down at the ground.

But then his father straightened up, wiping the sweat off his face.

'Buy them for him, buy them,' he said. 'He's never asked us to buy him a single thing before. Let him have them.' Kenju's mother smiled as though relieved.

Overjoyed, Kenju ran straight home, got an iron-headed hoe out of the barn, and began turning up the turf to make holes for planting the trees.

His elder brother, who had come after him, saw what he was doing and said, 'You have to dig deeper when you plant cedars. Wait until tomorrow. I'll go and buy the seedlings for you.'

Reluctantly, Kenju laid down the hoe.

The next day the sky was clear, the snow on the mountains shone pure white, and the larks sang their bubbling songs as they rose high into the sky. And Kenju, grinning as though he could scarcely contain his joy, started digging holes for the seedlings just as his brother told him, beginning at the northern edge of the land. He dug them in absolutely straight rows and at absolutely regular intervals. His brother planted one seedling in each hole in turn.

At this point, Heiji, who owned a field to the north of the piece of open ground, came along. He had a pipe in his mouth, and his hands were tucked inside his clothes and his shoulders hunched up as though he was cold. Heiji did a little farming, but he made a good part of his living in other, not so pleasant ways.

'Hey, Kenju!' he called. 'That's a daft thing you're doing, planting cedars there! In the first place, they'll shut off the sunlight from my field.'

Kenju went red and looked as though he wanted to say something, but he couldn't get it out and stood fidgeting helplessly.

So Kenju's brother, who was working a little way off, said, 'Morning, Heiji,' and stood up; and Heiji ambled off again, muttering to himself as he went.

Nor was it Heiji alone who poked fun at Kenju for planting cedars on that stretch of grassy land. Everybody said the same thing: no cedars would grow in a place like that, there was hard clay underneath; a fool was always a fool, after all.

And they were right. For the first five years, the green saplings grew straight up towards the sky, but from then on their heads rounded out, and in both their seventh and eighth years their height stayed at about nine feet.

One morning, as Kenju was standing in front of the grove, a farmer came along to have some fun with him.

'Hey, Kenju. Aren't you going to prune those trees of yours?'

'Prune? What do you mean?'

'Pruning means cutting off all the lower branches with a hatchet.'

'Then I think I'll prune them.'

Kenju ran and fetched a hatchet. Since the cedars were only nine feet high, he had to stoop a bit to get underneath them, but by dusk every tree had ruthlessly been stripped of all its branches save for three or four at the very top. The grass was covered with a layer of dark green foliage, and the little grove lay bright and open.

All of a sudden it had become so bare that he was quite upset, feeling almost guilty.

Kenju's elder brother, on his way back from working in the fields, couldn't help smiling when he saw the wood. But, seeing Kenju standing there looking blank, he said good-naturedly, 'Come on, let's pick up this stuff. We've got enough for a good fire here. And the wood looks much better now, too.'

This made Kenju feel easier at last, and they both went in under the trees to collect all the branches he'd lopped off. The grass below was short and neat; it soon looked like the kind of place where you might find a couple of old men playing chess.

But the next day, as Kenju was picking the worm-eaten beans out of the store in the barn, he heard a great commotion over in his wood. From all directions came voices giving orders, voices imitating bugles, feet stamping the ground, then suddenly a burst of laughter that sent all the birds of the neighbourhood flying up into the air. Startled, Kenju went out to see what was going on.

And there, to his astonishment, he found a good fifty children on their way home from school, all drawn up in lines and marching in step between the rows of trees.

Whichever way one went, of course, the trees formed an avenue. And the cedars themselves, in their green costumes, looked as though they too were marching in formation, which added to the children's fun. With flushed faces, calling to one another as shrilly as a flock of shrikes, they paraded up and down.

In no time at all, the rows of trees had been given names – Tokyo Street, Russia Street, Western Street. Kenju was delighted. Watching from behind a tree, he opened his mouth wide and laughed out loud.

From then on, the children gathered there every day. The only times they didn't come were when it was raining. On those days, Kenju would stand alone outside the grove, drenched to the skin in the rain that rustled down from the soft white sky.

'On guard at the wood again, Kenju?' people would say with a smile as they went by in their straw raincoats. There were brown cones on the cedars, and from the tips of the fine green branches cold, crystal-clear drops of rain came splashing down. With his mouth wide open Kenju laughed great gasps of laughter, and stood there for hours, never tiring, while the steam rose from his body.

One misty morning, though, Kenju bumped into Heiji at the place where people gathered rushes for thatching. Heiji looked carefully all around, then shouted at Kenju with a nasty, sly expression on his face:

'Kenju! Cut your trees down!'

'Why?'

'Because they shut off the light from my field.'

Kenju looked down at the ground without saying anything. At the most, the shadow of the cedars stretched no further than six inches into Heiji's field. What was more, the trees actually protected it from the strong south winds.

'Cut them down! Go on, cut them down!'

'No! I won't,' said Kenju rather timidly, lifting his head. His lips were tense, as though he might burst into tears at any moment. It was the only time in his whole life that he had ever said anything in defiance of another person.

But Heiji, who didn't care for being snubbed by someone as easy-going as Kenju, suddenly flew into a rage, and squaring his shoulders began to clout him about the face. He hit him heavily, again and again.

Kenju let himself be struck in silence, with one hand held against his cheek, but before long everything went dark and he began to stagger. At this even Heiji must have started feeling uncomfortable, for he abruptly stopped and, folding his arms, stalked off into the mist.

That autumn, Kenju died of typhus. Heiji, too, had died of the same sickness only ten days earlier. Yet every day the children gathered in the wood just as before, quite unconcerned about things like that.

The next year, the railway reached the village, and a station was built a mile or so from Kenju's house. Here and there, large chinaware factories and silk mills sprang up. In time, the fields and paddies all about were eaten up by houses. Almost before people realised it, the village had become a full-fledged town. Yet by some chance Kenju's wood was the one thing that remained untouched. The trees, moreover, were still barely ten feet high, and still the children gathered there every day. Since a primary school had been built close by, they gradually came to feel that the wood and the stretch of grass to the south of the wood were an extension of their own playground.

By now, Kenju's father was quite white-haired. And well he might be, for already it was close to twenty years since Kenju had died.

One day a young scholar, who had been born in what was then the village and who was now a professor at some university in America, came to visit his old home for the first time in fifteen years. Yet, look as he might, he could find no trace of the old fields and forests. Even the people of the town were mostly newcomers from other parts.

During his visit, the professor was asked by the primary school to come and give a talk about foreign countries in the school hall. When the talk was over, he went out into the playground with the principal and the other teachers, then walked on in the direction of Kenju's wood.

Suddenly, the man stopped in surprise and adjusted his spectacles repeatedly as though unsure of what he saw. Then at last he said, almost to himself, 'Why, this is absolutely as it used to be! Even the trees are just the same. If anything, they seem to have got smaller. And there are children playing there. I almost feel I might find myself and my old friends among them.' He smiled, as if reassured by the memory, then said to the principal, 'Is this a part of the school playground now?'

'No. The land belongs to the house over there, but they leave it for the children to play on just as they please. So in practice it's become a kind of extra playground for the school.'

'That's rather unusual, isn't it? I wonder why that should be?'

'Ever since this place became built up everybody's been urging them to sell, but the old man, it seems, says it's the only thing he has to remember his son Kenju by, and however hard up he is he'll never let it go.'

'Yes, yes – I remember. We used to think that Kenju was a bit soft in the head. He was always laughing in a breathy kind of way. He used to stand just here every day and watch us children playing. They say it was he who planted all these trees. Ah, well, who's to say who is wise and who is foolish? . . . But, you know, this would always make a lovely park for children. How about it – how would it be if you called it "Kenju's Wood" and kept it this way forever?'

'What an excellent idea! The children would love it.'

And so that was how it happened.

Right in the middle of the grass in front of the cedar grove, they set up an olive-coloured slab of rock inscribed with the words 'Kenju's Wood.'

Letters and donations poured in to the school from lawyers and army officers and people with their own small farms in lands across the seas, all of whom had once been pupils at the school.

Kenju's family cried, they were so pleased.

Who can tell how many thousands of people learned what happiness was thanks to the cedar trees in Kenju's Wood, with their splendid dark green, their fresh scent, their cool shade in summer, and the turf with the pale sheen of moonlight that lay beneath?

And when it rained, the trees would drip great, cold, crystal-clear drops onto the grass below, and when the sun shone they would breathe out clean, new air all about them, just as they had done when Kenju himself was there.

The Wild Pear

Two boy crabs were talking to each other in the dim depths of the water.

'Crambon laughed, you know, he did.'

'Crambon laughed: *glub, glub*.'

'He was laughing as he danced.'

'He was laughing, yes.'

Above and around them the water was blue and dark. Along the smooth ceiling, dark bubbles went flowing past.

'Crambon was laughing, you know.'

'Crambon laughed: *glub, glub.*'

'But why was he laughing, then?'

'I don't know.'

The bubbles streamed past. The young crabs, too, blew five or six bubbles each in succession. Swaying and gleaming like mercury, the bubbles climbed diagonally towards the surface.

A fish went by above them, flipping over his silver belly.

'Crambon died.'

'Crambon was killed!'

'Yes, he was killed!'

'But why was he killed, then?'

'I don't know,' said the elder of the two, putting two of the four legs on his right side on top of his brother's flat head.

The fish came gliding back again and went on downstream.

'Crambon laughed!'

'Yes, he laughed.'

Suddenly, gold sunlight poured down into the water as in a dream.

A network of light from the waves above swayed, stretching and shrinking, on the white rock of the riverbed. Straight sticks of shadow from bubbles and bits of debris stood in slanting, parallel lines in the water.

In a sudden flurry that played havoc with the golden light all around them, the fish went swimming off upstream again, his body gleaming with a strange, steely sheen.

'Why does that fish keep going backwards and forwards like that?' asked the younger crab, moving his eyes as though the light was dazzling him.

'He's doing something bad. Catching something.'

'Catching something?'

'Mm.'

Again the fish came swimming down from upstream. This time he swam slowly, calmly, without moving fins or tail, allowing himself to be carried on the current with his mouth open in a round ring.

His shadow slid black and silent over the network of light on the riverbed.

'Why does the fish . . . ?'

But then something startling happened. With a flurry of foam on the ceiling, what looked like a blue-gleaming bullet came diving into the water.

The thing – the elder brother saw quite clearly – was black and pointed at one end like the leg of a compass. But before he could take it in properly, the fish's pale belly gave a flash of light and seemed to be drawn upward. Then there was nothing; the blue thing and the fish shape both disappeared, leaving the golden net of light swaying and the bubbles streaming by.

The two of them stood petrified, unable to say anything.

The father crab came out.

'What's up with you, then – all of a tremble like that?'

'Something strange came down here just now.'

'What kind of thing?'

'All blue and shiny. But black and pointed at one end. Like this. It came diving down, and the fish went climbing up.'

'Did it have red eyes?'

'I don't know.'

'You don't, eh? . . . Well, it was a bird – a "kingfisher," they call him. It's all right, you don't need to worry. It's got nothing to do with us.'

'But where did the fish go to?'

'The fish? He went somewhere nasty.'

'Daddy, I'm scared.'

'Well, don't be. It's all right. Stop worrying. There, look – some birch flowers have come floating along. Aren't they pretty?'

A crowd of white petals was gliding along with the bubbles.

'Daddy, *I'm* scared, too,' said the younger brother.

The net of light swayed, stretching and shrinking, and the shadows of the petals slipped silently over the sand.

The Twelfth Month

The boy crabs were a lot bigger by now, and the scenery on the riverbed had changed completely from summer to late autumn.

Soft white pebbles came tumbling along; small, sharp slivers of crystal and fragments of mica were borne down on the current and landed there.

On the surface, the waves seemed alternately to flash and douse their pale blue fires. Down beneath the cold water, a moonlight the colour of green bottle-glass permeated everything. All about was hushed and still, save for the sound of the waves coming from what seemed a great, great distance.

The moon was so bright and the water so clear that the young crabs, instead of going to sleep, came out and stayed there a while, silent, blowing bubbles and watching the ceiling above.

'*My* bubbles are bigger, just as you'd expect,' said the elder boy.

'No –' said his brother. 'You're blowing them big on purpose. *I* can blow them big too, if I make a special effort.'

'Go ahead, then. There, see – that's all you can manage. Here, watch – I'll blow some now. You see? Big, aren't they?'

'They're no bigger. They're the same as mine.'

'Your own bubbles look big because you're close to them. Let's try blowing them together. All right? There!'

'But mine *are* bigger – look.'

'You think so? Then I'll blow some more.'

'That's no good! You mustn't stretch up like that.'

The father crab came out again.

'Come on, off to bed with you! It's late – I shan't take you out tomorrow.'

'Daddy, which of us blows the biggest bubbles?'

'Why, your brother, I suppose. Doesn't he?'

'No, he doesn't! Mine are bigger than his!' said the younger boy, sounding close to tears.

Just then, there was a big splash.

A large, round, dark object fell from the ceiling, came sinking down, then floated up again, with a flash of yellow patches as it went.

'A kingfisher!' cried the boy crabs, drawing their heads in.

Their father extended his two eyes like telescopes as far as they would go, took a good look, and said:

'No, it's not, it's a wild pear. It's floating away – let's go after it. Mm, it smells good!'

The water round about was, indeed, full of the fragrance of wild pears.

The three crabs went after the pear as it bobbed along on the water. The sidling figures and their black shadows on the riverbed danced together in pairs, all six of them, following the round shadow of the wild pear.

Almost immediately, though, the water began to gurgle, the waves on the ceiling gave off even more blue fires than before, and the pear tilted on its side, then stopped, caught in the low-hanging branches of a tree with moonlight rainbows playing about it.

'There, you see – it *is* a wild pear. It's nice and ripe – smells good, doesn't it?'

'It looks good enough to eat now, Daddy.'

'You just wait a while. Another couple of days and it'll sink to the bottom, then it'll produce some nice wine – all by itself, without our doing anything at all. Come on, now, let's get home to bed!'

The three crabs, father and sons, went back home to their holes.

The waves flickered still brighter with pale blue fires, almost as though exhaling a dust of diamonds.

Down in the Wood

'Our ancestors, now –' he said. 'Around the time when the birds first came down from heaven, they were white all over, every one of them.'

It was a quiet, windless evening with the Golden Sickle poised up there in the western sky, and the speaker was an elderly owl, sitting on a low branch of a pine tree in the wood.

But I didn't put much trust in what the owl said. At first glance, with his puffed-out cheeks, and the way he rarely spoke and then only in weighty tones, and his eyes wide open all the while, and his massive head nodding there in the blue-black shadows of the tree – why, he looked so honest and reliable that anyone might have been taken in at first. *I* wasn't going to trust him so easily, though.

Even so, on this idle evening, breathing in the silver moonlight, I was tempted to stop and listen to what the grand old bird had to tell, for judging from what I'd already heard, it might well be the famous story of the kite who took up dyeing. And it might be fun to see if he could get through it without getting caught out in contradictions. So I kept as serious a face as possible and said:

'Well – so the birds came dropping out of the sky like rain, did they? And every single one of them was white, eh? So how did they come to be all different as they are now – I mean, some of them tortoiseshell and some red and some a sooty colour?'

As I started to speak, the owl had given a swift blink of his eyes as though to say I'd taken the bait nicely, but when I said 'tortoiseshell' he suddenly turned peevish.

'That's going too far, now. "Tortoiseshell" is used of cats. There aren't any tortoiseshell *birds*.'

This time it was *I* who felt he'd taken the bait.

'So –' I said smugly, 'there were no cats among the birds, then?'

The owl fidgeted uncomfortably a bit, and I seized the chance.

'I'm sure I heard that there was a cat among the birds,' I said. 'The nighthawk mentioned one, and the crow too.'

The owl tried to pass this off with a rueful grin.

'You have a large acquaintance, it seems,' he said.

But I wasn't going to let him get away with it.

'Anyway,' I said, 'was there one? Or was your friend the nighthawk lying?'

The owl fidgeted for a while.

'Well, it's a nickname,' he said, coming out with it abruptly, then turning aside.

'Oh!' I exclaimed. 'A nickname? And whose is it, I wonder. Whose, eh? Come on, tell me whose nickname it is!'

The owl by now had one claw off the branch and was holding it up to examine it against the moon, looking terribly put out. But finally, with the most disagreeable look he could summon up, he was obliged to confess:

'Mine.'

'I *see*,' I said. '*Your* nickname, eh? So they call you "the Cat", do they? You don't look a bit like one.' And I directed a long stare at his face, thinking all the while that that was exactly what he *did* look like.

The owl, who had turned away from me, his eyes blinking as though dazzled by the moonlight, suddenly looked as though he might start crying.

I was thoroughly ashamed. I hadn't meant to make the poor fellow actually cry with my clumsy teasing. Besides, it would be rather a pity to tease him into not telling a story he'd embarked on so happily.

'If you think about it, though,' I said, 'there really are all kinds of birds with all kinds of shapes and voices, but it's quite possible they really *were* all white once. I wonder how they got to be so different? Admittedly, the heron and the stork are pure white even now, so some of them, I suppose, must have stayed as they were . . .'

As I talked, the owl had gradually turned his face towards me, and by now was nodding slightly in agreement.

'You are absolutely right in your suppositions,' said the owl. 'There was in fact a good deal of confusion, with them all being white.

'For example, the pheasant would call to another bird from behind, "Good day to you, Mr Tit", and the other bird would look around with a funny expression, and he'd see it was a siskin. Or some small birds would be up in a tree and would call out to another one they saw coming in the distance, "Hello there, Siskin!" only to have the other bird fly off in a huff because he was actually a meadow bunting.

'Not only did people get offended, but their practical affairs sometimes got so tangled up that they had to call in Judge Condor, they say – and even *he* couldn't unravel things.'

'I can imagine it,' I said. 'It must have been very awkward. So what happened then?' Actually, just as I asked this question, I'd noticed a leaf on an oak tree not far away shaking and glinting in the moonlight, and was wondering why an oak leaf should shake all by itself.

But the owl, not noticing this lapse of attention, looked pleased and went on, bit by bit, with his story.

'So all the birds were desperately thinking: unless we can find some way out of this, it's going to mean the end of bird civilisation.'

'Mm, I suppose it *would* have meant that. Anyway, what happened next?'

'Then the kite, who'd seen the way things were going, set himself up as a dyer.'

I found myself smiling: so it *was* the story of the kite, after all. The owl looked a bit taken aback, so I asked hastily:

'The kite started a dyeing business, did he? Yes, of course – he's got long legs, which must have helped, I imagine, when he got hold of the stuff and dipped it in a vat of dye.'

'That's right, and he was very good at it too. Of course, he started it all with an eye to making a profit, but, yes, those legs of his were just right for putting birds in the dyeing vat.'

I realised with dismay that what I'd called the 'stuff' to be dyed was of course the birds themselves; it was enough to make any owl angry. I felt nervous, but the owl continued with his tale. In fact, he seemed to be enjoying himself, for there was no wind that night and the wood was as still as a millpond, with an ageing silver sickle in the western sky, and oaks, pines and the rest all standing hushed – yet not asleep but listening, it seemed, to his story.

'You've no idea how pleased the birds were. The little ones who were forever being mixed up by the others – the sparrows and the tits, the wrens, the white-eyes, the buntings and pewees and bush warblers – they squeaked and hopped around the place in delight, then went straight off to the kite's dyeing shop.'

I was getting quite interested myself by now.

'I see,' I said. 'The birds all went to get themselves dyed, eh?'

'They certainly did! Even the big ones like the eagle and the stork, they all marched off to his place. And they all wanted it done differently. "Something perfectly simple for me, my good fellow," one would say. "Nothing gaudy," another would request, "just a tasteful grey at the most." And it was clever of the kite to get it all done just as he was asked, without turning anyone away.

'He dug five round pits in the clay in front of the bank of red earth by the river and dissolved the dyes in them. Then he'd grab a bird firmly in his beak and, standing with his legs wide apart, dunk him in the liquid. The thing that was hardest of all, and looked the most unpleasant, was doing the head and the face. You could manage the head by putting them in upside down, but in dyeing the face you had to put the beak in the stuff, which all the birds seemed to find hard to take.

'If you took a breath at the wrong moment, you got dyed – black, red, or whatever – inside your stomach and all the way down into your guts. So there was nothing for it but to make sure you took in a good chestful of air – like in deep-breathing exercises – before putting your face in, then let out all the stale air once the thing was over. Even so, they say that the little birds, with lungs too small to hold their breath for long, would poke their heads out squeaking in panic as though he'd been trying to kill them. So naturally it was a hard job to get their faces dyed. The white-eye, for example, got white bits left around his eyes, and the bunting on his cheeks.'

I thought I'd amuse myself by picking a few holes in this.

'I wonder, though ... Personally, I suspect the white-eye and bunting were left white in parts because they *wanted* it that way.'

The owl looked a little flustered and peered into the depths of the dark wood behind him before saying:

'No, I'm afraid you're wrong there. It was because they had small lungs, I'm sure.'

Got you, I thought.

'Then why is it,' I asked, 'that the white-eye and the bunting both have white patches of the same shape in just the same place on each side? It's too much of a coincidence. If they'd stopped the dyeing because they'd run out of breath, you'd expect them to have, say, white around the eye on one side and at the top of the forehead on the other.'

The owl closed his eyes for a while. The moonlight was heavy and bluish, like lead.

Eventually, he opened his eyes and said in a rather quieter voice:

'I imagine they dyed the two sides separately.'

I smiled. 'If they did them separately, that makes it odder still, surely?'

'There's nothing odd about it,' said the owl, quite calm and collected again. 'The size of the lungs stays the same throughout, so they run out of breath at just the same point.'

'Hmm, I suppose so ...' I said. In theory at least his argument held water. The fellow had got out of it nicely.

'And so –' the owl began again, then fell silent. I got the feeling that he was cross at having been argued with, and didn't feel like going on. That made me feel sorry for him again.

'So he went on steadily with it, did he,' I said, 'leaving only the cranes and the herons, who never got dyed?'

'Oh, but you're wrong there, too: in the case of the crane, he was asked to add just a little splotch of black at the top end of the tail. And it was done exactly as requested.'

The owl grinned. He'd turned my question to skilful use, I thought with some irritation. But, after all, I'd only put the question to cheer him up in the first place, so I nodded without saying anything.

'The kite, though – he got more and more self-satisfied. He made a lot of money, and he put on more and more airs; in fact he began to behave as though he were one of the greatest benefactors the birds had ever known, and lost interest in his work. He'd dyed himself, of course, in splendid stripes of blue and yellow – and very proud of them he was, too.

'Even so he continued, reluctantly, doing two or three jobs a day, but the work was slapdash. You'd ask him to do you in a fine mottle of brown, white and black, and he'd leave out the black; or you'd ask for red and black stripes and he'd produce something as untidy as the markings on a swallow. The work was becoming too much trouble for him. Admittedly, in the end there were only a handful of birds left to do. The crow, the heron and the swan – just those three.

'The crow turned up to bother him every day: "Now today you really *will* do it, won't you?" he'd say.

'"Come back tomorrow, try again then," the kite would invariably reply.

'It kept being postponed, so finally the crow got angry, and one day he tackled him in earnest: "What do you think you're up to?" he said. "I come here because you've got a sign up saying 'Dyer' on it. If you're closing down the business, close it down. You can't just go on putting things off forever. If you're going to dye me, then come and do it now. If not, then ... well, you'll soon know about it!"

'The kite was just lounging about as usual, but this outburst made him think a bit. Even if he did quit his job, he wouldn't be short of money, but he still hankered after the renown. On the other hand, he felt he deserved a rest. With these thoughts in mind, he said:

'"Mm, let's see. Just how did you want to be done?"

'The crow calmed down a bit at this.

'"I'd like big splashes of black and purple. A really stylish pattern, like you get on Kyoto brocade."

'That put the kite's back up again. He stood up promptly and said:

'"Right, I'll dye you. Take a deep breath."

'Delighted, the crow stood up and puffed out his chest as far as it would go.

'"Right – ready? Shut your eyes." The kite took a firm hold of the crow with his beak and plunged him straight into the vat of Chinese ink. Fearing that he was being done out of his purple splashes, the crow struggled and struggled, but the kite wouldn't let him go; and when, crying and shrieking, he finally managed to get out, he was black all over. In a rage, he flew straight out of the dyeing shop and went around the homes of all his acquaintances, telling them how awful the kite was. By then, most of the other birds, too, were fed up with the kite, so they all marched down to his shop and this time put *him* in the ink vat. They left him in so long that he finally lost consciousness. Then after hauling him, still unconscious, out of the ink, they smashed his sign to pieces and went laughing on their way.

'Later, the kite somehow managed to pull round; but he was completely black by then.

'And the heron and the swan were left pure white.'

As he finished talking, the owl turned silently away to face the moon.

'I see,' I said. 'Now I understand. Looking back on things, though, it was lucky you had yourself dyed early on, wasn't it? I mean, that's quite a delicate pattern you've got . . .'

And getting up as I spoke, I left the owl and headed home through the heavy, mercury-coloured moonlight and the black shadows of the trees.

The Nighthawk Star

The nighthawk was really a very ugly bird. His face had reddish brown blotches as though someone had daubed it with bean paste, his beak was flat, and his mouth stretched right around to his ears. His legs, too, were so unsteady that he could barely walk even a couple of yards.

Things were so bad that the other birds had only to look at the nighthawk's face to take a dislike to him. Even the lark, who was not a very beautiful bird, considered himself far better than the nighthawk. If he met the nighthawk as he was setting out in the early evening, he would turn his head away with his eyes closed, as though the sight was really more than he could bear. And the smaller birds who liked to chatter were always saying downright nasty things about him.

'Well! Here he comes again,' they'd say. 'Just *look* at that, my dear! Did you ever see anything like it? It's really a disgrace to us birds!'

'I couldn't agree more. Why, look at that great big mouth of his! I'm sure he's related to the frogs.'

And so on. If only he had been a proper hawk instead of a nighthawk, his name alone would have been enough to send those half-baked little birds into hiding, all quivering and pale-faced, hunched up among the leaves. But the fact was that he wasn't even related to the hawk. Surprisingly enough, he was in the same family as the beautiful kingfisher and that jewel of birds, the hummingbird. And the whole family was quite harmless to other birds. The hummingbird ate the honey from flowers, and the kingfisher ate fish, while the nighthawk lived by catching winged insects. The nighthawk had no sharp claws or sharp beak even, so that no one, not even the weakest bird, was afraid of him.

It may seem strange, indeed, that he should have been called 'hawk' at all. In fact, there were two reasons. One was his wings, which were exceptionally strong, so that when he soared through the air he looked just like a hawk. The other was his voice, which was piercing and reminded people of a real hawk, too.

This bothered the real hawk a lot, of course. If he so much as caught sight of the nighthawk, he would hunch up his shoulders and tell him in a menacing voice to get his name changed quickly.

Then, early one evening, the hawk actually visited the nighthawk at his home.

'Hey – are you in?' he called. 'Why haven't you changed your name yet? It's disgraceful! Can't you see that we're completely different? Look at the way I range the skies all day long, whereas you never come out at all except on dark, cloudy days or at night. And take a look at my beak, too. Then compare it with your own!'

'I'm afraid I just *can't* do as you say,' the nighthawk replied. 'I didn't choose my own name – it was given to me by God.'

'That's not true. With *my* name, now, one might say it was given to me by God, but yours is sort of borrowed – half from me and half from the night. So give it back!'

'But I *can't*, Hawk.'

'Yes, you can! I'll tell you another name instead. Algernon. Algernon – right? Now that's a nice name for you. And remember – when you change your name, you have to have a ceremony to announce it to everybody. You understand? What you do is you go around to everybody's place wearing a sign saying "Algernon" around your neck, and you bow and you say, "From now on I want to be known as Algernon."'

'Oh, I could never do that!'

'Yes, you could. You've got to! If you don't do it by the morning of the day after tomorrow, I'll come and crush you in my claws. Don't forget, now. The day after tomorrow in the morning, I'll go around to all the other birds' houses and ask whether you've been there or not. If there's a single one that says you haven't, that'll be the end of you!'

'But how can you expect me to do something like that? I'd rather die. So you might as well kill me right now.'

'Come on, think about it carefully later. Algernon's not really a bad name at all.' And the hawk spread wide his great wings and flew off home to his nest.

The nighthawk sat perfectly still with his eyes shut, thinking. 'Why on earth should everybody dislike me so much? Actually, I know quite well. It's because my face looks as though it's been daubed with bean paste and my mouth is slit from ear to ear. But in fact I've never done a bad thing in all my life. Why, once I even rescued a baby white-eye that fell out of its nest, and took it back home.

But its mother snatched it away from me as if I'd been a thief. Then she laughed at me. And now – oh dear! – they want me to wear a sign around my neck saying "Algernon"! Whatever shall I do?'

Night was already drawing in about him, and the nighthawk flew out from his nest. The clouds hung low, gleaming ominously, and the bird almost brushed against them as he flew silently about the sky.

Suddenly, his mouth opened wide and, setting his wings back straight, he shot down through the air like an arrow. Insect after insect disappeared down his throat. Then, before anyone could say whether he'd actually touched the earth or not, he swung up and was shooting skywards again.

The clouds were grey by now, and a forest fire glowed red on the hills in the distance.

Whenever the nighthawk decided to strike, he flew so fast that he seemed to cleave the sky in two. But tonight, among the insects he caught, there was a beetle that struggled dreadfully as it went down his throat. The nighthawk forced it down at once, but a little shudder went down his back as he did so.

Now the clouds were all black, except in the east, where the forest fire, a sinister red, was reflected on them. The nighthawk flew up into the sky again, with a heavy feeling in his stomach.

Another beetle went into the nighthawk's maw, but this one flapped about as though it were actually scratching at his throat. The nighthawk got it down somehow, but even as he did so his heart gave a lurch, and he started crying in a loud voice. Round and round and round the sky he circled, crying all the while.

'Oh dear,' he said to himself, 'here I am every night, killing beetles and all kinds of different insects. But now *I'm* going to be killed by Hawk, and there's only one of me. It's no wonder I feel so miserable. I think I'll stop eating insects and starve to death. But then, I expect Hawk will kill me before that happens. No – I'll go away, far, far away, before he can get me.'

The flames of the forest fire were gradually spreading out like water, and the clouds looked as though they themselves were ablaze.

The nighthawk flew straight to the home of his younger brother, the kingfisher. Luckily enough, this handsome bird was still up, watching the distant forest fire.

'Hello there,' he said as he saw the nighthawk flying down towards him. 'What brings you here so unexpectedly?'

'It's just that I'm going far away, and I wanted to see you before I go.'

'But you *can't* do that! Hummingbird, too, lives far away, and I'll be left all alone!'

'I'm afraid it can't be helped, so don't say any more. And remember – try not to catch any more fish than is absolutely necessary. Please . . . Goodbye.'

'What's happened? Here – don't go just yet!'

'No. It won't make any difference, however long I stay. Give Hummingbird my love when you see him. Goodbye. We'll never meet again. Goodbye.'

And he went home weeping. The brief summer night was already giving way to the dawn.

The leaves of the ferns swayed green and gold, drinking in the morning mist. The nighthawk cried out loud and harsh. Then he made his nest neat and tidy, combed every bit of feather and down on his body into place, and set off again.

The mist cleared, and as it did so the sun climbed from the east. It was so dazzling that the nighthawk wavered for a moment, but he persevered and flew straight ahead towards the sun.

'Sun, Sun,' he called. 'Won't you take me up with you? I'll gladly die in your fire if I have to. My body may be ugly, yet surely it will give out at least a tiny bit of light as it burns. Won't you take me up with you?'

But though he flew and flew, the sun grew no closer. In fact, it seemed to grow smaller and more distant still.

'Nighthawk, eh?' said the sun. 'Yes, I suppose you do have a hard time of it. Why don't you fly up into the sky tonight and ask the stars instead? You're really a bird of the night, you see.'

The nighthawk gave what was meant to be a bow, but suddenly lost his balance and started falling down, down into the grass on the plain below.

For a while, everything was a dream. It seemed to the nighthawk that he was climbing up amidst the red and yellow stars, or that he was being swept away, away by the wind, or that the hawk had come and was crushing him in his claws.

Then something cold fell on his face, and he opened his eyes. The dew was dripping from a stem of young pampas grass. It was quite dark, and the deep indigo sky was covered all over with sparkling stars. The nighthawk flew up into the sky. The forest fire was gleaming red again tonight, and the nighthawk as he flew about found himself between the faint glow from the fire and the cold light of the stars above. Once more he flew around the sky, then suddenly made up his mind and went straight up towards the constellation of Orion in the west.

'O Stars!' he called as he went. 'Blue-White Stars of the west! Won't you take me up with you? I'm willing to die in your fires, if you want me.'

But Orion was too busy singing his brave songs to pay the slightest heed to anything as insignificant as the nighthawk. Unsteadily and close to tears, the nighthawk came down until he finally reached a resting place. Once more he flew around the sky. Then off he went straight upwards again, this time towards the Great Dog in the south.

'O Stars!' he cried as he went. 'Blue Stars of the south! Won't you take me up with you? I'll gladly die in your fires, if need be.'

'Don't talk nonsense!' said the Great Dog, busily winking blue and purple and yellow. 'Whoever do you think you are? A mere bird – that's all. Why, to reach here with your wings would take hundreds and thousands and millions of billions of years!' And the Great Dog turned away.

Disheartened, the nighthawk wavered back down to earth. He flew around the sky twice. Then again he summoned up his courage and flew straight up in the direction of the Great Bear in the north.

'O Blue Stars of the north!' he cried as he went. 'Won't you take me up with you?'

'Now, you mustn't say things you shouldn't,' said the Great Bear softly. 'Go and cool off a little. At times like this, it's best to dive into a sea with icebergs in it, but if there's no sea handy, a cup of iced water will do nicely.'

The nighthawk zigzagged sadly down to earth again. He flew around the sky four more times. Then he called out one last time, to the Eagle, which had just risen on the opposite bank of the Milky Way.

'O White Stars of the east! Won't you take me up with you? I'll happily die in your fires if I have to.'

'Dear me, no – it's quite out of the question!' said the Eagle pompously. 'One has to have the proper social status in order to become a star. And it takes a great deal of money, too.'

All his remaining strength left the nighthawk. Folding in his wings, he plummeted towards the earth. But then, just when his weak legs were only inches from the ground, quite suddenly he began to shoot upwards again like a rocket. Up he went, and when he came to the middle regions of the sky, he shook his body and ruffled up his feathers just as an eagle does before attacking a bear.

He called and called again in a harsh, piercing voice. It was the voice of a hawk, and all the other birds who were asleep on the plains and in the woods below awoke and trembled as they looked up wonderingly at the starry sky.

The nighthawk climbed straight up and up, ever further up. Now the flames of the forest fire below were no bigger than a burning cigarette end, yet still he climbed. His breath froze white on his breast with the cold, and the air grew thinner, so that he had to move his wings more and more frantically to keep going.

Yet the stars did not change in size. The nighthawk wheezed at each breath like a pair of bellows. The ice in the air pierced him like a blade. In the end, his wings went completely numb and useless. Then, with tear-filled eyes, he gazed up once more into the sky . . . and that was the last of the nighthawk. No longer did he know whether he was falling or climbing, whether he was facing up or down. But his heart was at peace now, and his great, bloodied beak, though a little twisted, was surely smiling slightly, too.

A while later, the nighthawk opened his eyes and saw, quite clearly, that his own body was glowing gently with a beautiful blue light like burning phosphorous.

Next to him was Cassiopeia. The bluish white light of the Milky Way lay just at his back.

And the nighthawk star went on burning. It burned forever and forever. It is still burning to this day.

VINTAGE CLASSICS

Vintage Classics is home to some of the greatest writers and thinkers from around the world and across the ages. Bringing you not just the books you already know and love, but new additions to your library, these are works to capture imaginations, inspire new perspectives and excite curiosity.

Renowned for our iconic red spines and bold, collectable design, Vintage Classics is an adventurous, ever-evolving list. We breathe new life into classic books for modern readers, publishing to reflect the world today, because we believe that our times can best be understood in conversation with the past.

A Note on Our Sustainability Commitments

We create Vintage Classics red spine paperbacks with the environment in mind.

We have minimised the carbon impact of our books by using low-carbon FSC™-certified paper. Our covers use minimal, reduced-carbon finishes and we are working towards making all our books recyclable. All red spine editions printed in the UK use 100% renewable energy.

For more information on our sustainability commitments, please visit greenpenguin.co.uk.

Discover more in **VINTAGE CLASSICS** red spine

Brave New World	Aldous Huxley
To Kill a Mockingbird	Harper Lee
Catch-22	Joseph Heller
Native Son	Richard Wright
The Handmaid's Tale	Margaret Atwood
The Gulag Archipelago	Aleksandr Solzhenitsyn
The Master and Margarita	Mikhail Bulgakov
Beloved	Toni Morrison
Stoner	John Williams
The Sailor Who Fell from Grace with the Sea	Yukio Mishima
The Savage Detectives	Roberto Bolaño
The Joy Luck Club	Amy Tan
Autobiography of Red	Anne Carson
I Who Have Never Known Men	Jacqueline Harpman
Oranges Are Not the Only Fruit	Jeanette Winterson
Disgrace	J. M. Coetzee
My Left Foot	Christy Brown
Sugar	Bernice L. McFadden
Death and the Penguin	Andrey Kurkov
Persepolis	Marjane Satrapi